KALEIDOCIDE

ALSO BY DAVE SWAVELY

Silhouette

KALEIDOCIDE

A Peacer Novel

DAVE SWAVELY

THOMAS DUNNE BOOKS
ST. MARTIN'S PRESS
NEW YORK

This is a work of fiction. All of the characters, organizations, and events portrayed in this novel are either products of the author's imagination or are used fictitiously.

THOMAS DUNNE BOOKS.
An imprint of St. Martin's Press.

www.thomasdunnebooks.com
www.stmartins.com

The Library of Congress Cataloging-in-Publication Data is available upon request.

ISBN 978-1-250-00150-4 (hardcover)
ISBN 978-1-250-02074-1 (e-book)

St. Martin's Press books may be purchased for educational, business, or promotional use. For information on bulk purchases, please contact Macmillan Corporate and Premium Sales Department at 1-800-221-7945, extension 5442, or write specialmarkets@macmillan.com.

First Edition: December 2013

10 9 8 7 6 5 4 3 2 1

To Alfred Bester and Howard Chaykin,
who fueled a young imagination with their "kaleidocide"
of ideas and images in the graphic-novel version of
The Stars My Destination

KALEIDOCIDE

1
BEIJING

The *xing lu cai se* was now ready, and it was the best possible time for Michael Ares to die.

General Zhang Sun had decided to take his revenge in this manner a year earlier, when he had first received the information, but it took six months for the complex preparations to be completed. Then he had to wait for the fall season, when the leaves began to change, so that the assassination could be the most successful according to his *ban lan jiao,* or "religion of powerful colors."

He stood next to the transteel wall in his twentieth-floor office, staring down at the trees in the middle of the Beijing City Center and noting with satisfaction that they were indeed the epitome of *xing lu cai se*—a many-colored death, where the numerous shades of green, red, and gold on the leaves marked the end of their lives, and made it a beautiful thing. Sun knew that his target, on the other side of the world but in the same hemisphere, would also be surrounded by such majesty at this time of year. The trees and vineyards dominating the landscape around Michael Ares's home in Napa Valley would be adorned with the same hues, and Sun knew this was no mere coincidence. This was a sign that the ancient spirits were ready to use the modern technology at his disposal to balance the justice of the universe by the satisfaction of this blood debt.

The thought of modern technology reminded him that he still wore the net glasses that he had just used to issue the final orders for the *xing lu cai se,* and that they were still set in the secure mode that was necessary because those orders could not be public, owing to the factions within his country that he did not yet fully control. He had nearly absolute power in the ironically named "People's Republic," but *only* nearly. Yet Sun considered any risk he faced to be a small price to pay for the pleasure of seeing Michael Ares suffer.

To bolster his confidence, he took the glasses off and surveyed the impressive City Center with an unobstructed view. His tower and twenty other skyscrapers of various heights surrounded the trees and water in the massive park, under which was a geothermal heat-exchange system used to passively heat and cool all of the district's buildings. This was the crowning achievement of China's building craze in the years before and after the turn of the century, when they were in a race with the United States for the world's largest Gross Domestic Product. After building the infamous "ghost cities" (which now provided housing for Sun's growing army), the government hired the eminent architectural firm SOM to transform the Dawangjing District into a "sustainable city" that would be an urban center impressive enough to symbolize China's ascendancy among the nations.

The new Beijing did symbolize that reality well, and drinking it in assured Sun that there were few limits to what he could achieve with his power as supreme leader of his *Baquan* empire. And he was absolutely sure that even those few limits would be effectively removed by the *ban lan jiao* ritual he was about to perform. The demise of his enemy was a foregone conclusion in his mind, for the *xing lu cai se* had never failed to accomplish it.

He strode excitedly across the room, stepped into the elevator, and rode it twenty-two stories down to another of the architectural marvels of new Beijing, the reconstructed Underground City. Built during the Cold War by Chairman Mao Zedong to shelter or evacuate prominent residents in the event of a nuclear attack from Russia, the original complex included about thirty kilometers of tunnels, a thousand bomb-proof rooms, and seventy well sites. As the nuclear threat receded after the collapse of the Soviet Union, many of the tunnels were sealed off, a few remained in secret use by the highest officials, and still fewer were opened to the public as a tourist attraction. But when the new City Center became the seat of government, making it a target for terrorism or outside aggression, many of the tunnels were re-opened and improved to serve their original purpose again, as well as to provide exclusive transportation for the elite.

It was the latter purpose that General Sun appreciated the most, especially when he had discovered that one of the tunnels under his building led to the Western Hills, a quiet and picturesque area outside the city that both the twentieth-century builders and their twenty-first-century heirs thought would serve as a good evacuation destination for their influential customers. What they did not know, but was obviously no surprise to the spirits that guided Zhang Sun, was that one of the tunnels ran to Fragrant Hills Park, which contained the Temple of Azure Clouds. This Buddhist holy site was one of the few that actually had a color in its name, and was therefore a veritable capacitor for supernatural power in Sun's religion. And the general was able to leave his office building at any time and be in the temple within twenty minutes, by way of the tunnel and the miniature maglev train that was propelled by the same technology as the larger ones in the subways and on the surface.

As his custom car sped through the tunnel, Sun rehearsed in his mind the twist of fate that was perhaps the greatest gift provided by the *ban lan* spirits in regard to his worship in the temple: an effective alibi. He could not openly practice his cultic faith in the current political atmosphere because atheism, Buddhism, and Christianity were still the most prevalent worldviews among his rivals and the voters. But fortunately he had an acceptable reason for his frequent excursions to the blue cloud temple, because inside it was a memorial hall dedicated to Sun Yat-sen, a government leader from the early twentieth century who was China's most famous populist icon. His body had been entombed in the temple pagoda for several years before being relocated to Nanjing in 1929, and it had been replaced by an empty crystal coffin that the Soviet government had given as a gift "in memory of the great man."

Sun smiled at the thought of the autocratic Soviets honoring a democratic hero, for he knew they did it only for show. And it was for that same reason he himself told people that he had changed his name to Sun (pronounced "soon") in honor of Sun Yat-sen, and that his frequent visits to the temple were to meditate at the shrine of his "hero." But in fact he was practicing the advice of his real hero, the ancient war strategist Sun Tzu, who said, "When seeking power, make it appear that you are not doing so." It was Sun Tzu whom he secretly honored by the new name he had chosen when he first became a general, but it was useful to have his people think that he was cut from the mold of the other famous Sun.

When he arrived at the surface entrance near the temple, he waved off the security detail greeting him there and made his way through the courtyard and gardens toward the temple pagoda. As he did, he passed several of the resident monks, who were working in the gardens, but mostly working to conceal their perplexity or disgust at his latest visit. He wondered how many of the monks knew what he was really doing in the room he had commandeered in the temple, and was sure at least some of them did know and considered it a defilement of their holy site. But they wouldn't dare say anything publicly, of course, for fear of losing their government sanction, access to the temple, or much more.

Soon he reached the base of the Vajrasana, or Diamond Throne Pagoda, which was by far the most impressive structure on the temple grounds, and the largest of its kind in the world. Sun took in the intricate carvings in the brick and marble as he climbed the stairs to the top of the pagoda's base, and began to feel intoxicated when he stood at its edge with the five towers rising into the sky behind him and the exquisite view of miles and miles of brightly colored fall foliage filling the hills and valleys in front of him. Just as his high view of the Beijing City Center earlier had symbolized the modern technology available to him, this one represented the timeless occult power that would tip the scales in his favor and make his plans invincible. His enemy might have the former, but the *ban lan* forces were only Sun's to command.

Eager to do that, he left the crest of the temple and stepped into the small dark room with the altar, which he had chosen precisely because it was a tight space that enabled him to better absorb the primeval energies summoned by the ritual. As he fumbled to remove the first item from the small bag he carried, he began chanting the names of the *ban lan* colors and the foundational elements they represented.

"*Hēi sè . . . hóng sè . . . bì . . . bái . . . huáng,*" he whispered. "*Jīn . . . jiǒng . . . zhǎn . . . lún . . . rǎng.*"

As he repeated the words, he brought his OutPhone from the bag and opened two files on it, then sat it on the altar in the center of the chamber. The phone's projector soon filled the space with the colors he had named, switching locations every few seconds on the walls and ceiling above the little machine. Each one was a darker version than the basic color, because black was the most important one and it had to be mixed in with all the others.

The other file was being projected now as well, and a single stationary screen appeared on one spot of the wall in front of Sun, where a biographical clip lifted from the net began to play. It showed various pictures of his enemy as it described him, and Sun enjoyed the effect as the colors from the other file alternately tinted his face. The *xing lu cai se* was now being applied to its target, and there would be no escape from it.

"A little more than a year ago," the narrator of the bio piece said, "Michael Ares was virtually unknown outside the city-state of San Francisco, except in his home country of England, where as a young man he had been knighted by King Noel I for his distinguished military service in the Taiwan Crisis . . ."

"*Hēi sè . . . hóng sè . . . bì . . . bái . . . huáng,*" Sun continued to whisper, but more forcefully now. "*Jìn . . . jiŏng . . . zhăn . . . lún . . . răng.*"

"But Michael Ares has now ascended to what is arguably one of the most prominent positions in the new world order of our fast-approaching future. As the new CEO of the Bay Area Security Service, known more popularly as BASS, he now controls not only the government of that young city-state, but the exclusive rights to the most coveted scientific and technological breakthrough of our generation: the Sabon antigravity system, which was developed by a Silicon Valley firm under contract with BASS."

The screen now showed footage of the BASS "aerocars" floating above landmarks like Alcatraz Island, the Golden Gate Bridge, and the Bay Bridges, the last of which had been destroyed by the big earthquake and then rebuilt bigger and better. Sun grimaced a bit at this reminder of the prized technology that his country would probably not have anytime soon, because of what he was about to do to Michael Ares. But the Chinese leader knew that he had the power to procure it eventually, even despite whatever recriminations might occur. And the postponement was a minor inconvenience compared to the gratification he was already beginning to experience.

"Hēi sè . . . hóng sè . . . bì . . . bái . . . huáng." His voice rose higher. *"Jìn . . . jiǒng . . . zhǎn . . . lún . . . rǎng."*

"So far Michael Ares has kept his scientific secrets to himself, continuing the miserly policy of his predecessor Saul Rabin, who had become the dictator of the Bay Area after the devastating earthquake, when he was the only one able to restore order to the crippled city. The former chief of police did so by hand-picking a trusted and skilled force of cops and soldiers who were given a license to kill and came to be known as 'peacers,' probably because of Rabin's most famous saying, 'We *will* keep the peace.' British war hero Ares was brought in a few years later by the aging mayor to command the peacer corps, along with his son Paul and former star athlete Darien Anthony. These three executive peacers ended up as key players in the succession drama that became headline news just over a year ago . . ."

"Hēi sè . . . hóng sè . . . bì . . . bái . . . huáng. Jìn . . . jiǒng . . . zhǎn . . . lún . . . rǎng."

At the other times when Sun had performed this rite, he had pulled the drug out of his bag at this point. But he hadn't brought it along this time because he wanted to see the spirits do more than they had ever done before, and to rely on them alone to provide the ecstatic confirmation of the *xing lu cai se*. So he grasped the only other object in the bag, a very special one, and waited for the right moment to open it.

"When Darien Anthony, Darien's young son, and Michael's own young daughter Lynette were brutally murdered, Michael barely survived a plot to frame him, which was perpetrated by Paul Rabin. He was cleared by the intervention of the older Rabin, who sacrificed his own life to save Michael and recorded his son's confession in a dramatic scene that was released to the public and certified as genuine by Reality G. From the parts of the confrontation that are decipherable to those not involved, it appears that the senior Rabin was already dying, and that the gauntlet Michael had to endure in his final days was a test of his qualifications to inherit the throne of BASS. In some of his last words, Saul referred cryptically to Michael as 'the true peacer,' hinting at some mysterious destiny for the man."

Michael Ares has but one destiny, thought Sun as he repeated the chant louder, *and it has nothing to do with peace.* As he did this, he lifted the ecotube in his hand and moved his finger toward the button on the side. The vidclip was now over, and a picture of his enemy's face was frozen on the screen, the colors from the projector alternating on it with increasing frequency.

"*Hēi sè . . . hóng sè . . . bì . . . bái . . . huáng!*" He was shouting now. "*Jìn . . . jiǒng . . . zhǎn . . . lún . . . rǎng!*"

Sun pressed the button on the ecotube and one end of it slid out on two thin rods, separating from the rest and providing an escape route for what was inside. As he waited for it to discover this and emerge, he felt his heart beating hard and broke into a cold sweat, probably more from excitement than fear of being injured. He shouted the chant again, to draw the little dragon forth, and sure enough its darting tongue, and then its head, soon poked cautiously through the hole. Then part of its small body appeared, and on it the many colors that matched the ones playing on the walls and ceiling.

Sun's heart beat even faster as he slowly lifted his left hand to a spot just below the snake's head and tried not to flinch in fear—he must have faith the spirits would protect him. The serpent proceeded down his arm and half-coiled its body around it. Soon its tail was out of the tube and its whole body was resting on him completely. He raised his arm slightly so that the creature's head was near his face, and gazed at it with wonder. The colors were impressive, but what really amazed him was that he could have asked for no better accoutrement for the rite. A fellow devotee of the *ban lan jiao,* one of the few souls privy to this practice, had given it to him as a gift and explained that it was not only native to the area where his enemy lived, but it actually bore the name of his city. On top of that, its species was almost extinct. Yet this one lived and allowed him to handle it without harm.

"*Hēi sè . . . hóng sè . . . bì . . . bái . . . huáng! Hēi sè . . . hóng sè . . . bì . . . bái . . . huáng!*" Sun was now chanting only the names of the colors, so that they would be all in all, with the elements themselves being consumed by their power.

"*Hēi sè . . . hóng sè . . . bì . . . bái . . . huáng! Xing . . . lu . . . cai . . . se . . . Michael Ares!*"

He speared the image on the wall with a hateful stare, focusing all his spiritual energy in its direction, and then he felt the confirmation, as he knew he would. Without any chemical assistance, and with only the spirits themselves to thank, his whole body shuddered with an ecstatic rush that was something like a sexual climax, and just as rapturous.

Zhang Sun was convinced that his faith in the *ban lan jiao* had brought him to the throne in China, through circumstances that not even the most hardened skeptics could deny, if only they had experienced it. Every time he had performed this ritual and invoked *xing lu cai se* in the past, his enemies had died in prompt fashion, long before all the contingencies had been exhausted. So he was already a sincere believer, but the confirmation experience was so overwhelming that now, more than ever, he knew that his faith was real and that the multiple murder methods could not possibly fail. The *ban lan* spirits had made this clear in so many ways already, through the shared fall season, the snake, and the unprecedented feeling he had during the ceremony. Beyond that, the traitor in his employ had already borne the marks of the *ban lan* long before being enlisted, and would be close enough to the target to succeed even without the many other means unleashed upon him.

This was all too much to be mere coincidence, so Sun was confident beyond all doubt that in a matter of weeks, all future net bios of Michael Ares would be in memoriam.

2
SAUSALITO

It was a memorable calm before the storm. Lynn and I were enjoying each other more than any time in recent memory, as if we somehow knew that we would soon be torn apart. This little getaway must have happened at just the right time, because for once she wanted to make love as much as I did, if not more. During those afternoon hours of alternating tenderness and passion, even the slightest touch never failed to make my heart race, and it felt so good that I wondered why we didn't do this more often.

Now happily exhausted, we were enjoying the sunset from the divan, which had slid from inside the room to the deck outside it. We lay intertwined, as comfortably as we could manage with Lynn's pregnant swell. She was six months along—a factor that had contributed to the recent infrequency of our intimacy, but also had made this day all the more enjoyable. During her first pregnancy, I had found it hard to be attracted to her physically, because I was still so heavily influenced by the assumption that a woman had to be shaped like a model to be beautiful. But somewhere along the line, perhaps because we lost our first child, my perspective changed completely. I now loved her body like this, and I was telling her so as I moved my hand across the soft skin of her belly.

"I don't believe it," she said, as usual.

"How many times do I have to tell you?" I said playfully. "Or do I have to

9

show you again?" I nuzzled her ear, through the streaked blond-and-brown hair that always smelled so good.

"There are so many young and thin women," she continued. "Why would you want fat old me?"

I found myself wincing a bit, as the reference to women with nice bodies brought thoughts of Tara back into my mind again. I had been trying to keep them out during the trip, because I didn't want to let them ruin this good time with Lynn. So I focused on my wife again and made it seem like my expression was a result of what she had said about being fat.

"Don't talk like that," I said. "I want you because you're the mother of my baby—my *babies*. Besides, you're only fat in the right places." I spread my hand out and pressed slightly until I felt a little kick from the baby, and then moved it up to the other part of her body that had gotten bigger recently, and whispered into her ear. "You're beautiful everywhere."

"I think you have a mental problem," she said, "but I guess I won't complain." Giving up the argument, she gazed out at the wisps of orange cloud that hung above the bay, colored that way by the sun that was setting in the west. "Now that *is* beautiful."

I grunted in agreement, as the colors reminded me of Monet's painting *Impression, Sunrise*. The bright orange of the clouds was similar, of course, and so was the aqua blue of the deck of the house, which visually pulled the darker greens and blues of the bay beyond it in its direction. The only thing missing from Monet's vision was the sun itself, which was on the other side of the mountain from us. But the shining cityscape of San Francisco, in the distance to the right side of our view, provided an attractive alternative.

We had bought this hillside house for moments exactly like this. And we had bought six properties surrounding it, with my company's version of eminent domain, to create a cushion as a part of the obligatory security plan. I knew that my cyborg bodyguard was below us on the street in front of the house, probably worrying about our level of exposure on the open deck, and that there were seven other agents at various places around the perimeter of our little retreat. Wondering whether a machine-man like Min was capable of an emotion like worry, my focus drifted away from the sunset and my wife, and back to my job.

"What are you thinking about?" Lynn asked, pulling a light blanket over her.

"The same stuff, about BASS," I said.

"How ruling the world is boring?" she asked with a twinkle in her eye.

"You know, meetings and hearing about what other people have been doing was okay for an old man like Saul, but I miss the action of being a peacer, even if it was only occasional."

"Why don't you just go out and find someone to arrest, or shoot?" she asked.

"With my entourage of bodyguards and advisors, and half the world press stalking me?" I adjusted myself on the divan, so I could share some of the blanket. The sky had now turned darker, and the temperature was dropping. "I never asked for all this, you know. The old man brought me to BASS, and he cooked up the plan to leave me in charge. It's like I've been carried along to where I am today—it's not like I wanted it or chose it myself. Maybe that's why I'm not really that happy . . ."

We lay silent for a moment, then Lynn said, "Maybe you just need to find out why."

"Pardon me?" I asked, beginning to notice her against me once again. I shifted a little, and it felt even better.

"Do you know what part you're supposed to play?" she continued. "I mean, Saul brought you here, left you his empire. Do you know why?"

"Hmmm," I said, after thinking awhile. "I suppose I don't." I put my hand on her belly again. "You may be onto something there, Mama."

"If you find out what Saul had in mind for you," she continued, "maybe you'll like it. Maybe you'll like the part you're supposed to play."

"And then I'll be happy?" I asked.

"Maybe."

"That's a lot of maybes," I said, and tickled her side.

"Stop!" she growled through clenched teeth, and I did.

"What about you?" I asked. "Have you been thinking more about taking over the school?" Lynn had grown up in the orphanage that Saul's wife started on the grounds of the Presidio, and that kind of work was right up her alley, compassionate and domestic as she was.

"Yes, but I want to have the baby first and bond with her, before taking something like that on. I don't need a job to be happy."

"I don't need my job to be happy either," I said, not sure it was really true, but trying to forget about it for now and get back to enjoying the moment. "I only need you . . . and Lynley." I moved my hand back down to the baby. "You believe me, don't you?"

"Maybe," she said with a smile and turned from her side to her back.

"What will really make me happy," I said, touching her belly button now, "is when this gets all stretched out, so there's no hole anymore. That's cool."

"It won't be long," she said, and soon we were kissing and caressing again, with Lynn pausing periodically to stop the blanket from slipping off. She was insecure about her body, despite my compliments, and also a bit paranoid because she knew there were so many security people in the vicinity of the house.

Her modesty turned out to be providential, because just as it was getting good again, we were interrupted by what felt like an earthquake, as five hundred pounds of Chinese cyborg jumped from the ground below the deck, soared over the art-deco railing, and landed with a shocking thud on the floor next to us. Lynn shrieked and pulled the whole blanket to herself, as if the greatest danger was that Min might see her naked. The giant had no interest in that, however. He stood with his forearms extended in combat readiness, and his eyes scanned the inside room, through the wide doorway, with a superhuman speed and perception.

Then he spoke, which was a rare phenomenon. "I'm sorry, sir. My sensors had been registering some anomalies within the security perimeter—nothing to bother you with. But when one of the diagnostic programs suggested that a foreign object may have entered your vicinity, I felt it necessary—"

"You're saying someone's in there?" I looked toward the room. I felt naked without my clothes, but even more so without my guns, which were inside.

"I do not know," said the big man, his gaze never leaving the darkness of the room. "There is an anomaly in my readings, but I have now scanned the room in four modes, and found nothing."

"It *was* getting rather exciting out here," I said. "Maybe that set off your—"

"Michael!" Lynn scolded me, in disgust. She wrapped the blanket tighter around herself, and checked to see if anything was showing.

"I can turn the lights on from out here," I said, then to the room: "Lights on." Nothing happened, so I said it louder, and they finally came on.

Just inside the room, a man was sitting in one of the plush aqua chairs. He was holding both of my guns, and pointing them straight at us.

3
KALEIDOCIDE

I instinctively moved in front of Lynn, so that the bullets would hit me if the guns were fired, and Min moved in front of me faster than the eye could see. I knew the cyborg's augmented mind was calculating an angle at which he could disarm the intruder, and sensed his powerful body coiling to do that, when my non-augmented mind finally realized who was sitting in the chair.

"Stand down, Min," I said. "And tell the men coming up the steps to stay outside." The giant's head turned slightly toward me, the muscles and machinery inside him not relaxing a bit, despite my order. "It's all right, he's an old friend." Min's head turned back toward the figure in the chair, who smiled and lowered the guns. Then Min did relax, but remained still, silently issuing the orders with his brain to the approaching forces. The rumbling on the other side of the door stopped, and I stepped to the side so I could see the man in the chair better.

"Terrey?" I said, and then it occurred to me that he could be an impostor, though it would have been an impressive disguise, because my old friend was so uniquely handsome. The squiggly upper lip, imperfect complexion, short but wavy sandy hair, sad but tough eyes, and the overall boyish but intelligent look . . . only the biggest money and best science could have duplicated him. But this intruder had beat BASS security to get in here—marks of big money and top science. So I cocked my head to the side and spread my hands in a query toward him.

"Only one way to find out," he said in a half-Australian, half-British accent, which also would have been hard to duplicate.

"Live forever, man," I said in my half-British, half-American.

"Never die young, mate," he answered, and I knew it was Terrey, because this was the customary greeting from when we were younger. My part was from a song first recorded by Oasis in the 1990s long before I was born, then remade by Balls Out when I was a teen in England, and his part was from a popular movie made in Australia when he was young.

I started to step toward him to greet him further, but then remembered Lynn and looked back to see that she was white as a sheet.

"Bloody hell, Terrey," I said, gesturing to my half-covered wife.

"Had to be, Michael," he answered, studying the guns while he did. "Boas, huh? These are a bit of a step down from your Trinity, aren't they?" He smiled at me, trying to ease the awkwardness of the moment.

I ignored him and sat back down next to Lynn.

"I'm so sorry, sweetheart. You okay?" I put my hand on the part of the blanket where the baby was underneath.

"I think so," she said, breathing hard. "Can I just get dressed?"

"Yeah, sure. Absolutely." I stood up with her and walked her inside to the door to another room, helping her hold the blanket in place and keeping my naked body between hers and Terrey, in deference to her modesty and regardless of mine. When we reached it, I told Terrey and Min that I would be back in a second.

"Try not to kill each other," I added, and went into the room with Lynn, where I assured her further and slipped on some pants. Then I hurried back out to the main room.

Terrey had tossed the guns onto another piece of furniture, obviously wanting to pacify the big cyborg, who still stood motionless and wary in the same place.

"How did you get in here?" I asked.

"Magic," he answered, spreading his own hands now.

"How?" I repeated. "Tell me."

"Really, Michael." He smiled. "I can't reveal all my secrets, you know, but I did it to reveal one that I have discovered about you: you are in some *serious* danger." He crossed his legs and relaxed, now that any possible confrontation was past. "I could have taken you out easily before your machine-man arrived, and long before the others. And if *I* can do that, you're going to have to make some big-time changes to survive what's coming."

"Have the peacers outside conduct an investigation right now," I said to Min. "Find out how we were breached." The big man nodded very slightly, and dived into the net via the cyberware in his brain, while still listening to our conversation—something that not many creatures on the planet could do.

"I told you, Michael," Terrey said, "there's no existing tech that can make someone invisible to your people or to your scanning capabilities, let alone both."

"Were any of the guards taken out?" I asked Min, who shook his head no. "Any air traffic detected?" No again.

"So unless there's been an unknown invention that cannot be seen by the human eye or current surveillance," Terrey continued, "it's magic. Harry Potter, *Lord of the Rings,* Net Aura kind of stuff."

I frowned at him and looked at Min again, who shook his head one more time.

"And seriously, mate," Terrey continued, "that kind of mystical stuff may be at play in this problem you have, which is what you really need to worry about, not something irrelevant that I'll never tell you."

"Okay, what is it?" I asked, sitting down across from him.

"You'll be dead within two weeks."

"How so?"

"Ever hear of the word 'kaleidocide'?"

I thought for a moment, then said, "Yes, I have, because I met Zhang Sun once, and became curious, so I surfed the net about him. I saw some of the speculation—rumors that he's into some weird religion that includes a ritual he uses to kill people, political enemies and such. Looked like an urban myth to me."

"It's not," Terrey said. "And you're next."

"Excuse me, sir," Min interrupted. "Dead ends all around on the breach. Looks like the secret stays with him for now." Another understated gesture from the cyborg, in the direction of Terrey. "But I can confirm what he is saying about Zhang Sun. I heard about his cult from reliable sources."

"That's right," I said to Min. "You should know better than us." I had recently discovered that my bodyguard had fled China because of Sun's rise to power.

"I want to hear about this," said Lynn as she emerged from the other room, dressed and made up.

"That's fine," I said, and she sat down on the divan next to me after I brought it back inside and closed the big door. "Lynn, meet Terrey Thorn. Terrey, my wife Lynn."

"My apologies for the intrusion, marm," Terrey said to Lynn, who didn't reply. "I had to show your husband how vulnerable he is, so he would let me save his life."

"Michael?" Lynn looked at me.

"Terrey and I were in the British special forces together," I explained. "Then I came here, and he went into the personal security business. We've lost touch, but I take it from this visit, Terrey, that you're still in that business?"

"One of the top companies in the world."

"What's the name again? 'Terrey Will Take Care of You'?"

"Protection Guaranteed."

"Oh, right. Nice rip-off of Reality G."

"An homage. I want a monopoly like theirs."

"Michael," Lynn said again. "What's going on?"

"The most powerful man in the world wants him dead," Terrey said. "And he most certainly will have his way, unless you hire me."

"Why you?" Lynn asked.

"Because, trust me, I'm the only one who can protect you against *this*. And you can trust me."

"What's *this*?"

"A method of assassination that has never failed to end in the death of its target."

"What's so special about it? Michael and Min keep assuring me that we're as safe as anyone, with the BASS security measures."

"You know how in most assassination attempts, the bad guy sends just one killer, or plants one bomb, or uses one other method of some kind? He can't do more than that because of limits on money and ability to escape the reach of the law. So if the good guy manages to thwart the attempt, he lives happily ever after, right? Well, in this case there are almost no limits on the resources and power of the one ordering the assassination. He's not just *trying* to kill you—he *is* killing you."

"How?"

"He doesn't send just one assassin," Terrey explained. "He uses multiple methods simultaneously, usually five or more. And in the three cases I've personally investigated and confirmed, they were successful long before all the methods were exhausted. Make no mistake, kaleidocide is not just a threat . . . it is a *death sentence*."

All four of us were silent for a few fearful moments, and then I broke the silence.

"But you think you can protect me?"

"I'd like to try," Terrey said. "This is like the World Cup Final in my business. If I keep you alive, we won't be *one* of the top firms in the world, we'll be at the top. Plus I owe you one."

"That you do," I agreed.

"So that's the meaning of the term you're using?" Lynn said. "Killing by a lot of different ways, like a kaleidoscope?"

"Yes, but by a lot of different colors, too." Terrey started to explain this, but Min continued, probably accessing information from the net as he spoke.

"Zhang Sun is like many of his contemporaries in China," the big bodyguard said, "in that he has become religious in the aftermath of the atheistic communist era, as the cultural pendulum has swung in that direction. But he is unlike most in that he embraced a rare form of cultic belief called the *bin lan jiao*. It's a complex system of faith, but in short they believe that colors, or the spirits associated with them, are a source of supernatural power. And one of the more exotic uses of this power is called *xing lu cai se*, or 'many-colored murder.'

As some on the net have become aware of Sun's practice, different names for it in English have been proposed, but the one that stuck is 'kaleidocide.' Perhaps because it sounds something like the Chinese words."

"The leader of the world's largest country is into this kind of stuff?" Lynn asked.

"It's not so hard to believe," Terrey answered. "Famous people have often invented or adopted their own unique religion—it's a trapping of power. And China has long been one of the most superstitious places on earth. To this day, most Chinese cover the mirrors in their bedrooms because they think they reflect evil spirits."

"And colors have always been very important to my people," Min added. "Sun's religion is merely a modern modification and conglomeration of many ancient traditions, tailored to his purposes."

"Which are what?" Lynn asked Terrey. "Why does he want to kill Michael? Because of Taiwan?"

"Very unlikely," Terrey said. "Even if he knows of Michael's role there, that's not enough to drive him to this. He's very powerful, but this move is not without its political risks."

"I agree," Min added. "This must be something more, something personal."

"What risks?" Lynn asked. I was a bit surprised at how interested she was, but also felt a tinge of pride that she was.

"The *ban lan jiao* and the *xing lu cai se* are open secrets to some in the government," Min continued. "But not to most of the people. If they became more exposed, we could possibly gain enough popular support to turn the political tide."

"We?"

"The People's Party. The movement I was a part of before I left China."

"Besides, Zhang Sun has mixed feelings about the Taiwan Crisis," Terrey added. "In a way, the Allied forces, and therefore Michael, did him a favor. It was a serious embarrassment for his country, but it allowed him personally to consolidate his power because the precipitous decline afterward created a desperation and willingness to accept a militaristic dictator like him. It was similar to how Saul Rabin rose to power, right here in the Bay Area, but on a bigger scale."

"You're up on recent Chinese history, huh?" I asked.

"I've been studying," he answered with a proud smile, then had to finish his homily. "After China failed in the Taiwan Crisis, the Chinese people were afraid of Western aggression and were persuaded that the failure was a result of weak-kneed domestic leaders. If Sun and the military had possessed more power, the thinking went, China would have won. So like I said, the Crisis was a major stepping stone to the throne for the bloke . . . I don't think he's that upset about it.

"Plus," Terrey added, "this move by Sun endangers his regime's chances of buying or trading for BASS technology."

"Oh, you're up on that, too?" I asked, raising my eyebrows at him.

"I have to be up on everything pertaining to a client," Terrey answered, and then saw Lynn cock her head in surprise, as if to say *We haven't hired you yet*. So he added, "Or possible client. Either way, this has to be personal for Sun. He's spending his own fortune on it, and to some degree he's risking his political future. So it's something more important to him than money or power."

"But what?" Lynn asked again.

"I don't know," Terrey said. "I was hoping Michael could tell us." He looked at me, but I just shrugged.

"No idea," I said. "But I actually sensed animosity toward me the one time I met him, even though it was in a public setting—at one of Saul's 'summit meetings' where he showed off that tech you were talking about, to some world leaders."

"When was that?" Terrey asked.

"About a year ago."

"So he had a hard-on for you *before* you became CEO of BASS."

"Also," Min said, "in Mandarin *lu* and *sha* are the basic words meaning to kill, but *xing lu* means 'to kill as punishment.'"

"So you did something before you came to BASS," Terrey said to me, "that you need to be punished for."

"If it wasn't Taiwan," I said, "I don't know what it could be."

"Use your detective skills to figure it out. Who knows, anything you find might be helpful to us somehow." Terrey looked at both Lynn and me. "But we have to keep you alive for you to be able to do that."

"Yeah," Lynn said. "How can we keep him alive?"

"By hiring Protection Guaranteed, of course." Terrey stood up, and Min tensed again. "I breached your security to show you how much you need us—and now I'm going to show you how good we are."

4
EXIT

It was a dark room, in more ways than one. The site managers kept the envi-ronmental gamma levels low, because even in virtual reality, some works are not well-suited for the light.

"You're not really a little boy, are you?" asked the newbie observer, who seemed to be appearing as herself.

"No," he answered. "This is how I looked when I was five."

"Oh. And why is there no name or title on you when I select that option?" Her eyes were looking down as she said that, confirming that she was indeed using one of those "mirror" skins, which were nice in that you could see what the person really looked like, but irritating in that a holo that portrayed an object in the real world was not entirely compatible with the physics of the virtual room. So her eyes were looking down—at her keyboard, mousegloves, or whatever—when she should have been looking at the person to whom she was speaking.

Mirror skins also only worked for people who were not ashamed and had little to hide, which explained why this woman was the only figure in the room who looked like herself. She was also nice looking, which may have been another reason she was willing to appear this way.

"I just forgot to enter one when I imported the skin, I guess," the five-year-old answered, in a boyish voice. The software he was using simulated both the video and audio from the scan of an old family holo. "But you can call me J.J.—that was my nickname as a kid."

"Okay, J.J.," she said, looking down again as she made a note of his name. "I don't want to intrude—I know why you're here must be very personal . . . but since you're here, you also must want to talk about it with someone . . ."

"Actually I first came here just to find out some ways of doing it," the boy said, scratching his right knee violently. "But after I did, I ended up coming back to build up some more courage. Some people visit here a long time before they do it."

"Yeah, that's what I've heard," she said. "So do you mind if I ask you some more questions?"

"I guess not," the boy answered. He picked at his nose with his index finger, and then wiped whatever he had liberated on his bright red sweatshirt, which clashed happily with the yellow bell-bottom pants that had been all the rage thirty years ago. He was sitting, but seemingly only on air, because the program had imported the figure but not the furniture. The woman, on the other hand, was wearing a beige pantsuit and standing, with empty hands hanging motionless at her sides. Both his feet and her feet rested on the floor of the room, however, mercifully borrowing from its physics. Skins like the Sideways Man, whom they would meet shortly, were considerably more disconcerting than even the missing chair.

"Why do you want to ask me questions?" he said, his fingers now clasped together behind his head, where they would remain for a while. She studied him for a few moments, and then looked around at the other characters in the room, who all seemed to be engaged in their own conversations a safe distance from her.

"I'll be honest with you, uh, J.J.," she finally said, and he noticed that she *looked* honest. "I'm a freelance journalist, and I'm producing a net feature on . . . places like Exit." The boy sat silent, his hands still behind his head, rocking slightly forward and backward on the chair that wasn't there. So she continued: "Does that turn you off?"

"It doesn't turn me on," he said after some more silence. "But it doesn't bother me as much as it would some of the people in here."

Now they both looked around at the other figures in the room who were still engrossed in their own business. But then the woman jumped when a new one suddenly appeared near her. It didn't help that he was huge and green and had knobs on his neck, and she had visible difficulty regaining her composure.

"Frank, you should use the door," said another woman in an Erin Elly skin, as she glided halfway across the room to greet the monster, taking his oversized hand in hers. The famous actress shot an apologetic glance at the staring pair, then pulled her friend away from them, toward the group she had left. He mumbled something that sounded like an apology, but in another language.

"Anyway, where were we?" the pretty beige woman asked. "It doesn't turn you on."

"It's not that kind of a site anyway," he said, and she smiled nervously when she finally realized he was making a joke. "Though they have them, of course." He nodded at her, but when she didn't nod back, he added, "Erotic suicide sites."

"Oh, yes," she said, looking even more nervous. "I saw links to some on the way here."

The boy wondered why a net journalist would seem uncomfortable with something like that—weren't they all immersed constantly in every imaginable deviance? Yet this woman didn't seem so jaded. Bringing his right hand down to scratch his knee, he studied her a little more closely. A little paunch was showing, just below her waist.

"You're thinking more of a *family* feature?" he asked her.

"Yes, well, most of what I've done is oriented that way . . . so actually I'm trying to branch out, diversify. You know, do some things that are more for adults." He now knew for sure that she wasn't very experienced, because she had so easily surrendered control of the conversation. Intrigued, he continued with his own interview.

"Are you full-time in this business?" he asked.

"No," she said, the professional air gone completely now, and just a normal person left. "Actually I'm a housewife, mother of two with another on the way. We desperately need some extra money, and I took some classes in college . . ."

She was interrupted as the Sideways Man entered the room, his body starting very small in one corner then growing bigger as it spun around in various directions—something like a wobbling top that was almost done spinning. When it grew to about the size of an actual person it stopped, but was stretched out in a parallel position to the "floor," rather than a perpendicular one like the boy and the journalist. In the real world, they instinctively cocked their heads to the side to get a better look at the man, but it didn't work in the virtual reality of the room, so they were forced to look at him in this disconcerting manner. It was like trying to view a sideways picture that comes up on a screen, without the ability to turn the screen or rotate the picture. But they could at least see that he was handsome, and well-dressed in a designer suit. The boy had talked to him before, and gotten to know him well enough to find out that this was a video-shopped version of himself made thinner and more attractive, and the suit was something he could never afford in reality.

"Meet the Sideways Man," the little boy said about the figure, who like him had no name displayed. "You might want to talk to him, for your article. He's made three attempts so far, which obviously failed, but I've gotten some good information from him."

"Learning from my mistakes," the man said, in a voice that didn't seem to quite fit with the way he looked. "Did the three twins come in here yet?"

"Not that we've seen," the boy replied, not noticing the oxymoron about "three twins."

"Good," the Sideways Man said. "They're making the rounds of the rooms, and I want to try again. I got cut off after a couple questions, and I want to see if it was an accident." The boy and lady were puzzled, but didn't have a chance to ask what he was talking about, because he then said, "Here they are."

Appearing in the very center of the room, and forming a triangle so they could look in every direction, were three beautiful Asian women. They were identical in appearance except for the different shades of their business suits, which were at least as expensive as the Sideways Man's. The first thing notice-able about them was the extremely high projection quality—they obviously had the best net technology available. Better than anyone in the room had ever seen, in fact.

"Please pardon the intrusion," they all said at the same time, "but we have one million dollars and a new life to offer someone who meets our criteria. This is a legitimate offer that we are unquestionably able to fulfill, as you can see by our Reality G certification." They all held out a paper that had appeared in their hands; it contained the company's logo and a link that could be selected for confirmation.

"You don't have to open it," the Sideways Man said to the reporter and the boy. "Someone did in the other room, and it's for real."

"Well, they have to be pretty serious to just waltz in here," the boy said, picking his nose again and wiping it on his shirt. "I've never seen spam on this site."

"It's like playing the lottery," the three women in the ad construct continued. "But slightly better odds and you don't have to buy a ticket. You just have to answer some questions."

"I'll do it," the Sideways Man said, louder than necessary.

"Thank you." Only the one nearest to him spoke now. "Are you male, female, or bi-gender?"

"Male."

"How old are you?"

"Thirty-seven."

"What is your IQ or highest level of education completed?"

"Bachelor's degree."

"What is your approximate height?"

"Six foot."

"What is your approximate weight?"

The Sideways Man paused, then said, "Two-thirty."

"No more questions are necessary," she said almost immediately. "Thank you for participating."

"Damn," he said. "It stopped at the same place before. And I even said a lower number this time."

"Can they tell if you're lying?" the woman asked.

"No," the boy said. "Must be a weight range they're looking for." He leaned back and put his hands behind his head.

"Anyone else?" the triplets asked, all together again.

"Okay," the woman said. "I'll try." She giggled nervously and shrugged her shoulders toward the boy. "This could be that extra money I'm needing."

"Thank you," said the one nearest to her. "Are you male, female, or bi-gender?"

"Female," she said confidently.

"No more questions are necessary. Thank you for participating."

There was silence in the room for a while, and the boy felt like everyone was looking at him.

"Not interested," he said in his high voice. "I had a lot of money once. I lost it all and ended up here."

"Maybe you could do things differently if you had it again," the woman said, looking down. "Besides, what have you got to lose? If by some chance you win, maybe it was meant to be."

"You think this is a game that you 'win'?" the boy asked, then paused while he scratched his knee. "But what have I got to lose, indeed. I literally have nothing to lose."

"Thank you," the construct near to him said. It must have been programmed to recognize that as one of the possible "yes" answers. "Are you male, female, or bi-gender?"

"Male."

"How old are you?"

"Thirty-five."

"What is your IQ or highest level of education completed?"

"A Master's degree."

"What is your approximate height?"

"Six foot, one half inch."

"What is your approximate weight?"

"One-ninety."

"What is your physical location?"

"Fresno, California."

"Are you in good physical health?"

The little boy paused and started digging in his nose again. In the real world he was thinking, *Now we'll see if they can recognize a lie, or a half-lie at least.*

"Yes," he said.

"Besides depression and suicidal ideation, do have any other mental health issues?"

He was briefly taken aback by their apparent clairvoyance about his issues, but then remembered where he was.

"No," he answered. Another half-lie. At this point it *was* somewhat of a game to him.

"Do you have any neural implants? And if so, what kind?"

"Yes, the Allware 33 system." This was true, but he didn't tell them that his contract had lapsed.

"Why do you want to die?"

The boy found this question curious, but he answered: "Like I said, I lost everything."

"Could we have some pictures of you, or better yet some holos? We can either extract them from your device or cloud, or you can send them to this link."

"Nuh-uh," the boy mumbled, mostly to himself. "You better not touch my stuff."

"I'm sorry, but I'm having difficulty understanding what you're saying. Please try again."

No way was the boy going to allow this scary software access to his own files, but *What have I got to lose?* echoed in his brain enough times that he ended up sending three holos to them.

Finally, the Asian model asked for his name, social security number, and permission to verify his answers.

"I knew that was coming," he said, mumbling again.

"I'm sorry, but I'm having difficulty understanding what you're saying. Please try again."

Again, despite himself, he ended up giving them what they wanted. *What have I got to lose?*

Then they disappeared.

"That's it?" he asked no one in particular.

"That was interesting," the pregnant semi-journalist said. "She went on and on."

"Remember me if you get the million," the Sideways Man said, then started spinning and receding until he was gone from the room.

"Those women weren't actually online, right?" the woman asked. "It's just a fancy program sent around to thousands of sights, probably."

"It was ridiculous," the little boy said to her. "Some kind of scheme to steal my identity—can't believe I went for it." He leaned back on nothing again, and clasped his hands behind his head. "Fortunately I won't have an identity to steal after tonight."

After the brief spark of interest in the mysterious ad, and the temporary flash of what might have been called hope, the hell of a life he was left with seemed even more worthless. And he was more determined than ever to end it.

"I was wondering, J.J.," the woman said, looking down again. "Before you, uh, go, could you introduce me to some more of the people in here, help me get some interviews? I was even thinking, maybe someone would let me go with them into the private room, and be there with them when they . . . be with them at the end. You probably wouldn't want to do that, I'm sure, but maybe someone else would. Or would you . . . ?"

The five-year-old began to rock back and forth on his chair of air. He did that for quite a while, in silent contemplation, while the woman's eyes alternately looked up at him and back down at whatever in the real world was drawing their attention.

"Okay," he said at last, and reached down to scratch his knee.

5
THE RUINS OF OAKLAND

"Is this a net room?" Terrey asked, looking around the Sausalito house.

"Of course," I answered.

"Can I . . . ?" He looked at both Min and me. "I want to show you something." I nodded to Min, and the cyborg released the blocks on the wireless access to the room without moving or speaking. Apparently Terrey was free from any cyberware in his head, as most educated and wealthy people were, because he had to do more than just think about it. From his belt he removed an earpiece and inserted it, to provide two-way audio, and a small sheath for the top of his index finger, which would allow him to mouse the display that he was apparently seeing in his eyes.

"Contacts man?" I said to him, and he nodded. "I'm a glasses man myself."

"We can argue about that later," he said with a smile, while moving his finger almost imperceptibly against his thigh. "But for now, check this out."

One whole side of the room suddenly became a large screen with an aerial view of Treasure Island, the Bay Bridges extending from each side of it. Then the view zoomed in toward the flat part of the island that was originally a military base, and had been restored to that use during the Taiwan Crisis because of concern for possible Chinese retaliation from the Allies' maneuvers. Since the earthquake it belonged to BASS, with many of its best soldiers and its fleet of

Firehawk helicopters commandeered for the peacer force that restored order to the devastated city. That was one of Saul Rabin's many amazing feats, co-opting American military resources for his new empire, then keeping them when the Bay Area was granted independence from the United States. None of this could have happened without the numerous economic and foreign debacles the U.S. had experienced in the decades prior, and without its utter frustration in attempting to provide relief and order to Oakland and the East Bay, which to its regret still belonged to the mainland. But the coup Rabin had accomplished was still amazing, by any standard.

As a base for the helicopter fleet and other peacer resources, Treasure Island also served to bolster the new city-state's sense of security on the East Bay side, where just across the water lay the "wild west." Since the American government had run out of money and patience following the quake, Oakland especially was a postapocalyptic wasteland populated mostly by criminals and other malcontents, including people that BASS had exiled from the peninsula. Little did I know that we would soon be taking a virtual trip to that wasteland, as Terrey's camera view zoomed farther in to show a black SUV parked at one of the entrance gates to our base on Treasure Island.

"I'd like you to meet the rest of my team," Terrey said, and we could see three figures emerge from the SUV and approach the gate, their long black coats flapping in the fall winds. When they reached the guard house at the gate, Terrey manipulated his controls and filled our entire room with the holo projection, so that the three figures were life-size, and we were now facing them. It was as if we were there on the tarmac at Treasure Island, except that we couldn't feel the wind coming off the bay.

The rest of Terrey's team was three Asian women, Japanese if my guess was right. They seemed taller than most women, if indeed the scale of the holo was correct, and their faces and necks, which were the only parts of their body visible above the black coats, had some randomly placed spots that at first glance seemed to be covered with metal that was reflecting colors from around it. Upon further inspection, those patches seemed to be small video displays, like living tattoos.

"This is Ni, San, and Go," Terrey said, gesturing to the women. "Their surname is Shimomura, if you want to check them out, but that name means little to them. They are sisters, triplets actually, so I like to call them *Trois* together, but their names individually." I noticed that they did seem to be identical, except for the varying patches. They were attractive, but in an unusual way that would take some getting used to. And when they all said "Pleased to meet you" at the exact same time, I felt even more uncomfortable.

"Maybe you shouldn't do that," Terrey said to them, sensing my reaction. "I'm used to it, but it can be a bit disconcerting to others. *Trois,* this is Michael Ares, his wife Lynn, and his assistant Min." Just one of the triplets said "Pleased to meet you" this time, with a smile, and we all said hello.

"And yes, you heard right when I said this is the rest of my team," Terrey continued. "Fact is, I don't need anyone else on a permanent basis. These super-Sheilas are quite sufficient."

"Are you Japanese?" I asked, sensing in my subconscious that this was important, given the fact that I was being threatened by the Chinese. The same one answered "Yes" (Ni, perhaps, because Terrey referred to her first?). I also made the connection because there was probably genetic experimentation and manipulation involved in their creation, for which Japan was renowned.

"The girls need access to three of your Firehawks, the files for them, and enough onboard weaponry to start a small war," Terrey said, and both he and I immediately sensed Lynn and Min tensing again. So he explained: "One of the assassination methods is always a direct attack by an assault team. Sun's people hire mercenaries near the target's location, arm them, and embed them as sleepers until the best time for a strike. This usually happens before the other attempts, because of the preparation involved and the limited time they can stay hidden. So I took the liberty to imagine where I would place such a team, and investigated it, hoping that you would indeed hire me. This may be the easiest part of the kaleidocide to figure out, because of all the prep involved and because the Chinese are a little disadvantaged in their thinking regarding American culture, geography, etcetera. They picked a location without exercising much creativity, and I found it by simply guessing some spots that seemed workable from an outside perspective, and then hacking some of the cyberware in citizens who might live there or had passed nearby." He looked at the triplets. "Or I should say, my associates hacked them."

"So where is it?" I asked.

"In Oakland, of course. Like I said, not blinding creativity. The easiest place to hide vehicles and weapons within striking distance of BASS territory." That was certainly true, and one reason why we needed the deterrent of Treasure Island to make our people feel safe. Oakland had been in a state of urban decay even before the earthquake hit; now it was mostly ruins, and outside of our jurisdiction. Our satellite surveillance system, affectionately known as the Eye, could cover the devastated area, but couldn't really see *under* the ruins, where most of the surviving denizens lived and moved.

"Why don't you give us the coordinates?" I said. "And we'll take care of it."

"Well, frankly, no offense, but the Shimmies can do it way better. Plus as I said, I want to show you what we can do, so you can see why you need to hire us."

I looked at Lynn, who shrugged, which was her way of telling me that this decision and the rest from now on were up to me, because I knew about this sort of thing and she didn't.

"Give him what he wants," I said to Min.

Ten minutes later, three of the Firehawk helicopters were in the air over the East Bay, heading for Oakland as the sunset abated to our west. When our blocks were removed, the triplets had wirelessly downloaded the schematics and controls for those birds, and some smaller flying machines inside of them, into the cyberware in their brains. They were processing and integrating the weapons capabilities of the helos en route, and Terrey had shifted the displays in the room so that we could see from each of their perspectives.

"Isn't it a risk to use them for this?" I asked.

"Not really," Terrey answered. "They're that good."

"What if one of our Hawks malfunctions? Something out of their control?"

"They're good enough to overcome anything like that."

"The Hawks are augmented with our antigravity tech," I said, "so they'll handle differently than other helicopters."

"They learn very fast."

He was obviously not worried, so I changed the subject. "Why don't they use the Hawks by remote?"

"They're sharper when they're on site—broader angles, etcetera. But mostly they just love doing this kind of stuff. And any direct action against Red interests *really* appeals to them."

There had never been any love lost between the Chinese and Japanese, I knew, and the fears and resentment on the island nation's side had increased in recent years, with the Chinese military buildup, imperialistic dictatorship, and attempt to annex Taiwan, whose proximity to the mainland mirrored Japan's.

"So who are the mercs they hired?" I asked.

"Maybe some from farther east. But probably a lot of locals, because they know where to hide and how to get around."

"What's their exit strategy, do you think?"

"Well, I'm sure their contact told them that there would be other methods in play, so they're rolling the dice that they won't be needed, and can just go home with a fat paycheck and no action."

"And if they do attack?"

"Hope they survive and escape the area in their helos?"

I nodded, but also raised my eyebrows when it sank in that they had helicopters, and therefore how serious this threat really was.

"Wait a minute," Lynn said, still interested, as I was glad to note. "Why would these people risk their lives or freedom like this? Sounds like they have a good chance of ending up dead or in jail."

"Desperate times," Terrey said. "There are a lot of criminals, and even battlers, who are willing to take the chance at the big bikkies they're being offered, not to mention getting to play with some nice hardware."

Lynn looked at me, puzzled.

"Battlers are people who are working hard but barely making a living," I explained. "And big bikkies is Australian for a lot of money."

She said "Ohhhh," a bit playfully.

"Also, Oakland is a hotbed of resentment toward BASS," I added. "Don't ever take a stroll through there alone, okay?" I turned back to Terrey.

"What're you planning to do with them?" I asked, which for Lynn's sake was a softer way of saying *Will you kill them?*.

"If we capture some," Terrey said, subtly tipping me that at least some killing was inevitable. "It's my pretty educated guess that we'll get nothing from interrogating them or hacking any implants they have. Sun's people are too good for that—they'll have too many layers between them and anything worth tracing." He looked at me. "But it's your call."

"It's worth a try," I said, "in case we can head off some of the other assassins. Let's not have any unnecessary loss of life." I worded it that way for Lynn. I was always trying to keep her from thinking of me as a monster, especially after what we'd been through a year before in what we called the "silhouette" incident. But I was also telling Terrey to not worry about shedding some blood.

"Almost there," Terrey said, and we all watched the displays as the copters approached the ruins of Oakland, which were an astonishing sight at any time, but especially bathed in the dying light from the sunset. The mostly crooked buildings that still stood reflected it and cast long shadows across the gnarled remains of the ones that did not. I knew that some adventurous tourists braved the city just to see the kind of postapocalyptic landscape that only existed before in video games and movies, and I also knew that some companies provided flyovers so that the less adventurous ones could get a bird's-eye view of sights like Lake Merritt, the large tidal lagoon that had once been a downtown landmark but was now just a scarred ditch because all the water had dissipated through the cracks in the earth. At least it wasn't overrun by a plague of birds anymore.

"Will they see us coming?" Lynn asked, her use of first person hinting at how effectively the displays put us in the action.

"No chance, with the jamming capabilities of my girls," Terrey said. "In fact, considering that and how quietly the Firehawks run, you may see *them* before we even open fire." With that reference to a preemptive strike, any illusion of no casualties was gone, but Lynn didn't react to it at all. "Depending on how well-hidden they are. Look for teal vehicles and body armor—they'll all be painted that color."

"How do you know that?" I asked.

"We saw it on some of our surveillance shots," Terrey answered. "Blue-green is one of the elemental colors, significant in ancient China, and they make it darker by adding in black because that's the color of death, or maybe the 'king of colors.' Whatever. But knowing this might help us to figure out what other colors to look for."

As if on cue, one of the triplets used her augmented eyes to telescope to one section of the distant ruins; as a result our view in that display zoomed in as well. It moved rapidly across the nooks and crannies in the debris, following the red indicators of a targeting system until they locked together and lit up brighter in the middle of the display.

"There you go," Terrey said. "See that? San is saying it's one of their armored SUVs, only partially covered with the camo. They have to use their best big hiding places for the helicopters, because they're harder to explain away if seen."

We all strained our eyes looking for something teal, but in the fading light all we could see was blacks and grays.

"Bottom right corner," Min said, and I realized that he was probably plugged directly into the triplets' eyes. When he said it, I concentrated on that part of the slightly wavering display and thought maybe I did see something, but wasn't sure.

"I don't see a thing," Lynn announced. But then the two triplets on the outside swung their Hawks away from the middle one, all the while keeping their gaze locked on the neighborhood where the assault team had been sighted, which looked to be somewhere between the downtown ruins to the left and the crater that had been Lake Merritt to the right. And for the next thirty minutes, dark blue-green was about all we would see.

6

IMPRESSED

Obviously the mercs had seen or heard the approaching Hawks, because a camo canopy was thrown off the SUV we were trying to see, and it shot out of its hiding place onto one of the few drivable paths in that part of the dead city. Two more identical vehicles were soon visible on other roads, each of the three rushing in totally different directions. But they all had appeared on the perimeter of a center point, which they were heading *away* from—a fact not lost on a military mind like Terrey's.

"Those are the observation sentries," he said, "trying to lead us away from the bulk of the force." This fact was also not lost on the triplets, apparently, because each one maneuvered her craft closer to one of the streaking SUVs, released two guided rockets in its direction, and immediately turned back toward the center of the perimeter outlined by the decoys. Terrey switched our displays to the rear cameras of the Hawks for a few moments, so we could see the rocket tandems weave their way around all obstacles and explode each of the SUVs in a fiery cascade of teal metal and red body parts. So much for no casualties.

Then our three views returned to the triplets' perspective, looking toward the section of ruins they were all approaching from different directions. In two of the displays we could now see helicopters, painted the same color, that had been uncovered or moved out of a building, their rotors unfolding for imminent flight. One of them burst into flames before it could lift off, targeted and destroyed by one of the triplets. But the other managed to get off the ground and release some flak at the same time (a nice move), causing the projectiles coming its way to create some more debris where it had been parked. Soon it became apparent that at least three other enemy craft were in the air as well, and Lynn gasped beside me.

"Can they come and get us?" she asked.

"No," I said, putting my arm around her. "They're clear on the other side of the city. And at this point, they just want to escape."

"They were holed up there waiting for a strategic moment to attack Michael," Terrey added. "With the element of surprise, hopefully. But now the jig is up, and like he said, they just want to get away. Which is Buckley's." He saw Lynn's brow knit at the Aussie slang and added, "No chance." He had to raise his voice considerably now, because the seven helicopters had begun to exchange fire. "If any of their birds come this direction, the rest of your Firehawk fleet would take them out."

"But they can hurt your helpers," Lynn shouted above the din, and then Terrey turned down the audio with his finger mouse. So she finished at a normal volume: "They have more than you, and they look pretty fancy."

"Yes, those are a more advanced model—Sikorsky Primes," Terrey conceded. "Though more lightly armed, for stealth purposes. And they have even more of an advantage in numbers . . . look at that." He pointed to the right-hand screen, where one triplet was looking at a telescoped shot of a group of four more teal SUVs emerging from another hiding place. They fanned out and as they did, panels on their roofs slid open and armored soldiers holding RPGs extended themselves and prepared to fire. Judging by the quality of the other warware I had seen so far, I knew that these would be the kind that could fire repeatedly without reloading, and their projectiles would also be guided, to some degree at least. I was beginning to wonder myself if the triplets were in over their heads, when one of them announced that there were also RPG gunners on foot now in various parts of the rubble. She said this calmly, however, not seeming worried in the least, and even added the superfluous detail that the foot soldiers were "also attired in teal body armor."

The three views became harder to watch as the triplets pushed their Hawks into the spaces between the higher buildings that were still standing. But though it was difficult to follow, it was absolutely fascinating watching these "super-Sheilas" work. From their relative concealment, they took out one of the enemies' choppers before it realized it was a sitting duck in the open air. So now the three remaining Sikorskys entered the labyrinth of the higher ruins to play a cat-and-mouse game with the Hawks, and their ground forces were drawn into those areas as well, trying to get a clear shot at our three black birds. But when the teal forces fired, their shots always seemed to miss the Hawks, sometimes by inches, and explode harmlessly against the walls of the buildings, or the roofs if the triplets flew upward and circled back down toward their targets. On the other hand, the machine guns and rockets of the Hawks rarely missed, turning the ground vehicles into more sprays of metal and blood, and the mercs on foot into blotches of red on the concrete where they were standing or running. In a matter of minutes, another of the Sikorskys was down, too, having rounded a corner into the sites of a waiting Hawk.

"My *Trois* see everything through one another's eyes," Terrey explained with pride. "And they communicate everything simultaneously with no noise or jamming limitations. So it's like one pilot in three different locations. Like the perfect team, their movements perfectly synchronized. And they can see through the Eye as well." He modified one of the displays to show us a view of the entire battlefield from above, with several inset screens showing up-close details of the location and movements of particular enemy units.

"Your satellite system is also providing them warnings when entities and projectiles enter their proximity," he continued. "Which they programmed it to do in about three minutes on the ride in." He smiled like a father whose son has been drafted into professional sports, and as if on cue, two brightly colored indicators lit up on the Eye view to show that an enemy chopper and SUV had entered each end of a corridor between buildings, where one of the Hawks hovered in the middle. As soon as they saw our helicopter, the teal chopper fired from the air and the teal SUV from the ground. But Ni (I could see her name on the display) surged forward to a spot above the ground vehicle just in time, and the enemy rockets crossed paths and streaked into their counterparts, turning the blue-green into red flames.

We were duly impressed, but Terrey wasn't done.

"And guess what else they can see," he said, and changed the Eye display to another channel, which took me a few moments to identify. I soon realized it was a view from one of the two remaining enemy choppers, which I first thought was lifted from the HUD display or a forward camera. But then I realized the perspective was shifting, and it was coming from *inside* the cockpit.

"The girls can hack basic cyberware," Terrey explained. "Like this guy, who probably has an entertainment implant, for music, movies, porn. Some have comm imps for their InPhones . . . in those cases we can also access what they're saying or hearing."

"Wow," said Lynn, and like an exclamation point we watched from the Sikorsky pilot's view as he flew right into a trap and was shredded by Go's cannon fire. His head must have lolled to the side, because the perspective of the front of the cockpit was slightly askew as it dipped toward the ground and crashed into the debris.

"Way to go, Go," Lynn said with a nervous laugh.

I rolled my eyes and Terrey said with a grin, "She's never heard that one before."

Then we all stopped smiling, because of the display from the optic cyberware of the enemy pilot. His helicopter had not exploded in the crash, so his cocked view showed the wrecked front of the cockpit, lit by some outside light and some flames burning inside. The display was utterly still, so that meant that the man was dead, probably from Go's bullets while still in the air. But though the man was dead his implant was functioning, so we could still see through his eyes.

After an eerie moment of relative quiet, Terrey changed that display back to the Eye view, and we could tell that the one remaining Sikorsky had turned tail and was flying away from the battleground. All three Firehawks gave chase, bearing down from behind on the fleeing chopper like black wolves stalking some wounded prey. When in range, they opened fire with their cannons, and the beaten enemy met its end.

"No way to take them prisoner," I said half-heartedly to Lynn.

"But we can capture the rest if you want," Terrey said.

"The rest?"

"Yeah, according to some more 'ware that the Shimmies are scanning, some of them stayed in their base, which is in the bottom of that building." He pointed to the structure that was on all three screens now, because the triplets were approaching it. It was about five stories tall, but much wider, and leaning less than the others around it.

"That is the YWCA building," Min spoke for the first time in a while. "Designed by Julia Morgan, who did Hearst Castle and other famous projects. She lived through the 1906 earthquake here, so she must have designed it to endure the next one."

"Good for her," Lynn said. "A bright spot in Oakland's otherwise miserable history."

The Firehawks hovered near the building on three sides, and Ni's voice rang out on her bird's PA system.

"You are surrounded, with enough fire power to blow you all out. Please surrender, so we don't have to further damage that nice historic building."

They came out, but not in the way we hoped. And the triplets had one more surprise for us as well.

7
NAPA CITY

"You don't get nothin' for nothin', piece." That's what Simon had said when Angelee realized what he was all about. The "free" place he had given to her seemed too good to be true, and it was. It had a separate room for her little boy, more than she could have hoped for, but now she knew why that room was necessary. Simon's customers wouldn't be interested in that kind of audience (at least most of them).

At first she had blamed Mariah, the friend she made at the homeless shelter. But then she remembered that the big black woman had told her what was going on, in her own way.

"He'll get you some work," Mariah had said while nodding her head slightly—the only way she could have relayed such sensitive information in that cramped and crowded environment. And all Mariah's references to how pretty Angelee was were now starting to make sense. Angelee had thought her older friend was attracted to her, but she knew now that Mariah had been pointing to her only way out of that diseased death trap. But she wasn't sure whether she should be grateful or hateful to her "Mama," as Mariah liked to be called.

Angelee knew that she *needed* Mariah, however, so she couldn't tell her off, or otherwise spurn her "kindness." Mariah was her only hope in case the handsome rich man ever made it back to the shelter. Mariah had promised to watch for him or one of his assistants, and Mariah knew where to find her, if necessary. And Mariah was simply the best person for this job, because somehow she had managed to live at the shelter for years, when most arrivals either left or died within weeks.

Angelee lay on her new bed, the biggest thing in the room, and waited for her four-year-old son Chris to stagger droopy-eyed out of his room, which he did every once in a while until he finally got too tired and fell asleep. She looked around at the brownish colors on the carpet, curtains, and paint—Simon had said it was "like living in a sewer, pony, but without the smell." Remembering that, she noticed for the first time that there *was* a nagging odor, and tried to figure out what it was for a minute or two before giving up.

Then she closed her eyes and reviewed her meeting with the handsome rich man for the hundredth time, picturing it in her mind and savoring every detail to keep the memory alive. Even as she did, she wondered if this was good for her. Perhaps it was a dream that needed to die. But not yet—these were the last few hours she would have the room to herself (judging by what Simon had said), and the last time in her life that she would be Angelee. When the tricks started rolling in, she would become someone else, back to being just "Lee." Back to being some kind of monster? She didn't want to think that way—this was something she had to do, or else her little boy would never make it. But for right now she was still Angelee, and Angelee was the girl that the handsome rich man had come looking for . . .

They had tried to get him to wear one of those little masks that most of the visitors wore, but someone who saw him come in said that he had waved it off. He must have been a very important person, because the staff who saw him all followed him with their eyes—some of them even stopped working to watch him. (She got this information from other "residents" also, later on.) And then there was the seven-foot-tall Chinese man who stayed at the door, his eyes sweeping the room in a machinelike, measured cycle.

"Are you Angelee?" he asked from behind her. (She was changing Chris's diaper.) She looked back over her shoulder, and then did a double take because he was so good-looking and well-dressed—unlike anyone else she had seen at that place, including the staff. His voice was tinged with a slight accent, which someone later said was English. She didn't know about that, but she did know that it immediately struck her as dignified, kind, and even sexy. Maybe she was projecting a feeling back on her memory of the moment, but thinking of it now, it seemed that right away she knew that he was unlike any other person she had ever met. This was one of the *special people,* the ones who seemed so unreal when you saw them on TV.

"Mommy!" Chris had blurted out, and jerked her out of the seemingly eternal moment. The boy was old enough to be bothered by lying there with his diaper off, but unfortunately not old enough to be completely out of diapers yet. Angelee turned back to the little boy and finished with him, wondering if she should have said "Wait a minute" or "Excuse me" or something to the man, and wondering if he would still be there when she turned back around. While doing this, she briefly glanced up at some of her "bedmates" nearby, and noticed them staring past her at the man. Valya, a young Eurasian girl with only one eye, was moving a bandaged hand up and down in a futile attempt to beautify her greasy, matted hair.

Finally, after what seemed like another eternity, Angelee turned around to face the man. She stayed seated, clasped her hands down between her knees, and grew painfully aware of how unkempt she was. Why couldn't this have been shower day?

"Angelee?" he said in that heavenly voice. "Are you the wife of Peter Kim?"

Maybe it was the rush of odd emotions provoked by this unexpected visitor, or maybe it was because she had not heard a reference to her husband in a while, but she lost it. She began sobbing uncontrollably, her shoulders wrenching forward as though they were trying to touch each other. But she did happen to manage a nod or two in the midst of her blubbering and dabbing at her face with the bottom of her shirt.

When he was sure that she had nodded, the dark-haired angel sat down beside her on the cot and put his arm around her. The shudders of grief were now joined by euphoric waves of pleasure, which seemed to spread through her body from where his arm was touching her. This was the first time a man had touched her since Peter died, a fact that provoked more sobs and delayed her further from any kind of rational interaction with the man. But he just sat with her, squeezed her shoulder now and then, and waited for her to come out of it.

"Sorry. Very sorry," she eventually got out, but then jumped in her seat when she looked up and saw the Chinese giant, blocking half the light as he towered over them. He had left his post by the door, glided through the beds with surprising ease—since he seemed too big for some of the spaces between them—and was now holding out a tissue for her.

"Thank you," she said as she took it. The bald, brown monstrosity just nodded slightly, then made his way back to the door, scanning the room the whole time. As she wiped her nose, she looked again at the handsome man, who had now taken his arm off her and twisted sideways so he could see her better.

He chuckled, waving his finger toward the back of his head and said, "He has a bit of a leak from his upper cranial port." His mild amusement seemed to fade as he realized she had no idea what he was talking about. "The tissues," he added with a more serious expression. "That's why he carries tissues." He pointed to the one she was holding, and then grinned again. "We can engineer a cybernetic vascular system impervious to the common cold, but he still needs tissues. Funny."

He paused for a moment as she sat silent, studying his green eyes. Then he said, "Angelee, I came here to help you."

He explained that her husband had worked for his company and had provided some assistance to him personally before he had died "in the line of duty." Wanting to make sure Kim's family was cared for, and to thank them personally, he got their address and came to visit them in Napa City, only to find that they had been evicted because the BASS salary had been their only source of income. The apartment manager had mentioned the downtown shelters, because that was where he had directed the young mother when she asked, "Where can we go?"

"So here I am," the man concluded with that charming smile. "And I want to give you this." He handed her a wad of cash, and squeezed her shoulder with his other hand. "That should take care of you and your son for now, but I'll come back, or send someone to take care of you. I'll have to think about what else I can do for you, and check on a few things." He looked over toward the door.

"Well, I have to go now," he said, politely regretful. He gestured at the big cyborg by the door. "They have a security window for me—I can only be in public for so long. But I'll see you again."

He smiled and walked away, dodging the miscreants and their makeshift homes, until he and the bodyguard had disappeared. Angelee sat with her mouth open, clutching the money, realizing that she never got the man's name. Important people usually don't need to introduce themselves, and an utter nobody like her was too intimidated to speak, let alone ask for his name. But none of that mattered to her at that moment, as her homeless neighbors gathered around her to begin the gossip and speculation that would give them all a reason for living in the days to come. And he said he would come back!

Now, lying on her bed in the brown room, Angelee was crying again, much like she did on that day when the beautiful man put his arm around her. But he wasn't there to comfort her this time. In fact, more than a month had passed since he promised that he would come back, and apparently he had forgotten her. Thinking that he would be taking care of her, and knowing that holding on to that much money would make her a target for crime, she gave some of it to her extended family members who had qualified for federal housing. The rest she spent on food for herself, Chris, and Mariah, enduring the shelter until her knight in shining armor would ride in and take her away. But that day never came, and the money ran out. So here she was, about to return to the oldest profession.

"You got settled in by now, hoover," Simon had told her earlier today. "So tonight you open for business. Get some sleep now, baby girl, cuz you won't be sleeping much at night no more." He groped her with both hands and added, "You won't believe how they go for the new ones. Be real busy at first. But after a while, it'll slow down some. Won't be such new stew—be just like the rest."

She moved to take his hands off, but he drew his face up close to hers. "Ah, ah, stew," he hissed through chemical breath, "You mine. An' sooner you learn that, the better. You say no to me, or any my customers, you dead, and we put your kid to work. Simple as that, stew." Finally, he drew back from her.

"Sample some of the merchandise myseff," he said, "but wouldn't wanna dirty it for your first night. Expectin' to get some big money on that one. Good marketin' mierda, you know." He moved his hand across the air in front of him, as if depicting a billboard. *"Brand-new stew . . ."*

8
PREY

Not long after the triplets' warning boomed out of the PA into the dusty Oakland air, about ten of the teal-armored mercenaries ran out of the bottom of the YWCA building through several different exits. Some took off on surface paths—they could hardly be called roads anymore—while others disappeared into nearby tunnels that had been discovered or dug in the debris by survivors of the quake. They probably figured that the Firehawks couldn't shoot them all, and that we had no ground troops on site to chase after them. And on both counts they were right. But they didn't count on what happened next.

From the side doors of each helicopter sprang four dark shapes, two on each side, which hung in descending order next to it for a moment, making it look like the big birds were sprouting wings. But it soon became apparent that these were not wings, but smaller birds—the remote-controlled flying machines called "falcons" that we had built with the Sabon antigravity technology and used to assist our peacers in surveillance and pursuit. As these falcons now dove toward the surface in different directions, it was clear that the triplets were controlling them wirelessly with their cyber brains, and sending them in pursuit of the fleeing mercs. We had "falconers" who could control the flying robots, but only one or two at a time. The triplets were each controlling *four* of the black birds, while also piloting their Firehawks.

48

Terrey switched the displays so that twelve screens with a view from every one of the falcons hung around us in the room. Now I was really experiencing sensory overload, and I'm sure it was worse for Lynn, but our gazes darted among the screens nonetheless. This was just too good to miss.

The first falcon that reached a man running on the surface simply gassed him and left him lying unconscious (it did this by firing softshell pellets from its wings, which also contained killer and stopper rounds). But when another caught up with a merc in a rather big underground tunnel (the remains of a subway, perhaps?), it not only hit him with one of the gas pellets, but also hauled his body back up to the surface by shooting toward him an Immobilization and Retrieval Apparatus (IMRATS or more often RATS, for short). This device looked something like the back of an open wallet and was attached to the falcon by a plasteel cord that extended and retracted from the bird. The apparatus at the end, when contacting a human figure, would encircle the person and lock its ends together. Then it would contract, immobilizing the person and enabling him to be transported (usually without too much injury). By an interesting coincidence, the RATS was located on the bottom of the falcon, right about where a real bird would extend its claws to grasp its prey.

The falcons made short work of the fleeing mercs, with only a few incidents—one was accidentally flown into a wall and knocked out; another was shot by a merc and had to be brought back to the helicopter. But the others found and acquired their targets impressively, and we all watched the last two arrests because Terrey deleted the other displays and made those larger on one side of the room.

One man had escaped the pursuing bird earlier by being clever enough to put on a little gas mask from his utility pack, so that when a pellet struck his arm and discharged, he was able to continue moving and disappear into a small debris tunnel. The falcon pursued, and the man crawled on all fours through the other end and back to the surface. Then he blocked that end of the tunnel with a big piece of debris before the falcon could emerge, and took off running across the surface again. Unfortunately for him, the menacing bird fired killer rounds at the debris to unclog the exit, then rose into the air and put him down with stoppers. These rounds were often referred to as "Xs" (pronounced "exes"), because the plasteel contents expanded into the shape of a cross, about three inches in diameter, after being fired. They often left marks in the shape of an X on the body of the person who was immobilized by them.

The last merc tried to make a stand in another small tunnel, where he stopped after a curve and fired his handgun at the falcon when it came around the corner. But he missed, so the falcon merely backed up out of view, fired a gas pellet at the wall near the man, and waited until he collapsed to use the RATS and haul him to the surface. By that time one of the triplets had already landed her Firehawk and was skipping from prisoner to prisoner, checking if they had any cyberware she could hack, and also threatening the conscious ones with torture if they didn't talk. On the audio feed of a falcon hovering near one of the mercs, I overheard her say something about cutting off parts of his face and neck to match her "decorations." I imagined that an exotic cyborg brandishing a knife about a foot from your face was rather intimidating. But the man didn't talk, because he didn't know anything. None of them did.

"It's like I told you," Terrey said, summarizing the findings of his team. "The kind of people who organized this wouldn't take the chance of giving these people anything we could use." He turned off the displays and took the mouse sheath off his finger.

"Min, send a squad of peacers to pick up the survivors," I said. "Lock 'em in the cathedral and interrogate them, just in case they know something."

"Can my team join us here?" Terrey asked, to Lynn as much as to me. He obviously recognized her level of influence in our relationship. "We need to get started right now, if we're going to save your life. The other parts of the kaleido-cide won't be this easy to stop."

I thought for a moment, then said, "Terrey, will you excuse us for a few minutes? Min, you can stay, but tell the other agents to hang with Terrey outside until we call."

"Fine," Terrey said. "But I suggest you don't take too long, and in the meantime don't go near the window, don't eat or drink anything, and don't even wash yourself with any water, until we can get the safety measures in place."

He headed toward the door, and as he did I addressed him again.

"I will consider it bad faith if you planted any listening devices in this room—without telling us right now, that is."

He kept walking out, but glanced back with a mild smile, sideways nod, and a little wave of his hand that told me not to worry about it. Then he was gone.

9
ENIGMA

"Are there any bugs in here?" I asked Min, who turned his head and body slowly, scanning the entire room, and then answered no.

"So what do you think, Lynn?" I asked, and when she didn't answer right away, I said, "Keep in mind what we just saw, that Terrey was able to head off part of the danger already. He obviously knows what he's doing. And his team certainly is impressive, wouldn't you say?"

"Do you want me to say something?" she asked, bristling a bit. "Or do you just want to tell me what you think?"

"No. Go for it."

"I'm sure he's good, that seems obvious. But I would say the more important question is, can you trust him?"

"Of course. Farther than I can throw him, anyway. He's—"

"You're answering too quickly. Stop and think about it more. What's he really like?"

"Do *you* have some reason to distrust him?" I asked. "Some, uh, intuition?" I had learned to take seriously her intuitions, or instincts, or whatever they were.

She thought for a moment, then said, "No. But I don't know him. I want *you* to think more about it, and maybe do your thing, check on him or whatever you do."

"Okay," I said, and nodded to Min, who I knew would initiate a thorough combing of the net. "As for what I remember about Terrey . . . he was loyal to the king, if not to the entire chain of command, and he was loyal to me personally, especially after I did him a big favor. He talked a lot about money, how his only goal was to be rich." I thought some more. "But there seemed to be more to him, though he didn't want to admit it. I once referred to him as 'a man of principle in disguise,' something like that. But it could have been wishful thinking on my part. I've had experiences with other friends from my younger days, where I had idealized them, only to be sorely disappointed later."

I had little more to say about this, and I felt the urgency to do everything I could about the imminent threat to my life. In fact, I had to admit, despite my considerable experience with almost dying, I felt more fear now than any other time I could remember. This puzzled me, but perhaps it was because of Lynley, the little baby girl inside Lynn's belly, which I found myself staring at presently. She was our "replacement" for little Lynette, who had died a year previous, in violent circumstances like the one we were facing now. I hadn't known much about fear since I entered the military at age eighteen, half my life ago, but I knew enough that I didn't want to go through anything like that again.

"My instinct is to trust him," I said, looking back up at Lynn's face. "And I think we need his help." I shrugged and turned to Min. "What did you find?"

"Nothing very alarming," he answered. "His communications are hidden under an extreme amount of ice, which would be unheard of for an average person, but not too surprising considering his vocation." He looked at Lynn. "Hotel and other rental records show that he has had numerous female friends in various places around the world, but his only visible bank account is cosigned by one particular woman. It has to be publicly accessible for her sake, presumably."

"Hmmm, one true love, though a ladies' man?" I said. "That's the kind of disguise I was talking about. Bit of an enigma." I looked purposefully at Min. "What do you think?"

The big brown man was silent for a long time, perhaps finishing a sweep of the net.

"I agree that we need all the help we can get," he finally said. "From my knowledge of the resources and forces arrayed against you, I am surprised that he was able to expose and eliminate the assault team so quickly. I would be comfortable with hiring him, as long as we run a perpetual analysis. If he does happen to love money as much as he said, he has a good reason to do his best for you. But he could also be bought by someone else." He paused to change gears. "But what would really satisfy me is some time alone with the triplets."

"Really, Min?" I looked at Lynn, and we both laughed. "You're hoping for some cyborg 'fourplay'?" I couldn't resist the joke, even though I knew that the same injuries that had resulted in Min's cyberization had also rendered him unable to enjoy that part of life. He was like the eunuchs who long ago served in the palaces of royalty—in more ways than one.

"A poor choice of words," he said with a rare smile. "The triplets are undoubtedly the ones who conceal Mr. Thorn's communications and accounts so well, so they must be his confidantes. I would like to understand their perspectives and motives better. Perhaps I could ask them some questions while you take the call you have received from Stanford Glenn."

"Oh, my glasses," I said, instinctively patting my belt and pockets. "I left them in the bedroom, in all the excitement earlier." I looked at Lynn and winked. "And I mean *before* Terrey came."

"Stop," she said, blushing. She didn't like any talk about sex in public, especially ours, but I always thought she was too prudish.

"Come on," I jabbed at her while I headed toward the bedroom door. "You didn't have a problem laughing at Min a minute ago."

"'Cause that wasn't about me." Right. At least she was honest.

I grabbed the glasses quickly, then returned to the big room.

"You asked me for my opinion, sir," Min continued. "Would you mind if I added one more thought?"

"Absolutely, Min. You don't need to be so humble about it."

"I would suggest talking to Mr. Rabin before you make a final decision."

This reminded me that my personal "eunuch" had belonged to the king who ruled before me, and he was still keen on advancing his interests, even posthumously. But I thought it was a good idea, because this was the reason Saul's wisdom and experience had been downloaded from his brain before he died, into his Legacy Project.

"Tell Terrey we haven't made a decision yet," I said to Min, "but that he can bring the triplets here, on the condition that he lets you talk with them on the way. Or interface, or intercourse, or whatever you cyborgs do. I'll make a few calls and then give him our answer."

Min nodded and left the room. Lynn said, "I'm gonna take a shower" and did the same. I slipped the glasses on and saw that I had indeed missed a call from Stan Glenn's direct line, a rare and important enough phenomenon that I needed to call him back, even under the circumstances, though I reminded myself not to talk too long. I kept the glasses on so that my side would be audio only, since I expected to be on the defensive and didn't want my face to give away any lies I had to tell. He must not have had any such concern, because he answered with full video from his chest up.

He wore his trademark white sweater, which as always made the darkness of his skin more pronounced. I had wondered many times if he did that intentionally, like a megaphone announcement of his blackness, but had also always been afraid to ask him, because I was generally happy with our relationship and didn't want to endanger it in any way. He had been a professional athlete in the same sport as Darien Anthony, my late friend and associate, and had known and liked D. I think we developed a connection because of that, and because of our shared sympathy for what had happened to our mutual friend. Which was a good thing for both of us, because Stan was arguably the most influential government official in our neighboring country, the American Confederation. His office was a combination of the historic ones of secretary of state and minister of foreign affairs, charged with conducting all the interaction with other governments on behalf of the American people. And in today's global economy, that role may have given him as much power as the president herself, if not more. The health of nations depended more than ever on their relationship with others, and that was especially true of the decentralizing and destabilized AC, which had both lost the Bay Area and annexed Mexico in recent years. So as one news site had posted, referring to his characteristic appearance, Stanford Glenn represented "the great black and white hope for America's reputation in the world."

The fact that Stan was content to appear on video while I was only audio was a good sign for me. It suggested that his censure would have few teeth—as did his opening greeting.

"You know I had to make this call," he said.

"Why?" I responded, like an innocent lamb.

"We've had reports that BASS conducted some kind of military or police action on American soil . . . again." Occasionally we had to do something in the East Bay, but it was only a few times a year at most.

"You're calling Oakland 'American soil'? You're the ones who gave up on the East Bay after the quake."

"Now that's not fair. We can't help it if no one wants to live there, and we can't throw money at a place where no one wants to live."

"Only since the money ran out," I said with a smile he couldn't see. "Before that you were throwing it left and right at places like Oakland."

"I don't know about that—it was before my time. But I know we could make it a nice place again if we had more money, like the kind we could make if we become your business partners." He was referring to the Sabon antigravity technology, of course, which he and the rest of the world wanted BASS to share with them.

"I heard Oakland streets aren't even on your satnav maps anymore," I said, ignoring his plea.

"We call it GPS in America." Was he trying to remind me I wasn't from this country? "And that's because for the first few years after the quake, people were following their GPS—most direct route—to Frisco or Napa Valley, and they were getting robbed, killed, or at least badly lost."

"Yeah, not good." I laughed. "I was just there."

"Oh, you *were* there?"

"Well not really. Virtually."

"So your people were."

"What happens if I say yes?"

"It could be bad, unless . . ."

"Unless what?"

"We make some kind of deal, like for some kind of cutting edge technology?" He couldn't see my smile, but I could see his. "Maybe a flying car that would save me from the DC traffic?"

"I think you're bluffing. No one wants an incident. I'm guessing the Queen suggested, or even pressured you, to make an attempt with me." "The Queen" was our way of referring to the president.

"You're a quick study, Michael. Only one year under your belt, and you've already figured out how these things work. But you can't blame a guy for trying."

"I won't be surprised if it happens before long, Stan," I said, returning his familiar address, then turned more serious. "Saul's open to it, but he doesn't want it going to any governments with a penchant for warmongering or violence. That's why you shouldn't pick a fight about anything we do in Oakland."

"You're using present tense, for a man who's been dead a year."

"He being dead yet speaketh."

"Sounds like a ghost story."

"It is," I said, "and I actually have to talk to him now about some problems we're having."

"Okay," he said. "You've heard from me."

"That I have."

I hung up, imagining his next conversation, with the woman we called the Queen. *"Yes, ma'am, I talked to him personally for about five minutes. Yes, ma'am, I gave him a piece of my mind about Oakland and negotiated for the Sabon technology. No, ma'am, but I'm hopeful."*

It was interesting that when I mentioned my "problems," Glenn didn't bother to ask what they were. I wondered if he might possibly know about the kaleidocide, but I didn't have time to worry about that now. I was about to summon the dead man we'd been talking about, with a brand-new kind of séance.

10
NEW YORK

During the day, Lower Manhattan was a colorful place, visually and de-mographically. But late at night it became almost monochromatic in both.

An eye looking down upon this part of the city would see, for the most part, varying shades of gray—from the concrete and metal of the buildings on the dark end, to the soft whites of the evening lights and the new snow falling through the air. In between were all the other colors that had been visible in the daytime, but were now washed out into the middle shades of gray by the prevailing weather and indistinguishable from the old, dirty snow around them. The only nocturnal survivor from the bright colors of the day was taxi-yellow—not the thick river that carpets the streets during business hours, but smaller trickles flowing here and there, enjoying much more freedom of movement in the almost deserted sprawl.

A generation ago, no one would have believed that the business district around Wall Street would again become a veritable ghost town after dark, but no one would have predicted the destruction of the World Trade Center either, in the generation before. Crime always increases when an economic crisis occurs, especially after a series of them, and the recent proliferation in this area had been enough to justify the curfew. Just as the 9/11 disaster symbolized how vulnerable the United States had been to terrorists, the quiet on these night streets now showed how much of a threat organized crime was to the American Confederacy.

So the denizens of this New York night were primarily criminals whose hope of profit was enough incentive for them to risk breaking the curfew. They had dominated the night in this area for decades, ever since the gradual attrition of NYPD officers working the late shift had dwindled their numbers down to an ineffective ratio. In fact, there were times during that sad epoch in New York history that the only police on the streets at night were those who were paid to look the other way. This "surrender" of the night was understandable, because prior to it over 95 percent of all NYPD casualties had been occurring after dark.

But in recent years, things were changing, thanks to some more ambitious leadership in the city and the decentralization of the American government, which freed up more money and encouraged more self-interest at the local levels. Inspired by the grand experiment of Saul Rabin's Bay Area Security Service in San Francisco, the NYPD hired and heavily subsidized a native rent-a-cop outfit called Garden Safety Services, which was transformed into Gotham Security. City legislators instituted the curfew and (also following the BASS model) granted "freedom of deadly force"—a license to kill—to these "Dark Knights." During these early years of the program, however, they were often referred to as the "Dead Knights," because the criminal organizations that had become entrenched in the city night were not prepared to give up their own operations without turning the Big Apple into a bloody battleground.

Though the costs were already high, however, the New York government and Gotham Security were continuing the fight and expecting to win at least some modicum of law and order before too long. Enlistment had not been a problem so far—there always seemed to be people with a military or law enforcement background who wanted more action and were willing to put themselves at risk for a five-year term, after which they could retire comfortably. The "career path" was therefore similar to that of a professional athlete—except that an athlete doesn't find himself in a vicious firefight about once a week. Each agent had to take his chances for five hours every night, four nights a week, during the street patrol or "hard" shift. The other half of their night—the "soft" shift—was spent in a safer location, often babysitting one of the big buildings. And so far this had been a good year: in its first nine months, less than one in five of them had been killed or incapacitated. That was slightly better than the statistical average since the founding of the company—the employees all had about a 25 percent chance of buying it before their five years were completed.

On this particular night in early November, two future statistics named Korcz and Stephenson sat in their patrol car, moving slowly down a snowy street, surrounded by deserted skyscrapers. Their yellow vehicle was the only one within view, though a few blocks back they had passed a "real" taxi that had broken down and been abandoned on the street earlier in the day. It looked almost the same as the car they were driving, but it wasn't heavily armored like theirs, which was one from the fleets of "night taxis" that Gotham Security had purchased when the curfew went up. It had been a mutually beneficial arrangement—the cab companies had no more use for such heavy secure cars, now that they would not be driving at night anymore. And the armor on them was already so formidable that very little modification was necessary for their new work. Gotham also chose to keep the color, and to give their agents matching body armor, because the yellow was easily recognizable and distinguishable from the criminals, who were usually draped in blacks and grays to blend in with the night.

Korcz was a big Russian man, with a bald head and a pock-marked face. He appeared even bigger than he was next to his partner, who was a wiry little man no more than five foot six. Stephenson didn't look like a "Dark Knight," or any other type of cop, but was qualified based on his inner constitution. Unless he was lying about it, he had a doctoral degree in mathematics, but was so much of an adventurer at heart that he had become bored with teaching at a college. Korcz, on the other hand, didn't even speak English that well—his childhood in Eurasia had left him undereducated in the arts and sciences, but toughened by the third-world streets. He was more familiar with the art of pugilism and the science of ballistics, therefore, and he caught a break a few years back in San Francisco when a brother's friend took him on as a peacer with BASS. After he made some irreparable mistakes in that notoriously demanding organization, the brother's friend helped him to get this job on the other coast. After almost three years here, he had already faced death too many times to count, and every night he was more afraid of dying than he would ever show.

This dream thing with Stephenson didn't help, either.

"I tell you, it's odd," the little man was saying. "I'm a scientist, sort of, and you're a skeptic. But we both have to admit it's possible."

Korcz continued driving, not saying anything.

"Right?" Stephenson asked again. "They've worked this stuff out. It's not religious crap. They admit it's experimental, and all that, which makes me inclined to believe it more." He paused to see if his partner was ready to say anything yet, then went on. "And this one isn't just in their 'possible precog' range—it's off the charts, I'm telling you. I called the company today, I think they'll want to know about this one. I mean, if they got a lot like this during testing, or since it was released, they would have it in the manual. But the numbers aren't even in the manual!"

"Drimscepp?" Korcz finally said. It was his way of saying "Dreamscape."

"Huh?"

"You called Drimscepp, danyet?"

"Yes. I did."

"They did not answer?"

"No, of course not," Stephenson said. "I left a message. Hopefully I'll get something more than the usual construct reciting a standard response." He tapped his antique-style glasses to check the time. "But I think I will, for this one."

"Maybe it is broken," Korcz said.

"That's the third time you've said that since we started talking about this," Stephenson said, shaking his head. Then he shifted his small body to get a better look at Korcz. "Are you scared about this?"

"Are *you*?" Korcz answered.

"No, of course not. Do I look scared?"

"No, but my point. You think it is true, but you are not a 'fred. Why do you think I am a 'fred when I do not think it is true, ah?"

"Because that's why you're denying it." Stephenson pointed to his head. "You're denying it, because you're scared." Korcz snorted, but said nothing.

"Do you want to see it?" Stephenson asked cautiously.

"I will be tired when my work is done," Korcz answered, thinking he would have to visit Stephenson's apartment.

His partner shook his head. "I have it here," he said.

"You have it . . . here?" Korcz tapped the brake, as if there was some danger ahead on the street. The little man began searching through his wallet, looking for a tiny dot drive, and since his head was pointed down, Korcz could see the dime-sized jackpatch behind his left ear. It was yellow, the same color as the car and their uniforms. Korcz was surprised at this, because for years all such "headware" had come only in gray.

"You have matching color," Korcz said to Stephenson, who had found the dot he was looking for.

"What?"

"Your hole in your head," Korcz gestured at it. "It is the color of the car."

"Yeah, it's new," Stephenson said with a frown. Then he held up the dot. "Are you stalling? Do you want to see it or not?"

"You spend all that money for the machine," Korcz said. "You want to find something . . . ah, how do you say, spectacle?"

"Spectacular," Stephenson said. "Now quit stalling and watch it with me."

The bigger man sighed audibly. "We have to go to the back."

"Right," Stephenson said. "Stop the car for a minute. We'll hear it if they call."

Korcz pulled over a little toward the side of the street, though that was hardly necessary in this ghost town. Both men exited the front doors of the cab and climbed into the back. The passenger compartment doubled as a net room, and after fiddling with the controls for a minute, Stephenson found the dream he had recorded on his new toy.

"I'm gonna show you the enhanced version, because it's so much better," he said. "But I've seen the other one, and it's pretty clear what's going on."

With this he pushed his last button, and the compartment filled with a hologram. They were seemingly suspended in the sky, looking down on a yellow car similar to theirs, but with less detail. On the top of the car stood two men, one much taller and bulkier than the other. The faces vaguely resembled theirs, but the difference in size between them was exaggerated in almost ridiculous fashion.

"I must see myself as *very* small compared to you," Stephenson said with a chuckle. "I wonder what my analyst would say about that."

"Do you have one of those?" Korcz asked.

"No, it's a joke," Stephenson answered. "Now watch what happens. It's quick, so I'll slow it down."

The yellow car began erupting into an orange ball of flame, engulfing the two figures. The sound of the slow-motion explosion roared painfully in their ears for a few moments until Stephenson turned it down. The explosion gradually subsided, leaving a pile of wreckage where the car had been. But the two figures hung suspended in the air, apparently unharmed, hugging each other.

"I wonder what your anal person would say about that?" Korcz said.

"Funny," Stephenson said. "Now watch this."

The two attached figures rose up slowly into the sky, as if by levitation, and disappeared into a bright light there. The hologram ended and disappeared, leaving the two real men staring at each other.

"That was our souls, or spirits, or whatever, going up to heaven, right?" Stephenson said. "We're gonna get blown up, and then the afterlife."

"You are talking like it will happen," Korcz observed.

"Valeri," said the little man, with a grunt of disgust, "let's review the facts here. I have been recording my dreams every night for two months. The Dreamscape console logs the recurring ones, and it has these categories, one of which is 'Precog Potential.' *Precognition,* my friend. From all their endless research and cutting edge technology, which is way over my head, they've determined that dreams falling into this category may point to some future event."

"*May* point . . ."

"Yes, may point. But I've had a form of this dream over ten times. And the potential precog levels on the console were way higher than any of the examples in the tutorial. Plus I've had the dream *more often* lately." He paused for effect. "If these tech wizards are even close to right, Valeri, this is gonna happen, and it's gonna happen soon."

"What the hell are you two doing in the backseat?"

It was Arvit's voice from the front, and her face was on the dashboard screen. Korcz and Stephenson both jumped, and then clambered back into the front of the taxi. They looked at each other, each waiting for the other to say something, which made the moment more awkward.

"Listen, I don't want to know," Arvit said. "Go to the Aegis building, north side, right now." Korcz spun the converted cab in that direction, as the middle-aged woman continued. "This is the Ponchinello 'Money' lab we heard about, the one where they produce it and supply it to the employees right in the building itself. Our mole in the lab finally came through with the location, just now. And damn me if my sister doesn't work in that building during the day. Small world."

Korcz and Stephenson had heard about this case that the day cops were working on, and had been close to breaking for weeks. Money was a designer drug that increased memory, stamina, and other capabilities necessary for "getting ahead" in the Manhattan rat race. Unfortunately it also turned many of its users into psychotics or catatonics after prolonged use. Of course that didn't matter to the people selling it, who in this case were a mob family known popularly as the Black Italians. A few generations back an Italian mob family had united with an African-American one, and like medieval kingdoms of old, their union was cemented by intermarriage. Only this time, in a subsequent flurry of marital concupiscence, many more mixed couples tied the knot, now that it wasn't taboo anymore, and what could basically be called a new race of criminals appeared on the streets of New York. This was all common knowledge now because the genesis and rise of the Black Italians had been immortalized in the long-running net series *Duets*.

"The lab is in a hidden room three floors deep in the basement parking garage," Arvit continued. "I guess the customers pick it up before or after work, or maybe they have it delivered to their desks along with the mail, I don't know. But I do know that we're gonna bust the building supe who knows about it, and anybody else in line, but I need you and the others I'm sending to take the lab before they can clean it out and blow it up." She paused for a couple seconds. "Do you want to say something? You're looking at each other? No, okay. We're uploading the schematics for the garage now, and the info on your squad. Stephenson, you can make the call."

"Thank you, ma'am," he answered.

"Oh, and one more thing," she added. "Tyra Ponchinello, Tyrone's daughter, is in that lab tonight." A picture of a pudgy, rather odd-looking woman appeared on the screen. "Don't kill her, bring her in. Understood?"

"We'll do our best, ma'am."

While Korcz sped through the gray streets, Stephenson put together a plan to approach the lab discreetly. But by the time they joined two other Gotham cars at the big building, that plan was out the window. The criminals somehow knew that the police were coming, according to the mole in the lab, and were already cleaning out the operation. So it was to be a frontal assault, and fast, because once the mob got what they wanted out of the lab, they would most certainly obliterate it with explosives.

As the squads readied their arsenals and prepared to enter the building, the two rent-a-cops were plagued with the images and sounds from Stephenson's dream, so freshly implanted in his mind and so eerily resonating with a ring of truth.

11
GHOST STORIES

I didn't talk to Saul's ghost for several months after I became CEO of BASS, first because the emotional wounds from my ordeal were too raw, and I didn't want to reopen them by talking to the man who was at least partly responsible for them. He was also responsible for the good things that happened to me as a result of the ordeal, so my feelings were mixed, but the confusion of not knowing how to classify the old man and his role in my life created some additional hesitation. Another reason was that I was creeped out by the idea of communing with the dead—you could read about it or see it in fictional books or movies, but actually doing it, even in this virtual format, felt something like attending a funeral. And doing it regularly seemed like attending the same one over and over again.

Only one of those problems was alleviated to any degree when I finally decided to access the construct. By the third or fourth time I'd used it, I wasn't as uncomfortable, because the ghost took on a "life" of its own, and I thought of it more as a different version of Saul Rabin, rather than the man himself. But the mixed feelings transferred to this new "person," whom I was getting to know better than I ever knew Saul himself while he was alive. The more I found out about my former boss's history and perspectives, he became even harder to categorize in my mind. I couldn't prove most of his opinions wrong, but I instinc-

66

tively knew there was something off about at least some of them. And I just couldn't get my mind or heart around the reasons he had for many things he had done, nor for many things that he advised me to do.

When the Mayor, as he was often called, found out that he was dying of one of the few types of cancer that even great wealth couldn't cure, he resurrected a secret cyberware project that his son Paul had started for the nefarious purpose of controlling people's actions through a chip implanted in their brains. (It wasn't technically a computer chip, but that was a lot easier to say than the scientific name for it.) Saul didn't want to waste all the time and money that had gone into the project so far, but he also didn't want it to continue in that direction. Nor did he even think it would ever be *possible* to control someone else's moral decisions, because he believed in the existence of an immaterial soul— one of the unconventional ideas of his that I was still trying to understand. So he came up with the idea of using the technology to record and preserve his knowledge and experience for future generations, renamed it the Legacy Project, and had the implant installed in his own head.

Saul was nothing if not a visionary, foreseeing that he might be the first of millions to download the contents of a brain, which he called "the physical storage center for the soul," so that the resulting construct could tell ghost stories of their lives. The idea was that most people didn't have the time or skill to write autobiographies for their progeny, but could do it this way with little effort. However, I thought it was questionable whether it would catch on when BASS was done perfecting it, because the kind of people who had enough money to afford quality wetware were still almost unanimously wary of it. They didn't share Saul's confidence that the seat of the human will resides somewhere other than the brain, and wanted to avoid any outside control at all costs. I myself had once lived under an extreme version of that fear for several days, and I was still thoroughly unwilling to take a chance with it.

Saul was also nothing if not a private recluse, so he protected his own Legacy files with typical ferocity. They were initially stored in the cyberbrain of the only person he fully trusted, who was Min, until the bodyguard could vet me and other potential heirs. Then they were copied to a Fortress Cloud, the most secure location on the net, and coupled with the alpha version of the personification software being developed by BASS techs. Part of the security strategy was that there would be no connection whatsoever between Saul's ghost and the rest of the net—it would only know what Saul had known by the end of his life, and whatever information was shared with it by the privileged few who had access.

As one of those few, I had to provide voice recognition by speaking into my glasses, DNA validation by pressing my fingertips to the sensors on their arms, and a retinal scan by holding my eyes open for five seconds. Only then did the virtual 3D bust of Saul Rabin appear, suspended in front of a nondescript background and looking almost exactly as I remembered him from his final days: an expensive but out-of-style shirt draped over shoulders that were still broad but slightly slumped from aging, a thick lightning scar stretching from temple to cheek on one side of a heavily wrinkled face, and a receding shock of gray hair. I had asked the ghost about its appearance in an earlier conversation (Why not appear as a younger version?), and it responded with a rather cryptic explanation to the effect that other than his marriage, Saul considered his last decisions to be his best . . . an answer that elicited in me some of the mixed feelings I mentioned earlier.

"Hello, Michael." The audio was not as accurate as the video, since human vocal cords and larynx were such a complex organic system. But it captured the basic impression of Saul's cracked voice at nearly eighty years old, and the somewhat impolite, order-barking manner in which he had talked. "Is my empire intact?"

The almost imperceptible grin on the construct's lips was reminiscent of the living Saul, but it could not approximate the amused sparkle that had been in the old man's eye when he said things like that.

"It's fine for now," I said, "but I could use some advice on how to keep it that way."

"Well done, Michael." One of the minor glitches in the programming was that the ghost said my name more often than a human would. "A fool trusts in his own heart, but a wise man listens to counsel."

"Last time I asked you for advice," I said, "you quoted Confucius. Before that was Aristotle, and the time before you said the same thing you just said, which I'm guessing is from the Bible. Your programmers should have anticipated this happening more than three times." I liked to point out things like this, because it reminded me that I wasn't talking to a human, and I felt more in control that way.

"I can adapt," it said. "Plans succeed with many counselors." There were pauses before the response and between the two statements, which I had noticed quite often when it talked. I assumed they were built in to make it seem more human, because I knew this kind of high-powered A.I. would definitely not require any time to think.

"What's that one from?" I asked. "The Book of Mormon?"

"Right," it said. "Spoken in the deformed Egyptian by the angel Moronic himself."

I squinted at the construct for a moment, because even though I knew very little about Mormonism, that answer didn't seem right to me. "Really?" I asked.

"No, Michael, it's from the Good Book also." I had heard Saul use that expression when he was alive, and it always struck me as a subtle way to lessen the embarrassment of saying "the Bible," because it was in such ill repute in our culture. Then the ghost let out a grating laugh that was not exactly like Saul's, but just as awkward. And it added, "I'm programmed to spice up every tenth answer with some humor."

I squinted again, realizing that it had used humor twice in a row. The ghost was as enigmatic as the man. But I was short on time, and that mystery was too minor to be worth solving right now. So I merely thought about what I wanted to ask next, and as I did the ghost sat in absolute silence with an utterly fixed expression. That was one of its major glitches: unlike a human, it didn't seem to mind an awkward silence, and appeared willing to go on forever without breaking it. A similar glitch was that it had no compunctions about going on forever when given the opportunity to provide pedantic explanations that seemed to come straight out of a book. That hiccup became apparent when I asked it how to survive a kaleidocide.

"No one ever has, as far as I know," the ghost said. "I don't know what the success rate was in the early days of the religion, when it developed among the rank-and-file soldiers in the Red Army as a way of preparation for battle. Of course, we *do* know that the Chinese have succeeded in every annexation of neighboring territory they have attempted, as well as every 'police action' they carried out in those territories afterward. But no record exists of the specific rituals by the sons of the *ban lan,* or whatever the groups of soldiers called themselves at the time. They must have been successful to some degree, however, or a rising star like Zhang Sun would never have adopted the religion as a means of personal power. He saw something in those early days that made him believe in it.

"But since Sun adopted the *ban lan jiao,* he has been nothing but successful in his quest for power, specifically in the elimination of his enemies by way of the *ban lan* ritual. This could be simply because none of his targets had a snowball's chance in hell of surviving multiple assassination methods thrown at them simultaneously from a murderer with almost unlimited resources. But we must also consider the possibility that there are actually supernatural forces at work in the kaleidocide."

I was initially surprised at this, but then realized that the idea was consistent with Saul's belief in an immaterial or spiritual part of life.

"If I were in your position, Michael," he droned on, and I wondered how he knew that I was the one being threatened, because I hadn't revealed that, "I would hire some outside help and pay them more than they could possibly be offered by the other side, because in every situation we know about, Sun has infiltrated or turned someone against the target. Betrayal seems to be one method that is a part of every kaleidocide . . . maybe because the supernatural forces are especially fond of it."

"How can I be sure the outside help won't betray me?" I asked. "Besides paying them a lot?"

"You can't be sure—risks are unavoidable either way. But before you hire someone, see how up front they are about that particular danger. If they are, that's a good sign. The ideal situation would be to surround yourself with only those with whom you have a personal connection, or with those who have had no contact with you before, or both. You want to avoid people with no sense of loyalty to you, Michael, or those who have been around you and may have been contacted and corrupted." The ghost paused again, for human effect. "And try to get someone who knows what they're doing. There are personal security companies that are good enough that they only work for clients who are in significant danger and can afford an exorbitant fee. Relate to these professionals like you do a doctor: follow their instructions unless you have a really good reason not to, and don't think you can protect yourself better in your own way."

Through the other side of the glasses, which did not contain the image of Saul, I could see that Min had re-entered the room, obviously finished his reconnaissance and ready to report. So I said thanks to the ghost, and asked him if it had any last word of advice.

"Pray," it answered. "Pay a lot and pray a lot. That about sums it up."

I was about to hang up when Min spoke up in an amplified voice, designed to supersede any audio in my glasses: "Sir, do I hear the shower running? Is Mrs. Ares in there?"

"Yeah . . . ?" I said, puzzled at first, but then realized why he was asking. Terrey had said not to touch any water until safety measures were in place, and neither Lynn nor I had taken it seriously enough to remember it.

I shot to my feet and held out a hand to Min, communicating that I would check on her myself. Then I moved toward the door, fast at first, but then slower because I realized that if the shower water was booby-trapped in some way, Lynn would already be dead. She would be slumped on the floor of the tub with the deadly acid or poison or whatever still spewing out from the showerhead.

I stepped through the door to our bedroom and then to the threshold of the big bathroom, the sound of the water now seeming overamplified in my ears, and my heart pounding in my chest. I was filled with dread as the shower came into view and I called Lynn's name. There was no reply, but soon I could see her pregnant shape through the semiopaque door, and I could see that she was rinsing her hair. I was so relieved that I punched the button and slid the door open without thinking how it might scare her, and sure enough she jumped and let out a little shout when she saw me. I only refrained from hugging her because I didn't want to get soaked, and I reminded her of what Terrey had said and asked her to shut off the water. She said "I'm done anyway" and obliged.

While she was replying, a voice in my ear said something also, like "Pardon me, Michael?" I was still connected to Saul's ghost, who had waited silently in the glasses for my next question or comment.

"Lynn was almost killed," I said, blurting out the first thing that came to mind.

"You can't make an omelet without breaking a few eggs," said the ghost with a sad expression on its face. Apparently it had misunderstood what I was saying, because of the time lapse, the background noise, or my exaggerated comment. Another glitch.

"Sorry," I said. "I gave you the wrong impression. Lynn's fine. You were saying something about paying and praying, to save me from the kaleidocide."

Another pause, then the ghost said, "Pay a lot and pray a lot. That about sums it up."

I thanked it again, and hung up. Why I was thanking a computer program, I don't know, but I just shook my head and went back out to the living room to see what Min had learned about the triplets.

12
SAVING LIVES

"I interviewed them," Min said about the triplets, **"and they allowed me a** limited look inside."

"Inside their minds," I said. "Their cyber whatever . . . not their bodies, right?"

"Right. But I could see their physical capabilities as well, which are considerable, though not at my level." Was the big machine-man capable of pride? I supposed so, though he didn't show it. "Their mental capabilities, however, are unprecedented. The fact that they were engineered from birth by the Japanese scientists allowed their systems to accommodate the wetware more successfully than those of us who have added it later. And the fact that they share the same DNA gives them a unique ease of interaction, because they can totally avoid the translation problem that limits most other neurocybernetic communication. They are like one person with three brains, which of course they were originally."

"They were?" I said, catching some of it. "Oh, the same DNA. They were 'Siamese triplets.'"

"Yes, separated and augmented at some time after they were born. If they were born." He paused and looked away, either processing more of his data or deciding whether to say something. "But I have to say that there seems to be even more to them than can be explained by their distinctive physiology."

"What do you mean?"

"Their capabilities exceed their augmentations. In other words, they seem to have supernatural powers—and I use the term in a technical sense—or at least natural ones that I cannot see."

"Do you think there is such a thing?" I asked, referring to supernatural powers, of course, because the ghost had just mentioned the idea. And it had become a topic of mild interest to me in the last year, since Saul Rabin was by far the most intelligent person I had ever met who believed in them. As to whether the old man was entirely sane, however, that jury was still out in my mind. So I was curious to know if Min shared his metaphysical perspective.

"My background is purely atheistic and naturalistic, as is much of China, of course. I have to admit that Mr. Rabin challenged my assumptions, but they remain basically unchanged. Perhaps I am more of an agnostic than an atheist now, but until proven otherwise, I would still say that the mysteries of life are a result of natural causes we simply have not discovered yet."

I wondered briefly why Saul had hired and confided in Min, knowing the big cyborg didn't share the beliefs that seemed so important to him, or at least to his late wife. For that matter, I still hadn't figured out how religious the Mayor really had been, and how much was merely in deference to Mrs. Rabin.

"What are those designs on parts of their skin?" I asked about the triplets. "It looks like the decorative nanotech that I've seen, but professionals don't usually wear it at work." Nanotechnology hadn't turned out to be the wonderware that many had predicted, because there wasn't yet a power source small enough to extend its life long enough to accomplish significant tasks. But it was big in the clothing and "new tattoo" markets.

"That's what it is," Min said. "The metal patches underneath could be removed or covered up with cosmetic modification, but they leave them intentionally as a mark of identity, as most of us do." He gestured to the two jackpatches clearly visible at the bottom back of his bald skull; I knew they were only necessary for emergencies, because he could do almost everything wirelessly. "The colorful ornamentation added by the triplets is, we could say, the female version of this tradition."

This reference made me wonder whether the triplets were "sexless" like

Min, but the clock in my head told me I had indulged too much curiosity already. I needed to proceed to what really mattered.

"Should we hire them?" I asked.

"From what I could tell in a brief interview, I don't see any reason not to. I asked them why they chose this line of work, while I was far enough in to confirm the truthfulness of their answers. Their special talents, combined with the fact that they enjoy money and thrills, like anybody would, leaves them with basically two options: they can either be paid to end lives, or to save lives. They chose the latter because, as they said, 'We died many times during our creation, and we know how bad it hurts.' Also, they have no love for China and its current leader, and they seem eager to act against his interests."

"You say *current* leader," I said, "as if you don't expect him to rule for too long."

"One can only hope," he answered.

"Okay," I said, making up my mind. "Bring Terrey in. I'll ask him a few questions, and if it looks okay, we'll go for it. Then we'll hope there *is* a God out there, and that he or she's on our side."

"But we'll take five stones," Min said as he turned toward the door, to unlock it for Terrey to enter.

"What?"

"Mr. Rabin used to say, 'Trust in God, but take five stones.' From David and Goliath, I think."

"Oh," I said, but the reference was lost on me, and soon Terrey was back in the room.

"Tell me what I have to do to survive this," I said to him.

"You have to do exactly what I tell you to do," he answered.

"Which is what?"

"I can't tell you much now, because it's fluid and you haven't hired me yet."

"Help me to hire you. Tell me some things we would do."

"Well, the first thing is to get Lynn away from you and secure so she won't become collateral damage."

So far so good, I thought.

"Then the next thing we would do," Terrey continued, "is change up your entire security force, remove anyone who's had any prior access to you." He looked at Min. "With one exception, of course."

"Why the changes?"

"Because one thing that happens every time Sun wants to kill someone," he said, "is that his people manage to turn a mate against the target, or plant someone close to him. I think there's something about betrayal that turns him on."

"You just passed Saul's hiring test with flying colors," I said, no pun intended. "What else?"

"I'd rather get paid for the rest."

"How much?" This was Lynn, coming through the door to the bedroom, through which she must have been listening. I was reminded of the running joke between us that she was a better detective than I.

"The bad news is that I get a million dollars a day for every day I keep you alive," he said matter-of-factly. "The good news is that all our expenses and salaries come out of that."

"Big bikkies," I said.

"You can afford it," he said. "And you have to."

"For how long?"

"Thirty days max, then renegotiation if necessary. But it will all go down in half that time, I assure you. You'll be dead by then or the attempts will have failed or been exposed."

"But you don't know how many attempts there will be, right? So how will you know if they're done?"

"Good question. It's never happened, because no one's ever survived that long. So we'll play it by ear, hence the thirty-day limit."

"Why can't we just pay the Chinese guy thirty million dollars," Lynn said, "to call off his kaleidoscope thing?"

"Good luck with that" was all Terrey said.

"I don't think money's a big priority for him, Lynn," I added, then glanced at her and Min. "Listen, I think I've heard enough. Let's get on with this, unless anyone has an objection."

No one said anything, so we got on with it. Terrey gave us the info on a havened bank account hidden under enough ice to sink the *Titanic*, and we transferred one million BASS dollars to it, to be repeated once a day at the same time until I was dead or free from danger, whichever came first.

Just seconds after the payment was confirmed and Terrey was officially hired, he reached out and touched Lynn's damp hair and asked her if she had taken a shower. She pulled away and said yes, and my old friend turned toward me and singed my ears with a string of military-style profanity. The gist of his rant, interspersed between vulgar references to human anatomy and maternal intimacy, was that I had better pay attention and do what he says, or I would regret it deeply.

"I didn't even think about it when she said she was taking a shower," I said. "Sorry, Lynn."

"You *are* sorry, you . . ." And Terrey let out another string, and then sent some Lynn's way because she should have known better.

"Can we still get our million dollars back?" Lynn said to me.

"No, he's right, honey," I said. "We'll listen, Terrey. But if you don't mind, BASS has kind of an unwritten rule about bad language."

"What's up with that?"

"In honor of Saul," I said with an embarrassed shrug. "Who probably did it in honor of his wife."

"I thought you were in charge here."

"I am," I said. "And it makes sense to me." Not an entirely truthful answer, but one I thought both Lynn and Min would appreciate. In Mrs. Rabin's orphanage, where Lynn had been raised, such moral traditions were an important part of the curriculum, and Min valued respect and respectfulness as high as anything.

"Professionalism, intelligence, and distinctiveness," a raspy voice suddenly rang out, and a holo of Saul Rabin's ghost was standing in the room among us, leaning on his cane. Min had obviously accessed the construct through the net room, probably because he knew it would do a better job explaining this than I could. Min's reverence for the old man was creating an awkward moment—not the first time it had happened—but out of deference to him I let the ghost talk.

"First, at least some people consider it unprofessional to use profanity on the job, and any benefit it might possibly provide is not worth the risk of potential marks on our reputation. Second, profanity is often a sign of a limited vocabulary, a lack of creativity, and a lapse in mental discipline, and if someone cannot find a way to communicate effectively without it, he or she is not capable of functioning at the level our work demands. Third, this policy sets us apart from other organizations and shows how serious we are in our pursuit of excellence. Professionalism, intelligence, and distinctiveness."

"Sounds like something from a Middle School speech class," Terrey said to me, and I shrugged again. "State your main points at the beginning and the end . . ."

"I can hear what you're saying, Mr. Thorn," the ghost said in a gruff voice. "I am a fully interactive construct, and I heard what you said before, also, because all oral and textual data that Min receives is passed on to me. "

Silently, Terrey mouthed to me the words *Can he see me, too?* I shook my head no, and he promptly gave Saul the backward peace sign that was known in England as "the two-fingered salute" and in Australia as "the forks."

"Fine," Terrey said as he made the gesture, which is similar to "the finger" in America. "Look, I'll cut the shite if you'll tell these two to do what I say." He now gestured toward Lynn and me, already forgetting that the ghost couldn't see him. "So I can save the buggers' lives."

"I will encourage them to do that," the ghost answered, then added, "Within reason." It was apparently smart enough to decipher to whom Terrey was referring. But the construct's intelligence had some limits, as my friend now pointed out to me.

"He didn't seem to register the limey substitutes," he said. "Could it be that he's only programmed to recognize American slang? So I can speak down under and call you freckles and clackers, doodles, frangers. I can talk about your Mappa Tassie . . ."

"You are correct," Min spoke up. "Mr. Rabin's Legacy Project only preserved what he knew at the time of his death, and he never learned to speak 'down under.'" Was that a slight edge of wit from the straight-faced giant? "But Mr. Ares and I are able to load information from the net into the construct, like a dictionary of Australian slang, so that he will know what you are saying."

"That won't be necessary, Min," I said. I guessed that my friend's belligerence about this minor issue was only to make sure his point was made, and to show that he wouldn't be intimidated by anyone—even the legendary Saul Rabin, and especially this virtual version. "Let Terrey have his fun. We need to get to work now."

"The download is already completed," Min replied.

"Oh," I said.

Terrey asked, "Who's in charge here again?" I didn't answer, but told Min to shut down the ghost, and reiterated that we needed to get to work.

13
BODIES

"Okay," Terrey started, and looked at Lynn. "The first step, as I said, is to get this very tidy spunk out of harm's way."

"All right, that's it," Lynn said, highly offended. "What's with you?"

"Sorry, marm," Terrey said before I could defend him. "I'm still in the slang mode, I guess."

"It was actually a compliment," I told Lynn. I had heard Terrey use those words many times for the women he chased during our military days.

"Oh," she said, and silently mouthed the words herself. "Really?"

"Yes, really. How do we make her safe, Terrey?"

He explained that as soon as the triplets arrived, they needed to take Lynn to a location that could be secured sufficiently. Various options were discussed, but Terrey said that it would be much easier to add the scanning equipment and make changes to a property that we already owned. So when Lynn realized that our home in Napa Valley was on the list, the matter was settled quickly. Lynn said she would rather be stuck at home than anywhere else, and "frankly I'd rather die there, too." Terrey asked me about the security there, and I told him it was beyond his wildest dreams because the house was protected by the same measures installed for my new operations center, which was built into the moun-

80

tain below. He seemed pleasantly and genuinely surprised by this—apparently the homework he had done on BASS had not yielded all of this information, and it gratified me to know that we still had some secrets. Hopefully Terrey would keep them, as his contract required.

Lynn gathered her things, and when the triplets were outside, I kissed her good-bye and said I would fill her in on the rest. The cyborg girls had figured out how to fly an aero while riding here in one of them, which I'm sure was beyond easy for them because the flying cars were very user-friendly. We gave them the security clearance they needed to use them, and San took Lynn home in our personal aero. Ni and Go stayed to secure our perimeter and scan the area while we made some more plans.

"Now we need to phase out the rest of your on-site staff as quickly as possible, both here and at the house." Terrey said this in a much more serious and businesslike manner, which confirmed what I thought about the purpose of his earlier behavior. "But we'll need a few more capable bodies, and some expendable ones, too, if we can. They need to be people who have had little or no connection with you, because anyone known to be around you could be contacted and turned by Sun's agents. Same reason I don't bring any staff except the *Trois*, who are inviolable. Can you think of anyone who is qualified but you don't know well enough for anyone to predict they'd be here? Maybe a former peacer working somewhere else, someone that you know good things about?"

"We don't have much of a turnover here," I said. But I thought for a few moments, and Min processed.

"What about Keren Reyes?" I asked the big man. She was a good peacer who had requested a leave of absence to take care of a relative of some kind who had refused to move to the Bay Area from her native El Salvador.

"A possibility," Min said. "But it would be unfortunate for her to have to leave her mother at this difficult time." *It was her mother, right,* I thought. *That would be pretty coldhearted.*

"She's on my list," Terrey said. I noticed that his mouse sheath was back on and he was checking some information in his contacts. "We don't have much time, so I had the triplets do some research." A screen appeared in the room again, this time filled with various mugshots. "Here's an option where we could possibly get two good men in one try." One of the pictures was maximized, and I recognized the face immediately.

"That's the guy from the 'silhouette' incident," I said to Min, using the term that had become shorthand for the worst few days of my life. "What's his name?"

"Valeri Korcz," Terrey said.

"Didn't you shoot him?" Min said.

"Only a little," I said, raising my eyebrows.

"He may not be very eager to protect you."

"He will when he hears about the pay," Terrey said. "And he has a partner with a good résumé as well." Another picture appeared next to Korcz's, of a man with a lot less size but a lot more hair.

"I remember being impressed with Korcz's skill," I said, then shrugged. "Until he got shot, of course. But I also remember that he doesn't seem the type to be easily corrupted, or even a good liar. How did Saul like to describe some people? 'Without guile,' I think."

"He always said that about Lynn," Min said. "That's why he liked her. And he thought you had some of that in you, too, and she would bring it out."

"Can I make an offer to these two?" Terrey asked, interrupting the personal reverie and pointing toward the pictures of Korcz and his partner. After I said yes, he added, "Do you have anyone in New York that could help with the contact?"

"Yes, we have ambassadors in all the major cities. They liaison with the movers and shakers and show off some of our tech. You know, stimulate salivation in case we decide to release it for sale, or to make friends."

"Have Min send that contact info to the triplets," Terrey said, and I nodded my permission to the giant. "Now, the next thing we have to do is make you disappear, if we can. You need to think of a place you can go where no one will know where you are."

"Run away? That's not gonna happen." I stuck out my chin. "You of all people should know that."

"What I know is that if you stay visible, the chances of you dying are about ninety-eight percent. There's probably a bomb and sniper being put into place right now, plus some form of poison and lethal gas, an accident being arranged, other kinds of sabotage, the betrayal of someone close to you, and who knows what else. One of those methods are bound to work, and then you don't get to see your baby. And I don't get enough money to even pay my expenses."

I didn't care about the last part, of course, but I did about the one before it.

"Tell you what," he went on. "Let's see if it's even possible before we argue more about it. Indulge me for a moment . . . there are two things you would need to make this work really well: a place and a person. Can you think of a place where you could go and stay for a while, that no one would know about? You can't have been there recently, you can't own it, and ideally it's secluded and you don't have to pay anyone for it, so there's no data trail. Second, can you think of a person you could trust who is unrecognizable and not traceable in connection with you, and who would be willing to bring you things you need, or even stay with you? Because you wouldn't be able to leave the place.

"That's the ideal scenario, and the next best option is a major step up in risk, but still doable. You pick a random hotel and a random person, and pay them cash to get a room in their name. You stay in the room and keep paying them to keep confidence and bring you food and such, so as far as the outside world is concerned, they're staying in that room by themselves. The problem with this approach is that there are too many variables—too many people around, what to do about the maids who will start to wonder why the 'Do Not Disturb' sign is on the door every day. Your helper may have a job or a family or both to juggle. They may recognize you and be tempted to say something, despite the large amounts of cash you throw at them. They might realize they could get even more money from the media or the other side . . ."

I wasn't even listening to Terrey's last few sentences, because the strangest thing happened to me while he described the ideal scenario. Against all odds, I actually thought of both a place and a person that fit his description. I couldn't believe it, and immediately (and quite involuntarily) thoughts about the supernatural started bouncing around my brain again, no doubt because of the conversation with Min and the nature of the "ideal" person who came to mind. *This must be what the fanatics mean when they talk about God "showing up,"* I thought. It seemed too uncanny and coincidental to be explained by natural causes. *But that doesn't mean it can't be,* I reminded myself, and came back to earth.

"You're not gonna believe this, Terrey," I said, "but I know a place and a person that I think will work even better than you're hoping. Lynn wouldn't like either one of them, but—"

"She doesn't need to know," he interrupted. "And none of us should know anything about it, so keep the details to yourself. But you really think it'll work?"

"Yeah, it's bizarre. It's like the situations are ready made for what you're talking about, and the fact that they came to mind as you were talking is amazing, too. I had completely forgotten about the person until now. It's like the thoughts were . . . downloaded into my head on schedule."

"Positively Dickensian," Terrey said, after grunting a couple times. "So you'll do it?"

"Well, wait a minute." I was still amazed at what was happening, but I wasn't ready to base my decisions on an experience. In the words of a classic British song, *just 'cause you feel it doesn't mean it's there.* "I don't like the idea of being away from Lynn for who knows how long."

"If you get killed, you'll be away from her a lot longer. And your baby—don't forget her."

"People will figure out quickly that I'm gone. There'll be a media circus, and Sun has considerable resources at his disposal. His forces could probably find me."

"Only if they're looking," Terrey said. "This is the best part. We'll get someone to sleep with your wife."

"Excuse me?"

"Well, maybe not sleep with her, but at least live with her, and go to a few places you would go." He sat back and crossed his arms, obviously proud of himself. "A double, to take your place."

"Is that possible?" I asked. I had heard of the idea, and even of it being done, but I wasn't up on it.

"Not for most people. But we can do it."

"How?"

"Find someone who's desperate enough to make a new start." He was leaning forward now. "And willing to be physically altered and risk his life for the big bikkies."

"Where, a prison?"

"Maybe, but not the best sort to choose from there, plus you have to circumvent the justice system somehow, which is not easily done." He paused for effect. "There's a better way."

"Okay," I said, impatient with the pauses.

"Hospital psych wards and online suicide sites."

"A mentally ill person would be better than a criminal, for living with my wife?"

"Not everyone who wants to end it all is mentally ill," he said. "Sometimes they've suffered a lot and just have no reason for living."

"So you give him one," I said, nodding. "Have you done this before?"

"Yeah, mate. And it worked, to answer your next question."

"Wow," I said, shaking my head. "This is . . . weird."

"This is life and death," Terrey added. "And time is of the essence. You're gonna have to trust me on a lot because we have to move fast."

"I should talk to Lynn," I said.

"No, I wouldn't do that. Don't want too much emotion in the mix. Plus it would be fun to see if she can tell that he's not you."

"Hmmph," I snorted. "To use your words, good luck with that." I thought a little more about whether I should talk to Lynn, and decided against it because I didn't think her opinions on this matter could possibly be more educated than Terrey's.

"I'll go for it," I said. "But I want to approve the double before you hire him, if he's going to be living in my house."

"Fine. The triplets already have a search running throughout North America, screening about a half million candidates who have responded. I'm sure we'll find at least one that works."

"That many people responded?" I asked, incredulously.

"That many are interested in the million dollars we're offering," he answered, "and we're certified by Reality G. Of course, most of them are eliminated right away, because we're looking for a very specific set of qualifications."

"And there's a fine line between desperate and too desperate, I'm sure."

"Right."

"Can we please make sure we stay on the safer side of that line?" I pleaded. "He'll be living in my house, remember?"

"No worries, mate," Terrey said with a smile.

14
EXIT INTERVIEW

"So you really think you're ready to . . . do it?" the amateur journalist with the baby bump asked the five-year-old boy dressed in bright red and yellow, who picked his nose and wiped it on his shirt. They had moved to one of the many private rooms in the Exit website, where every day thousands of customers around the world recorded their last words (or thoughts, if they had implants), in the latest version of the timeless convention known as the suicide note.

"Yes, that's what I'm here for," the boy answered, "and that's exactly what I'm going to do." Adult terms like "exactly" sounded incongruous in the lisping voice of a small child, but the thirty-five-year-old man speaking the words had chosen this net skin for a reason. He had created it by importing video of himself from thirty years before because it reminded him of a time of innocence, long before his life had been ruined in so many ways. He wasn't a religious man, but as death approached most people had at least *some* thoughts of the afterlife, and he preferred to enter it this way, even though it was only a virtual construct. In a way, it actually mattered more what he looked like inside the site, because the woman was there to see him, whereas in the real world he was totally alone.

"So I thought that maybe I could be with you when you . . . do it," she said, clearly uncomfortable with this but needing to produce a web article to help pay for her two kids and one on the way. "But you could tell me your story first, and I can sell all the footage to HoloFare for enough that I could send some to your family."

"I don't have any family," the little boy said. "That's part of my story."

"Your friends, then? A girlfriend or boyfriend?"

"I don't have any of those either."

"I'm sorry, I . . ."

"You keep the money," he said. "For your kids."

"You'll do it, then?" she asked excitedly, despite her misgivings. It was worth it for the kids, as he had seemed to imply.

He said yes, knowing that the only reason was because of those kids, and the fact that she had the same number that he had lost. If it wasn't for the guilt and disease he carried around with him, he might have thought he could go on with the hope of experiencing again what the woman had.

"Should I take the pills now and then tell the story on my way out?" he asked. "If I tell the story first and then take them, you'll have to be here longer. If you want to see it through."

"That's how you're going to do it?" she asked. "Pills?"

"Yeah, I'm not brave. I just want to go to sleep."

"Maybe," she said, then paused as she looked down and bit her lip. "Maybe, as much as I need the money . . . maybe you shouldn't do it? Or maybe I can do an article on your story, and how you didn't do it."

"What?" the boy said, the real man behind him immediately feeling irritated that she would meddle like this.

"Well, you were thinking of me, weren't you? By agreeing to the interview, and then by worrying about me having to stay too long?"

"So what?" That exclamation did sound perfectly juvenile, spoken in the five-year-old's voice.

"Well, you still have . . . what do they call it? Empathy. You could do some good, J.J. It would be a shame if you—"

"Just write your article," the little boy shouted, "and stay the hell out of my business!" Now the woman was looking down again, and her lip was quivering. She put a hand on her belly, a protective instinct, as he continued. "And I wasn't worrying about you—that's deluded."

The boy leaned back on the "chair" that was conspicuously absent from the construct, and folded his hands behind his head.

"I'm sorry," she said. But then she showed a resilience that only motherhood could have produced in her and added, "But don't take the pills yet . . . until after you tell me your story." In his anger the boy didn't recognize her ulterior motives, nor how she was effectively mothering him. But perhaps his subconscious did, because he calmed down considerably and followed her cue. Or maybe he felt compelled to tell his story as a justification for why he was about to take his life.

"Three years ago, everything was fine, more or less," he said. "I was teaching history and my wife was making good money as a medical lab tech, and we had three children, a girl and two twin boys. On the way home from daycare one night, their car was hit by a truck. Two of them died instantly, and the other two soon after. The report said that they thought my wife had drifted off the road, then jerked the wheel to compensate, hit the lip, and rolled the car into the oncoming traffic. But whatever, it doesn't matter, they were all gone."

"I'm so sorry," the woman said.

"Yeah. So I didn't take it well, as you could imagine. I quit teaching and started traveling, when I couldn't stand being around home anymore. So my family and career were gone, and I was gone from everything else in my life. I was cut off from all my moorings. The only thing I had was money, at that point, from a big insurance policy we had on my wife, because she was the main breadwinner." He paused, deciding how much of the story to tell. "One thing led to another, and I ended up with AIMS, so now I can't even have . . . a relationship with anyone."

"Oh, my," she said, and studied the boy as if she might see some signs of the dreaded STD, or how he might have contracted it. She added the words, "Aquired Immune Mutation Syndrome," just in case anyone who would watch the recording didn't know what it stood for.

"Now you see why I'm here," he said.

"Aren't there some treatments?" she asked. "I've heard—"

"Experimental ones," he interrupted. "And only if you have a small fortune."

"You said you had money, from the insurance policy."

"I spent it all," he said testily, still irritated at her. "I had a small fortune, but I spent it all." He let out a sad laugh. "I spent it all getting AIMS."

"How do you mean?"

"I had a lot of money and a lot of time," he said. "So I . . . tried to fill the holes, I guess. With women. I made it my goal to have as many as I could, as often as I could." The little boy's voice had now taken on a tone that was both regretful and nostalgic. "I bought an expensive car and wardrobe, worked out every day, then bought a whole new wardrobe when I got thinner and figured out what was more effective with the ladies. I thought that money and a sad story might work."

"Did it?" she asked.

"Oh, yeah," he said, with the same mixture of regret and nostalgia. "I started at the obvious places, like bars and vacation spots, where they were looking for some action, or open to it at least. In those places, if I talked to enough of them, or even propositioned one after another, I hardly ever went back to my room alone. Usually a few drinks was enough, but sometimes I had to buy them an expensive dinner, enough to impress them or maybe give them hope that they might end up with a wealthy boyfriend or husband. The hotels were very expensive, too, by the way, since you asked where all the money went."

She hadn't asked, in fact, but was silent and let him continue.

"After a while I got bored with that, and wanted some new challenges and thrills. I was willing to endure a lot of rejection for the kick of succeeding with someone who wasn't looking or even wanting it, at least at first."

"What do you mean?"

"I was on the prowl everywhere, in the normal places of life, like grocery stores, gas stations, business hotels."

"What did you do?"

"I would find a woman who looked good to me and tell her how beautiful she was, or ask her if she wanted some excitement in her life, or if I could take her to lunch or dinner or whatever. Sometimes I would just lead with 'My family was killed and I'm really hurting,' and go from there. If they didn't say no right away, which many did, I then kept trying to work it out with them."

"Did they ever ask you to verify your story?" she asked. "I would do that." Then she regretted what she said, and added, "Not that I would even consider a one-night stand like that."

"Well, they weren't all one-night stands," he said. "If they were worth it, I'd meet them a few more times before moving on." The woman shook her head slightly at this, but was trying not to look too disgusted so she wouldn't endanger the interview. "And yes, they sometimes did want verification, so I would just give them a link to a story about the accident. It had a picture of me on there."

"How many women did you . . . have?"

"I don't know. Hundreds. I didn't count, but I did try to sample every kind, all shapes and sizes and races. The only requirement was that they had to be beautiful . . . and willing, of course."

"I'm sure the money and the sad story helped," she said. "But that alone wouldn't do it. You must be attractive."

"I guess I am," the five-year-old boy said as he picked his nose and wiped it on his shirt. "I've kept in shape, too, because I didn't want to go back to my old flabby self."

"How did you get AIMS?" she asked.

"Like I told you, after a while I wanted more of a challenge, so I would try for the ones who weren't looking, or two or more at a time. Those took some time and patience, and by then I was used to getting some almost every day, so I started to fill in the gaps with the bar scene, prostitutes, etcetera. I think I got AIMS from someone that way."

"Etcetera?"

"I bought a state-of-the-art implant," he said, now speaking without the tinge of nostalgia, and only with regret. "For porn and virtual sex. Using it by myself got old eventually . . . you want to hook up and share with others in person sometimes, to multiply the thrill, and the kind of people you find aren't exactly the most savory types. Or safe."

"Did you . . . ?" She hesitated, already uncomfortable getting this far from her domestic existence, and now she was heading farther out. "AIMS started with zooies, right? Besties?" She wasn't sure how to pronounce "zoophiliacs" or "bestialists" so she used the slang terms, but immediately regretted it. She was afraid the boy might be offended if he was one of them.

"It appeared and spread in the bestie community first," he answered, and she was relieved to hear him use the word. "But I don't think they know for sure how it started, and it definitely is not limited to them. I'm not one, if that's what you're asking."

"How long ago did you find out you had the disease?" she asked, wanting to change the subject.

"About a year ago."

"So you stopped then?"

"Ummm," he said, then paused, clearly not wanting to discuss this part. "Initially I tried just using the implant. But I was so in the habit by then—it was what I'd been living for, for two years. I couldn't stop . . . everywhere I went I would see beautiful women . . . I couldn't help myself."

"So . . . you . . . ," she said, trying to get her mind around this. "Those women wouldn't have been interested if you told them you had AIMS." She stated the obvious: "So you didn't tell them."

"I know it sounds terrible," he said, and she thought, *It is terrible.* "But you have to understand. I'm a poly. I realized that I was born a poly, and that my trauma and coping methods triggered the genes."

"Polyamory," she said, making sure she had heard the word right. "Did you learn about that from the net, or therapy, or what?"

"Both. When I kept relapsing and endangering these women, of course I felt bad, so I tried to figure out what was wrong with me. Then I found out that there's nothing really wrong with me—I'm constitutionally unable to be celibate or have just one partner."

"Couldn't you just have many virtual partners, on the net, so you wouldn't spread the AIMS?"

"No, my therapist said I'm a 3P," he said, and starting rocking back and forth on nothing. "Physical Proximity Polyamorist."

"Oh, there's different kinds?"

"Yes. So you see why there's no reason for me to go on living. By nature I'm made to have multiple partners, but I can't be who I am without hurting others. That's a living hell, too much for anyone to bear."

"There must be a way," the housewife/journalist said, her mother instincts kicking in again. "If there's no affordable treatment for AIMS, is there some kind of therapy for polyamory?"

"At first I took some medication, but it was basically a chemical castration. To the extent it worked, which wasn't completely, it just made me depressed and unable to get out of bed. And then I realized, this isn't something I should change about myself. Can you imagine someone trying to not be black or white anymore, or straight or gay? No, I realized that either I need to be who I am, or die if I can't."

"You sound like you could be a preacher," she said admiringly, "or an activist."

"I did end up giving some speeches for PRIDE."

"I've heard of that. What does it stand for again?"

"Polyamorist Rights in Discrimination and Equality."

"Right," she said, and the mother in her wouldn't give up. "Why don't you give your life to that cause? You could be the Martin Luther King of poly rights."

"With AIMS?" he said, getting exasperated again. "Someone will find out, and all the women I've been with would sue me."

"Oh, right," she said, realizing this was getting nowhere. Then a thought struck her. "Why did you tell that survey, with the Asian girls, that you were in good physical health?"

"Because I don't have any symptoms at this point. I feel fine, and the AIMS can lie dormant for years."

"And mental health? You said you didn't have any problems with that, either."

"I don't," the boy said, his child's voice still irritated. "I was born a poly, I can't help it, and that's the point of poly rights. Again, would you tell someone that being black is a 'problem,' or being white, or gay or straight?"

"I guess not," she said, and then finally went too far. "But still, maybe you could . . . change somehow."

"Listen," he said. "If you're going to be a journalist, you'd better read up on your science. The experts say that kind of ignorant talk fills people with guilt and shame, and kills their self-esteem. I don't think I can change what I am. When I took the medication I told you about, I was different. And when I stopped taking it, I went back to the way I was. That's proof this is the way my brain works. And someone else may want to go on living without being able to be happy, but not me."

The boy reached down to scratch his knee, and the pantsuited woman could somehow tell that in real life he was reaching for the pills. The interview was now over, and the Exit was about to begin.

15
ONLY YOUR LIFE

The five-year-old boy in the Web site sat still and didn't move, since it was a rudimentary net skin not slaved to the man's body. But the man himself, in the real world, had been lifting a bottle filled with pills and another one filled with water, which he'd placed by his feet.

Then the Asian angels appeared.

They gently faded into the middle of the room and formed a triangle, facing out, like last time.

"Excuse me," all three said at the same time, "but are you still alive?" The skins often remained in the rooms at Exit for a while after someone committed suicide, until they were cleared out by the site's monitor constructs. Since this particular skin wasn't moving at all, it seemed like a prime candidate for that ghostly effect.

"J.J.?" asked the slightly pregnant journalist, who wore the much better skin that looked and moved like she did. More silent moments passed, and she feared the worst. "Did you take the pills?"

"No, not yet," said the young voice finally. "My mouth was just hanging open when I saw them. How do they get into these places without permission?"

"Jonathan James Cates," the one closest to the boy said, ignoring his question.

"You have been selected to continue toward a possible one million dollars and a new life, in exchange for a brief employment. If you are willing to take the next step and be interviewed, please respond by saying 'Yes, I am willing to be interviewed,' or select this link." It appeared in her right hand. "And remember that our ability to deliver what we promise has been certified by Reality G." That link appeared in her left hand.

"Asked to do two interviews in one day," the boy said. "I'm Mr. Popularity all of a sudden. I should kill myself more often."

"Do it, J.J.," the woman said, not hearing his joke because she was intent on making use of this opportunity to save his life. Her mothering instincts were in full gear after spending even this short amount of time with him.

"Kill myself?" he asked, genuinely confused.

"Heavens no," she said, aghast. "Do the interview!"

"Why should I?" he asked, though he probably already knew the answer.

"What have you got to lose?" she answered, echoing what he had said earlier. "And look what you could gain. With that money you could buy treatment, and start over."

"Yeah, but what they want me to do for that money could be worse than what I'm running from."

"All you have to do is be willing to die, which you already are." This came from the ad construct, which was apparently programmed to respond in this way to questions like "What do you want me to do?"

"The rest is not difficult at all," it continued.

"What have I got to lose?" the boy said to himself, or the woman, or both.

"Only your life," the construct replied, with another programmed response. "The same thing you came here to lose."

The boy leaned back and put his hands behind his head, and after a few moments said, "Okay, I'll do the interview. What have I . . ." He paused.

". . . got to lose," the pregnant woman said with a smile, and the construct did not respond this time. In fact, the three Asian models didn't say anything and there was a long, awkward silence.

"Oh, sorry," the boy said with his prepubescent lisp. "What are the code words you said . . . Open Sesame?"

"I'm sorry, but I'm having difficulty understanding what you're saying. Please try again."

"What am I supposed to say to agree to the interview? I forget."

"Please respond by saying, 'Yes, I am willing to be interviewed,' or select this link."

"Yes, I am willing to be interviewed."

"Thank you," they all said, and then they disappeared.

"Not again," the boy said, and began rocking back and forth on the air. "I'm not waiting around for—"

They appeared again, looking the same, but the boy could sense that there was something different about them.

"Mr. Cates," the one closest to him said. She immediately seemed more human somehow, in facial and body movements. "It is a pleasure to meet you. I'd shake your hand, but . . ." She shrugged and smiled, something that the construct would not have done previously.

"Who are you?"

"My name is Ni. The advertisement A.I. you spoke to was designed by my sisters and me, based on what we want to look like. Sometimes. But we are short on time, and must get down to business. Before we go any further, we have to ask you another question that wasn't on the survey."

"Okay," the boy said.

"Do you have any opinions about the current Chinese government?"

Which way does she want me to answer? he wondered, but then decided that honesty was the best policy.

"Not really, except they seem a bit scary to me."

"How so?"

"I was a history teacher, so I know enough about China to know that they have an imperialistic streak. And the guy who they say is really in power was involved in Taiwan and the annexations, right?" He paused. "Why are we talking about this?"

"Because our boss just wasted twelve minutes and thirty-two-point-four seconds of his precious time talking to the last candidate, before we realized that he was a Chinese sympathizer."

The little boy had no response, except to pick his nose again.

"Here, let us fix that for you," Ni said with a grimace. Almost instantaneously the little boy disappeared and a well-dressed adult male with a beard took his place, still sitting, but now with a chair under him. The resolution was much higher.

"How did you do that?" Jon Cates asked, speaking now in his own voice.

"We took over the net closet you're in at the library and upgraded it," Ni answered, "and used one of the holos you gave us for your skin."

"You *are* good-looking, J.J.," the journalist on the other side of the room said.

"He'll be even better looking soon," Ni said with a wink. "Now, Mrs. Lang, we're afraid we have to say good-bye. The rest of our discussion is confidential."

"But . . . my interview isn't finished."

"Yes, it is," the cyborg's avatar said. "In fact, you'll find that it has already been erased from your net room and cloud." The pregnant, tan-suited woman looked down frantically, checking to see if this was true. "But don't panic, your two children and one on the way will not starve. We have just deposited some money into your account." As she said this, the interface for the woman's bank account appeared in one corner of the room and zoomed in on the most recent item, a $10,000 deposit with no description, that might reveal where it came from. The housewife's eyes widened when she saw the number.

"You didn't even need my password?" she asked.

"No, and now comes the more unpleasant part of our good-bye." The bank interface disappeared, and a security camera feed from an office building interior appeared. This also zoomed in, but on a woman who was working on a net pad in a cubicle.

"That's my wife," the journalist woman said, even more aghast now. "She's at work."

"And she'll be able to stay working there," Ni said in a threatening voice, "as long as you don't talk about what happened in this room. But if you do, especially to the media, the other Mrs. Lang will be out of a job." As if on cue, the pad on the desk began blinking off and on in bright colors, startling the woman in the cubicle and causing her to move her chair away from it, as if it might explode. Then it went back to normal, after which the woman looked all around for a while and eventually got up to ask other workers about the anomaly. Then the security camera view faded from the room.

"We also know where you live," Ni continued. "Nine-eighty-six North Washington Street, Pittsville, Wisconsin. We can crash all your net equipment permanently, and probably some other appliances, if you don't honor our agreement." To illustrate, the cyborg turned off the housewife's net room, and her skin disappeared briefly until it was turned back on. When she reappeared, the tan-suited woman's mouth was hanging open.

"Can't the police arrest you, if you do something like that?" she finally asked.

The three Asian women looked at each other and laughed. After they were done, Ni spoke, and the other two figures were still again.

"Remember what we said, and enjoy the money." Then the pregnant woman disappeared for good, and Ni turned back to the man.

"You go by Jon, right?" When he said yes, she continued: "Let me tell you about this job, Jon. But we won't be able to talk about it long—you'll have to make a decision very soon."

He said okay and she proceeded to explain about the upcoming assassination attempts without giving the name of the target. She explained that Jon would be physically altered and be in the line of fire, with a slim chance of surviving but a hefty payday waiting for him if he did. And that the money could be given to family or friends if he didn't. She told him that her team would do their best to protect him because they wanted to keep the double alive as long as possible, so that more of the attempts would run their course and there was more of a chance that the party behind them could be exposed. He told her about the AIMS, because after that display of net mastery he figured that they would find out anyway. She said, "We did find out, thank you," but to his surprise it wasn't a deal breaker. She explained that it wasn't her decision, but there were no other viable candidates at this time, and reiterated that time was of the essence. She also added that the process of physical alteration he would undergo could possibly cure him of the disease, the science of which she would explain later. She answered a few questions he had, then reiterated again that time was of the essence and asked for a commitment on his part.

He made the commitment, because by now he felt like he had already been carried along too far to turn back. It reminded him of the feeling he had when his old life was slipping away, never to return, like it was spiraling out of his control. But this time he felt a spark of curiosity and interest (the first in a long time), and had a desire to learn where these new forces were taking him.

"Our boss will be here soon," she said to him. "Along with the man whose place you would be taking. In the meantime let us ask you about this. We can't detect the brainware you said that you have—is it broken?"

"No," he said. "I had to cancel the account—couldn't pay for it anymore."

"What company was it? Allware, or another one who used their stuff?"

"Allware."

"Can you give us your idents so I can activate it? We could crack Allware's ice, but it would take a little while." He gave her the information, feeling carried along again.

"I thought you wouldn't hire me till I talked to your boss," he said.

"That's right, but we're trying to save some time." *Time is of the essence,* he remembered. "There. You're back online. Now you can leave the closet if you want or need to—you can get a cup of coffee or use the bathroom. Or you can turn the closet off and just use your eyes, which would probably be good. A public net room like that is easier to hack than your brain."

He did as she suggested, and turned the closet off. He was now out of the virtual room and back in the real library cubicle, and all he could see besides its walls was the small standby icon flashing in the top left of his vision. For a few moments he sat there in the library cubicle, staring at the door and thinking about running away while he was temporarily disconnected from the super-woman. But he was almost sure that she could reconnect with him remotely in a split second. Inexplicably he felt more fear of these strange people, and of the unknown world they represented, than he had felt about committing suicide.

"N, R, U, T, N, O, M, E, T, S, Y, S," he said. The chip was set for vocal commands rather than thought controls, because he had used it too sparingly to master the latter, which were more complicated. The purpose for spelling the words in the command backward was so that features of the cyberware would not be activated by random or unrelated speech or thoughts. For the same purpose, all the commands had to be at least seven characters.

A moment after he issued the command he was back in the same Exit room with the Asian women, which showed that they were in fact connected to and even controlling his cyberware, because this site wasn't his homepage.

"Let's see what you've got in here," Ni said, and he could almost feel her rooting around in his head, though he knew it was psychosomatic. "You have a lot of interesting material in your cache." She was referring to the porn, of course, and he was embarrassed despite himself. "And some bad viruses."

"That's another reason I canceled my account," he said. "I couldn't afford all the security systems you have to buy. That's where they get you."

"We'll have to wipe it all if you're hired," she said.

"Fine with me," he said, and meant it. As fun as the virtual sex had been at first, he only had bad memories of it now. "Do it now," he said, somehow knowing that she could.

"Done."

Then the three female figures moved to form a row facing him, and started looking at each other and themselves as though they were now uncomfortable in their skins.

"Jon, meet our employers." The woman's voice came from everywhere now, not out of the mouth of any of the skins. "They don't look anything like this, of course, but they're using our skins because you can't see their faces until you're hired. On the left is our boss; you can call him T.T. In the middle is the man you would double for . . ."

"You can call me M.A.," the middle one said in a male voice.

"And on the right is his assistant."

"You can call him 'Ass' for short," the middle one said again, then looked to his left. "Sorry, big guy, I couldn't resist."

"You have a pretty good sense of humor," Jon said, "for someone whose life is in danger."

"It's not the first time," he said. "And I'm excited about meeting you, because I hear you're willing to help me save it."

"I guess I am."

"Good," said the Asian woman on the left, also in a man's voice. "What do you think about China?"

"I already asked him," the disembodied woman's voice said.

"This must be confusing for him," the middle one said to the ceiling. "Why don't you vary the skins somehow?"

"How's this?" the voice said, and the skins changed. The one on the left now had sandy and wavy hair, the middle one short black hair, and the one on the right had become much larger than the other two and had no hair.

"I hope you can agree to hire me soon," Jon said, "so I don't have to look at this mess for too long." The Asian women with the men's hair laughed.

"It doesn't have to be much of an interview, if you're willing," the middle one said, turning more serious. "I'm told we don't have much choice, and we don't have much time. But I just wanted to make sure you'll do what we say, and that you're at least somewhat normal, because over the next few weeks you'll be spending a lot of time in my house, and I'll be spending a lot of time in your head."

16
SAVIOR

Angelee was dreaming about her late husband again when her mind recognized a new sound, and her eyes slowly opened. The ceiling was a blur at first, but then her vision cleared enough to see a huge mosquito hawk flitter across it to join a gang of them near one of the corners. She lay on her back on the bed of the brown room at the Cadillac Flats Apartments in Napa City, feeling the rumble of the subway outside under Soscol Avenue. And as awareness fully dawned, she realized the sound that woke her was Simon unlocking the door and entering the room.

She sat up abruptly and pulled her knees up to her chest, hoping that the space around her on the bed might keep him from groping her again. Unfortunately it didn't work, because he just jumped onto it and helped himself to whatever he could reach. At least it was only one hand, because in the other he held up his InPhone.

"Juss in time," he said proudly. "Got me the app for your switch, hoover. Hadda go to the libree to find oudabaddit and download it. Hadna been *there* for a while."

The birth control switch had been installed during her first gig as a prostitute, before she had met her husband, and she wasn't looking forward to it being turned on again. But without ceremony or warning, Simon started tapping the screen to activate it.

"Say the password." He held it up near her head, even though he didn't have to.

"Lady Lee," she said weakly, and after a few more taps on his phone, a blinding pain seared through the base of her brain.

The implant sent neural signals into the pituitary gland, preventing the release of FSH (follicle-stimulating hormone) and stopping ovulation at its source. The initial disruption of the additional electricity had an effect on the nerves not unlike a bad tumor. Angelee didn't understand any of that, of course—she just knew it hurt really bad, and was soon gripping the back of her head and knocking the front of it against her knees.

"Hey, ho," Simon started, when he saw how bad she was hurting, and rubbed her back in an awkward attempt to help her. "Don' wanno babies, but don' wanno dying, either. You gonna make me too much money."

"You . . . have . . . to . . . ," she barely managed to say. "Turn . . . it . . . off!"

"Oh, oh, right." He fumbled at the phone, realizing that he hadn't completed the activation process, and accidentally dropped it on the brown blanket because he was only using one hand. He fished for it while Angelee continued to suffer, then finally located it and hit the "Finish" icon. The little Asian girl stopped twitching, but curled up in a tighter ball for a few moments.

"You okay?" Simon asked, patting her back again. "Memmer I told you how much we gonna make tonight, cuz you're brand-new stew. Got summun who's payin' biiiiig money cuz you're so young and fresh. Drives 'em loco, they line up . . . highest bidder, baby."

The pain had receded some, so Angelee lifted her head and opened her eyes. The left one was drooping and cloudy, but she knew that it would return to normal before too long.

"Okey, hoover," Simon said, relieved that she was recovering. "Lessee if it worked." He triggered the app again on the phone, and waved it up and down, from her head to her bottom, though he didn't have to do that either.

"Says you're safe," he declared happily after a few moments, then leaned in close to her, swamping her with his chemical breath. "Like to test it, me, but the johnny boy gonna be calling soon . . ."

Suddenly Angelee came fully back to life when she heard a soft voice say

"Mommy" from the doorway to the other room. Her little son Chris was staggering through it, trailing a blanket and rubbing his eyes. She shot out of bed and crouched next to the boy to comfort him, while Simon also clambered off the bed and stood up, with concerns of his own.

"Thought you said he was gonna sleep at night," the pimp shouted.

"He will," Angelee answered, the pain of the switch a forgotten memory now.

"It's night, and he ain' sleeping." Simon stepped over and crouched next to the boy, with the opposite effect that his mother had. "Lissen ta me, lamb meat. You better stay in that room over there, or I'll hafta throw you in with the package." The boy had no idea what the man was saying, but he cowered nonetheless at Simon's bad breath and bad teeth. "Or you gonna be sleeping forever." The pimp stood up and pulled aside his jacket to show his gun to both of them, and as he did his phone vibrated with the call from the customer who would turn Angelee back into Lady Lee.

"Now you stew," Simon said quickly to her before he answered the phone. "Getcha bitchass in that room and get that boy to sleep, while I talkit."

She did as he said, hustling Chris through the door and swinging it almost shut behind her. In his bed was the tiny amp (all-media pocket) that she used so often to settle him down or lull him to sleep. Cheap apartments like these didn't have net rooms, so the holo was simply projected in the air above the amp, with a rather low quality. The audio was also muted, because she didn't want Chris to turn it up too loud and draw attention to himself. So while they were here he either had to watch it silently, or Angelee had to reproduce or improvise the sounds for him.

In this case she could do the latter, because it was a holo that they had watched repeatedly with Peter before he died, and many times since then. It was both Peter's and Chris's favorite movie—the father had even named his son after the main character. Angelee started to describe the current scene to Chris, one which contained two men walking along a path in the woods, but then she noticed that she could hear Simon talking on his phone in the other room. So she tucked Chris in and crept over to listen through the crack in the door.

"Yeh, no, I unnerstand," Simon was saying. "You like ta hurt 'em. But can't afford to lose this one, or have her damaged bad." A pause as he listened to the other party. "Yeh, no. I know there's always a way, but not this time." Another pause.

"Collaterwhat? Naw, I'm juss playin' witcha. I know what it is. I'll bet my butt ring you don't have anything good enough . . . No, too hard ta fence . . . Already got one."

Simon paused longer this time. "Now you're playin' wit *me*. You serious? What's wrong with them? . . . Okey, deal. But if she dies, I'm keepin' both."

He hung up and called to the other room in a much louder voice, "Get youseff ready, hoover. He be here in ten."

Angelee tiptoed back to the bed and cuddled with Chris.

"What's wrong, Mommy?" the little boy asked softly.

"Shhhhh. Can we watch the part at the end, please?"

"Okay," he said. She selected the scene that they had viewed more than any other since her husband died, and narrated it for the boy.

"Christian and his friend," she said softly, and was choking up already. "They've seen the Celestial City, but to get there they have to pass through a river. And there is no boat, and I guess they can't swim too well, because they ask the Shining Ones, 'How do we get across these waters?'

"*'You have to walk through them!'*" She said this with a low growl, which she imagined to be the way an angel would talk. "And when the pilgrims ask if they were deep or shallow, the Shining Ones say, *'They are deep or shallow, depending on your faith!'* So they start through the river, and sure enough, one of them starts to sink—I can't tell which one—because he didn't believe very much. But the other one says, 'Remember the promises that the king made!' That's the king of the city where they were headed, of course."

Angelee stopped to look toward the door into the other room, because her voice had grown louder.

"Well," she continued quietly, "when the man who was sinking remembered the king's promises, when he had faith instead of so much fear, he found that his feet touched the bottom of the river, and he could walk across! It got more shallow, because he believed now, you see?" She stopped again, this time to see if her son was really asleep, or just keeping his eyes closed. It looked like he was out cold, but she continued anyway, for her own sake. She had difficulty getting the words out, because she was straining to hold back tears.

"By the time they got to the other side of the river, their old clothes were gone and they had new ones. Really nice new clothes." She looked down at hers, then closed her eyes and imagined herself dressed like an angel, in shining white. But when he opened them, she still wore the slinky dress that Simon had given her.

She kissed Chris, looked up at the cracked ceiling, and did something she hadn't done since her husband died. She had prayed many times with her little boy, but that was more out of a sense of obligation to his father. It seemed ironic that this would be her first time praying on her own, because she thought it would also likely be her last, especially when she heard the door open in the other room and Simon say, "Lady Lee . . . c'mon out here."

She wiped the wetness from her eyes, stood up and went through the door, which she closed firmly behind her. Then she turned to face Simon and a much fatter man, who was wearing a coat and tie.

"You two kids have fun," Simon said with a smile that was now more nervous than mischievous. "I'll be outside." Then he left the room.

The fat man didn't waste any time or words. He moved closer to Angelee and pulled out a small but very sharp knife, which he used to saw through the front of his belt and waistbands so that his pants fell to the floor. Then he held the knife ready and lurched toward her. Whether in her traumatized mind or in reality, she wasn't sure which, she saw saliva dripping from his mouth.

As she closed her eyes and felt the cold steel of the knife on her skin, under the strap of her dress, she suddenly heard the lock open on the door to the outside. She opened her eyes, and then was *really* not sure about what she saw . . .

Simon stumbled into the room through the door, having been pushed from behind. Half of the pimp's gun was in his hand, but the other half was stuffed into his mouth, painfully straining his lips and cheeks. Another man stepped in right behind him, and this one had a very intact gun in his hand, a wicked-looking thing with two barrels.

The fat man wheeled around and put his hands up, dropping the knife on the floor.

Angelee instinctively moved away from her molester to one side of the room, and it was only then that the shock lifted and she recognized the new person. He was the beautiful rich man who had visited her at the shelter a month before. Her body shuddered—this was all too much for her to take—and she staggered back against the table behind her.

The man with the gun waved it toward the door just once, and the fat john immediately scrambled to gather himself and waddled out of the door faster than one would think he could move. Then the handsome angel pushed Simon's neck down with his free hand and held the gun to his head with the other. He pointed the pimp in the direction of Angelee and told him to apologize to her.

Simon couldn't speak with the gun in his mouth, of course, but he forced out something that sounded like he was trying to say "Sorry." So the man lifted his head back up and spun him around.

"Does your mouth hurt?" he asked. Simon nodded furiously. The man said, "Good," and pistol-whipped him right across that part of his face. The half-gun stayed inside his bloody mouth as he fell to the floor, groaning in agony. "Now it's worse."

Despite her resentment toward Simon, Angelee cringed and recoiled at the violence, because she wasn't used to it. But that reaction quickly faded when the man moved close to her and tenderly grasped her arm.

"Angie," he said, and she didn't correct him. "I am so sorry I didn't come sooner, but I need your help. Please get your boy and your things and come with me."

He's asking me for help? She couldn't believe it.

"Are you okay?" he asked, when she didn't move or speak.

She nodded, then practically skipped past Simon's sprawled form and into Chris's room.

As soon as they were safely in the man's car and moving north across Napa City, Angelee began sobbing uncontrollably. She alternated between tears of trauma and tears of joy, but it must have seemed all bad to her savior, because he was visibly worried about her and obviously searching for something to say. Chris, on the other hand, rested quietly on her lap, being used to his mother crying, especially in the last month or so.

"Do you not want to help me?" he asked. "I won't make you."

This gave her the motivation to gain some control of her emotions, because there seemed to be an implication that he might leave her somewhere if his plans didn't work out.

"Your boss could come looking for you, though," he added before she could respond. "So it would be good for you to disappear with me for a while, until he moves on with his life and forgets about you." She wondered briefly if he had let Simon live for this reason, so she would be inclined to accept his offer. But she didn't care if he was manipulating her, because all she wanted to do was please him and be with him. Besides, she knew that Simon was too much of a coward to take the chance of tangling with this kind of man again.

"Disappear?" she asked, wiping at her face.

"Yes. I know this will sound odd, but I'm going to a place for a few weeks where no one will know, and I can't leave there and risk being seen. So I need someone to stay with me there, who can go out to get food and other things I might need. *We* might need."

Angelee's body shuddered again, and she felt light-headed.

"It's only for a few weeks," he said, misreading her reaction. "And it's a very nice place, nicer than you've probably ever seen." As soon as he said that, he cringed. "I'm sorry, I didn't mean to say that. Please don't be offended."

"No" was all she could get out, feeling like she might faint.

"It has a pool, and everything else," he continued. "Your son will like it there. And remember your boss . . ."

"No," she said again. "I'm not offended."

"Good. So you'll help me? You know, I feel like this is all meant to be, somehow."

She overcame her hesitation to look his way, and moved her eyes more than her head, so she could stare at him. As she drank in the sight, she started to feel faint again, so she looked away. *I can't believe this is happening to me* ran like a loop through her mind.

"What's your son's name again?" he asked.

"Chris," she said.

"How old is he?"

"Four," she said, then blurted out, "My husband died."

"I know. That's why I came to visit you at the shelter, remember? He worked for me."

"Right, I'm sorry. I'm a little out of it right now." The reference to the shelter made her think of Mariah, and the agreement they had. "How did you find me this time?"

"I went to the shelter asking for you, and a lady there told me what you were doing and where."

"Was she big and black?" she asked, and he said yes. "She was the friend who got me the job with Simon."

"With friends like that, who needs an enema?" he said, laughing.

"Well, at least she kept our deal," Angelee said. "I went to work for Simon, she got some cash, and she promised to watch if you came back."

"Hmmm," he said, smiling warmly. "I guess there *is* honor among thieves."

He was not only her savior, and one of the best-looking men she had ever met, but he was able to put her completely at ease, too. He even reached out to her son . . .

"Chris, do you like to swim . . . in a pool?"

"I can't swim by myself yet," the little boy said sheepishly.

"Yes, he loves it," Angelee said. "But we haven't done it very much."

The man wore the same apologetic look as before, realizing that they were too poor to enjoy a pool very often, and there were probably not many in the urban sprawl of Napa City.

"What's *your* name?" she asked, feeling comfortable enough now to do so.

"Oh, I'm sorry. I never told you? It's Michael Ares."

"That's what I thought, but I wasn't sure. Some of the people at the shelter said it, but I never know whether to believe what they say."

"You didn't look me up on the net?" he asked.

"No," she said, and then hesitated, feeling embarrassed about what she was about to say, and fearful that he would dislike it. But she was nothing if not honest. "We try not to use the net. My husband had to at work, of course, but our church didn't believe in going on there for entertainment, or even to learn things."

"So you don't know who I am?" he asked incredulously, and when she said no, he shook his head and said mostly to himself, "This couldn't have worked out better."

Angelee didn't know what he meant by that, but she knew what it meant to her. God was back in her life, and He had not only sent her a savior, but hopefully a new lover, too. And she wanted to thank him for saving her, in any and every way she could.

17
FIRED AND HIRED

Stephenson and another Gotham Security agent, who was also tech savvy, transferred quickly to the backseat of one of the converted taxis. They called up the access to the two other ones on the scene, and placed their hands and feet on the virtual steering wheels and gas pedals that appeared from the holo projectors. Then, by remote control, they sent the two empty cars screeching into the underground parking garage as their diversion maneuver.

As he watched them go and made his way with the other three agents toward the elevators inside the garage entrance, Korcz couldn't help but think about the dream his partner had shown him earlier. According to Stephenson and the precognition software at Dreamscape, both of them were destined to die in a fiery explosion in one of the taxis, but that was clearly not going to happen right now. One or both of those cars might end up being blown up by the armed criminals coming out of the hidden drug lab three stories down, but they were empty, and Korcz himself would be on foot in another part of the facility. All of which confirmed his skepticism about Stephenson's dream theories.

But he didn't have any time to think about it more, because he and one of the men had reached their destination, and the other two had rushed into the stairway nearby.

"At the elevator," he said into his comm.

"Okay, we have control of it," Arvit said from back at the base. His boss must have had a tech with her, because Korcz knew she wasn't skilled enough herself to do things like that. "Have fun, and remember we want Tyra Ponchinello alive."

Korcz watched as the door slid open and the elevator moved down, stopping just low enough that he and his partner could step onto its top. As they rode downward for three floors, the other agents on the stairs encountered some of the Black Italians trying to leave that way, and engaged them with grenades and gunfire, killing some and forcing the rest back toward the room that was serving as the lab where they made and stored the drug called Money. The criminals were effectively trapped now, not even trying to use the exit on the third level of the garage, because Stephenson's two empty cars had arrived outside it, their sirens blazing and windows tinted to preserve the illusion.

When the elevator reached the lab, Arvit sent it past the door, and stopped it when its top was about four feet lower than the bottom of the door. Korcz pulled out something that looked like a black curtain rod, stretched it out so it reached from one bottom corner of the doorway to the other, and pulled the thin film off the adhesive on its bottom. Then he positioned it across the bottom of the doorway and pressed it down till it held fast. When he turned it on, a crackling transparent wall of energy filled the doorway behind the closed elevator door.

This contraption was commonly called an OWCH. Korcz knew that it stood for "one-way" something, but he didn't know the fancy words that the other two letters represented. He knew that he was glad for it, however, because when Arvit opened the elevator door everything within a few feet of the doorway was now suddenly pushed back, including some boxes, a chair, and two men who were standing near it. Most projectiles would not penetrate the field, or at least would be slowed and diverted by it. And most importantly it would repel any grenades, which were the biggest threat to them in their current position. But the "one-way" of the OWCH was the most helpful part—unlike their opponents, Korcz and his partner were able to shoot through it unobstructed. And they had to start doing that right away, because the noise of the field and the sirens outside in the garage prevented them from telling the criminals to put down their weapons. It didn't matter anyway, because the mob men were shooting at them before the door was even completely open.

The OWCH gave the yellow-armored Gotham agents a major tactical advantage, providing cover for most of their bodies. So they made short work of most of the criminals who were visible to them, with the exception of the mob boss's daughter, who was crouching on the right side of the room, not too far from them. Perhaps she knew that they were told not to shoot her, because she didn't seek cover on the other side of boxes or tables. Or maybe she knew that the other Gotham agents would be coming through the door to the stairway soon, and there wouldn't be a safe angle for hiding.

The agents on the stairs hadn't fought their way through to the room yet, so some of the armed criminals were well covered for now, even by small obstructions, because Korcz and his partner were basically firing from the floor. When Korcz figured this out, he told Arvit to raise the elevator under him, and when she did, a few more of the crouching enemies suddenly became visible, much to their surprise. Then they would never be surprised by anything again, as the caseless hollow points from the agents' rifles rained down on them.

Just as Korcz was deciding whether to have the elevator lowered again, because of the greater exposure and risk of a bullet getting through the field, one of the thugs in the room threw a golfball-sized grenade at the elevator, obviously not knowing how the OWCH worked. Korcz yelled some profane words ending in "You idiot!" and at the same time Tyra Ponchinello said some other profane words ending in "idiot!" The similarity of their reactions was so uncanny that they actually looked at each other for a second until the grenade, which had bounced off the force field, exploded with a deafening concussion that killed or immobilized half of the resistance left in the room.

Tyra was among the immobilized, and Korcz immediately felt responsible for her, because of his orders but also because he felt like he may have delayed her from diving away when their eyes locked. It wasn't really his fault, but he was moved to help her nonetheless. So when he saw the other two Gotham agents coming through the stairway door, he told Arvit to lower the elevator, turned off the OWCH, and stepped through the elevator doorway toward the wounded woman. His partner looked nervously at him, then back to the room, tensing at the increased danger they were in without the barrier. But he didn't know the half of it yet.

Korcz strafed the rest of the room as he moved to Tyra's side, then stooped to check her out, leaving the other three armored men to mop up the resistance. She was bleeding, but not profusely, so he was hopeful that no artery or major organ had been hit by the shrapnel. He was even more hopeful when he heard the firing cease and one of his fellow agents yell, "Clear!" But that hope faded fast when the same man called him over with a panicked voice and showed him the explosives that were rigged to blow in less than three minutes, according to the timer that was counting down.

"Can you or anyone else in here turn it off?" he asked, returning fast to Tyra's side.

"No," she croaked. He thought this was strange, but he didn't have time to confirm it by torturing someone. So he just said, "Neither can we, danyet?" in the direction of the other agents and his comm link. The other men in the room all shook their heads, and Arvit's voice soon confirmed their dilemma:

"We have a bomb man here who was ready," she said hurriedly, "but he says three minutes is *not* long enough to talk you through it over the comm. Damn! How did they get the jump on us?"

Before she even finished talking, Korcz had lifted Tyra to her feet and sent the other three agents into the stairway ahead of him. He made the five unarmed criminals who were still alive stay behind him, however, as he started to help the wounded woman up the steps. They were visibly nervous and resentful about the slow progress, but Korcz figured if he was going to die, they should too. For all he knew, one of them might have triggered the explosives.

After about a floor's worth of steps, he realized the assault rifle was inhibiting him from moving Tyra fast enough, and he began to worry about the criminals jumping him so they could get out faster. So he made one of them help her, and moved backward behind them so he could cover the others. It was amazing how fast a lab worker could move two bodies when a bomb was about to go off.

It seemed to take forever, but they made it to the surface level of the garage before the blast. The four other Gotham agents and Stephenson were waiting for them just outside the entrance, and all three converted taxis were also back on the street. Stephenson told the other agents to take the surviving criminals in, and he and Korcz escorted Tyra to their car.

They were almost there when the lab exploded. At first Korcz thought that the Money makers overdid it in their zeal to erase their operation. The ground shook like a major earthquake and a heavy cloud of debris, gas, and liquid chemicals burst out of the stairway, the elevator shaft, and two grates on the street. Then the ground suddenly began catching fire everywhere the cloud landed. As the flames started to spread out in every direction, Korcz realized it was actually the snow that was reacting with the burning chemicals from the lab, and from the recesses of his brain remembered hearing that there were often deadly accidents involving water when Money was being synthesized. He even remembered hearing that people had been burned alive, and now he saw it firsthand as the flames caught the fleeing criminals and agents and literally consumed them from their feet to their heads, the incendiary chemical mixture reacting with the few flakes of snow that had fallen on them, their sweat, and maybe even the moisture in their bodies.

It was like a science experiment from hell, but Korcz and Stephenson didn't have time to gawk at it, for the deluge of fire was headed their way, and was about to surround them. They moved quickly toward their taxi, dragging Tyra with them, but then saw that two of the other agents had managed to jump into theirs and start to drive, only to have the flames overtake the vehicle. The balls of fire seemed to jump onto the snow that had accumulated on the car and then into the inside of it, and the yellow on the taxi and the men's armor soon was turned to red and black.

The last place Korcz and Stephenson now wanted to be was inside their car, so they instinctively and pointlessly fled to the only place they could go, which was the top of it. They scrambled onto the trunk, pulling Tyra with them, and then to the roof as the flames reached the tires and very quickly climbed the sides toward them. This progress of the fire up the car probably took only three or four seconds, but time seemed to slow to a crawl for Korcz. He could even see that some of the snowflakes falling through the air near them were sparking into tiny flames. It would have been beautiful, in a way, if he wasn't about to die.

The trio held onto one another, again purely by instinct, as they stood on the top of the car and waited to catch fire.

Then a small slab of plasteel, about the size of a hand, slammed into Korcz's shoulder. Two small snakes of the same material shot out of each side of it, flashing around the three bodies till they joined at the ends and constricted painfully. Then all three of them were jerked up and away from the engulfed car and carried gradually higher and away from the apocalyptic scene below.

Korcz looked up and saw that the other end of the tether was attached to one of the flying cars owned by his former employer, the Bay Area Security Service. Some other recess of his mind informed him that he had been rescued by a RATS, which stood for "retrieval" something. He couldn't remember the other words in that acronym, either. But he was definitely grateful for this fancy tech, because a look back down revealed just how apocalyptic the chemical and water fire really was. He could tell that it had already spread beyond the street outside the garage, and he later heard that it consumed over two whole blocks before it petered out.

The aero dropped them on a nearby rooftop, and then landed next to them after it had released and retracted the RATS. A woman with beautiful long blond hair stepped out of the passenger side and greeted them, periodically looking in the direction of the fire to make sure it hadn't moved faster and farther than she thought.

"I'm Raylyn Young," she said, "the BASS ambassador to the Big Apple." They shook hands with her after they had helped each other to their feet. "I was coming to make you an offer in person that was too important to do over the net, and too time sensitive to make an appointment. Seems a good thing that I came when I did."

"She is wounded," Korcz said about Tyra.

"Yes, I see. We'd better get her to help, and I can talk to you on the way."

She gestured toward the aero and joined Korcz in helping Tyra, supporting her other side without concern for the blood she might get on her stylish clothes.

When they were helping her into the backseat of the aero, Korcz noticed that Stephenson hadn't walked with them, but was still standing in the same spot, his arms limp at his sides and his mouth hanging wide open.

"Lawrence?" Korcz said, and when the short man didn't answer, the big one walked back to him and waved a hand in front of his glazed eyes.

"Holy Shiva, mother of all fuhhhh . . . ," Stephenson mumbled until he ran out of breath. Then he came alive again. "Did you see that?!"

"Yeh . . . ?" Korcz replied. Then it starting dawning on him. "Daaa." Then it dawned on him more. "Ohuitelno!"

"It was exactly like in the dream." He gripped the Russian's shoulders, which he had to reach up to do. "The precog dream. They were right! There was the car, the fire, and us going up. Except I thought that was our souls going to heaven. But it was actually us going up."

"You forgot the hugging."

"Yeah, and the hugging thing. Unbelievable. I can't believe it. I knew it was real, I knew . . . I believed it."

"Wait now, not so fast." Korcz was thinking further. "The woman was not in the dream."

"Hmmm," Stephenson said, grabbing his chin. "I wonder why. But it doesn't matter, it's still the most amazing thing ever. This proves . . . something, that's for sure. Did you see it?!"

"Ohuitelno. I was there. But we have to go now."

"Yeah, okay, right," the little man said, and practically skipped to the car, making Korcz have to double his stride to catch up.

The BASS ambassador turned on the holo projectors in the backseat of the aero, and soon the three passengers were facing the top half of Terrey Thorn, as if he were there with them and not three thousand miles away in San Francisco. The handsome Aussie knew a lot about each of them, including Tyra, whom he had researched just prior to the call.

"I don't really believe in destiny," he told them. "But if I did, we could put this night on the poster for it." They looked at him and each other quizzically. "Something's going on here, I don't know what. But I'm going to ride the wave . . ."

And then he proceeded to offer a ridiculously high-paying, short-term job to Korcz and Stephenson, plus an opportunity to stay with BASS afterward if they did well.

"And I hope you say yes," he added, "because I've had four others turn me down while we were locating you, and I'm running short on time."

The two men accepted his offer with little hesitation, partially because an idea like destiny was on their minds, too, and they felt like they might miss it if they didn't "ride the wave" themselves.

"Hah! Fired and hired in the same night," Stephenson said, positively giddy with the buzz from the dream thing, not to mention being alive. "Fired and hired, get it?"

Then Terrey surprised even himself by offering a job to Tyra as well, as the destiny wave kept rolling and the details coalesced in his mind.

"You'll need some place other than New York to recover," he said to her. "Won't you?" She looked perplexed again, but a little less this time. "And you might be needing that place and a new life just enough to do a dangerous job for me. Plus you're no stranger to walking the edge."

"What's he talking about?" asked Stephenson from the other side of Korcz, whose big bulk filled the middle of the seat. "Why would you have to leave New York?"

"My papa will know now that I'm not with him," she said with the unique Black Italian accent.

"You were the police mole in the lab?" Stephenson asked, realizing why she would be in trouble with the mob.

"Papa has known it's been comin' for a while now. He won't be surprised, and he loves me too much to kill me. But he can't have me around doin' damage to the business. Even doh I cut his losses."

Stephenson pondered for a moment, then said, "You were the one who tipped the mob off too?"

"I have . . . uhn . . . interesting relationship with my father," she said, nodding.

When Korcz heard that this woman had basically caused the explosion that almost killed them, he bristled visibly and scooted over away from her in the seat, far enough that he was crunching Stephenson. He also gripped the rifle resting between his legs.

"This gives new meaning to the term double agent," Stephenson said, trying to lighten things up a bit. "Working for both sides at the same time."

"I'm on your side for good now, feel me?" she said to Korcz, touching his knee with her hand. "You saved my life." The big man relaxed a little.

"And we did, too," Terrey interrupted. "So would you risk it for us a little while, for a pile of money and a better future?"

"Yes, I guess I will. Don't have to think about it much, 'cause you're right about no place to go. And besides, I like this one." She squeezed Korcz's leg this time. "Being serious, doh, I do owe you BASS people, and I don' wanna any money, juss what I need to heal, and to live after that."

"Wow, okay," Terrey said. "Are you sure?"

"No extra money. It's a blood debt."

"Whadda you think of that, mates?" he asked the men.

"I owe BASS also, two times now," Korcz said, holding up that many fingers. "But I do want the money."

"I want the money, too," Stephenson chimed in. "And I also want you to replace something that I lost in the fire back there." He leaned forward so he would be less crunched. "Ever hear of Dreamscape?"

18
LOVE NEST

As we drove through the urban sprawl of Napa City, I noticed how over-
crowded and poverty stricken it had become, since the flood of refugees had
transformed it after the quake. And I looked forward to the stark contrast we
would experience when we passed through the Oak Knoll Gates into Napa Valley, which was now one of the world's largest private communities, walled off by
an electrified strip of metal that protected the wealthy residents from their not-
so-wealthy neighbors and anyone else who might not be privileged with access.

The home I shared with Lynn was inside this beautiful area, located on a
secluded set of high hills known as Stags Leap. But I wasn't going there right
now, nor for a while; instead I was headed to a secret place that Lynn herself had
never been to, and wouldn't be happy if she knew I was going there. I didn't
think she would be very happy with what was happening in this car right now,
either—the girl I had rescued was curled up against my side, resting her head on
the side of my shoulder.

Angelee had situated her little son on the right side of her seat after he fell
asleep, and then moved over toward me. I thought she would soon become uncomfortable sitting on the emergency brake and cup holders like that, but she
didn't seem to mind at all. In fact, she seemed downright happy to be there. At this
point I thought that perhaps she was viewing me as a father figure, and I had just

been with Lynn earlier that night, so I wasn't turned on at all by this. But I had definitely noticed, as any man would, that she was a very attractive young woman.

I used an anonymous BASS identification card at the East Gate so I could enter the Valley without anyone knowing I was Michael Ares. The scanners wouldn't read the car as belonging to me, or even to BASS, because it was one of a number that we kept as "blank slates" for this very purpose of being able to move around the Bay Area without being detected or located. So right now, this Asian girl was the only person who knew where I was, and she didn't even know who I was. I marveled again that I had actually found someone like her to hide with me, and that the place I was going was also perfect for what I needed in order to be invisible while the kaleidocide ran its course. It was within "striking distance" of my home, about fifteen to twenty minutes by car, but no one knew about it except the owner, who was hardly ever there.

The girl's eyes were closed, either sleeping or just savoring her safety, so she wouldn't even see where I drove, and probably wouldn't recognize anywhere we went anyway. It was still well before sunrise, and I was sure she had never been inside the exclusive Valley. I thought of telling her where we were, because I was already beginning to enjoy the innocent, childlike pleasure she took in everything that was happening, but I also didn't want to disturb her. I had seen people sleep for days after trauma of various kinds, and wondered if she would be like that. It made me feel good to be protecting her, despite the danger I was in myself, and I wondered briefly if I would have had that feeling if she weren't so beautiful.

In twenty minutes we were deep inside the Valley, and with little trouble I found the long driveway through the vineyards that led to our destination, even though I hadn't been there in about seven years. The memories started flooding back as I approached the house, and were surprisingly fresh considering all the time that had passed, and all the circumstances, like a wedding and two pregnancies. They also were rather guilt-inducing, considering those circumstances.

We reached the end of the long dirt path, and the external house lights lit up when they sensed the car. The place looked basically same as it had years earlier, with some minor landscaping changes. An inside light near the front door came on at the same time as the outside ones did, which confirmed to me that no one was there, as I had fully expected.

"Stay here," I said to the girl. "In case this doesn't work." As I left the car and stepped toward the side of the house, I thought again about what I would do if it didn't work. But somehow I knew it would, not because I was so smart, but because I was so *weak* that I had failed to completely break off a relationship that shouldn't have existed in the first place.

I found the light casing in the flower bed, and as I expected the keycard was still there. I pulled it out and walked around to the front door, and as I did the words I had heard in many conversations played in my head. *Our love nest is still there, waiting for you. Go there anytime, call me, and I'll be there as soon as I can. Even if I'm at work—I have plenty of vacation time saved up. You know where the key is . . .*

Tara had even programmed the card so that my entry would not be registered on any security grid, and I didn't have to be afraid that someone would find out I was there. She wanted to make it easier for me to commit adultery with her, of course, but little did she know the much better purpose it would end up serving. *Not more enjoyable,* I thought to myself, *but better.* It struck me as ironic that I had always thought if I ever came back here, it would be for the purpose of renewing my relationship with her, but now a plan had already occurred to me how I could use this situation to finally put an end to it.

Not long after these thoughts about avoiding adultery were in my head, however, I found myself faced with the issue again. I carried in the girl's bags to the master bedroom, saying "Here you go," and watched as she laid the boy down in the big bed and tucked him in under the covers. But then she followed me out of the room, leaving the door slightly ajar, and stood looking at me when I turned to face her in the foyer. It took me a few moments to realize what was happening, but then I started to understand, and she soon removed all doubt.

"I owe you everything," she said nervously. "But I would feel a lot better about this if we were married."

She was used to men wanting only one thing from her, and she was assuming it was included in my intentions for this arrangement. Her religion apparently limited sex to marriage, and she was obviously thinking that I was single. I had never worn a wedding ring, partly because of the nature of my initial work as a peacer, and she didn't use the net, so I realized that she could go on thinking that indefinitely unless I corrected her. I realized that this could serve my purposes well, and also give her a safe place to stay for a while. She would go on thinking a relationship with me was a possibility, and that would give her hope and string her along sufficiently until enough time had passed and she didn't need to be here anymore. If and when she found out the truth, I could honestly say that I had never confirmed her hopes. So I let her have them for now.

"I wouldn't ask that from you," I said, "unless we were married." I thought that would end the conversation, but she surprised me with her response.

"Thank you," she said with relief, but then grew nervous again. "So . . . did you want to get married now?"

"I, um, I told you that I can't go anywhere for a while," I said with a puzzled look on my face, "especially not to a courthouse or a church."

"Peter and I said our vows by ourselves, and we were married right then."

"Didn't your religion have a problem with that?"

"No, our church didn't believe in ceremonies, like with the government. 'Cause of the gays and besties getting married, and all that."

It seemed that she wasn't only willing to do this, but actually desired it. And I didn't want to reject her too strongly, because I needed her for now and didn't want to send her out into the world just yet, while her pimp might still be looking for her.

"You're very beautiful, Angie, but—" Then I had a second thought. "Am I getting your name right? Is it Angie?"

"It's Angelee," she said proudly. "Thanks to you."

"What do you mean?"

"The first time I became an escort, I was sixteen." She started to choke up as she told the story. "One of my regular tricks was Peter, who became my husband. He had a lot of guilt being with me, because he was a Christian who had gotten into a bad habit, you know. So we ended up talking a lot, and he didn't want me to be with anyone else, so he took me home and took care of me. I didn't have to . . . give myself up anymore." She was sobbing now. "Then he died and I had to take care of Chris. The only thing I have . . . they say I'm pretty . . . I took the place Simon gave me, and was going back to where I was before I met Peter. But then you came—that man you saw was my first customer. You saved me like Peter did, you're like him coming back to me. I belong to you now—all of me."

"I'm glad I could help," I said, and had to admit that it did feel good. "But what does that have to do with your name?"

"Oh, sorry," she sniffled, wiping her face with her sleeve. "My name was Lee, working name Lady Lee, when I met Peter. He changed it to Angelee when we were married, because he said I was a new person, like an angel. I was ready to change it back tonight, but then you came. So my name is Angelee. Unless *you* want to change it . . ."

"No, no. That's okay, I like Angelee. Listen, can we talk about this more later? Right now I have to set up some things in my room, because remember I'm hiding from some powerful people who want to kill me."

"Won't they be able to find you here at your house?" she asked.

"No . . . this isn't my house. It belongs to a woman I know, a woman I work with. Her name's Tara."

"You have a key to her house?" she asked. I ran through the options quickly in my mind and decided there was no reason to keep her in the dark about this.

"We were together a long time ago," I explained. "She has a place in the city, where she works. But she bought this as a second home, so we could come here to get away. And she keeps telling me that she wants me to come back to her, to come back here." I left out the part about needing a private rendezvous spot because I was married. "I knew she wouldn't be coming here anytime soon, because she hardly ever does, so this was a perfect place for me to disappear."

"So you're not . . . with her?"

"No, not for years," I said, again leaving out the part about marrying someone else. (Now she would be even more convinced that I was single.) "But I haven't really made a full break, if you know what I mean. I actually plan to do that really soon." Angelee clearly didn't understand all this, but she brightened at the last statement. So I continued: "And to do that, I have to set up a net room. So why don't you get some sleep with your son. Chris, right? And I'll see you in the morning."

She nodded, wiping at her face again, and then tiptoed back into the master bedroom.

I let out a long breath and proceeded to bring my things into the second bedroom, on the other side of the kitchen and living room. When I had everything inside, I locked the front door manually, stood next to it, and spoke into the air just loud enough that the Living House A.I. could hear me.

"Vera, are you there?" I said. A code word had to be spoken at the beginning of every sentence, because otherwise the house would always think you were talking to it. And since it spoke in a woman's voice, Tara and I had picked "Vera"—she liked it because of something in an old TV series, and I liked it because of something in a classic British rock album.

"Yes, Michael," the house responded, only through the walls in my proximity, so it wouldn't disturb any other guests. "Is that you?"

"Yes, Vera, it's me."

"It's good to have you back, Michael." Like Saul's ghost, this A.I. had the irritating habit of using names too often. But I supposed that was necessary for this kind of communication to work well, because others who were present would know to whom it was speaking. There was no other way to know, because it couldn't "look" at anyone.

"Thank you, Vera. Please make sure that your external security settings for the property are as high as they go, and please disconnect any possible communication with the outside world. Please terminate any net connections . . . I'll use my own. Oh wait, Vera, before you do that, I should ask: Are there any scheduled security or utility reports that would be missed by Tara or anyone else, if you shut them off?"

"Tara and the security company are only notified if an alarm goes off, Michael."

"Good," I said. "Vera, make sure any incoming calls will go directly to voice-mail, so that no one here could pick one up by mistake."

"Consider it done, Michael," she said. "Would you like me to tell Tara that you're here?"

"No, Vera, please don't tell her. Don't tell anyone."

"Very well, Michael. Would you like me to play a holo for you, that you and Tara filmed on one of your previous visits?"

"No thank you, Vera," I said quickly. "You can shut down for now, after you set the temperature at seventy degrees Fahrenheit. And don't film anything on this visit, okay?"

"Okay, Michael."

This all made me think of Lynn, not just because I wouldn't want her to know those holos existed, but because the Living House showed how different she and Tara were. Our home was equipped with this same technology, but Lynn never turned it on, because she always said, "When I talk, I like to talk to *people*." Tara, on the other hand, loved it and played with it like a toy. And unlike her, Lynn hated being filmed by anyone in any situation, let alone private ones.

I stepped back into the second bedroom and pulled out the netkit that we had requisitioned from the castle. It was only the size of a large book but worth as much money as a large yacht, and contained everything I needed to communicate with Lynn, Terrey, and the protection team at any time, without any security risk. I pulled out the projector patches that would make the room into a net room and stuck them onto the wall at various places. Then I unrolled the three paper-thin monitor screens and pressed them to the wall above the desk, situated the keyboard scroll and airmouse patches on its top, and activated the system with my handprint, retinal scan, and voice identification.

"Live forever, man," I said when Terrey's face appeared on one of the monitors.

"Never die young, mate," he responded. "Hey, before anything else, let me get my *Trois* to test your equipment, make sure it's the bee's knees."

According to the techs at BASS, this system was connected to the ultimate Fortress Cloud, which would filter any data so thoroughly that no one on the planet could scan it, hack it, or otherwise know that it even existed. Terrey was so concerned to keep me hidden that he was originally going to suggest I have no contact at all with anyone for the duration. But the triplets were very impressed with the capabilities of the BASS technology and convinced him that it would keep me safe, especially when combined with their own. Plus the ability I would have to "ride" with my double would make it so much easier for him to pass for me when he had to go into public places.

Apparently the netkit and Fortress system was as good as advertised, because

Terrey soon gave me the thumbs-up and a report about what had happened in the few hours since I had left the vacation house in Sausalito.

"The triplets combed your property for every possible sabotage device or method, and installed sensors on the air system, electrical, water, you name it, so that if any foreign element is introduced, we should know about it."

"Should?" I said.

"Well, mate, like everything in life, it's not perfect. That's why we'll have backups, like the cupbearer."

"You found someone for that?"

"Yes, but in an unusual place. The two friends you suggested were not good enough friends to agree to risking their life for you. They said no."

"Figures."

"But we got someone better, someone who has had no prior contact with you at all, which is always the best in this situation, because of the traitor factor. And at the same time, I kid you not, we got the other two security types we needed. I keep saying it, but the way this has all worked out is really bizarre. It's like the hand of fate, or the stars are lined up, some weird shite like that. I still can't believe we got a double this good, in less than an hour of interviews."

"Good except for the AIMS," I said.

"You still worried about that? Like I told you, the only way someone can get it is by sleeping with him, and that's not going to happen. The incredibly minor risk of transmission by some other means is a wash, because the fact that he has the disease motivates him to follow through with what we need him for. He's hoping to survive and get treated with the money he makes, or be healed by the Makeover. I didn't even have to give him a self-destruct imp to threaten him and keep him in line, like the other times I've done this. He's committed, and he's a fast learner. He'll be awake by morning."

Terrey's mention of an implant reminded me of a year before, and made me shudder.

"Speaking of imps," I said, "tell me again how you didn't do anything to my head while I was out for that half hour." The triplet who stayed at the house had anesthetized me briefly for a procedure before I left Sausalito to get Angelee.

"You're really uptight about that issue, aren't you? But you're the boss with the bikkies, so I'll tell you again. We just had to lift some paths from your brain and transfer them to the double's, so he can walk and talk like you." The triplet had explained back at the house, in layman's terms, that much of what makes people appear the way they do, and even talk the way they do, is determined by the neuropaths in the brain.

"And when you say 'lifted,'" I asked, "you mean copied, right? You didn't actually take anything away from me."

"Do you still walk and talk like you did before?" Terrey asked rhetorically. "No worries, mate."

"Okay, just one more thing," I said apologetically. "On my drive after you did that to me—it all happened so fast—I looked up implants on the net. It said that some of them can be inserted quickly, like through the nose?" Terrey snorted and shook his head, but I pressed on: "Min was outside getting the netkit and other stuff from the peacers who came from the castle, so it was only you and the cyborg girl for a while when I was out, until Min came back in. I started to think . . . I know, it's paranoid—"

"Bloody hell, Michael," my friend said, frustrated with me. "I told you we have to do things fast, your life depends on it, and you're gonna have to trust me. There's no other way." He calmed down, and asked rhetorically again, "Does your nose hurt? Does your head hurt?"

"Actually my head does hurt a little. It reminds me of the feeling I had during the 'silhouette' incident."

"When you *didn't* have an implant, but only thought you did." He shook his head again. "Listen, you can have Min scan your brain if you're gonna worry about this."

I thought about that for a moment, then said, "No. I'm fine. I'm guess I'm just shaken up by all this. I need some time to process it."

"That's cool," he said. "Take your time. But *trust me,* and try to get some sleep. We'll meet the team in the morning when you and Lynn are both awake. And we'll see how good my *Trois* and the Makeover are, and whether she'll be fooled by the double."

I seriously doubted that would happen. I could never fool Lynn myself, so I didn't think it could be done by someone who was almost me.

19
MAKEOVER

I slept a few hours, just enough to meet my body's needs (another ability I still had from my military days), and then stumbled out into the kitchen to check the fridge for some breakfast, even though I knew there was probably nothing in there. I was reminded immediately of Angelee, and how I needed her to shop for me, but the master bedroom was quiet and I wanted to let her and the boy rest as long as they could.

I noticed it was almost 10:00 A.M., so I gave up my search of the cabinets and went back into my room. I washed up in the bathroom and called Terrey first, rather than Lynn, because I knew he wanted to have his fun with the double, and I had to admit I myself had a guilty curiosity to see what would happen. Lynn wouldn't be happy with me for being a part of it, but she would recover.

It took me a few minutes to reach my Aussie friend, because he had slept a few hours and was washing up when I called, his military habits exactly mirroring mine. And speaking of mirrors, it took me a minute to realize that I was looking at one when Terrey appeared on my wall screen. He had just finished dressing at the mirror in his room, and was now looking at himself so I could see his face, because he had answered my call in his contacts.

"I know you're not a contacts man," he said, "but look how natural they

130

are. Nothing to take on and off, and you can see my beautiful face with no obstruction. But for someone who looks like you, I can see why you'd want to cover up some." He was referring to my preference for glasses over contacts, of course, and we were now having the same conversation that was repeated constantly among people who could afford tech like this.

"Yeah," I responded, both hearing him and talking to him through his earpiece. "But I have to watch you blink all the time."

This was the classic criticism of contacts used for such purposes, because the average human being blinks twenty-five times per minute and there was no way to eliminate the effect on the camera function. I had to admit that the blinking effect wasn't really more noticeable than that of normal eyesight, but it was enough to prevent use by law enforcement agencies such as BASS, because of our dependence on complete and accurate video recording in much of our work. The audio recording by glasses was also so much better than even the best contact systems, and many of the latter didn't have audio at all, or had to be augmented through an earpiece like Terrey's. So I was, by necessity, a glasses man. Plus I liked the way I looked in them—it was nice to have a good excuse to wear cool shades at any time—and I liked how no one could see where I was looking when they were darkened.

"And you have to look in the mirror for me to see you," I added to Terrey. "While I can just take off my glasses and put them down in front of me."

"Touché," Terrey said. "But I'm gonna leave mine on. You have a lot more interesting things than me to look at this morning."

With that he walked out of his room and into the hallways of the BASS base built into the mountain under my house on Stags Leap, which we called "the hill" to distinguish it from "the castle," our base in the city. Saul Rabin had ordered the complex to be constructed in secret while they were building my house and another for Darien Anthony on the next crest over. He wanted to see if D and I would pass his tests and prove worthy to be his successors, when he passed away from the cancer that was eating him alive. Saul's son Paul, angered by his father's rejection and jealous of us for taking his place, had killed D (along with my daughter Lynette, who happened to be with him) and framed me for the murder. With Saul's help, however, I had turned the tables on Paul and inherited all of BASS, including the house that was built for D, under which was the rest of the mountain base. That part of it was not in use right now, because I had given D's house to Paul's widow and children, and some security concerns involving his teen son kept me from fully confiding in them.

The part of the base under my house was completely functioning, however. It contained state-of-the-art communications and surveillance equipment, research labs, a well-stocked armory, and other peacer supplies. It also had staff housing, an aero hangar bay camouflaged by a huge holo on one side of the hill, and a high-tech infirmary that Min had used to bring me back to life and patch me up after my confrontation with Paul. It was there that Terrey was headed, as I noticed through his lenses that the halls were deserted.

"Pretty quiet in here," Terrey said, reading my mind, "because I sent all the staff away. We'll just run with my team and Min from now on. You never know who Sun's people may have gotten to."

"You like the security there, huh?" I asked.

"That's an understatement," he said breathlessly. "I'm positively orgasmic about it. Triple redundancy on the internal systems, external scanning backed up by the Eye, five coordinated smart missile cannons on the perimeters of the property, S-laser umbrella shields. If the Chinese knew about even half of this, I guarantee that assault team was waiting for you to show up somewhere else, 'cause they would never try to attack you here. What was Rabin planning for when he built this, the next world war?"

"Maybe," I said. "Or maybe he thought that some factions might stop at nothing to get the Sabon tech."

"Hmmm," Terrey mused. "But the tech and its secrets are spread out in several places, right? Here, the castle, Silicon Valley. Seems to me he wanted to be able to protect a *person*. In fact, at the risk of sounding like a bloody broken record, it seems like it was all set up for a situation like the one we're in." He had reached the door of the medical suite. "Ah, here we are."

Inside, sitting on one of the examining tables and surrounded by the triplets, was the double. He was wearing my clothes, or at least a perfect facsimile of them, and he was looking down at the inside of his arm and injecting something into it.

"We're showing him how to take the Makeover I.S.," one of the *Trois* said, and I knew from what Terrey had told me before that those letters stood for "immunosuppressants." The Makeover was an elaborate chemical cocktail of modified genes and stem cells synthesized from the subject's skin and muscle that could be programmed and molded like an intelligent form of clay. Introducing it to a human body caused the immune system to panic and go into murder mode on a molecular level. The good news was that ADA, a key protein in the human immune system, was actually prone to meld with the Makeover when it flooded the "infected" areas, but the bad news was that it left the subject with no ADA for his own immune system, and he would therefore not be able to survive even the most basic forms of bacteria. So for the first few weeks, until the body adapted, a synthetic form of ADA had to be added into the body on a regular basis to maintain its health and strength. This was the agent that was a possible cure for AIMS, but could only be afforded by the wealthiest of the wealthy.

Terrey arrived next to the bedside, and I watched through his eyes as the double pressed one tip of a dime-sized triangle to the vein he had located with the help of the triplets. The triangle's air-delivery system opened a microscopic hole from the epidermis to the bloodstream, sending the tiny sphere containing the ADA into it. Then the vacuum it created pulled all the skin and muscle back together so that there was no mark left, or damage done. White collar drug users loved this undetectable delivery system, and often paid more for the triangles than they did for the drugs themselves. Now the double would have to carry a stash of them with him at all times, in a fold on his belt, and shoot up two times a day until the Makeover stabilized and the transformation became permanent.

"What happens if he doesn't take it?" I asked, trying to be nonchalant about how I might feel when the double finally looked up at me.

"He would get very sick," one of the triplets said, obviously monitoring my audio in that seemingly omniscient way of theirs. "And because of the ADA imbalance, the Makeover would fail and his face and ears would become unstable."

"It would look like hell," another of the triplets said, "and feel worse."

"Well," I said to the double, "I certainly appreciate you doing this."

"You're welcome," the triplet said. "Or were you talking to Mr. Cates?" I then realized that the double couldn't hear me, because my voice was only in the cyberspace between Terrey and his *Trois*. I said yes, and she added, "Say it again . . . now."

Suddenly my sitting form appeared on one side of the room, the holographic image coming from the cameras from the netkit in my room. So now I was looking at myself through Terrey's contacts, and my voice was recorded by my net room and broadcast into theirs.

"I appreciate you doing this," I said again.

As if on cue, the double handed the used triangle to a triplet, and looked up at my figure on the screen. He and I both watched my chin jerk up slightly from the inevitable shock of seeing two of myself, but my first thought after that was that he didn't look as much like me as I thought he would.

"You don't see yourself as often or as accurately as others do," Terrey said, reading my mind again. "But we're more objective, and we're happy with the likeness."

"The hair will actually be better," said a triplet, "when the cut and color aren't so fresh."

"I'll miss my beard more than anything," the double spoke for the first time, causing me to knit my brow at the sound of his voice . . . or my voice.

"Our voices are very different from when we hear them in our own heads," Terrey explained. "The combined effect of the throat patch and your copied neuropaths will be sufficient to trick most people, if not the best voiceprint systems. But in case of the latter, you can talk through the speakers on his glasses when you're riding with him."

"Did the Makeover change his eye color, too?" I asked, knowing that the double's eyes had been blue, while mine were green.

"No, we did that the old-fashioned, low-tech way," Terrey said. "Green contacts."

"Should we be calling him by his name?" I asked. "From now on?"

"We won't, when we're in his presence. But I don't have a problem with us or you doing it when we're secure online."

"Won't that be confusing for him?"

"Not enough to cause a problem. He'll be concentrating hard, earning the big bikkies and saving his life, as well as yours. And he's a well-educated man . . . another coup for us. I think he can handle it."

"That's right," I said to the man who looked like me. "What did you teach?"

"Mostly history," he answered in my slight accent, which must have been the neuropaths at work. "Some literature."

"Not British, was it?" I said, my mind on the accent and Terrey's comments about uncanny coincidences.

"Some."

"What's a favorite?" I asked, trying to make a connection with him, but feeling like maybe I shouldn't, for some reason that was still at the back of my mind.

"Oh, I don't know. Tennyson's 'In Memoriam'?"

"Yeah, good stuff."

Then we both froze and stared at one another, like twins who realized something at the same time. For me, it related to the thought that had been at the back of my mind, and was now passing to the front. "In Memoriam" was about a dead friend, and this double was a dead man walking. Multiple assassination methods were about to rain down on him in a storm that had taken the life of everyone who had faced it so far. And he would be dying in my place, so I had to try to push aside the natural guilt I felt for this by reminding myself that he had been planning to kill himself already, and that he might possibly survive and become a rich man. Rich, and maybe even healthy.

Terrey cleared his throat. "As much as I would enjoy a poetry recital right now, we have other business to attend to." He placed his hand on the double's shoulder, which turned out be a symbol of how I was about to go from being inside Terrey to being inside the other man. "While we make our way up to the house to meet the rest of the team, you two can get used to riding together."

A link appeared at the bottom right of the wall screen, beckoning me to open it. I did, and now found myself looking through the eyes of the double as he followed Terrey and the triplets out of the sickbay. I knew that these "eyes" were more literal than Terrey's, because Jon wasn't wearing cyber contacts. The neuroware in his brain actually allowed me to use his optic nerve in the same way he himself did. I saw exactly what he saw, though without the peripheral vision, because I was looking at a 2D screen right now instead of using the 3D hologram of the entire net room. (I wasn't ready to become that intimate with him yet.)

The first thing I noticed about my double's view was that he was blinking noticeably more than Terrey, probably because he was nervous. The second thing I noticed was that his gaze was often directed at the bodies of the two triplets who were walking in front of him—especially one particular part of their bodies. I found myself unconsciously participating in this examination, my eyes drawn to the strategically placed holes in their black bodysuits, where the multicolored, moving nanotech tattoos covered the jackpatches that were used for access to their cyber systems. There was one on the side of each of their shoulders, one just above the back of each knee, and a big one down low on their backs, just above the body part that Jon was looking at the most. I wouldn't say their figures were highly attractive, not in a classic sense at least, because their shapes were slightly different from most women. But like the whole impression given by the triplets, it was interesting and attractive in its own peculiar way.

The other part of their bodies that the double obviously found interesting, and I did too, was on their backs above the big jackpatch. Something protruded there, like a thin backpack, which probably contained some of the extra hardware that made them so superhuman in their abilities.

"Can you hear me, Jon?" I said, interrupting his ogling. "I think it's just you and me on this line."

"Yes," he said, too loudly.

"You can talk as softly as you want. I can hear everything through the implant, except your thoughts."

We could have upgraded his 'ware to accommodate thought commands and communication, but it would have taken too long to install, and had a steep learning curve beyond that. So he would have to communicate with me verbally, unless it was impossible for him to do so, like in a situation where he had to impersonate me in a conversation with someone else. In some of those cases, he might be able to communicate with me using texting, a finger mouse, or electronic paper, but those methods would often be too suspicious. So I knew there might be times when he was on his own, with only my voice in his ears to guide him. That's why we would keep him in the hill as much as we could, and another reason we were very grateful for his higher education and extra motivation.

"Can you hear me?" Terrey said into his earpiece, and both Jon and I answered "yes," so he was obviously broadcasting into Jon's cyberware and into my wall monitor. We were now all riding in the elevator that led to the garage that was attached to my house on the surface. Lynn and I had joked about how at the end of the workday I walked into the house from the garage like other men, except that many times I had been working underneath the house instead of somewhere else, and arrived in an elevator instead of a car. On those days "Honey, I'm home!" meant I was just a few hundred feet higher than I was before.

"Do you have a term of endearment for Lynn?" Terrey asked me.

"Pies," I answered, knowing where he was going with this, then felt like I needed to explain. "Like in sweetie pies."

"Yeah, I get it," Terrey said, and through Jon's eyes I could see the mocking look on his face. "Jon, I'll do most of the talking. Just say 'Hi, Pies' at first and try not to say too much else, because the voice emulation is probably the weakest part to someone who talks with Michael all the time."

Terrey, the two triplets, and the double stepped out of the elevator and over to the door leading into the house, and then through the hallway and into the foyer, where Lynn and the rest of the protection team were gathered, sipping coffee and nibbling on snacks that she had made for them. She was always eager to play the hostess, even in an extreme circumstance like this.

"Lynn, I didn't tell you Michael was coming," Terrey said to her as we entered the room, "because I wanted it to be a surprise."

"What . . . ?" she said and stopped as she looked at the double, but I couldn't tell whether it was just surprise, or whether she was already realizing it was not me. But when Jon said, "Hi Pies," all doubt was removed. She gasped and almost dropped the coffee cup she was holding, fumbling with it as the black liquid slopped over the sides.

"Oh God, Terrey," she finally said. "Who the hell *is* that? What kind of . . . monster did you bring into my house?!"

"Told you," I said to Terrey.

"Can you do better?" he asked the triplets.

"Don't panic yet," one of them answered him. "She's not exactly a typical test case. Try the Russian."

"Don't ignore me," Lynn broke in firmly. "What are you doing?"

"Bear with me for a moment, marm, please." Terrey said this as charmingly as he could, and then looked at a bald, pockmarked man who was the biggest figure in the room, except for Min. Terrey approached him and beckoned the double to do the same.

It took me a few moments to realize that I recognized the big Russian, and had actually met him before, so the Makeover job by the triplets was about to get a second test that would be much more fair than the first one that was just blown up by my dear wife. She had always been clairvoyant when it comes to anything about me, and in fact another nickname I had for her was "Claire," because of that. I should have told the double to use that one.

20
HOME INVASION

"Valeri," Terrey said as he reached the Russian man, "you met Michael one time before, right?"

"Da," the big man responded, too puzzled by Lynn's hysterics to remember to speak English. The double stepped closer to him, and I told Jon what to say.

"We only seem to meet in unfortunate circumstances," Jon said, and put out his hand.

"Da . . . ," Korcz said again, hesitatingly shaking his hand.

"I'm glad you could come back to BASS," the double said, repeating my words to him again.

"Valeri," Terrey said after a moment, "do you know why Mrs. Ares responded that way to her husband?"

"Nyet," Korcz said, still confused. "I do not understand. I think she said you changed him, but he look the same to me."

Terrey looked pleased and nodded to the triplets.

"We didn't tell you all about this," he said to everyone, "because we wanted to see how well we had done, and Mrs. Ares and Mr. Korcz were the only safe way to test it, because they know Michael. But I'd like you all to meet Jon Cates, who from now on will be Michael Ares until the danger is over." He could have added *or until he is killed,* but I was glad he didn't. This wasn't the right time for that unvarnished truth.

"Who is he?" Lynn said, still disgusted, but trying to hide it for the double's sake. Her sensitivity to others' feelings extended as far as her hospitality instincts.

"He's a man who was wanting to have a new life, and willing to take a significant risk to get it. More than that, no one has the need to know, nor do we have the time to discuss it right now."

"I'll say what I need to know," Lynn barked. "Min, were you a part of this?"

"Yes, ma'am," the big cyborg answered. "Considering the time constraints Mr. Thorn just mentioned, I think we did as well as we could in choosing him."

"Well, if Min says that, it makes me feel better," she said to Terrey. "You can talk about what you need to now, but we'll discuss this more later."

"Yes, marm," my friend said. "Thank you." Then he addressed everyone again. "The real Michael is in hiding at a place known only to himself." Then when he saw Lynn frowning again, he added to her, "Something we can also discuss later. But Michael can communicate with us through a net link that is more secure than Fort Knox, and he can ride with the double, as he is now."

"Hi, everyone," I said in my net room at the cottage in the vineyards.

"Hi, everyone," the double said in my house on Stags Leap.

"We'll keep the double here most of the time," Terrey continued, ignoring further looks from Lynn. "But occasionally we will have to take him out in public, to avoid suspicion and perfect the ruse. When he's here and when we go out, you all will guard him with everything that's in you, because the longer we keep him alive, the more assassination methods we can smoke out, and the better chance we have of our Chinese friend giving up. We also may be able to find something we can use as leverage in the public arena, and make it too much of a risk for him to try again.

"So let's finish our introductions," he continued, "and then we'll get to work." He moved over to a short man, who looked even shorter next to Korcz. "This is Lawrence Stephenson, Korcz's partner from Gotham Security. Lawrence, this is Michael Ares and Michael Ares." We shook hands with the little man, and I noticed that he had a boyish face with a thick head of slightly gray and slightly wavy hair. "And this is Tyra Ponchinello. She has graciously agreed to be our 'cupbearer,' as I call it."

"It's a blood debt," the dark-haired, dark-skinned woman said as Jon shook her hand and looked her over. He didn't spend as much time checking her out as he did the triplets, because she was overweight and not nearly as attractive. "Thank you for the chair," she added. She was sitting in a floating wheelchair, or really an "airchair," which was powered by the Sabon antigravity system.

"And you both know everyone else," Terrey finished, and Jon's eyes surveyed the room, taking in the triplets, Min, and Lynn, whom he looked up and down several times. I didn't blame him for it, because she *was* the best-looking woman in the room, even with her pregnant swell.

"The first thing we did," Terrey said, "was scan the entire property with equipment too expensive for most countries to afford, doing our best to make sure there are no explosives, poison, or any other kind of booby traps that could have already been planted on the grounds. And then we installed scanners all around the house to make sure nothing gets past them from now on. In one of the kaleidocide killings, a bomb was found and deactivated barely in time, and in another a postal envelope emitted a gas that killed two of the target's family members. In the third, the target died of poison introduced into his food by a lover who had been turned against him."

There was the idea of betrayal again. As Jon glanced at the different people in the room, I noticed how well Terrey had done at staffing this security team with those who had no prior relationship to me. I hoped he could prevent them from being contacted or turned by the enemy in the coming days.

"Poison is a favorite method of assassins," Terrey continued, "especially those who betray someone close to them, because it gives the killer an opportunity to escape before the method is discovered, yet assures that it will be fatal." He moved closer to the Black Italian woman again. "This is why we must begin right away with our cupbearer here. That term comes from the practice of ancient kings who would have someone else taste their food before they ate it. I know it sounds bizarre, and will be inconvenient and hard to get used to, but from this moment on, no one who's in this house can eat or drink anything, take any pills, or even wash with water until Tyra has tested it first."

"What are the chances that something would get past all the scanners you've installed?" Lynn asked, clearly uncomfortable with this invasion of her beloved home.

"Does it matter how unlikely it may be?" Terrey said right away, as if he had faced objections to this before. "Do you want to take any chance at all with your life, or the life of your baby?"

Lynn didn't answer the question, which was clearly rhetorical.

"One of the *Trois* will give Tyra a crash course on cupbearing," Terrey continued, looking at the triplets until one gestured to herself. "So rather than taking the time to educate everyone here, you'll just have to listen to Tyra's instructions and trust her. Do what she says or you could be endangered—"

"How can I trust her with something like my food," Lynn said, "when I don't even know her?" Food was as close to Lynn's heart as her house was. I was really starting to feel bad for her.

"That's the point, Lynn," I said from the cottage, and Jon repeated it to her, already getting the hang of the double routine. "We can trust her more *because* we don't know her." As Jon said this, Lynn looked visibly disoriented.

"Is that you talking to me, Michael?" she asked, and I and the double both said yes.

"Please don't," she said. "I can talk to you later on the phone. I don't want to do it through that . . . thing."

I said okay, and Jon wisely changed it to "He said okay."

"Sorry for calling you a thing," she said to him, her tone softer now. She took a step toward him and raised her hand slightly, like she might touch his shoulder, but then looked at him again, hesitated, and stayed where she was. "Everyone please bear with me. This is a lot for me, on top of being pregnant and all."

"So do you understand what I explained about the danger of a traitor?" Terrey asked her with a gentle voice. He gestured around the room at the new team members. "And how these are the only people who couldn't have been approached by the Chinese, because they didn't know Michael before?"

"I understand," she said, and rubbed her belly a bit as if to remind them all to be patient with her.

"Good," he said, back to business, and looked around at everyone. "So follow Tyra's instructions and be prepared to 'rough it' a bit. It could be much worse—I would prefer if we only ate food out of tubes, like the astronauts do, but Mrs. Ares would have none of that. So we'll have to order only certain kinds of foods, with certain kinds of packaging. For example, if you wanna slip some shrimp on the barbie . . ."

As he was going on, my attention was caught by one of the screens I had unrolled on the wall, which had been unused until now. It started to flash with a jumble of data that seemed like a lot of computer code with some Asian letters and a little English, and then it coalesced into some English words:

YON: I CAN SWITCH YOUR VOICE TO THE HOUSE SPEAKERS IF YOU WANT TO TALK TO ALL OF THEM.

I assumed this was coming from one of the triplets, because other than Min they were the only ones with the capability of thought communication, and it wouldn't have been in character for the big bodyguard to concern himself with anything but security. I didn't recognize "Yon" as one of their names, so I thought it was either a nickname or not a name at all, but just happened to appear where a name would usually be.

"How can I answer you?" I said aloud, to see if she could hear me.

"What?" said Jon, in the meeting. Terrey stopped his exposition, and looked at him until Jon said "Sorry," and then Terrey continued talking.

"Sorry, Jon," I said. "I was talking to someone else."

YON: USE THE KEYBOARD appeared on the screen, so I pulled my chair closer to the paper-thin device I had unrolled on the desk, and typed in "That would be nice, but I might want to talk to the double only sometimes."

YON: I WILL SET UP SO YOU CAN TOGGLE EASILY.

I typed "ok," and sure enough, the screen soon contained two icons, one for Jon and one for the room, and a note to use the arrow and select keys to choose which one. The room icon was currently selected, and without thinking I said "Thank you," which was broadcast to everyone and caused Terrey to stop his speech again and look up in the air as if to say, "Where did that voice come from?"

"Sorry, Terrey," I said. "I'm on the house channel now, so Lynn doesn't have to talk to . . . that thing." A few of them chuckled, and Terrey finished his spiel.

YON: YOU ARE WELCOME appeared at the top of the screen, above the icons, and then disappeared.

"What about our bananas?" Lynn asked, when Terrey was done. "They're not packaged and sealed in groups. So does that mean she has to take a bite of each one before we eat it?"

The bioengineered, organic bananas (or "biganánas," as we called them) were a staple in our home, since recent medical discoveries about potassium and B6 had proven them to be one of the healthiest foods, and they had also turned out to be very compatible with the new methods of adding nutrients and medications to food, rather than taking them as pills.

"Yes, but she can cut off an end and then test it," said the triplet who would be training Tyra, showing a domestic sensitivity that I had not expected from a cyborg, even a female one.

"We have to have our bananas," Lynn said, with a nervous laugh, and then looked up at the ceiling. "Right, Michael?"

"Right, sweetheart."

"Funny you should mention that," Terrey said. "Because one of the kaleidocide attempts I researched included poisoned bananas. I'm not kidding. They found them after the target had already been killed by another method. Apparently the thick peel prevented the poison from being detected by the scanners."

I could see Lynn gulp after hearing this, the danger seeming much more real and closer to her now.

"Okay," she said, "we'll hold off on the bananas until this is over."

"So San will take Tyra to the kitchen and get started on her little tutorial," Terrey continued, shooing the ladies off. "And now we have to talk about a sniper. Along with explosives, which we've pretty much ruled out—around here anyway—a sniper is most likely to strike at the beginning. Like a bomb, he or she could have been fixed in a spot before we were aware of the threat and put the extra security measures in place, and now be waiting for a good opportunity. But they can't wait too long, because the body can only stay stationary and awake for so long without impairing ability. So if there *is* a sniper in place, we're looking at a strike within the next couple days.

"The longest distance currently possible for a rifle, even if we figure in the possibility of a secret Chinese upgrade, is less than three thousand meters with a straight line of sight. Fortunately, with mostly open space on the hills around here, and mostly vineyards within that range, it won't be too hard to scan and clear. It would be even easier if all we had to check were the line-of-sight locations, but unfortunately with the possibility of them using guided bullets, we'll have to check everything within two thousand meters, because that's the range of self-guided bullets, and they can be fired from anywhere, and curve around obstacles."

"But they have to be tagged with a laser," Stephenson spoke up. "By a spotter who transmits to the shooter."

"Right," Terrey said. "And the laser sight has a direct-line range of up to five thousand meters, so if we have time we'll look at line-of-sight locations that far out, in case we might find a spotter first and eliminate the threat that way. But our first priority is everything up to two thousand, and line-of-sight up to three thousand. We're already using the Eye to scan everything out that far, both visually and using its weapons location capabilities. But as you probably know, there are limitations to satellite systems, and people like we're dealing with are aware of them. So my lovely ladies are also using the Eye and other tools to calculate every possible sniper location within range, and we're going to send out our mates here to investigate them personally." He gestured to the remaining two triplets first, and then to Korcz and Stephenson. Then the short man became visibly excited when Terrey added, "The locations will be downloaded into the nav program in your aeros, which will take you right to them."

"You're gonna let us . . . ," Stephenson said, then was thinking about whether to say more, and I knew what he was thinking about.

"Yes, we'll let you fly our aeros," I said through the house. "But I have to tell you what your partner already knows, because he used to work here, that our surveillance system sees everything you do. If you try to go anywhere you shouldn't with the aeros, or even mess with them thinking you might sell some information about their engineering, you will be fried right where you sit, and the whole car will self-destruct before it gets into anyone's else's hands."

Those security measures had been instituted by Saul Rabin, of course, to remain until such a time that BASS decided to share the secrets of the Sabon antigravity technology with others. The only way they could be turned off was by me, or Min, or our designated successors if we should be killed.

"In the meantime," Terrey said, "until we finish our sweep, or actually find and neutralize a sniper, anywhere within view of a window in this house is a potential danger. That's why we're meeting in this inner room now. So Michael . . ." He was speaking to the double. "You should stay in the base below, and Lynn, you should, too."

"Oh, boy," she responded in a flabbergasted voice. "Can't you secure the windows somehow so I could stay in the house?"

"We could OWCH up all the windows," he said reluctantly, "but that would be a pain, and might tip our hand to a keen observer earlier than we'd like to."

"Do it," I said to Terrey, knowing that he wouldn't be able to budge Lynn on this one.

"I suppose we can," he said, probably realizing the same thing, then addressed Lynn again. "If you insist on staying in the house . . ."

"I insist," she said.

"What colors are we looking for?" Stephenson asked Terrey. "There's a color associated with each method of assassination, right?"

"Yes, but they're assigned by Sun in a ritual he conducts, so they're not always the same ones, or attached to the same methods. In one of them, the bomb was red, which kinda makes sense. But in two of the others, the envelope with the gas and the assault team were each blue, which seemed pretty random to us."

"And the poisoned bananas were yellow," Lynn said.

"What was the color of the traitors?" Korcz asked.

"Now that has been fairly consistent, as far as we can tell," Terrey answered. "All the traitors seem to be associated with black in some way. When the lover poisoned the one man, she was wearing black, and the poison itself was also black."

"You are wearing black," Korcz said to Terrey. This didn't phase me in the least, because I wore a lot of that color myself. It was par for the course for former special forces like us, because we were always ready for something to happen, particularly at night, when we might need to conceal ourselves.

"I guess I am, mate," Terrey laughed, as he looked down at his clothes. Then he looked at the big bald man, and his eyes narrowed. "But do you think that if I was a traitor, I would wear black at the same time I was telling you that traitors wear black?"

"Mebee," Korcz said. "You could be doing . . . ah, what is it? Reverse psychosis?"

Terrey laughed again, but then said to Korcz, "You're wearing black, too, mate." He said this more seriously, in almost a confrontational manner, but then added, "And Tyra has black skin."

Korcz nodded in agreement and dropped the subject. But this was the first small seed of the suspicion that would grow between the two of them.

21
HEGEMON

After the briefing was over, Min took Korcz and Stephenson to the aero bay in the base below the house, to send them out on their sniper search. Terrey asked Lynn which rooms in the house she most wanted to use, and told the two remaining triplets to secure those windows first. Lynn asked about talking to me on the net, and he assured her that the house systems, my netkit, and even our glasses had been routed through the Fortress Cloud and were safe. "But don't call him from anywhere else," he added.

"I'll take Jon with me to the base while I supervise the sniper search," Terrey said. "So if there's one watching, he won't see Michael in the house. But stay away from the windows anyway, until the Shimmies are done securing them."

"Okay," Lynn said, half-nodding. "Michael, I'll talk to you in our room. I have to go to the bathroom . . . again." She had to do that a lot lately—one of the plagues of pregnancy.

I switched off my view of the empty room after Lynn headed up the stairs, and Terrey and my double disappeared in the other direction. After a couple minutes, a bleeping and blinking icon informed me that Lynn was calling me, so I opened the link and could see her waddling around our room, making the bed as she talked to me.

"I should probably sleep some, because I didn't much last night," she said, "but I'm too worked up. I hope all this doesn't affect Lynley."

"She'll be fine," I said. "Let me see her." Lynn turned toward the side of the room where I was displayed on a 2D holoscreen, and where my voice was being broadcast from as well. She had the net-room equipment configured this way, because she didn't like the total immersion of a full 3D holo surrounding her.

She lifted her shirt a little and pulled down the elastic wasteband of her pants so I could see all of her belly. Then she took her phone out of a pocket and opened the BabyView app, moving it around near her belly button as it showed our little girl from different angles on the small hologram it projected.

"Awww," I said, "I miss her already."

"How about me?" she said as she turned off the phone app and put her clothes back into place. "Where are you?"

"Of course I miss you," I answered the first question, not wanting to answer the second.

"Good," she said, and asked again: "Where are you?"

"Like Terrey said, I'm not sure you should know."

Fortunately for me, another issue came up as she moved closer to one of the windows in the room, to look out of it. She was standing beside it, more than in front of it, but it still gave me the opportunity to change the subject.

"Terrey said you should stay away from the windows, Lynn."

"Is it really that much of a danger, or is your friend just being overcautious?" She said this as she moved closer to the wall next to the window, ignoring my warning and peering out of it guardedly.

"With a good location and a cyborg eye linked to the rifle sight, they can be accurate within an inch from almost two miles away."

"Sounds like some of the movies you watch," she said, referring to the ones she didn't. "Besides, they want to kill you, not me."

She leaned closer to the glass at the edge of the window, studying the lower hills near the house, and the valley with the vineyards beyond that, for any sign of this phantom killer, and . . . BAM! A sudden impact shook the window and made her jump back and grab the baby with both hands. Then another slam startled her again, and a dark shape appeared outside the window. But then it became clear that it was one of the triplets, who had climbed up the wall to the second-story window like a spider, and was anchoring herself next to the window so she could install the OWCH security measures on it.

"Oh, God help me," Lynn said with a gasp, using a phrase she had learned growing up at Mrs. Rabin's orphanage, but didn't really mean.

"That'll teach you," I said, smiling a little despite my concern for her nerves and the baby, both of which she now addressed.

"She can't take much more of that kind of stress."

"They can take a lot," I said, "and she'll have to. This isn't going to be over anytime soon, unless of course they get me. We have to hang in together and make it through—"

Then I heard another loud crash, this time not from my house on the video where Lynn was, but from another room in the vineyard cottage where I was.

"Hold on a second, Lynn, I'll be back."

I stepped quickly toward the door of my room and moved one of the boas around to the front of my belt as I passed through it.

In the living room, Angelee was picking a tall decorative lamp off the floor while her little boy stood nearby, looking guilty. Some of his toys were spread around on the floor, but he obviously had gotten bored with them and decided to push or climb on the lamp.

"I'm so sorry," she said, straightening up and brushing the black hair from her face. She gestured toward the kitchen. "I made you some coffee." She moved toward the kitchen, keeping half an eye on her son. "I couldn't find any food to make you breakfast, but there was some of this in the cabinet." She held up an opened bag of Tara's fancy Blue Mountain beans.

"Thanks," I said, and sent a silly little wave toward the boy, to put him at ease. "You'll have to get some groceries for us today." I reached in my pocket as I moved toward her, and she met me halfway with the coffee, bowing slightly and placing it on the island counter near me. For some reason, a recent episode popped into my mind when Lynn had been cranky and told me, "Make your own coffee."

"Here's some cash," I said, handing it to Angelee. "Get whatever you want, enough to last for a week or so. Whatever you and Chris like to eat and drink . . . I'm not picky." I *was* rather picky, actually, but I didn't want to make this hard for her.

As she took the money and our hands touched briefly, the look in her eyes grew more longing, and before I knew it she lunged toward me and was hugging me with a ferocity that was surprising for a woman her size.

"What are your favorite meals?" she asked, her accent muffled because the side of her face was pressed against my chest. "I'll cook for you like I did for Peter."

"No, really. Anything is okay with me." I didn't know what to do with my hands while she was attached to me like this, so I patted her back gently. But when I did, she seemed to take encouragement from it, and pressed in harder with her whole body, and maybe even certain parts of it. I was hoping it was my imagination, but then remembered what she had said the night before about her version of "getting married." Now, as then, I didn't want to disappoint her too much, but I also didn't want this to go too far and further complicate my already complicated life. I wasn't sure what to do, but was fortunately "saved by the bell" when the glasses in a case on my belt started buzzing with an incoming call.

"Oh, no," I said, breaking away and fumbling for the glasses. "Lynn."

"It's Angelee," she said, straightening her shirt and her hair again, only slightly embarrassed. "My name's Angelee."

"Right. Angelee." I let it alone. "I have to take a call in my room. Why don't you take the car and find a store." I backed toward my room. "Take Chris with you. There's a child seat in the back of the car, it'll come out when you activate it on the dash." I looked up at the ceiling and spoke to the house. "Vera, the next person who asks you to unlock the front door will be Angelee. Please key her voice and allow her full security access."

"Certainly, Michael," the house answered. I nodded to the girl, as if to ask if she understood what to do, and she nodded back.

"Thank you," she said. "Thank you!"

I disappeared back into my room, and called Lynn on the netkit. She came back on, sitting in her chair in our room at the house.

"What happened?" she asked.

"Nothing," I said. "I heard something, and had to make sure it was nothing. It was. Are they finished with the windows?"

"Yeah, I think so."

"Terrey probably knows this, but they're already bulletproof. I guess another layer of protection can't hurt, though, with the ballistic power we might be up against."

"How long do you really think this will take?" she asked. "I don't want us to be apart for a long time."

"Me neither," I said. "Hopefully we'll find the assassins before they strike, or they'll expose themselves by striking soon—"

"Terrey said something about getting the Chinese guy, what's-his-name, to back off?"

"Sun, his name's Zhang Sun," I said. "If we were able to link the murder attempts to him and prove it publicly, or discover some leverage on him . . ."

"So the more you know about why this is happening, the better." Her wheels were spinning. "You should talk to Saul about it." For some reason, she didn't share my aversion to using the old man's name when referring to his posthumous construct.

"Why?"

"I just have a feeling that this is all related to him somehow."

When she said that, our conversation in the Sausalito house about why the Mayor had brought me here came to mind, and so did something that I couldn't fully remember from my last talk with the ghost.

"You may be on to something, Marlowe," I said.

"Who?" She loved books like I did—one of the few things we had in common. But she only read nonfiction—one of the many things we didn't.

"I think I'll take your suggestion," I said, "so I'll talk to you later. In the meantime, please follow Terrey's instructions. I know you don't like doing what anyone says, but remember Lynley needs a daddy, and we need her mommy to stay safe, too."

"Okay," she agreed. "Love you."

"Love you, too."

I closed the link to Lynn on the screen and put on my glasses, going through the three-step security routine to access Saul's ghost. When his face appeared in my view and he said, "Hello Michael," I forwarded only the audio to the room, so I could be free from the glasses and more aware of my surroundings.

"I have some more questions for you," I said, dispensing with the pleasantries to remind myself this was not a real person.

"Wonderful," the disembodied voice said, echoing throughout the room and seeming more like a ghost than ever. "How can I help you, Michael?"

"Last time I told you that I'm currently the target of a kaleidocide initiated by General Sun of China."

"I remember," the ghost said quickly, seeming like it was proud of its capabilities, or maybe eager to approximate a real person. "Let me tell you some things you need to know about General Zhang Sun."

"I'm wondering if you can tell me why this is happening to me."

"I don't know, Michael," it said, after what seemed like a brief pause.

"Is there some reason you know of that Sun wants me dead?"

"I don't know, Michael." The same apparent pause again. "But let me tell you some things you need to know—"

"Why would General Sun want to kill me?" I persisted, trying a different wording.

"Perhaps he found out about your role in the Taiwan Crisis," the old man's voice said.

"But even if he did, that doesn't seem to be enough motivation for a move like this. Everyone I've talked to thinks it's something more."

"I don't know, Michael. But let me tell you some things you need to know about General Zhang Sun."

This time I let it continue, hoping I could get some more help from this path in its programming.

"General Zhang Sun is utterly committed to the concept of Chinese hegemony, or the *Ba*, as it is known in China. He is the modern incarnation of the *Bawang*, or hegemon-king, who is seeking to establish its *Baquan*, or hegemon-power. For thousands of years China exercised primary authority over its 'known world' of Asia—that's why it was always called the Middle Kingdom, which really means Central Kingdom. Each of China's historic dynasties—the Han, the Sui-Tang, the Song, the Yuan, the Ming, and the Qing—had no contemporary peer. But since their 'known world' grew much larger in the age of global travel and communication, and because of the rise of superior powers like the European empires of the 1800s and the U.S./Russian dominance in the 1900s, the leaders of China have endured two centuries of shame in which they have been unseated from their rightful place of world domination.

"Even during that time, however, China consistently sought to expand its borders and possessions as much as those other powers would allow them. In the mid-twentieth century, the Cultural Revolution was also a *Ba* revival—communist leader Mao Zedong fancied himself as the first emperor of a new imperial dynasty, and even wrote a famous poem called 'White Snow' in which he recounted the names of past emperors and then referred to himself as the 'True Hero.' So the communist government annexed Mongolia and Tibet, went to war with India over border territories, and reclaimed Hong Kong. After Tiananmen Square and the rise of the worldwide web, Westerners wrongly assumed that China would eventually become more democratic and would not use its growing power in an imperialistic or colonialist fashion. It may have become more like the West *economically* in recent decades with the introduction of more capitalistic principles, but that has happened in service of their hegemonic goals, not in opposition to them. The desire of nationalistic leaders like Zhang Sun to dominate the world has continued unabated, and in fact has increased since their failed attempt to reintegrate Taiwan. Sun's rise is the pinnacle of modern imperialism in China . . . the militaristic faction put him in power because they knew he would devote himself to expanding the *Baquan* as far as it could go."

"How do you know so much about this?" I asked the ghost.

"I was always a student of history, Michael, especially modern history, and I knew that Chinese issues were the most important in our lifetime. I also have numerous books on the subject downloaded into my memory banks. I would like to read to you, in fact, my favorite one, a book called *Hegemon* by Steven Mosher. It was published in 2000 and almost everything he said about China has come true, like he was some kind of prophet."

"That's okay, you can just tell me about it." Before he could continue doing that, I added: "You mentioned the militaristic faction. Are there any opposing ones in China today?"

"Yes, Michael. The People's Party has emerged in recent years, having consolidated most of the smaller democratic parties under its umbrella now. But its growth has mostly been accommodated by the spread of Christianity throughout China. Some have estimated that the number of Christians in China is approaching twenty percent of the population, and these are committed people who have kept their faith through the fires of persecution. They are beginning to make their voices heard in the social and political arenas. In fact, one of the strongest young leaders in the People's Party, Gao Dao, actually claims to be a Christian."

"Min said he was involved with that group," I said. "Does that have something to do with why he is here?"

"Yes, Michael." And then an irritating silence.

"Why did Min come to BASS?" I said.

"Min was a colonel in the Chinese PLA—that's People's Liberation Army, in case you don't know. He was given an order by Zhang Sun, at a time before the general ascended to national power, to wipe out an Orthodox community in the countryside outside Shenyang, where they were forced to live after they were driven out of the city. Min refused, and half of his battalion stayed with him to protest the injustice. Sun sent two full battalions with a kill order, and Min barely survived the attack. Fortunately, the People's Party leaders found out, including Gao Dao, who happens to be a cousin of Min's. They used their contacts in Shenyang to save Min's life by cyberizing him, and then smuggled him out of the country to San Francisco, because I had heard about this and been in touch with them."

"So you—I mean Saul—brought him here to BASS."

"Yes, Michael. I brought him here, hired him, befriended him, and had the cyber techs in Chinatown Underground significantly improve his augmentations. Which they were more than glad to do, because most of them are political exiles themselves."

"So could that be the reason why Sun is so pissed at us?"

"Could be," the ghost replied quickly, but even as I said it, I realized it didn't add up. People were escaping China left and right, especially under the new regime, and they found asylum in many places. What's more, Sun didn't seem to be angry at Saul or Min, and had never tried to kill them or anyone else at BASS—only me.

"Did Darien Anthony have some connection to China as well?" I asked. D was the other executive peacer, high up in BASS leadership, who had been killed by Paul Rabin last year.

"No, I brought him in because of his ties to Stanford Glenn, from when they played in the WFL together." So Saul had hired D to improve BASS's relationship with the American government. Did he hire Min because he had a *bad* relationship with China? I was beginning to feel like I was on to something.

"Why did you hire me?" I asked, letting my pronouns slip.

"You're smart, skilled, responsible, a hard worker . . . and you look good on camera."

"Did my hiring have something to do with China?"

A brief pause, then: "I don't know, Michael."

"What . . . ," I started. "Did you bring me to BASS because of Zhang Sun?"

"I don't know, Michael. But let me tell you some more about Zhang Sun—"

"Dammit, old man," I shouted in frustration, "answer the bloody question!"

"Professionalism, intelligence, and distinctiveness," the construct began, launching into Saul's standard litany of why he didn't allow profanity at BASS.

"Oh, Christ," I sighed, and then the ghost told me that was "blasphemy, which is actually much worse than other swear words." That diffused my anger a bit, and brought on a hint of shame, because I remembered a conversation with Angelee's dead husband where I understood how that could be offensive to him and others who shared his faith. I looked around instinctively to see if she was within earshot, because she might share that faith herself, but then remembered that she was at the store.

"Will you be able to tell me more when the kaleidocide is over?" This was my last attempt for now to get more information out of the ghost.

"You won't be happy when it's over," it said.

"Why?"

"I don't know, Michael."

I hung up, muttering that I would have to find out for myself, and pulled a goggles rig out of a bag I had brought with me, so I could relive my assault on the nuclear power plant in Taiwan during the Crisis. Hopefully my "detective skills," as Terrey had called them, would help me learn some more about the questions that Saul's ghost was refusing to answer.

22
INSERTION

The Taiwan Crisis was the only connection I knew of between myself and Chinese interests, though I didn't know yet how Zhang Sun himself was connected to it. He had been a highly ranked general during the Crisis, but was not in Taiwan himself, as far as I knew—the Chinese operation there was led by a lower general named Ho (a romanized version of He'). So I wasn't sure what I might learn from reliving my part in the Crisis, or whether I would learn anything at all, but it was the only lead I had to pursue right now in an attempt to discover the reasons for Sun's animosity toward me, or any other information that might be helpful in abating it. Plus it had been years since I last watched the holo, which I had been allowed to keep as a reward for my heroics, contrary to normal procedure. And I won't deny that it was a major rush to experience the assault again in this way, much like an athlete who watches his greatest game on video, but many times more intense.

When I slipped on the goggles containing the file and opened it, I was transported back into the insertion coffin as it left the submarine in the East China Sea off the northeast coast of Taiwan. The file was video and sound only, of course, but I immediately started feeling echoes of the other sensations that I had experienced back then. It seemed like I was lying on my back again in the cramped interior of the coffin, feet forward and adrenaline coursing through my body as I imagined the immense volume and pressure of the water all around me, with only about three inches of the world's best plasteel protecting me from it. I felt disembodied again, too, because most of what I could see in the combat goggles that I was wearing inside the coffin was the view from the front end—headlights shining into the darkness of the ocean ahead of me, with only occasional dots of sea life flashing by.

I also had status displays in part of my view, of course, and control icons that I could select and manipulate using the mouse equipment that each of my hands rested on inside the coffin. I knew this part of the operation would be uneventful and take about ten minutes, but rather than fast forwarding it to the exciting part, I let it run and mentally reviewed the reasons for the assault I was about to relive.

The People's Republic of China (PRC) had been seeking to extend its hegemony over the island nation of Taiwan for over a hundred years. The island nation had been a part of China since ancient times, but became independent from the mainland in the mid-twentieth century, when Chiang Kai-shek and his government fled from the Communist revolution and found haven there with the support of western nations, especially the United States. Then in subsequent years Taiwan became more democratic, capitalistic, and economically successful, which was a constant insult to the PRC. So numerous times during the years to come, China tested the waters with saber-rattling and military maneuvers, to see if the U.S. would really stand by this "rebel nation" and protect it.

In 1954 Mao Zedong launched an invasion of some islands in the South China Sea and bombarded Taiwan with artillery. The U.S. Seventh Fleet moved in and he backed down, agreeing to peace talks. In 1958 he repeated the artillery bombardment, added air and naval assaults, and threatened a landing. The United States sent troops and a plethora of modern weapons to Taiwan, and signed a mutual defense treaty with the beleaguered country. Mao gave in again, and that uneasy peace more or less held until 1995, when President Jiang Zemin threatened force against Taiwan and even fired several M-9 nuclear capable missiles in the direction of the island. In 1996, the Red Army began rehearsing an invasion, forcing the Americans to send an official warning to Beijing and two carrier battle groups to back it up.

Since the United States had proven its resolve to defend Taiwan against Chinese aggression in the twentieth century, the first part of the twenty-first century was relatively quiet on that front, as China bided its time before acting again, waiting until it had grown stronger and America weaker. When that time came, the Middle Kingdom did act, but in an unexpected way, reflecting and honoring the stratagems of surprise advocated by the ancient general Sun-Tzu, from whom the present General Sun took his name.

Even though China had grown stronger and America weaker, the outcome of a frontal attack on the island was still risky because of the formidable Taiwanese military and the likelihood of escalation by the western powers. So the Red leaders decided to take a page from the playbooks of terrorists and guerrilla warfare groups, and sent General Ho and a company of "Flying Dragon" special forces from Nanjing to take over the Lungmen Nuclear Power Plant on the northeast tip of the island. The soldiers were transported by night in stealth aircraft to the airspace above the plant, and used the latest "Skyfall" backpack equipment to reach the plant with a combination of powered skydiving and powered paragliding. They easily neutralized the security measures, which were notoriously lax in Taiwan, and rigged the plant for sabotage before the Taiwanese government could intervene. One push of a button in the hand of General Ho could now release enough radiation into the air to kill all seven million people in the capital city of Taipei, which was forty kilometers downwind from Lungmen. Taiwan's military surrounded the plant, the army on the three land sides and the navy off the coast, but they didn't dare to do anything as long as General Ho had his finger on that button.

Ho demanded reunification with the mainland, of course, and the Chinese thinking behind this unorthodox move was that if it was successful, the loss of life from a war could be avoided by giving everyone an opportunity to agree to an outcome that was inevitable anyway, but now had the noble purpose of saving millions of lives. There was also some ambiguity, at the public level at least, as to whether General Ho was an extremist acting on his own, and combined with the threat of nuclear catastrophe, that made the situation much more complex than a direct invasion, and caused the western powers to hesitate in sending their forces to the area. Also, if the ransom attempt was unsuccessful, the Chinese could simply deny that they sanctioned Ho's operation—no one would be hurt, and things could presumably return to their former stalemate.

The unusual nature of this Crisis could also work against China, however, and that's where I came in. A counterespionage operation was a viable option, because the Reds were obviously not eager to launch into a world war. But the Taiwanese themselves didn't have the tech to pull it off, and their current government wouldn't be able to stay in power if Taipei ended up becoming irradiated because of an attack. The American government had the ability, but also preferred not to be the one to blame for whatever might happen. So they did what they had been doing ever since they funded and promoted "the revival of the British Empire" under King Noel I—they asked us to do the dirty work for them, and gave us the means to do it.

This was one of the most interesting global political developments in the twenty-first century—how the American populace had grown more and more isolationist as a result of numerous recessions and secessions, but also how some shrewd politicians cooked up a scheme to arm and empower other like-minded nations to create a buffer of security for their suffering society. This was all done in the name of "global sharing" and "reverse colonialism," and so was more palatable to the tastes of the voters. I didn't understand much of that, but what I did know was that I was gliding through the depths of the ocean in one of the most amazing machines I had ever seen, armed with American wartech that was worth a fortune, and could never have been developed by my own country.

Resting between my legs, in the storage spot carved out for it, was a gun with three barrels called the Alliant Trinity. (That was the only place in the thin coffin where there was room for the weapon, but that didn't stop everyone on the sub from cracking jokes about it.) The Trinity could fire a monofilament grappling wire and two kinds of projectiles—for this operation it was loaded with caseless explosive and killer rounds, both of which were "smart" in the sense that they could change direction in midair and be guided to their targets. This was achieved by a link to the other ridiculously expensive piece of wartech, which was the eye rig I was wearing that stretched around to the back of my head, allowing me not only to see in the dark and identify targets for the Trinity, as many combat goggles could do, but also to have a 360-degree view of my surroundings. This was accomplished by cameras on the outside of the rig that projected into the view inside, with a technology similar to the net glasses many people used, but much more complex. So in the center of my view was what I normally saw in front of my head, but on the peripheries were the input from the cameras showing what was behind and above me. If I kept my head still, but moved my eyes to those peripheral images, I literally had eyes in the back of my head (and the top). I remembered how I had loved practicing with the gun and the goggles on the day before the operation, and how excited I was about using them on real targets.

Since I was thinking about the 360-degree capabilities of the eye rig, and guessing that the holo would soon show the part where I reached the island, I decided to transfer it to the whole net room and take the simpler goggles off, so I could see everything I saw that night in Taiwan. When I did, I told Vera to interrupt my viewing only if Terrey or Lynn called, or if the cottage's security was breached. Then I imported images of Zhang Sun and all of his close friends and family members into the projection system, directing it to alert me if any of the faces I encountered in the power plant matched with any of them. I wondered if maybe one of the Chinese that I killed or maimed in the operation was someone close to Sun . . . it was the only possibility I could think of at the time for why he hated me so much.

I turned in my chair to face the coffin's headlights, so I would be oriented in the correct direction to catch all the action. Other than those lights and some navigation displays that were on the edges of the goggle's front view, the room was totally dark. That was because the sea around the headlight beams was dark, and because the inside of the coffin was, too, so the peripheral cameras weren't projecting any images yet. I reached behind me to the only other thing I could see in the room, which were the softly lit controls of the keyboard and mouse, and fast forwarded the holo until I could see the big pipe that was my destination. I shifted in the chair until I was comfortable, and let myself drift into this virtual world that had been very real just eight years ago.

"This is Talon 3," my voice rang out from the holo. "I've reached the insertion point."

The Americans had not only provided us with the most cutting edge war-tech, but they had also lent their strategic and simulation prowess to the planning of this operation. The Taiwanese had shared with them and British intelligence all the information about the Lungmen site, of course, to give us an opportunity to come up with a plan that could neutralize the Chinese threats without Taipei being endangered. But the natives didn't expect that to happen, and were genuinely surprised to find themselves agreeing that the plan could work and giving their approval for it to go ahead. One of the keys was that there was a desalination plant that had been built in the tight space between the nuclear power plant and the ocean, which enabled the Taiwanese to kill two birds with one stone and address their water crisis as well as their energy crisis. Many of these plants, which converted salt water into potable, had been added to nuclear sites all over the world, because they needed tremendous amounts of energy to make their contribution to the global water shortage, which had become almost as much of a threat to the world's population as the global energy shortage.

I was being inserted through the seawater intake of the desalination plant, because we knew that the primary security measures would be on the nuclear facility itself. For example, there were no sensors on the protective grill at the end of the large pipe, so the tool array on the front of the coffin merely projected a laser oval and cut a hole that I would fit through. I then proceeded down the long tunnel at a faster speed than I had come in, because the strategists had not been completely sure (as they never are) that this wouldn't be detected. We expected that the primary surveillance of the Chinese, if they even had any on this part of the site, would be heat sensors tuned to detect human activity. But we knew this wouldn't be a problem, because both the coffin and every inch of my body were "cold." The coffin was lined with a polymer that hid all heat signatures, and the black bodysuit that covered every inch of my skin was made out of a similar substance.

The pipe stretched far out to sea and disappeared into the ground well before it reached the coast, because the builders wanted to protect the marine environment as well as the beach and dunes. But I proceeded at a fast clip, only stopping twice for other safety grates, and before I knew it I was inside the underground portion of the desalination plant, as far as I could go because the water was now funneling into smaller pipes. Before I exited the coffin, I checked the HUD displays in my goggles to make sure there was no indication of Chinese alarms or other security issues detected by our tech people on the sub. There were none, so I opened the coffin and swung my legs out, crouching by its side so I could pull out the Trinity and hang it on the back of my left shoulder. (The insertion suit was ingeniously designed to hold it in place, while still allowing me sufficient freedom of movement.) Then I shimmied to the front of the coffin, detached the tool array from its front, and used it to open a hole in the high side of the pipe, so that no water would escape when I climbed out. I then slung the tool array, which looked something like a small oblong steering wheel, over my other shoulder so it was fastened there. The two pieces of equipment felt like wings on my back, and in a very real sense they would fly me where I needed to go.

I made my way through the desalination plant without incident—as we expected, the Chinese didn't even bother to post guards in it. They should have, though, because the turbine end of it was built very close to the reactor, so that energy from it could be channeled to the desal plant at the times when the grid was low, and untreated water could be channeled back into the reactor for cooling use. Also in our favor, and more evidence that the special forces gods were smiling upon this operation, was the fact that the Lungmen plant had two reactors, but the Chinese only had to rig one of them in order to achieve their goal. And that one happened to be next to the desalination plant.

So before long, I was on the bottom floor of Reactor Building 1, crouched between a big purplish heat exchanger and some gold hydraulic system pumps, manipulating the display in my goggles so I could see where the Chinese soldiers were stationed on the path to the explosives they had set. Unlike me in my suit, they were not "cold" or hidden from a thermal scan, so I could see that there were too many of them along both routes that I could take, one of which was a stairwell and the other a utility elevator. The explosives had been placed three stories up from where I was, in a room with one of the backup diesel generators, which was to the side of the tall reactor core, just below the pool of spent fuel, and right beside the north wall of the building. That was the reason the generator room had been chosen, because the only way radiation could be released into the air was if the water was drained out of the spent fuel pool, and if there was a hole in the side of the building for it to escape from. The room with the diesel generator, which was ironically one of the safety systems, was in a perfect location for both. A big enough explosion there would open holes both in the bottom of the fuel pool and in the side of the building.

Of course the Chinese had to disable the rest of the backup safety systems in order for this to happen as well, so that's why we knew that Ho and some of his men would be in the control room at the south end of the reactor building, where the general could also be safe from the explosion he would trigger by re-mote control. But he had stationed a good number of his force in and around the generator room, just in case we tried something like we were trying. Review-ing the numbers and positions again in my goggles, I was convinced that I wouldn't be able to reach the explosives without engaging too many of the guards and bringing the rest of Ho's force down on my head. Killing even one before I disabled the detonators could easily alert them, so I really needed to accomplish this part with complete stealth.

So, as much as I regretted what would probably happen to my two friends, I had to call them in as distractions.

"This is Talon 3," I said, not worrying about being overheard because of the hum of the machines around me. "My path is not clear enough. Send in Talon 1 and Talon 2."

The staging crew at the sub acknowledged my request, and I pictured in my mind the two other insertion coffins floating in the deep water off the coast. They each entered one of the two discharge pipes from the power plant, where the "clean" water used by it was released into the sea. The two pipes were similar to the one from the desalination plant that I had entered, but they were parallel to the ocean floor rather than perpendicular. The other difference was that the two discharge pipes were more likely to be monitored, and where they led to was much more likely to be guarded. We had hoped that Talons 1 and 2 would make it into the interior of the site without being detected, to serve as backup or even accomplish the mission if I couldn't, but the sober reality was that we all knew they probably would only serve as a misdirection for the Chinese.

Sure enough, about ten minutes later their presence was detected below the control room building, which sat between the reactor and the big turbine building where the nuclear energy was converted to electricity. I was aware of this because I had placed a feed in my goggles' view from Talon 2, since I knew him much better than the other British soldier. I also saw that most of the Chinese guards between me and my target were suddenly called away from my location, opening a path for me to the generator room.

I wasted no time weaving my way through the big machines, the rooms full of pipes and electrical equipment, and the long stairway that led to the spent fuel pool near the top of the building. Not too far before I reached the top of the stairway, I exited it through one of its few doors, because I knew that I could get to the generator room that way, and because my display showed the heat signature of two Chinese guarding the door at the top of the stairs. This was presumably to keep anyone from entering through the roof, as some of them had done when they infiltrated the plant.

When I reached the door to the generator room, I pulled the Trinity off my shoulder and cradled it with both hands. I felt the trigger with my index finger, and moved my thumb over the controls to make sure the killer barrel was selected, rather than the one with explosive rounds or the other with the grappling line. Then, because I had no choice in this situation, I flashed into the room as quickly as I could and shot the two guards inside. I was lucky that they'd both been facing the other way at the time, and even luckier when I checked their comm rigs and saw that they weren't open or broadcasting. So the gunfire wasn't heard by anyone on their lines, and I was hopeful that my distractions would give me a good chunk of time before the other Reds realized these were gone.

I wasn't disappointed, because for the next half hour or so the Reds were quite preoccupied with their two prisoners and one of the coffins, which they had hauled up to the control room for General Ho to see. I watched through Talon 2's goggles, which the Chinese had left on for some reason, as I began removing the remote detonators from the large stacks of C-7 and clamping them to my tool array, which I had now magnetized. After I removed all the detonators, I turned the array around and started spraying all the C-7 with a chemical called Lexout that would render it inert. These two measures would ensure that the Chinese could not rearm the explosives before the Taiwanese army arrived.

And we were quite confident that they didn't have any more C-7, because they had to bring these blocks in piece by piece on the backs of the soldiers who had powerglided in.

As I was sabotaging the sabotage, a window in my goggles showed me the drama going on in the control room, and another program in them translated the Chinese into English. The translation program was flawed, as they always seem to be, but I could tell what was going on. General Ho examined the coffin his soldiers had carried there, and was informed by his assistants that there were two coffins inserted, with one man in each, and that they were identified as Talon 1 and Talon 2, with schematics loaded for an assault on the control room. He then turned his attention to the two captured men, telling his helpers to leave the goggles on Talon 2 because he wanted whoever was watching to see what was going to happen, and had them hold Talon 2's head in place so that we had to watch what he did to the other Brit.

The Chinese general pulled out a big knife and went to work on the man, smiling the whole time. He didn't ask any questions during the torture, proba-bly because he didn't think he would get many answers, and was banking on getting some from the second man after he saw what happened to his friend. I was a pretty hardened veteran by this time, even though I was only twenty-six, but even I flinched and looked away when Ho reached the man's lower parts and castrated him. Rage toward Ho surged inside me, along with guilt for my part in this, but I forced myself to continue the job of removing the detonators and neutralizing the explosives. Then I *really* had to work hard at finishing the job, because Talon 1 passed out and the bloody knife was turned on the other man, who was a close friend of mine. Ho proceeded slower this time, thank-fully, because he paused for some questions in between the cutting, and soon I was done with my work in the generator room. I manipulated the controls on the tool array until it was keyed to all the detonators attached to it, in case I wanted to use them at some point, and called in.

"This is Talon 3," I said. "Mission accomplished."

"Affirmative, Talon 3," came the reply. "Proceed to the extraction point. We'll send in the hoverjet for you now, and the army assault will follow on its heels, now that there is no more radiation threat."

I did the mental math in my head, and was quite sure that my friend wouldn't make it until I was extracted and the cavalry arrived.

"Request permission to engage the enemy and rescue Talon 2," I said.

"Request denied. Proceed to the extraction point."

"I don't have time to argue this with you," I said, as I stepped out of the generator room. "Let me talk to Admiral Carter."

Howard Carter's voice came on the line momentarily, and I repeated my request to him.

"Follow your orders, son," the man said, even though he wasn't much older than I. "We don't want to lose you in this operation, too." When I was silent in response and he sensed my intent, he added, "If you disobey my direct order, I will not offer you another extraction or delay the attack. And from what I've heard, the Taiwanese will probably level the site before they endanger themselves in a firefight. Do you understand what I'm saying to you?"

I understood what he was saying to me. But I turned off the comm and headed in the direction of my friend, his screams still echoing in my ears.

23
MEANT TO BE

The car that Angelee drove to the store, with Chris in the backseat, was the nicest one she'd ever been in, even though it was intentionally plain so as not to be noticed. She was so glad that her late husband had made her get a driver's license, even though they had never owned a car and she only drove his uncle Otto's truck once in a while when Peter was at work (he rode the bus and train). Shopping for her knight in shining armor, and planning to cook for him, made her feel happier than she had been since her early days with Peter, or maybe when she first met Michael at the shelter a few months before. "Michael"—Did she dare call him that? If they were going to be married, then she would have to, right?

She pranced proudly through the store while Chris watched TV in the cart, the wad of cash burning a hole in her little purse made of cracked imitation leather. When she reached the cashier, she felt the urge to tell the man that she was shopping for—and living with!—a very important person who had saved her life. But then she remembered her vow of secrecy and felt ashamed that the thought of betraying his trust had even entered into her mind.

On the way back to the vineyard cottage, she was ruminating (again) on the new man in her life, and the thought that he didn't seem to share Peter's faith, or her weaker version for that matter, flashed unwelcomed into her mind. Would her late husband not approve of her marrying an unbeliever? He had

169

told her several times that she should remarry if something happened to him, but surely that would be a condition. And would she be really happy if they weren't on the same page spiritually? But she pushed such thoughts out of her mind, reasoning that God had brought them together, for sure, so He would take care of that. And then God gave her an idea right then, when Chris pointed at the car's entertainment system and asked, "Can you play my movie?" She knew he was referring to the treasured holo that his father had given him, which he played over and over again.

"No," she answered, "but when we get home, you can watch it on your amp. Maybe Mr. Ares would like to see it."

This, she thought, would be a good way for her savior to be introduced to her other Savior. So when she reached the cottage, the first thing she did after announcing her name at the front door and watching it open for her was to make a beeline to her room and get the old amp that contained the movie. She turned it on and watched the crude holo appear above it. Then she turned up the volume higher than usual, and told Chris to sit and watch it in the room next to the kitchen, hoping that Michael would overhear it. The door to his room was closed, so her next step was to knock on it. She heard him say "Wait a minute" from inside the door, and then soon he was opening it. Once again, she caught her breath merely at the sight of him.

"I-I wondered . . . ," she stammered. "Would you like to help me carry in the groceries, and see what I got?" He answered "Um" and looked back into the room behind him, so she added, "I know you're busy."

"No, what I'm doing can wait," he said, and closed the door when he exited the room, as if what was going in there had been private.

"What were you doing?" she asked, because it was the only thing that came to mind, but immediately regretted invading his privacy.

"I was . . ." He hesitated, as if he was thinking about whether there was any reason to lie or refuse to answer. He must have decided there wasn't, because he eventually said, "I was watching a holo from my past."

"Oh," Angelee said, as they reached the car and started carrying the bags in. "Chris loves watching an old holo of his own. He's watching it now."

She was all in, with no hesitation to work her plan, because she was so confident that this relationship was meant to be. But he didn't take the bait, and changed the subject.

"Did you have any problem at the store?"

"No, everything went great."

"Well, I really appreciate you doing this." He smiled kindly, and she melted inside again. And for the next half hour or so, he helped her bring the food in, watched her put it away from a stool at the kitchen island, and listened to her explain some of the meals she was going to make for him.

In the background, especially when she wasn't talking, the narration and dialogue from Chris's holo could be clearly heard in the kitchen. She was excited about some of the parts that wafted through the air, knowing what they said and some of what they meant, because she had heard it so many times before, and Peter had explained it to her and Chris.

"I perceive by the book in my hand," the main character said, *"that I am condemned to die, and after that to come to judgment, and I find that I am not willing to do the first, nor able to do the second."* A little later Angelee caught a glimpse of the face of the man named Pliable, who smiled a big smile and said, *"This is very pleasant"* when told about the Celestial City, then shortly after she could see him covered with mud from the swamp and not smiling anymore. Instead he was saying angrily, *"Is this the happiness you have told me all this while of?"*

Michael didn't seem to notice or care about this background noise for a while, so Angelee thought the silent prayers she had been throwing up were all in vain. But then after a lapse in the conversation, when she was almost done putting away the goods, he did say something about it.

"Is that the Bible?" he asked, looking toward the little boy and his old holopad.

"Almost," she said, hiding her excitement.

"That's funny," he went on, ignoring her enigmatic answer. "I talked to your husband about that when he helped me. I got the impression he was trying to convert me."

"He probably was," she said. "He did that a lot."

"And what about you?" He made a circle with his hand, obviously finding it awkward to even discuss this. "Are you . . . ?"

"Peter was always more committed than me," she said. "But I believe, too . . . especially now that God brought you into my life."

"Let's just . . . take it slow," he said, standing up from the stool and clearing his throat nervously. "Do you understand?" She nodded. "So you said that Chris likes the pool, right?" She nodded again, trying not to look too disappointed, and he added, "Let me show you something."

Michael led them both outside, and for the first time Angelee noticed just how beautiful this location was, since the pool deck was raised slightly, affording them an amazing view of the vineyards all around, and the hills in the distance. There were a few tall winery buildings a good distance away, but no houses in sight, only the rows of dark yellows, maroons, and some remaining greens of the autumn grapevines. Angelee was rather naïve to the ways of the rich, but she knew enough to know this was prime real estate. Michael's former lover must have been an important person, too—or maybe he had helped her to buy it.

"Vera," he said to the lukewarm air, "make the whole pool two feet deep." And she did; in a matter of seconds the water dropped down to that height, the broad steps at both ends reaching down that far, obviously designed to accommodate any depth desired.

"So Chris can play in the water as long as he wants, without you having to worry about his safety. Or if you want to swim yourself but keep an eye on him, you can do this: Vera, return half the pool to five feet."

The water immediately rose on the far side of the pool, and with it a transteel barrier that held it in and allowed the near side to remain shallow. Michael also explained that there was an invisible canopy over the whole pool area made of the same material, which allowed the air inside it to stay warm, and blocked only the harmful rays from the sun. He told Vera what temperature the air and water should be.

"Can I go in the water, Mommy?" the little boy asked, his attention finally diverted from the holo, which he had paused.

"I think so," she said, then looked at Michael. "There's only one problem. I don't have a swimsuit." He grunted a "Hmmm," and they both thought for a moment.

"Why don't you look through Tara's stuff in your room?" he said finally. "I'm sure she has something you can wear in there."

"She won't mind?"

"She won't know," he said. "So I'm sure she won't mind."

"Okay. Come on, Chris, let's get changed." And they both hurried off excitedly.

Once in the room, she put some shorts on Chris, over his pull-up, then rooted through the closets and drawers for a swimsuit. The most modest one she found was a white two-piece with a brand name that made it more expensive than a month's rent in the apartment she and her husband had lived in. She went into the bathroom and put it on, looking at herself from various angles, feeling a little guilty, but only a little because of the overwhelming sense she had that she was destined to be with Michael, because of all that had happened and the fact that she felt the same way she did with Peter before they were married. She knew that she might have to wait a while for that physical union with this man, judging by some of his reactions, but she believed the spiritual connection was already there because God saw all of time at once, as Peter had taught her. So in God's plan and in His eyes they were already together.

Back in the room, she found a beach shawl in the same drawer, to cover up a bit until she got out to the pool, and as she was slipping it on she noticed a frame sitting on top of the drawers. In it was a picture of a slightly younger Michael, with his arm around a woman that she presumed was Tara, the owner of the house. They were by the pool, and were both wearing swimsuits, the woman in the same white suit. The first thing Angelee noticed about the picture was Michael's body, which was as nice as she had imagined. Then she noticed that the woman was very beautiful herself, a milky skinned mixture of black and white who was much taller than Angelee. The next thing she thought about, which had the effect of dampening some of her excitement, was that the picture was still displayed, so it seemed to contradict Michael's claim that he and Tara had broken up years ago. But then Angelee realized that the picture did seem to be taken a while ago, and the woman may have still been pining for him after all this time. *I can understand that,* she thought to herself.

She looked around cautiously, even though she knew Chris was the only other person in the room, and turned the frame facedown on the shelf. Then she grabbed Chris's hand and led him out to the pool.

Michael was still out there, sitting in a chair and soaking up the sun and the view. She took hope from this, because he was a busy man and could have easily disappeared back into his room. Maybe he had wanted to see her again . . .

"I found those toys in the shed," he said, pointing to the colorful objects lined up by the pool. "I remembered Tara got them for her niece, who visited once in a while."

She took off the shawl and helped Chris into the pool, and he started splashing almost immediately. She pulled most of the toys into the pool for him one by one, and as she did, she got the impression that Michael was trying not to look at her, but not entirely succeeding.

"Do you want to come in?" she asked him. "I think Chris is okay—we could swim in the other part." She gestured to the deeper half, behind the transteel barrier.

"Uh, thanks," he said, "but no, I have some calls to make. Gotta get to work, you know?" He stood up and tossed the last remaining toy to Chris, and added, "Have fun, and let me know when dinner's ready."

"Okay," she said, and studied him as he walked into the house, comparing him to her first husband and thinking there wasn't much comparison. But Peter was a very spiritual man, and this one wasn't—she could just tell, by spending even this small amount of time with him. So she resolved again to introduce him to Chris's holo whenever she could, so that if they did come together, they could be one in every way.

24

SPECIAL HELL

When I got into the house I realized that I was sweating, and it wasn't from the California sun in November. I grabbed a glass of ice water, retreated into my room as quickly as I could, locked the door behind me in what was mostly a symbolic gesture, plopped down in my chair, and tried to get a handle on the emotions and impulses colliding inside me.

While I had been sitting outside waiting for Angelee to return from getting changed (*Why did I do that? It wasn't just the toys*), my mind began replaying some of the many times Tara and I had been in that pool, somewhere around it, and even walking in the vineyards nearby. And I found myself wanting that again, and let my mind replay far too much of it. But then I thought of Lynn and felt so bad, because she was carrying my child and we had just had such a great time a few days before at Sausalito, and so many other times before that. My mind replayed some of those times, too, and I felt mystified once again that I could have so much but still want more. I loved being with Lynn, but the fact that Tara and Angelee were something different from her seemed to make them desirable, too, not to mention their sheer physical appeal.

Then Angelee had come out to the pool, right when I was trying to think about Lynn and rebuking myself for these bad thoughts, and it became more difficult for me. *I guess I shouldn't have stayed outside—that was the bottom*

175

line—because deep down I hadn't been there for the right reasons. She was such a beautiful young woman, inside and out, and she actually thought God wanted her to be with me!

I didn't really even think about telling her the truth, ostensibly because I wanted her to remain loyal to me and not upset her too much. But again, I had to admit that part of my motive was that I enjoyed her adoring me and wanted to leave the door open more than a crack. That was exactly what had been happening with Tara for almost six years now, and when I thought about that, it became clear to me that the way to deal with all this was to work my plan to finally tell Tara that it was over and would never happen again. That would solidify my relationship with Lynn more, and make me stronger to resist other temptations like Angelee—or so I thought at the time. *And why am I even thinking about all this when I'm the target of the deadliest assassination method known to man? Then again, that's why I have the opportunity to finally put Tara behind me . . .*

I turned on the netkit, to use one of the wall screens to talk to Terrey and the double and pursue my "amputation" plan, but it immediately informed me that I had a message from Lynn. I opened it.

"Michael, I've called you three times with no answer," she said. "Is something going on? What's up? Call me back."

I thought for a moment, to get my story straight, and called her back.

"Why didn't you answer?" she said. "I was getting scared."

"Sorry, I had to step out for a few minutes."

"I thought you couldn't leave the place where you are. Terrey told me that when he was trying to reassure me that you'd be okay."

"I didn't leave the . . . building." I almost said "house" before I stopped myself. "I just left the room and forgot to take my glasses with me."

"You should have them with you at all times."

"Yeah, I know. I'm sorry. Won't happen again."

"When you do stuff like that, it makes me really want to know where you are."

"Why did you call, Lynn?" I asked, ignoring her comment and hoping the issue would go away.

"That's actually why I called," she said. "I was thinking, for this plan you and

Terrey cooked up to work, you'd probably have to be staying with someone who could go out and get things for you." There was the detective in her, at work again.

"Lynn, we've already agreed not to talk about this," I said, then realized we really hadn't.

"And I can tell you're in a house," she pressed ahead, "from what I can see behind you. So I'm worried."

"What are you worried about, Lynn?" *Could she really be that good of a detective?*

"Are you with that woman? I know she has a house in the Valley somewhere."

"I am *not* with Tara, Lynn," I said, glad that I could say something true. "I promise."

"Good. But it made me think about her again. I had pushed it out of my mind when we were having trouble the last few years, but since things have been better lately, I guess I have enough courage or something now to ask. Have you been with her?"

"No, Lynn, I haven't. I promise."

"Because I know she's still working at BASS, so you must see her at the castle." She paused before the next part. "Does she have to be working there?"

"Actually, it's funny that you're asking about this," I said, thinking quickly. "I was going to talk to Terrey first about it and then you, but since you brought it up, let's talk about it now. I have a plan for her to move on from BASS, now that I'm in charge."

"So you *are* tempted by her," she said.

"No, no, it's not like that," I lied. "I just know it's hard for you, and I want to clear out anything that could come between us. From the past, you know."

"So what's your plan?"

"Okay, but listen to the whole thing before you react," I warned her. "First, I give Tara a promotion."

"What?!"

"I said listen to the whole thing. Terrey said we can't put the double in the public eye much because the switch could be detected, with all the video that's shot and studied by the media, and maybe even our enemies. But we also don't want me to be conspicuous by absence. So he suggested that a way to deflect the problem would be for me to appoint a spokesperson, which BASS leaders have never had. The double could appear one time to appoint Tara, and then she could handle most of the communication while this is going on. That would keep the double off the net, in a way that seems to fit the normal flow of business."

"Okay," she said, "but how does it get her out of town?"

"I'll tell her that she needs to leave, but that I'm setting her up so well by this promotion, she'll be able to get any job she wants. When she puts her résumé out after earning this position, they'll be lined up offering her more than she ever dreamed of as an Internal Security Officer. Plus, she fits this job and will do it well."

I regretted saying the last line, because Lynn was smart enough to know that it meant Tara looked great on camera, and was intelligent to boot.

"What if she doesn't leave?" Lynn asked.

"She will," I said. "I'll make sure she does. I'll tell her that she'll be fired if she doesn't."

"You think you can do that?" She was asking the same question as before, but in a different way, which showed that she didn't fully believe me. I marveled at her sixth sense, as I had many times before.

"Yes, absolutely," I lied again. "I just didn't want to fire her without giving her a chance like this. It wouldn't be fair."

"Well, get on with it," Lynn said after thinking awhile. "As long as you do this, I guess I can live without knowing where you are, or who you're with. For now."

"Okay, I'll get on with it." I blew her a kiss, feeling much better about myself. "Love you."

"Love you," she said, and added before she hung up, "Lynley does, too."

The mention of my preborn daughter made my adulterous thoughts sting even more, and gave me some more motivation to "get on with it," as Lynn had said. So I called Terrey and ran it by him, saying we could have the double travel down to the city on Monday (this was Saturday) and make the appointment at the castle, where security would be optimal. I didn't tell him about the other issues involved with Tara, of course, just that she was such a perfect fit for the job that no one would question the decision to create this position for her. He was good with the idea, and said that he would plan the trip for Monday and announce it at the team meeting that night. He also said that I should "coach up" the double before then, since this would be his first public appearance and a key to maintaining the illusion and keeping the enemy focused on killing him, rather than looking for me.

After that call, I sat for a while in the chair thinking about how to coach the double about the main thing I wanted to accomplish, which was to use him for the purpose of ending the relationship with Tara—something I had failed to do myself, time and time again. I thought about how much to confide in the double, and decided to tell him what was going on because it might be too difficult to keep him in the dark and still accomplish my goal. And of all people he should be able to understand my dilemma, having contracted AIMS through his sexual adventures. But I also decided to wait until Monday morning to talk to him about it, so I didn't waste the time and energy in case he was killed before then, and so there was less of a chance that he might share my secrets with Lynn or someone else.

Now that this plan was formulated and prepared, I felt a sense of relief from the tension I had experienced by the pool, and thought I was calm enough to catch some sleep to make up for the few hours I had the night before. So I climbed onto the bed and told Vera to wake me up at five, which she did after a fitful rest that included half-remembered dreams about the women in my life and a Chinese army surrounding the cottage. I could recall Saul Rabin showing up with an Alliant Trinity to fight them with me, but the rest was foggy.

Knowing that Angelee would be preparing dinner for us, I took a shower and made myself presentable. I really wasn't thinking of doing anything with her that night—I had a Protection Team meeting scheduled for 10:00 P.M., after all. But I did find myself wanting to look nice for her sake. It reminded me of the early days with Lynn, and all my days with Tara. Probably for the same reason, I didn't dive into any more work at this point, but stepped out of the room even though she hadn't called me yet.

Sure enough, she had the table set and was finishing her prep in the kitchen, dressed in a pretty Asian garment that looked like a cross between a robe and a dress.

"Hi," I said.

"It's almost ready," she responded, moving a little quicker around the kitchen.

"No hurry," I said. "Where's Chris?"

"He's still sleeping, tired out from swimming. Would you like to get him up for dinner?"

I said okay, and went to her room. The boy was curled up on the bed, with the bedclothes swirled around him, but other than that the room was immaculate—obviously Angelee valued it and was keeping it in order. Except for a picture frame turned down on a piece of furniture . . . I turned it up to look at it and then put it back down, realizing why it was like that. I sat down on the edge of the bed next to Chris, and studied the sleeping boy. I had guessed that he was four years old before his mother confirmed it, because that was the age of my first daughter Lynette when she was killed, and most of my memories of her were at that age. And looking at this child, who was almost as cute as mine had been, I had a new appreciation of why Angelee would resort to selling herself in an attempt to keep him and provide for him: I would do almost anything to get my daughter back. I also was struck by how helpful it would be for him to have a father again, and felt a natural desire to help him myself. But though I could make sure they had enough money to live on—even Lynn would understand and approve of that—I couldn't be a daddy to him. Lynn wouldn't like having a sexy young thing like Angelee around our house much, that was for sure, and when Angelee found out that I was married, she probably wouldn't want anything to do with me anyway.

I tapped the boy's shoulder softly and watched as he stirred and fumbled at his sleepy eyes, like Lynette used to do. Then he climbed on to me like I was his father, and I carried him out to his mother. She comforted him until he was more awake, then sat him down at the table. Soon we were enjoying a terrific meal, with some Asian and American elements, in case I didn't like the Asian parts.

"Is that a kimono?" I asked.

"Yes, kind of an American version."

"Are you Japanese? I'm not an expert, but you don't really look Japanese to me, and Lee's not a Japanese name."

"I am half Japanese and half Korean," she said. "Not a good mix."

"Why's that?" I was thinking, *You look like a good mix to me,* but didn't say it because I didn't want to lead her on too much.

"Japanese and Koreans have hated each other for a long time," she said. "There's been some change these days, but when my parents got together it was taboo for most people."

"So that made it hard for you?"

"It made it hard for my parents. They were already immigrants, and then they lost all support from their family or anyone from the Japanese or Korean communities. So they had trouble getting jobs, finding people they could trust, things like that. They were robbed a bunch of times, and unemployed a lot . . ."

"But they made you," I said. "That was good." And it occurred to me that this may have been the reason she was so noticeably attractive: she was a unique combination of races that didn't often come together.

"Yes, but they didn't stay together. I think the pressures got to them. So I ended up on my own, long story short. And on the street, until I met Peter." Now I felt even more sorry for her, and for Chris, and we sat in silence for a while.

"Mommy," the little boy spoke up, having finished gulping down his food, "can I go in the pool again?"

"I think you've had enough for one day," she answered. "Why don't you watch your movie over there?" She pointed to a plush couch in the living room, where the amp was sitting.

As I watched the boy with the outdated piece of equipment, an idea occurred to me.

"Has he ever seen his favorite movie in any other way?" I asked. "Like in a holo theater or net room?"

"We never went to the theater," she said, and I wondered if this was a religious thing, or just a poor thing. Then again, it may have been both, because she added, "And we couldn't afford a net room."

I asked Vera if she could detect the boy's amp wirelessly, and she said yes. I asked her if the file he was watching was compatible with her surround system, and she said yes again, except that it wouldn't be the highest quality available.

"Cue it up, Vera, and have it ready for us to watch after dinner, in this room." I turned to Angelee. "He's gonna love this."

I helped Angelee with the dishes—it was the least I could do—and thanked her repeatedly for the meal. Then we sat down to watch the movie, ending up on the couch next to each other, because although the system could accommodate different perspectives, it was optimal to all watch from the same basic location and direction. Angelee was on my left, and the boy on hers, perched on the front edge of the couch in anticipation.

I told Vera to play the holo, now with its resolution and other features set at their highest levels, and the boy was blown away from the opening scene. Because we were next to each other on the couch, the system didn't block us from one another's view, but treated us as one party. So anytime the scene and room around us weren't pitch black, I could see his expressions to one degree or another, and saw his lips mouthing the word "Wow" over and over again at each new scene. And I could hear him say it when there was a lull in the music or other audio. But his eyes and face were saying "Wow" perpetually, as the scenes he had enjoyed so many times in the antiquated medium of the little pad were now displayed in their full glory in 360-degree 3D.

As Vera had warned, the resolution wasn't nearly as high as the cutting edge holos I usually watched, nor were the production values of this apparently independent movie very impressive, but that didn't diminish Chris's excitement in the least. And that excitement was contagious, of course—I stayed to watch the movie, and Chris's reactions, even though I had plenty of work that I could be doing.

The movie was the first of a three-part series called *Pilgrim,* and the opening credits said it was based on the complete original text of a book by John Bunyan. That name sounded vaguely familiar to me, which made sense when I could tell that the language was Elizabethan or close, and therefore originated in my native country. It didn't take long for me to tell that it was an allegory, from the name of the main character alone, which also gave me a clue to something else.

"Is Chris named after him?" I said to Angelee.

"Yes, his name is Christian," she whispered back. "Her father loved this book, and didn't even like for me to call him Chris. But like I said, I'm not as committed as he was. Now shhhhh."

She obviously wanted me to see this, so I settled in and watched it with an open mind, as best I could. As I did, I alternated between confusion and comprehension, and experienced a variety of emotions, most of them negative.

My confusion was the most pronounced when we reached the part where Christian approached a cross on a hill and the burden on his back fell off—and some irritation flared in me as well. I wondered how something that happened over two thousand years before could actually help anyone in this modern world, and whether it ever really happened anyway. And the implication that we all have a "burden of sin" that only God can remove bothered me. I had experienced some kind of spiritual awakening a year prior when I had talked to Angelee's husband, and prayed repeatedly for deliverance from death, but that had all faded into the background when my life returned to normal. And Lynn was liking me better since then, so I didn't feel so in need of forgiveness anymore.

But in the darkness of that room with Angelee sitting next to me, I did feel a tension that weighed on me like a burden. And then when I shifted nervously in my seat and unintentionally brushed against her, she put her hand on my arm and leaned her head on my shoulder. And despite how much I loved Lynn and knew I shouldn't hurt this innocent girl, that tension increased inside me.

I squinted my eyes shut, cursing myself for those thoughts and feelings, and when I did a seemingly random series of images entered my mind. But then I realized they weren't random at all, considering the situation, because they contained a religious character and were from another holo I had watched right here in this room with my other extramarital problem. Tara had been in love with an old classic flat TV series called *Firefly* that had been doctored into a 360 version with the latest technology—that was where she got the name "Vera." And in that series there was an episode where a "shepherd" warned a man not to take advantage of a naïve girl who was a lot like Angelee. If he did, the man was told, he would "burn in a special hell."

I had felt a periodic sense of déjà vu since I arrived at the cottage, and this was probably the reason why. And the term "special hell" was now stuck in my mind, so I shifted in my seat again in an effort to stop Angelee from leaning on me. She got the message and sat back up in her former position, and stayed that way for the rest of the movie. My inner conflict didn't go away, but it did help me to understand a later part of Chris's movie better . . .

Christian found himself at the foot of a Hill of Difficulty, which neither of his companions were willing to climb. But he said,

> *This hill, though high, I covet to ascend,*
> *The difficulty will not me offend.*
> *For I perceive the way of life lies here:*
> *Come pluck up, Heart, let's neither faint nor fear;*
> *Better, though difficult, the right way to go,*
> *Than wrong, though easy, where the end is woe.*

I wished that I could have the kind of resolve that character did, to stay on the straight and narrow. And because I didn't, I did have to admit to feeling some of that guilt that had been on the back of the pilgrim. But I didn't understand until much later how the other hill could solve that problem. I did, however, do the right thing after the movie that night, and told Angelee that I had a net meeting to attend, and would see her and Chris in the morning.

25
DREAMS

"Okay, mates," Terrey said, "let's hop to it, as we say down under."

The Protection Team was gathered in our living room, I assumed because its windows were now fully secured, and Lynn refused to travel down into the base below for the meeting. She disliked the fact that there was a huge facility hidden underneath her beloved homestead, and liked to pretend that it didn't exist.

I was watching the meeting through the two-way netroom equipment, and because it was state-of-the-art, I could switch between four perspectives and zoom in on individuals whenever I wanted to. I was currently having a closer look at the cupbearer named Tyra, who had painted multicolored decorations on her floating wheelchair, which had formerly been all black. I assumed she had gotten permission from Terrey to do that, and that she had used the removable paint that was all the rage lately, but I was a bit taken aback that she would use so many colors in the situation we were currently facing. Like Terrey wearing black, however, I supposed that if she was a traitor among us, she wouldn't broadcast it so blatantly.

While I was checking out clothing and colors, I noticed that Korcz was *not* wearing black, perhaps because Terrey had pointed out that he was the day before? Terrey himself was wearing it again, though.

But Terrey was starting the meeting, so I forgot about the probably point-less clothes issue and listened to him. I drew back my view so I could see every-one in the room. Besides Terrey, Tyra, and Korcz, there was Lynn, Min, the triplets, the double, and finally Stephenson, who looked rather nervous about something (*Was he sweating?*).

"We've made it through our second day," Terrey said. "Which is a good start. But we've got a long way to go."

"At least you hope so," Lynn chimed in, rubbing her big belly. "Since you're getting a million dollars a day." She smiled at this, but only a little.

"And many expenses to pay from that, as you'll remember, marm." He gestured around the room. "Like paying these fine people. So let's talk about what they've been doing. The triplets have upgraded the already stellar security measures to prevent or prepare for any threat. No one can get anywhere near this place unless we want them to, and the only one we do is the food truck, which we'll meet at the gate down below. The air defenses on the hills around here are quite sufficient to protect from any local air attack that might ensue, and we don't have to worry about a long-range jet. The Chinese would never send one into our airspace, because that would be an act of war with no deni-ability, and we're protected by NORAD anyway.

"Car accidents are a favorite method of political assassinations, because they appear random and intent is deniable, but we don't have to worry about that because we knew ahead of time and can keep you off the roads. And when we do need to go somewhere, such as the little trip we have planned to the city, we can use the aeros. Very convenient . . . I like to think that there will be some very frustrated mercenaries driving around the Bay Area this week, waiting for a car ride that will never happen.

"This whole hill has been scanned so well that the only way a bomb could have been placed and remain is if it was made of something no human has ever encountered before, and if that's the case, we have bigger problems than the Chinese. And the whole hill is being *continually* scanned by the sensors we've installed, so no explosive or gas or poison could be introduced. But just in case, Tyra has been testing all the food and water, and thankfully she's still okay . . . except for her leg." He gestured toward the plump lady. "I like what you've done with your chair. Those colors could help offset the *ban lan* of the enemy . . . I'll get to that more at the end of this meeting.

"But back to the measures we've already taken, the *Trois* and their faithful assistants"—he now gestured to Korcz and Stephenson—"have electronically and physically examined every possible sniper location up to three thousand meters. That's two hundred meters beyond the current range of any rifle in the world, and even beyond any possible upgrade we don't know about yet, because none of the last ten upgrades, over the last twenty years, have exceeded ten meters."

"That's a little too much math for me," I said through the netroom, so they all could hear me. "What's the bottom line?"

"The bottom line is that it's Buckley's—no way in the world—that a sniper could hit anyone in this house. I am very confident that you could sit on any of the porches, or even hang by the pool, without any fear of being shot. In fact, I'm thinking we should set up a photo op so the media could show the double and Lynn somewhere outside the house."

"I thought you were keeping Lynn and the double separate from one another, so it would be safer for her, if he becomes endangered."

"We *are* keeping them separate," Terrey said. "Jon is staying below in the base. But just like he needs to be seen in public sometimes, he and Lynn should occasionally be seen together, to head off any suspicion or attention drawn to an obvious change in your patterns. Of course, as you know, I'd much rather be keeping Lynn in an entirely separate place, because the rest of us have to be here, at the most secure location. But she wouldn't leave."

"If and when I'm going to die—" Lynn started.

"I know," Terrey finished. "You'd like to die in your house."

"Speaking of the trip to the city," the double spoke up. "How will we avoid a sniper during that?" All this talk of dying must have reminded him that his life was on the line more than anyone's.

"That was on my agenda," Terrey said, "so let's talk about it now. Once again the gods of personal protection have been smiling on us. You will enter one of the aeros in the hangar bay of this mountain base, fly in it to the castle in the city, exit the car inside the bay there, conduct your business inside one of the most secure buildings in the world, and then come back the same way. You will *not* be at risk. However, just in case something bizarre happens, like the aero goes down or someone infiltrates the castle, we have an extra safety measure for you."

One of the triplets stepped toward the double and handed him a piece of equipment about the size of her hand.

"This is an Atreides shield, designed by BASS about a year ago and recently cleared for safe use. If you're in danger or expect it, you can wear this on a belt or waistband at your right hip, like you would a phone. When activated, it will protect your body from almost any weapon, but for only about half an hour, so only turn it on when necessary. There's one for Lynn, too, courtesy of her husband, in case she does go outside the house at some time." The triplet gave another one to my wife. "It took this long to get them to you because they have to be programmed to your body specifically in order to be safe. They also cost a small fortune to build, so unfortunately the rest of us won't be so blessed."

That wasn't entirely true, I knew, because Min had a version of the shield built into his body—one of his many combat augmentations. He could activate this "second skin" at any time with his mind, and instantly become even more indestructible than he already was.

"Could we be alerted visually to potential dangers?" the double asked. "You said this lunatic has colors for everything he sends, right? Like the blue color on that assault team in the holo you showed me. Would it help to watch for certain colors?"

"Maybe," Terrey said, "but the problem is we haven't been able to identify a common pattern in the kaleidocides that have already happened, or that there necessarily is a common pattern. There could be different colors, depending on the situation. There are five that figure prominently in the Tibetan Book of the Dead—and there are some Buddhist elements in Sun's religion: red, yellow, blue, white, and green. But that doesn't explain the black that we've seen associated with betrayal and poison, unless the black is simply added to those five."

"Or it could be the five elements," the triplets said, briefly forgetting their protocol and all speaking at the same time. So now I knew that they were capable of making a mistake. But they corrected it quickly, and just one of them continued. "Throughout the Shang, Tang, Zhou and Qin dynasties of ancient China, which is the referent for much of Sun's faith, the emperors selected colors as symbols based on the theory of the five elements, which are water, fire, wood, metal and earth. These correspond with the colors black, red, greenish blue, white, and yellow. Ancient Chinese people believed that the five elements were the source of everything in nature, including the colors that come from each of them. They had a saying, 'Colors come naturally while black and white are the first.'"

"So that's the working hypothesis of the *Trois*," Terrey said. "And I don't think I've seen anything to disprove it yet. If it's true, and that's a big if, then we've already seen greenish blue—"

"The teal color of the assault team was greenish blue," the triplet interrupted again, "with black mixed in because it is the color of death, or maybe 'the king of colors,' as it was referred to in ancient China."

"So the greenish blue and the method of direct assault are off the table now," Terrey resumed. "And we'd be looking for the other methods to be black, red, white, or yellow, according to the Shimmies' theory. I don't know if that helps us much, Jon, because like I said, we don't really know."

"You said something about a car accident in one of the assassinations," the double added. "What color was the car?"

Terrey looked at the triplets, and they remained still for a moment as they were accessing their data files. Then one of them said, "White."

"So we should be especially looking out for black, red, and yellow," Jon said, and Terrey shrugged his shoulders and said "Maybe."

As they were talking, the second screen on my wall flashed like it had before, and some letters unfolded across it again:

YON: I DO NOT COMPLETELY AGREE WITH MY SISTERS. BE CAREFUL ABOUT OTHER COLORS TOO.

As I was wondering which triplet was texting me these words with her mind, and why she didn't speak up in the meeting, the words disappeared off the screen and Terrey wrenched my attention back to him.

"But overall we're in good shape to hold out for a while," he said. "And speaking of that, Michael, have you come up with any more clues as to why

Sun wants you dead, or anything we could use to expose him and get him to back off?"

"Nothing yet," I said, and felt guilty again, this time because I had been watching a movie tonight instead of investigating the mystery.

"All right," Terrey said. "Then the next agenda item is our man Lawrence here." He pointed to Stephenson, who was definitely sweating now. "He shared something with me after dinner that I thought would be best discussed with everyone, rather than being whispered down the lane. Go ahead, mate."

"Well, I'm sorry to have to bother you with this," the little man said, starting out nervously but soon gaining confidence because of his conviction about what he had to say. "For the past year or so, I've been experimenting with a Dreamscape rig that records my dreams and calculates their precognitive potential. Which means their ability to tell the future. I know some of you may think I'm crazy—heck, my partner doesn't even agree with me. But I believe that there's really something to this. I've had numerous dreams that have come true in one way or another, most recently the exact circumstances of our rescue from a fire in New York, when we were brought here."

"Is that true, Korcz?" I asked from the peanut gallery.

"Yah, that one is true," the big, bald Russian replied. "But the others, not really."

"The Dreamscape system is in continuing development," Stephenson countered. "They're learning how to identify precog dreams better as time goes on, and so am I."

"I'm sure we can respect your right to your hobby, Stephenson," I said, "as long as it doesn't interfere with your work. But why are you telling us about it?"

"I'm getting to that, sir. When I met Miss Ponchinello and saw her interest in Valeri . . ." I raised my eyebrows at this, and saw Lynn do the same. "It reminded me of something I had seen before, kind of like a déjà vu. So I searched my dreams that had been recorded and found images of a dark-haired, dark-skinned lady who was in love with Valeri."

"Hold on a second," Lynn said. "Tyra, do you even have this interest that he's talking about?"

The woman in the floating chair hesitated for a moment, so Stephenson spoke for her: "Last night she told Valeri that when she was recovered, she wanted to . . . celebrate with him."

Lynn asked Tyra if that was true, and the woman smiled and nodded. Everyone then looked at Korcz, who just shrugged his shoulders.

"That may have happened very fast," I said. "Love at first sight, I guess. But it hardly qualifies as a convincing case of predicting the future."

"Right, but I'm not done yet. I not only had a dream where a dark-haired, dark-skinned lady was with him, I also had a dream where a dark-haired, dark-skinned *man* was with him."

"So?"

"So, I searched the net about Tyra, trying to scratch my déjà vu itch, you know, and I remembered from working security in New York that boss Ponchinello had a son named Tyrone Jr." He looked across the room at Tyra. "I'm sorry if this is too personal, but it *is* well documented on the web, so it's really public. But Tyra used to be Tyrone—she's a transgender person."

There was a bit of a gasp around the room, not because Tyra was transgender—that was very common—but because this must have been an interesting surprise for Korcz, especially if the feelings had been mutual.

"The relationship is over," Korcz said with a slight grin, removing all doubt about his opinion regarding this. When he said it, I noticed Lynn trying to suppress a laugh and found myself smiling at her, since no one could see me.

"Valeri," Terrey said with a bemused look on his face, "you're as mean as cat's piss."

"She is still a man," Korcz said matter-of-factly. "*He* is still a man. No matter what you cut off—"

"Wait," Tyra said, holding up a hand in her chair. "Since this relationship is bein' ruined before it starts, all my secrets should come out."

She paused for effect, and it was effective indeed. We were all waiting to hear what she had to say.

"I was only Tyrone for five years. Before that I was Tyra again. I mean before. I didnta have a healthy childhood, ya feel me? Got the idea that becoming a man would solve my problems. It didn't, so I went back to what I was. Long story short: Valeri, I'm all woman, and I'm sure not gonna go through that again."

I had heard about "double trans" people, and despite Tyra's personal pro-testation, I had also heard of "triple trans" people. This was more and more common now that the technology for the treatment had evolved so far, and was so readily available. But this was the only time I'd ever met one—at least as far as I knew. We all looked at Korcz to see how this mini-saga would end.

"We may be able to celebrate," he said finally, much to her delight. And Lynn laughed out loud this time.

"This is all very fascinating," I said, "but let's get back to the point. You're telling us all this, Stephenson, because you think we should include your dreams in our protection plan. Right?"

"Well, right, I think that would be smart. But I'm not sure it would actu-ally do any good, because they may come true anyway." A collective sigh rang through the room, but he continued: "Look, I didn't know that she was a woman before, but even with that it all fits. My dreams predicted he would meet a woman who was also a man, or vice versa, or whatever versa."

"It could easily be coincidence," I countered, "even the trans-transgender thing. There could be all sorts of reasons why you might have a dream and then it, quote, comes true. What about all the other ones that don't? So let's do this, if it's all right with you, Terrey. Why don't you just tell us, Stephenson, if you happen to find something with your machine that pertains to our situation here, and then we'll cross that bridge when we come to it."

"Well, I already have one," he said. "And I'm afraid there's an ethical bridge to cross, too—that's why I'm telling you. In the dreams I found with Korcz and Tyra, there is one where she dies from eating something."

A pall fell over the room, not so much from the idea that Tyra might die—that was already possible. But we all immediately felt the weight of the moral dilemma that Stephenson had referred to: Should we continue on our present course if we knew that she would die?

"Let me see the file," I said, and Stephenson sent it to me. I watched it on my second screen and found it to be a blurry kaleidoscope of mostly indecipher-able images, though there was a ten-second segment where a black woman (darker than Tyra, if I recall correctly) did gag at a table and fall over. But the woman didn't look exactly like Tyra, and the table didn't look like anything in our house.

"Upon review," I said to the room, "I think we should postpone any action based on this, and consider it further. Stephenson, I appreciate you sharing it and want you to continue to do so, within reason, but we have to stick with what we can see clearly at this point. Is that all right with you, Terrey?"

"It's all right with me," he said, "but I think we should use any possible advantage, whether we believe in it or not. In fact, my last agenda item for this meeting is something that you might think is even stranger."

"Really?"

"Yes, really. I'm gonna suggest that we all participate in a *ban lan* ritual, the kind that General Sun uses to empower his kaleidocide."

I was stunned, but managed to say, "He doesn't empower it at all; the power comes from money and equipment and people. His religion is just a primitive cult that doesn't really do anything."

"He thinks it does," Terrey said. "And if you look at the sheer facts of what has happened over the years, it seems to be working for him."

"Terrey, you can't honestly think it would help us to pray to some eastern mystical force, or whatever it is?"

"I don't really know, mate. But I know I want to keep you alive, and the rest of us, too. And if it's even a possibility that there is something supernatural going on in Sun's religion, I say we use it ourselves in the hope it might counteract. I've done some of the rituals myself already, and we're all okay so far. So I thought we should all do it, just in case it actually works."

"Wow," I said. "I'm *really* gonna have to think about this one. So the answer's no for tonight. It's late, everyone should get some rest. I'll see you tomorrow."

As it turned out, we were all going to need the rest, because the next day we would find out how deadly the colors yellow and red could be.

26
QINGDAO

"China is the *Middle Kingdom*," Zhang Sun said forcefully to his chief advisors, "not the Peripheral Kingdom."

That was one of his favorite sayings, and he pulled it out again in this meeting because he felt that Li-Zhan Wei was challenging his authority. Wei was respectful and subtle but challenging nonetheless, and the age-old imperialistic ambitions of Sun's country were an effective tool for solidifying and maintaining his own power over it.

"I am concerned that your government," Wei said, "which is good and necessary for the prosperity of China, may be put at risk if you step out too far. The Communist party made sure long ago that the citizenry could not be armed with guns, at least not any that were comparable to what the military has. But now the people are armed with an even more powerful weapon—they are armed with the vote. You used that weapon to procure for yourself special powers in the wake of world recession and the Taiwan debacle, but the masses can be fickle."

Sun looked around at the other faces in the meeting while Wei was talking, to see their reactions. He had to strain his eyes a little because they were not really present, only virtually. The meeting was being held in the back of his limousine, as he traveled from the airport to his next destination. The windows were completely darkened, and the car's projectors simulated a conference table

194

with chairs around it. The holos of his advisors were imported from Beijing and other locations around the country.

"We talked a lot about the rights of the people," Wei continued, "and how they had a right to be protected from outside aggressors and overpopulation within. But now that they have been made more secure by our military buildup, and the economy has been improved by state-sponsored birth control and euthanasia, they don't have the same fears they had before. So they start to turn their ears to the latest fashions in cultural and political ideology, some of which are directly contrary to what they wanted previously. There is still much talk of rights, but with the western religions becoming more prevalent, we are hearing more about the right to have a larger family, or the right to keep their aging parents in the home with them. And we have agitators like Gao Dao suggesting that money should be taken from the military budget to support practices like that."

"Do you have to mention that name, Li?" Sun said, only half joking, because other than Michael Ares, this up-and-coming leader from the People's Party was the man he would most like to kill. But he couldn't do so at this time because his hold on power wasn't yet strong enough to survive the kind of martyr Gao Dao would become.

"We *must* mention him," Wei answered. "He is young, articulate, attractive, and some dare say that he is a term or less away from being electable. Which brings me to the specific concern I have right now. Dao has also been agitating, though at a more private level, about the vast amounts of money that have been directed to your special military technology project. He knows that it would not be feasible to produce or use on a broad scale because of the cost involved, so he is pointing to it as an example of you spending the people's money for something that will never benefit them. There are also rumblings from him and other pacifistic factions that the project does not contribute to national defense, but is only useful for assassinations."

Sun had always liked Li-Zhan Wei—the man had been loyal to him and his principles. And he especially liked Wei's name, which could mean "stand and fight" or "instigate war." But as far as Sun was concerned, this faithful advisor was the one who was overstepping his bounds. The pet project Wei spoke of was one that could possibly make his revenge upon Michael Ares infinitely sweeter, if it worked out the way he hoped. And the truth was that he did plan to use it to eliminate others, even in his own country, who might incur his wrath. But that was not something that should be discussed in a meeting like this.

"I appreciate your concern," Sun said, and the man seemed to breathe a sigh of relief. "But this is the second time you have raised it, and the first time should have been sufficient. If I wanted to change anything as a result of what you were saying, I would have done it after the first time. So if you do this again, I will have to conclude that you require some further education about the interaction within authority structures, and I will send you to one of our correctional facilities in Siberia."

He intentionally did not say whether Wei would be sent there as a person in authority or as a prisoner, but both were very undesirable positions in that endless frozen tundra. This had been an effective threat for many years in the former Soviet Union, and Sun was glad to revive it now that China had procured much of Siberia for the purpose of drilling for oil there.

"Does anyone else have any concerns?" Sun asked, and of course there were none, which was a good thing because his limousine had arrived at its destination, and the meeting was now over.

"Hēi sè . . . hóng sè . . . bì . . . bái . . . huáng," he whispered to himself as he exited the back of the big black car and walked toward the church building. "Jin . . . jiǒng . . . zhǎn . . . lún . . . rǎng."

As with the first ritual at the Temple of Azure Clouds near Beijing, Sun was experiencing a feeling of euphoria even without drugs, because this setting was so perfect for his purposes. As was the timing of what was about to happen in the Napa Valley of California.

He stopped in the courtyard to study the Protestant Church of Jiangsu Road, thinking how worthwhile it was to travel over four hundred miles from Beijing, as he had done several times before. The church had an interesting history, having been built in 1910 by the occupying Germans to match an identical twin building in Germany, which was destroyed in World War II. But its history was not what attracted General Sun to the church—it was its colors. The walls were dark yellow stone, the roof was burgundy red tiles, and the bell tower and windows were a deep green. The darker shades of the colors had no doubt been chosen by the architects to give them harmony with one another, but this also made them more harmonious with Sun's *xing lu cai se*. And even the name of the city where it was located had a color in its name—Qingdao meant "green island."

Sun recited the names of the elements and colors again as he resumed his walk to the front of the church, knowing that his people had made sure that the door was unlocked and the building empty. He entered the sanctuary, found a place in the center of it to stand, and now took in the colors on the inside of the church. In addition to yellow brick on the walls and the green of the stained glass windows, the floor was covered with dark red ceramic tile, and the altar and raised platform with carved gray marble. Gray was not a color he was invoking in this *xing lu cai se,* nor was the brown of the large wooden cross hanging above the altar. That was one reason why he stood in the center of the room, rather than at the front near the altar. And if he was honest, he would have to admit that the Christian iconography made him uncomfortable—a reaction he didn't have toward Buddhism or the other Eastern religions that were incorporated into the *ban lan jiao.*

But on this trip, his uneasiness was offset by the fact that a location like this was another coincidence that pointed to his inevitable victory. The wife of Saul Rabin, founder of BASS, had been a devotee of Christianity, and her husband had followed her to some degree at least. Sun didn't know whether Michael Ares shared those beliefs or not, but he did know that Michael's wife had been raised in the orphanage started by Mrs. Rabin. Yet he still stood in the middle of the room, rather than at the altar, because though he appreciated the harmonic convergence of all these dynamics, he doubted that the Christian God would be of much assistance to him in this situation. On the other hand, Sun imagined that the *ban lan* spirits would enjoy demonstrating their superiority in a place that symbolized the presence of a competing deity.

"*Hēi sè . . . hóng sè . . . bì . . . bái . . . huáng,*" Sun said again, out loud this time, as he slipped on the net glasses in which he would witness the assassination. "*Jìn . . . jiǒng . . . zhǎn . . . lún . . . rǎng.*"

He made sure that the glasses' path to the net was secure, taking two extra steps to ensure that even those who programmed them would not be able to trace or record what he did. Then purely for the sake of theatricality, he traveled to the location of the man he was calling by way of the Earth program used by the Chinese military. It started with an orbital view of North America, then zoomed in to California, and then further to the Napa Valley. As it continued to grow closer to his man, Sun reveled in the rich reds, golds, and greens of the vineyards, which almost exactly matched the colors surrounding him in the church. Finally, the program came to rest on one particular swath of gold vineyard, and Sun imagined the man lying prone inside one of the rows of dying grapevines, dressed head to toe in the same yellow color, and gripping a rifle that was also painted with it.

Then his view switched to the sniper's augmented eyes, and Sun could see the yellow barrel of his rifle propped on a yellow stand in front of his face, pointed toward a gap in the yellow leaves of the grapevine in which he was concealed. Through the gap Sun could see a hill in the distance.

"Some of the vines turn red at this time of year," Sun said, "because the anthocyanins, which make tannin in wine, are trapped in the leaves and give them a burgundy color. But on others, like the ones in this vineyard, the petiole or leaf stem swells with the onset of colder and longer nights. This causes the palisade layers in the leaf to collapse and chlorophyll production to cease, turning the leaf yellow instead of green."

"Yes, Sunzi." The man said this very softly, but it was quite legible because he had audio implants as well. The suffix "zi" meant "master," and Sun especially liked it because his role model, Sun-Tzu, was also sometimes called Sunzi.

"Why are you not looking through the gun sight?" Sun barked at the man. "The time is at hand."

"I have a smaller window open in my eyes," he answered. "Which is linked to the sight. I can watch the hill through the sight, but also see around me in case someone approaches. Your link connected with the one and not the other, but I can change that."

The sniper spelled two words backward, and his cybernetic system responded by altering Sun's view so that he could also now see through the gun sight, which was fixed on a brown hill with five white stones protruding from it.

"They are late, Sunzi," the man said. "It has now passed nine o'clock. Are you sure the intelligence is correct?"

"It is my own, that I have seen with my own eyes."

Sun was bothered that the man would even ask this question, but his irritation was tempered by the knowledge of his impending victory, and the sacrifices this man was making to assure it. This "sleeper agent" had lived in the United States for over two years and had taken up this concealed position almost three days ago, subsisting without moving or eating any solid food for the entire time since then (he sipped liquid nutrients from the chinrest attached to his neck). When the sniper's work was done, he would spell a few more words backward and all of his cyber implants would self-destruct, burning his brain out along with them, so that BASS investigators would have nothing to trace and no one to question.

"Because you have the honor of assisting me in the *xing lu cai se*," Sun said, "I will show you how I know they are coming."

He manipulated his glasses to access a vidclip, which began to play in a subwindow that appeared in both his glasses and the sniper's eyes. It was a net interview broadcast about a year before, when Michael Ares first became the primary leader of BASS.

"Tell us more about your daughter Lynette," said the woman conducting the interview, "how you plan to honor her memory."

"Well, in addition to the trust fund established in her name for the Presidio School," Sun's enemy said, "Lynn and I visit her grave every Sunday morning at nine o'clock, and talk about how great she was." He flashed the charming smile that Sun so deeply resented, and added: "That's our church."

The clip ended, and General Sun said, "They will be there. The *huáng* and *hóng sè* will fly with the power of the *ban lan* spirits, and will rain down the death of *xing lu cai se* on the enemy. I will wait with you to witness this, and then to discharge you with honor."

He tilted his head back and sent one upturned hand out away from his body, to welcome the *ban lan* into him, while the fingers on his other hand found the tiny pill in his belt and dropped it into his mouth. He stared at the dark yellow leaves and gun as he recited the words again, until his eyes shut and his mouth opened wide at the rush he felt when the chemicals reached his bloodstream, and the spirits entered his soul.

27
GRAVESIDE

The unwanted thoughts that I had the day before—about the two women who were not my wife—turned into a dream, as they were prone to do, and lingered in my head even when I awoke in the morning. But as I lay in bed blinking the sleep out of my eye, something else scratched at the back of my mind . . . and then it hit me. It was Sunday morning!

I scrambled out of the bed and called Lynn from the netkit. She was fully dressed and sitting on the edge of our bed, obviously waiting for me to call.

"It's 9:07," she said, perturbed. "I was about to go by myself."

"I'm so sorry, honey. It's all this stuff going on. Just the circumstances. You know I would never forget Lynnie."

She stood up, straightening her nice clothes with her hands, and said, "Well, get your clone and tell him to meet me by the pool. I'll try not to look at him."

Then I realized that I could keep our weekly appointment if I rode with the double. Unlike me, Lynn had obviously thought this through ahead of time. It would have been even easier if she had an implant herself—then I could visit the graveside inside her. But like most educated people, she was very averse to that kind of "mind invasion," especially since I had faced a threat like that when Lynette was killed.

I told her okay, signed off from her, and chose the link to the double. It didn't work, so I had to leave an urgent notification and wait a couple minutes. Then Jon received the call, and I was looking through his eyes at the bathroom mirror again.

"Sorry," he said, toweling himself off. "I was taking a shower."

"I wonder if we should have the triplets set it up so I can access you at any time," I said.

"Is that necessary?"

I thought for a moment, then said, "I guess not. I don't see why you can't have a little privacy. But don't leave me waiting long." I looked at his body in the mirror, and added, "You're even built like me."

"They were glad to know that I work out regularly like you do. I guess it's hard to fake being in shape."

"I suppose it would be," I said, and then remembered my business. "Listen, I need you to meet Lynn by the pool and take a little walk with her. With me, too. It's something we do every week together, usually alone, but you'll have to join us this time."

"Okay," he said, now slipping his clothes on. "Does Terrey know?"

"We should let him know. It's not that private. Go by his room, or wherever he is, on the way up there."

Jon did as I said, and we were soon face-to-face with my old army buddy, who was dressed in black again. I started to tell him what was going on through the double, but that was inconvenient, so he patched my netkit through to his earpiece and we were all able to hear each other.

"That's fine," he said. "I told you how safe you are outside the house, though I wouldn't linger too long. In fact, this would be a good opportunity for that photo op I was talking about. Perfect, in fact! Would you mind if one of the *Trois* ran out and took your picture, so we can get it out on the media?"

"No, that would be okay. But give Lynn and me about ten minutes by ourselves first."

"Ace!" Terrey said. "Just leave your line open so I can call you when she comes out."

We made our way to the pool, where Lynn was waiting for us, and Jon put on the light jacket he had brought with him because of the slight chill in the autumn morning air. Lynn just started walking without taking Jon's hand, as she usually did with me, and true to her word she kept looking ahead and not sideways at him as we walked. The gravesite was on a smaller hill to the west, between our house and the one that was now occupied by Paul Rabin's widow and her three children. That house was built for Darien Anthony, but he couldn't use it now because his body lay in one of the five graves in the little cemetery, along with his young son, who had died with him and Lynette when his car was bombed. The other two graves belonged to Saul and Paul Rabin.

As Lynn and Jon walked silently along the unpaved path that led to the site, I watched Lynn through my doppelganger's eyes. He didn't look her up and down as much as he had before, probably because she had a modest coat on and there wasn't much to see. He did look a few times at her protruding belly, and many more times at her beautiful profile and the streaked blond hair that was blowing in the slight breeze. I found myself enjoying looking at her through these new eyes, literally and figuratively, and I was about to say something complimentary to her when the double beat me to the punch.

"You're very pretty," he said, watching for her reaction.

"Which one of you is saying that?" she asked, still looking straight ahead.

"Both, I would think," Jon said without hesitation. "Who wouldn't?"

"That's flattering," she said. "But I would rather just hear from Michael while we're doing this." Her notorious sensitivity to people's feelings then gave her pause, and she added, "You can practice talking for him, for when you go out in public."

"No problem," Jon said. "It's all yours, Michael number one."

"Thanks," I said in my room at the cottage.

"Thanks," Jon said on the deserted hillside.

"No, I was saying that to you, Jon."

"I know, I was just kidding."

"What?" Lynn said, finally turning to Jon in bewilderment, because she couldn't hear what I was saying. "You were just kidding that I'm pretty?" Now her equally notorious sensitivity to what others thought of her was coming out.

"No," Jon said. "You're very pretty. From now on I'll only say what Michael says."

I didn't have anything to say at the moment, so we walked the rest of the way in silence, and finally reached the gravesite. Lynn approached Lynette's blank marker and placed a fresh flower there, next to the toys and holo pictures that always rested against the bottom of the stone. The double was reading the inscriptions on the other markers, so I told him to step over next to Lynn.

"I'd put my arm around you," I said, and Jon repeated it, "but I wouldn't want you to freak out."

"Thanks," she said, cracking a little smile to go with the tears that were now trickling down both sides of her face. "She would have been six this Christmas."

"She was so sweet," I said, starting the long litany of descriptions and memories that I always repeated on these Sunday mornings at the grave, but then suddenly a shout from the netkit speakers broke my reverie and pierced my ears.

"Michael!" It was Terrey, from back at the base. I could almost feel Jon jump at the voice—he could hear it, too. But Lynn couldn't, and she was in front of him staring at the marker, so she didn't notice his reaction.

"Don't panic yet," Terrey said, "but when I told the triplets what you were doing, they had a conniption and wanted to check the numbers on your location. Just in case, get ready to take cover, if I tell you to."

"What's going on, Terrey?" I said.

"When we did the sniper sweep out to three thousand meters, we didn't know you would be walking out this far. I'm really sorry about this, it may be nothing—" He asked the triplets something, and then spoke to us again. "It's close enough that it might be best to head back to the house, just to be safe."

"Jon," I said, "tell Lynn that Terrey says we should go back, and that I'm sorry."

"Terrey says we should head back, Lynn. I'm sorry."

"What?" she said, and began to look around instinctively, which the double was also doing. We could all see the hills on three sides of us, and a nice view of the vineyards down in the valley to the west.

Jon reached out and gently grabbed Lynn's arm, to direct her back toward the house, but she shrugged his hand away and said, "What's going on?"

"Okay, the girls are done," Terrey said in staccato, "and you could possibly be too far west. Better take cover till we can get there." I noticed he was breathing hard from running through the hallways in the hill.

"There's no cover out there!" I said. "Jon, take Lynn down to the ground now, and cover her with your body, to the west!"

"Which way is west?" he said, and Lynn shouted "What?" again.

"The vineyards. Take her down, now!"

Jon dove into Lynn and pulled her toward the ground, and I heard through his ears the unmistakable sound of a bullet hissing by his head. Then I heard two more hit the gravestones near him, and even saw the chunks fly from one of them as his bouncing view pointed in that direction. Then I heard Lynn screaming something like, "Get off me!" and told Jon to ignore her protests and hold her tight.

"Is your body west of hers?" I yelled, because I couldn't tell from the shaky, chaotic images coming from his eyes.

"Yes!" he yelled back over her shouts and another bullet hiss.

"Turn on the body shield that Terrey gave you," I yelled at him, remembering that from our meeting the day before.

"I didn't bring it!" he yelled back again. Then I could hear him asking Lynn if she had hers, but she didn't either.

I could sense how exposed his body was in the direction of the shooter, and could almost feel the impact of the rounds that were about to slam into it. *Please don't let them exit into Lynn and the baby,* I thought.

Then I heard numerous bullets slam into something, but it didn't sound like flesh, and Jon's view didn't jerk from the impact as I expected it to. He heard this new sound, too, and while still holding Lynn to the ground, he turned his head so that we both could see what it was. It was Min, who had reached the gravesite from the hillside hangar bay in about three jumps. (This looked like flying when he did it, but it was actually a superhuman leap powered by some augmentations that made use of the Sabon antigravity technology.) The Chinese bodyguard now stood just to the west of Jon and Lynn, blocking the sniper's line of fire with his big body, and more than that. His arms were extended out from his sides, and the Atreides shield that was slaved to his skin also spread out away from his body, emanating vertically from his arms in both directions and creating a barrier about ten feet wide and high.

The shimmering semi-transparent shields to each side of Min looked like the wings of a high-tech protecting angel, as they repelled many more shots from the valley below. I was sure that the shielded front of his body, which was facing away from us, was also being hit by the barrage. But he stood his ground, and the shooting soon stopped after three aeros from the hillside base streaked overhead en route to the vineyards below.

"Are you hit?" I shouted to the double. "Is Lynn okay?"

"I think so," he said, shifting on the ground to see.

"Stay down. The shooting stopped, but don't count your chickens. Tell Lynn."

"Michael says stay down," he said dutifully. "And don't count our chickens."

Min and his shield also remained in place, as we all waited for a report from the valley below. It didn't take long.

"We've got him," Terrey said. "He's dead—fried his own junk. But have Min take you back to the house, just in case there's another one somewhere down here."

"I'm on the line," Min said. "I hear you." The big cyborg turned his body 180 degrees to face Lynn and Jon, with the extended shields staying exactly where they were (another impressive trick). He moved slowly toward the two bodies on the ground, telling them that they could stand up when he was close enough.

"Thank you, my friend," I said to him. "How did you know where to land and stand?"

"As I was making the jumps," Min said, wrapping Jon and Lynn in his shimmering wings, "the triplets calculated the only possible trajectory of the bullets, using the Eye and their sweep data, and they transmitted it to me right before my last jump."

"What about the baby?" Lynn asked, and I could see she was worried about being thrown to the ground so violently.

"Do you have your phone?" I said, and she got the idea. She pulled it out, brought up the BabyView app, and was relieved to see Lynley's heart beating—though it was beating slightly faster than usual.

"She'll be fine," Min said. "It takes a lot more than that to hurt a baby inside its mother. And this will make your hearts race even more . . ."

He gathered both Lynn and Jon into his arms and leapt into the air, carrying them back to a safer place closer to the house. It made me wonder how far he could jump without the weight of several people in his arms. I also wondered what we might learn from the body of the sniper and the ballistics he had fired, when Terrey and his *Trois* were done examining them.

28
ARMED TO THE TEETH

"The good news is that we're all still alive," Terrey said, when everyone was gathered together that afternoon for the first time since the gravesite episode. "The bad news is that we almost weren't."

We were meeting in the cafeteria of the mountain base, which was one of the few parts of it that had a view. It was toward the top of the hill, and one wall of it was transteel, which allowed the people inside to see out, while from outside they were hidden by a large holographic cover, similar to the one that concealed the mouth of the hangar bay, which was several floors below. The protection team had eaten some lunch—mostly the astronaut food in tubes that Terrey had brought along. They were too rattled from the events of the morning to eat normal food, even though Tyra had been faithfully testing all of it. But the sniper had gotten by Terrey and the *Trois,* so clearly something else could as well. My friend was presently addressing this failure.

"Our opponent had us in check, and almost in checkmate," he said. "Somehow he was more informed and aware than we were about the Ares' Sunday morning habits, and managed to plant the sniper just beyond the range of our sweep. He also must have correctly calculated how far out we would conduct the sweep, and he knew that when Michael and Lynn walked that far out to the graves, they would pass just barely into the sniper's range. I'm very sorry that I botched this, and put you both into danger." He nodded at Jon and Lynn, who was still too shaken to go back up to the house.

"At least we know what the yellow part of the kaleidocide is," Stephenson said. Terrey had told us that the sniper was wearing dark yellow and camouflaged in a grapevine of the same color. "And we know that part is over." Stephenson and Korcz had spent the rest of the morning extending their sweep another five hundred meters on all sides of the house, and were fairly confident that the sniper had been the only one.

"Yeah," Terrey agreed. "And we actually might know more than that. I thought to myself, *How did Sun know about your Sunday mornings?* And I had the triplets search the net about it. They found an interview where Michael was asked about remembering his daughter and shared how they visit her grave every week—obviously that was the source. Then it occurred to me: What else could the enemy have gleaned from information on the net? So we searched it from his perspective, trying to find data that could give him ideas, and we found another interview where Michael said that he and Lynn have a glass of red wine from Artesa almost every night."

That was true. I didn't remember saying it in an interview, but we did love the exclusive wines from our favorite winery, which was built into a hill between Napa and Sonoma. We kept a stash of their limited release and single vineyard wines, at over $100 per bottle, in our Le Cache portable wine cellar (over $7,000 for that beast).

"So you think he might try to poison us through the wine," I said through the room speakers, and tried to introduce a little levity: "At least Tyra will have a good time tasting all of it."

"I don't think anyone should taste or drink it," Terrey said. "It's too high on the possibility scale."

"First you tell me I can't have my bananas," Lynn spoke up, "and now you want to take away my wine? Sheesh." She was smiling, but I could tell that her hands were shaking a little.

"There's too good of a chance that Sun heard that interview."

"What about the bottles that were already here?" she said. "We can drink from them . . . I did last night. We just won't buy any new ones."

"I wouldn't even mess with the ones you already had," Terrey insisted. "At least not anything you bought in the last year or so, since that interview was broadcast. I've underestimated Sun once already, I won't again. It's too easy to substitute a bottle or introduce something into one." He shrugged at Lynn, as if to say "Sorry," when he noticed her head sagging down. "But I would keep buying them."

"What?" she said.

"Order more bottles from Artesa, to draw out any possible attempt. We'll scan the packaging for explosives, and we'll open the bottles and test the wine. If we get a positive, at least we'll know what that we found the red-colored threat, and smoked it out. And maybe we can trace the foreign elements.

"Speaking of traces," Terrey continued, "Go is working in the lab right now, a couple floors below us." I noticed for the first time that only two of the triplets were in the room—Ni and San, presumably, though I couldn't tell them apart yet. "She has the sniper's body there and will be seeing if we can retrieve any information from his implants, which is unlikely because they were so well-fried when he killed himself, and if his rifle can be traced, which is also un-likely. He's not even Chinese, so I'm assuming any connections between him and Sun are quite well-hidden. We also extracted two of the fired rounds from the ground near the graves, and she'll be studying them as well.

"There was one curious thing about the sniper, in case any of you might have any ideas. I don't know what to make of it, if anything at all. His ammuni-tion had been stored in a belt that was painted red, unlike the yellow that covered every other part of his clothing."

"So maybe the sniper was the yellow *and* the red," Stephenson said, obvi-ously interested in the colors like he was in the meaning of his dreams. "And we don't have to worry about the wine so much."

"I don't know," Terrey said. "Seems odd to me, two colors. But what was also odd is that the cases on the belt, which held the bullets, were not the typical equipment used for that purpose. The belt was a highly secure, waterproof con-tainer like we used for amphibious operations." He looked up as if he were think-ing about me, his fellow soldier, and added, "When we were in the military."

"Do you have any theories?" I asked.

"Not really," he said, "except that I'm wondering if he traveled to his position through water. But there's not any around there. Like I said, it could be nothing, but colors never seem to be random with this barmy Red wanker."

"What I'm most concerned about right now," I said, "is that Lynn was involved in this. I want her as far away from the double as possible, starting now. And Lynn, if you don't feel safe enough in the house, Min should stay with you there. Her safety is a priority over the double, Terrey. No offense, Jon."

"I agree," Terrey said. "No offense, Jon. That's fine for Min to stay with Lynn, but you should know that a tech from Chinatown Underground is on his way here to take a look at the big guy, because he took some serious pounding acting as a shield earlier. Do you have a problem with the tech coming up to the house?"

I told him I didn't, because I knew that the techs from Cyber Hole who did maintenance on Min were also refugees from Sun's autocratic regime, and had always been trusted implicitly by Saul Rabin. Besides, even if something really weird happened with the tech, I was confident that Min could protect himself and Lynn quite well, even if he was a little banged up.

"So, Lynn, you go up there," I said to her, "and I'll talk to you at the house. Okay?"

"Okay," she said, still shaken but trusting in me, and in Min. The big brown mountain of a machine-man escorted her out of the room.

"One more thing, for Lynn and Jon." I said this because looking at Min reminded me of something. "If you do go out of the house together again, for Terrey's photo op or whatever, make sure you have the shields he gave you. Now that you know why he did, hopefully you'll think to use them."

"You should be in the personal protection business, Michael," Terrey said after Lynn and Min had left.

"You're not gonna be," I barked, rather impulsively, "if you don't take care of my wife."

"Easy, mate," he said, holding his hands up. "I wanted to store her somewhere, but she—"

"I know, I know. She insisted on staying in the house. But you've got to juggle all that. That's what you're being paid for."

"Actually, it's not—I'm being paid to keep *you* alive," he said. "Anyone else is usually extra."

"Are you serious?"

"Of course I'm serious. You want me to thin out my team more, or you want me to focus on her more, you should pay me more."

"So you're saying that if I pay you a million five per day, instead of a million, my wife will be safer?"

"Yeah, she'll be on my radar more. She'll figure into the plans more."

"Okay, done. You're now being paid to protect her, too."

"That was easy," he said, and raised his eyebrows at the others in the room, who had been listening to our conversation.

"I'm not laughing, Terrey," I said. "If anything happens to her, I will hold you personally responsible."

"Whoa, mate," he said. "I'm not the one trying to kill her."

"Me. You mean trying to kill me."

"I mean I'm trying to save her life, too. Always have been. But now I'll try even harder."

A little later, I plugged one of the screens on the wall into the system at my house atop the hill base, and found Lynn moving around the kitchen, organizing and apparently beginning to prepare some dinner. She didn't like to sit still for very long under normal circumstances, and probably felt an even stronger need to keep busy under these. She also didn't like to wear an earpiece or glasses, and was one of the few people I knew who actually held her OutPhone up to her ear when she was talking on it. I had given her various earpieces and glasses over the years, and even tried an expensive gold necklace with tiny speakers and a mic built in, telling her that she could hurt her neck by working around the house with the phone wedged between her ear and shoulder, or get into an accident by holding it when she was driving. But she had consistently refused to use any of those beyond the first week or so, and usually ended up losing them (including the necklace, unfortunately). So I had given up trying to get her to change, and that's why I often used the net room equipment initially when calling her, and only switched to a more private means when necessary.

In this case I could not only see her in the kitchen, but from the cameras up on the high walls I could also see three figures in the adjoining living room. They were Min, the Chinese tech who had just arrived, and a tall A.I. tool chest that followed the tech into the room on its own power. The white robot looked something like a refrigerator with controls and displays added to its surface, and treaded legs protruding slightly from its bottom.

"I've never seen any of your maintenance, Min," I said, genuinely interested. And I became more so when I realized that I had never taken the time to find out all of the giant's capabilities. So I said to the tech, who was fiddling with the refrigerator thing, "Could we have a tour of his augmentations?"

Min and the tech said something to each other in Chinese, and I remembered that the Cyber Hole employees didn't speak English.

"Here," I said, "let me turn on the room's translation grid." I did, and then spoke to the tech again: "Can you understand me now?"

"*Shi*," he said, and right after the room said "Yes."

"Do you want me to say to you the augmentations of this man?" The room translated this with an impressive speed also, and it was surprisingly good translation. But then the man added, "Good apples." These programs were always a mixed bag, because of the complexities and colloquialisms of all languages. But I got the idea, from the "eager to please" expression on his face.

"Lynn," I said, "I think you'll find this interesting."

"Yeah, go ahead," she said distractedly, continuing whatever she was doing. "I'll be listening from over here."

The front panels of the tool chest swung open, like arms awaiting Min, who stepped into it. As he did, the whole machine sunk lower, hiding at least half of the apparatus that had been showing at the bottom, and making me glad for Lynn's sake that our wooden floors were built and treated so well. Between the outstretched "arms" of the "medical closet," as it was called, appeared a digitized display. From directly in front of the closet, where the smaller Chinese man stood, the display was overlaying Min's body and showing the tech everything he needed to see inside of it.

"I can see already what we must do," the tech said. "The shield repelled all the bullets. The clothing is not even holes, and not the skin damaged. But the force of blows on the shield pushed right shoulder back, out of line, and right hip. And plate of chest also must be moved forward tiny piece." *A little bit?* Seemed like it, but I wondered if the Chinese really used that expression. I also realized that the area around Min's right side must have been where the sniper repeatedly fired, which meant that the double and my wife had been just behind him at that spot, and well protected by him. It made me grateful again for the loyalty and help of the big bodyguard.

"My tool box can change to operating table," the tech continued. "But I do not understand if you want me to work on him here. He will be, ah . . . . without clothing, and with blood."

"You can use the medlab below," I said. "But first tell us about his equipment." I switched cameras on my screen and zoomed in so I could see the body display better.

In the halting translation, but well enough that I could understand most of it, the tech then proceeded to show me what made Min the most state-of-the-art, kickass weapon I had ever seen, even after the many years I served in British special forces. In addition to the Sabon antigravity augmentations in his legs and the Atreides shielding I had just seen in action, the seven-foot cyborg had plasteel armor plating under the skin throughout his body, and retractable rail cannons in his forearms that energized tiny caseless bullets, making them as powerful as a .50 caliber machine gun but only needing a small tunnel in his upper arms to store hundreds of them. They were also able to be fed thousands more from a rig that Min could strap on at a moment's notice, for combat or high-danger situations.

Then the tech told the cyborg to turn around, so that we could see the display of his back, which gave the term "shoulder blades" new meaning. In recesses of the plating on his upper back were stored two three-foot swords, which he could reach back and pull out anytime he wanted to wreak hand-to-hand havoc on some unfortunate enemy who would soon be "resting in pieces." Min could wield the blades with the Atreides shielding extended to his hands, so that he could wade into opponents while repelling their ballistic fire, in the event he ran out of ammunition himself. And below that was something that left me speechless—I wasn't sure whether to say "Wow" or break out laughing.

"Min," I said incredulously, "am I mistaken, or do you have a cannon in your arse?"

The weaponry was actually more in his gluteus maximus, but the big cyborg still seemed embarrassed by the question. He stepped backward, out of the medbox, to defend himself like an insecure teenager.

"I must have some way to eliminate threats from the rear, in the melee of battle. So I can fire gas and explosive rounds when needed." He lifted his big hands and shrugged his massive shoulders. "Where else could I have something like that? Not in my torso, near my vital organs. But there's plenty of room back there."

"'Rear' and 'butt' being the key words," I laughed, prodded on by his very human discomfort—a side of him I had never seen. "Let me see . . . clearing out the area with posterior emissions. Well, I guess skunks have been doing that for a long time."

"And football fans," Lynn added, from out of my camera view. I didn't even know she'd been listening.

I noticed that even the Chinese tech was smiling, though I wasn't sure it was from what Lynn said or what he was about to say.

"He has weapons in his mouth," the room's grid announced after the tech said something in Mandarin. I figured this was a wooden translation of "armed to the teeth," and again was surprised that the Chinese used that expression, too.

I didn't have long to think about it, though, because at that moment the entire mountain shuddered below the room, causing Lynn to scream out as the lights and her kitchen appliances flickered off and on with several rapid-fire tremors that grew in magnitude. Even though I was only watching from the cottage far away, I was struck hard with the sense that people were dying in the hill below, and that what killed them was racing upward toward the house.

29
FIRE

"Min!" Terrey yelled into all channels. "Get Lynn into the air—the aero in the garage." The big cyborg had already forgotten about his human embarrassment, and began to move again with the efficiency of a machine, escorting Lynn out of the kitchen before Terrey could even finish. "The lab caught fire while Go was working there, and it's spreading fast in all directions. I don't know if any of us can get to the hangar or another exit without being blocked by—"

"Wait," Lynn said, grabbing the doorway as she was ushered through it. "They told us the fire system is really good."

"True," I said quickly. "But take her up anyway, just in case." Min moved her through the door with a perfect balance of gentleness and force.

As if in response to Lynn's statement, the hill shuddered once more, presumably from the fire causing another explosion, and then the lights went completely out for a minute or more. By the time they came back on, everything was still and quiet, and the almost extrasensory perception I had developed in the military told me that whatever happened had stopped. Terrey confirmed this shortly after.

"Is everyone okay?" he asked, on all channels again. Everyone responded that they were, except for Go, so he continued. "Ni and San are plugged in to the base, and they tell me that it has an EM suppression system, so once it identified

215

the fire locations and allowed a few moments for any humans to escape, it killed the flames." This was the latest development in indoor fire safety: scientists had discovered that physics actually worked better than chemistry in fighting fire, and that waves of the right kind of electromagnetic energy could disrupt the cold plasma that made up a flame. So rather than a sprinkler system, the rooms of the base and the house above had been built with the ability to send a blast of electricity into them when a harmful fire was detected.

"The girls are making their way into the burnt area right now," Terrey continued, "to find their sister and find out what happened. In the meantime, I suggest you all make your way to the aero bay, so we can debrief but also be able to take to the air at a moment's notice. In case something else happens."

While I was telling Min to keep Lynn in the air for now, until we knew for sure what was going on, I noticed on my screen that the medbox was still standing in the living room, but there was no sign of the tech from Cyber Hole. I was thinking that he must have panicked when hearing of the fire, and run off in some random direction, until I switched cameras and noticed that he was hunched up *inside* the box. Its doors were still open, presumably because there wouldn't be enough room inside if they were closed, so I wasn't sure how he thought this would protect him from a rabid fire.

"You can come out now," I said, and the room translated it into Mandarin. He stirred slowly and sheepishly emerged from the box, only to run right back in when I added, "The fire is out." He must have been unsure about my first statement, and the translation of the second must have given him the impression that the fire was outside the room, or something frightening like that. I tried a few other ways of saying it, and finally broke through the communication barrier. I told him the way to the aero bay in the hill below, because I knew he still had to work on Min in the medical bay (if it wasn't burnt to a crisp) and wanted him to be at a place where he could be evacuated easily, like Terrey had said.

Not long after, everyone was gathered in the bay and I was looking in on them through the surveillance system there. I had to fiddle with the zoom and the audio more, because this was a very large room, since it had to be big enough to hold a number of aeros and a couple Firehawk helicopters as well. The hillside entrance, or "mouth" of the bay, also had to be quite large, of course. It was hidden from the outside by a huge holo that made it look like part of the hillside. The protection team, minus the triplets and with the addition of the Chinese tech, were huddled near several aeros at the mouth of the bay, ready to jump into them if a wave of lethal fire should suddenly start heading their way.

To make sure I could hear everything, I tuned the second screen on my wall to the double's eyes and ears, and when I did I could hear Stephenson talking to his partner as they waited for Terrey to begin the debrief (Terrey was currently talking to the triplets on his earpiece).

"You're not gonna believe this," the little man said to Korcz, with his trademark wide-eyed enthusiasm.

"Another drimm come true?" the big man said, with no enthusiasm whatsoever.

"Yeah, I had a dream about fire, since New York. I thought it was just a recapitulation of that episode, but it could be prophetic. I'll have to run the precog scale on it. But we just escaped a fire." Then his enthusiasm dimmed a bit. "Although in the dream I'm running from it."

"The more you see the dreams come true," said Tyra, who was also eavesdropping, having planted her floating chair near Korcz as she usually did, "the more you think I'm gonna die." It occurred to me that this woman was safer than anyone from the threat of a fire, because she could simply fly out of the hangar on the chair—she didn't even need a car.

"Don't listen to him," Korcz answered instead of Stephenson, requiting some of her affection, or at least showing some concern for her feelings.

"You don't think it's God, or voodoo?" Tyra said to Korcz. "I've heard a lot about both in my life. But the Catholic hoodoo isn't much different from the African voodoo, ya ask me."

"How many drimms you have at night?" Korcz asked Stephenson. "How many on the machine?"

"About ten to twenty."

"Can see anything," Korcz said with a grunt, talking to both of them now. "Can see anything you want to see."

"But you're forgetting," Stephenson objected. "We're talking statistics here. They don't all have the same precog value."

"Did you ever have a high precock," Tyra said, "and it didn't come true?"

"It's *precog*. And yes, sometimes."

"Then you don't really know, danyet?" Korcz said, "It's ahhh . . . what you call it? *Presvorninck?*"

"Random?" Tyra said.

"Da," Korcz said, still in the Russian mode, and more delighted in Tyra. "You know Russian?"

"No, I guessed," she said. "But I could learn." She sent a big grin his way, and I noticed she was prettier when she smiled. And he actually returned it, though his version of a smile made him look worse.

"I thought it was 'precock,' too," Korcz whispered to her, after Terrey had started calling the team to order, and the triplets came into the room, two of them carrying the scorched body of the third on an unfolded stretcher. I noticed immediately that a pall hung over both of them, and their skin patches were now a flat black. They had obviously turned off all the moving colors in the nanotech decorations, in honor of their sister's suffering. They asked the Chinese tech (in flawless Chinese) if they could use his box, because they didn't want to be in the med lab right now, for the same reason everyone was gathered in the bay. He was more than willing, and soon the refrigerator transformed itself into an operating table and both triplets went to work on the third. Their hands moved much faster on the table, and their bodies around it, than I was used to seeing. It was like watching a normal operation in fast forward.

"She's alive?" Stephenson asked Terrey, not wanting to bother the Asian superwomen.

"Right now she is," he answered. "It's hard to kill a cyborg."

It was difficult to tell exactly what they were doing, because they moved so fast and I didn't have a close angle, but I did notice that they turned the body over at one point and were working on the apparatus that looked like a backpack. But then Terrey interrupted my spectating of the high-speed procedure.

"Let me tell you what happened," he said. "And Ni and San can correct me if I get anything wrong. They're good at multitasking." Terrey was no longer referring to them with terms like "the Sheilas" at this time, or even the *Trois*— that and the slight change in his visage made me think he had some decent amount of concern for them. But I also realized that he may have just been worried about the tremendous amount of money they were worth to him.

"When they made their way to the lab," Terrey said, "they found that the fire had spread one floor up and down, and about fifty meters in every direction before the suppression system stopped it. But the floors and walls retained integrity for the most part, so the girls were able to get to the lab and examine it briefly before bringing Go over here. That combined with their watching of the security video leading up to when the first explosion destroyed the camera, this is what we know: Go had finished her exam of the sniper's body and had turned to the ballistics that we took out of the ground near the gravesite. She put the first bullet under a faucet to wash it off, and it practically exploded in her hands. It dropped in the sink, of course, and then the sink flared up and the faucet itself blew off its base, with balls of fire showering out into the rest of the room. Then the whole cabinet down into the floor was on fire. Go herself was on fire by then, but she grabbed the extinguisher on the other side of the room and tried to use it on the flames around her. But when she did, they exploded more and the camera was knocked out."

Stephenson looked at Korcz, Korcz looked at Tyra, and Tyra looked back at both of them.

"We know what that is," she said.

"Yes, you do, and if I hadn't seen the report of what happened to you all at the Money lab in New York, I wouldn't have realized what happened nearly this soon. But we're looking at the same kind of chemical concoction that reacts with H_2O. It was in the Money lab that day, and it was in the bullet that the sniper fired this morning. We don't see it too often, because I guess the only people crazy enough to use it are the mob and Chinese assassins. No offense." He said the last to Tyra.

"No, s'okay," she said. "I think my people are crazy, too—that's why I ratted on 'em."

"What is actually a more amazing coincidence," Terrey continued, "is that this base has an EM system, instead of a sprinkler system. I'm sure that bastard Sun was assuming that there would be a sprinkler system, and when the bullet ignited by contact with water, there would be a flood of more water coming out of the ceilings, and that would ignite, too, and we'd all be toast in about five minutes, with no time to escape the firestorm. It's an ingenious plan, actually, but we were very lucky."

We all then became aware that Ni and San had finished their work at the table, and both of them were now slumped down to the ground, crying hard. It was obvious to all of us that Go had died while they were working on her, until just a few moments later, when her charred body began moving on the table. She sat up slowly, but everyone watching still jumped a bit when she did. She slid her feet out over the edge of the box, so the other two sisters could clearly see her, but strangely they didn't react at all, or even seem to care that she was alive. And then she started weeping, too, burying her head in a blackened hand. I was really confused, but I didn't have time to think about it, because Stephenson was about to discover the next threat we would face.

"So this is the red color of the kaleidocide," the little man said. "Explosives, red, makes sense."

"Yes, I suppose," Terrey said, distracted and looking back and forth between Stephenson and the triplets. His distraction, and that of the triplets, was undoubtedly why Stephenson was the one, rather than they, who figured out the danger we were all in.

"And you said that the sniper had a red belt that held all his ammunition," the ex-professor said. "A belt that was waterproof."

"Yes," Terrey said meaningfully, starting to catch on.

"So it probably wasn't just one of the bullets that was engineered to react with water, it was all of them. And they couldn't count on us bringing the bullets into the base, and they couldn't count on us getting the bullets wet. So there must be another way that this red method was supposed to work."

"They're not catching fire in the ground," I said, partly to let them know I was still watching them. "So it must take more water to cause the reaction than what's in the ground, or in a human body."

"Right," Stephenson said, and then added what most of us were already thinking. "Is there any rain in the forecast? We'd have to find the bullets before it rains, or at least be prepared to stop the fire if it starts."

"How could we stop something like that out there, while it's raining, for

God sake?" This was from Tyra. "Even in the city with just snow on the ground, it ate up three blocks."

"Girls, I'm so sorry," Terrey said to the triplets, who were already wiping the last tears off their face, and bringing themselves back to their feet. "But you're gonna have to help us with this. Can you start by checking the forecast?"

"Yes," one of them said, either Ni or San. Then right after, Go said from the table, "I'm in a lot of pain." She said this in the direction of the Chinese tech, presumably because he was the only one there who could do anything about it. But he just stared into space, so then, with an amazing presence of mind considering her condition, she said the same thing to him in Mandarin. When she did he scurried into action, liberating a needle from the side of his medbox and sticking her with it. In no time she was lying prone again, out cold and with no care in the world.

"No rain in any of the forecasts online," said the triplet who had dived into the net.

We were all silent for a while, as if we knew there was something else, and yet couldn't place it. Finally, I was the one who broke the silence.

"Aw hell," I said, and the others looked up in the air when they heard my voice coming from the faraway speakers. "When does the dew form?"

"Aw hell is right," Terrey said, as everyone else realized it, too, and the triplets silently conferred with the net and with each other, and did some fairly complex calculations.

"Dew point in this area," one of them said after a few moments, "should be in about twenty minutes, with a four-minute margin of error either way."

"Wow, okay," Terrey said. "Let's get everyone in the air right now." The triplets carried their sister to one of the flying cars and everyone else moved toward one—except for Stephenson, who stepped over to Terrey.

"Drop me at the gravesite and I'll find the bullets," the little man said, and saw Terrey's puzzled look. "I had a dream that I'll survive the fire."

"What if it was the fire that already happened?" Terrey asked as he walked toward a car.

"No, I know how this works, trust me."

"Well I sure don't," Terrey said. "But I'd rather you do it than lose another of my *Trois,* so fine. Let's go."

I made sure that Min was keeping Lynn in the air in our aero, and high enough that there would be no possible danger to her. I even told him to check the fuel gauge, just to be safe, and there was no issue with that. Then I sat back and mentally strapped myself in, feeling helpless as usual to do anything about what I was watching, but also a bit relieved that I wasn't there on the hill. The prospect of such an aggressive fire was frightening, even for a hardened veteran of combat like me. I went so far as to wonder whether a fire started there by those chemicals and spreading by dew could possibly reach as far as the cottage, four or five miles away. This prompted me to tell Terrey to notify the Valley's emergency services, informing them to ready themselves and not to use water— or anything containing water—on this kind of fire. Preventative burning on swaths of ground would probably be the only recourse. Terrey thanked me and said that the triplets were already on it.

Three aeros exited the hill through the holo and flew toward the gravesite. In one was Terrey, the nervous Chinese tech, and Jon, with whom I was now riding so I could see what happened through his eyes. In the second aero was Korcz, Stephenson, and Tyra. And in the third were the triplets, with two in the front seat and their unconscious sister lying in the back. Forgetting their grief for now, they were busy reviewing video from the sniper attack, calculating where the bullets could have ended up, and preparing some handheld equipment that could locate the bullets on and in the ground. I was amazed to think that they had something like this on hand, but I found out later that they actually had equipment built into their own cyborg bodies that could be removed and customized for emergency use.

When the aeros reached the gravesite, Terrey stayed high in the air to overlook the operation and protect the double, while the other two aeros flew down close to the graves. Stephenson jumped out onto the ground, and despite Terrey's hesitations so did one of the triplets, who handed Stephenson a scanning device. They both immediately went to work under the instructions of the triplet who stayed in the aero, and who knew what direction the bullets had gone. Many of them were on top of the ground where Min's shield had blocked them, but others had lodged in the hill beyond the little cemetery. When Stephenson and the girl found them, they were simply sticking them in their pockets, because there had been no time to get any kind of bags or containers, and the protective belt worn by the sniper had been destroyed in the fire, of course.

"I have to admire the plan," Terrey said from the seat next to me—or next to my double, I should say. "If the sniper doesn't hit his target, the bullets he fired become bombs that can start a chain reaction and spread to the house. I'm glad that the ground slopes up from the line of fire, with the hills in that direction. Imagine if the bullets traveled for miles before lodging . . . we'd never have a chance of finding them before they were ignited by the dew."

At his mention of the dew, both Jon and I looked out the window of the aero at the hills and the descending sun. I didn't know much about science, but I remembered that dew forms when a surface cools fast enough that the water in the air near it condenses into droplets, and that was the "dew point" that the triplet referred to. Obviously the combustive reaction with the chemicals could only take place with water in its liquid state, and probably with only a certain amount of mass. So to keep the bullets from igniting, we just had to get them off the ground before the droplets formed on or around them.

"Get all the rounds off the surface first, the ones that Min blocked," I said, thinking about this more. "The ones that were unblocked entered the ground, and won't come in contact with the dew, because the dew's only on the surface. We'll have to dig them out later, sometime before it rains, but they're not a danger right now."

"Did you hear that, Stephenson and San?" Terrey said, not sure whether my audio was still on all channels. They said that they did, so obviously it was.

Ni, who was the triplet in the aero, started to count down the minutes as time progressed, which became nerve-racking as the projected deadline approached. Her sister even seemed rattled when there were three minutes left before the possibility of combustion, and she asked Terrey if he wanted her to stay on the ground or get back in the aero. It occurred to me that even a superhuman like her could be fearful of fire, especially when her own sister had just been fried by it. Terrey thought a moment and told her to get back in the aero, which implied rather strongly that he was more worried about losing her than losing our house. But I guess it made sense—he wasn't being paid to protect our house.

After swooping lower so that her sister could jump into the door of her aero, Ni announced that there was one minute left until the danger point. But Stephenson kept hopping around, eagerly scanning for more bullets and stuffing them in his pants pocket when he found them. Korcz was flying the aero that would pick him up, but fairly high in the air, probably because he and Tyra had recently experienced the fearsome power of the kind of flames that might ignite here at any moment.

Ni announced that we had now passed the point where dew might form and combustion could begin. In fact, she added that a lot of dew may have already formed, but none of it had contacted a bullet yet. So Terrey said that Stephenson might want to think about getting some altitude.

"I think I got all the ones on the surface here, where Min was." He started walking past the graves and toward the hill behind them. "Let's see if any of the ones that went past are close to the surface. You know they could be, depending on the angle. Better safe than sorry."

Right after he said this, we could see him stop in his tracks and listen as behind him there was a loud hiss, then another, and then another, all at the gravesite. We hadn't realized that a few of the sniper's bullets had hit the gravestones themselves, one lodging halfway in a marker and the others falling to the ground. Whether they all got wet at once, or whether one did and then ignited the others, a conflagration immediately engulfed the gravesite and started spreading outward.

I couldn't believe that such a tiny object could start something like this, or that such an uncommon chemical reaction could spread and sustain as it did, but I watched it with my own eyes (through Jon's, of course). *This is what it was engineered to do,* I thought, *and it's doing it.* The torrent of fire was so violent that Stephenson took off running in panic, rather than wait for the aero to come down and get him, and the flames followed so hard on his heels that he couldn't even put enough distance between him and them, or stop running long enough to get picked up.

30
THE CHOSEN ONE

I'm so glad I did all that biking back in New York, **Stephenson thought as** he raced for his life from the fire spreading behind him. He could have such a casual thought because he was utterly confident that the flames wouldn't overtake him, since this was déjà vu all over again. Early that morning he had watched a recorded dream on his new rig in which he was running from fire and made it safely. The precog rating was high, according to his Dreamscape software, and here he was living it out. Nothing had ever seemed more real to him than this.

"You have to jump so we can grab you!" Korcz was yelling in his earpiece, over the din of the fire behind him. "Or stop so we can pick you up!" He saw the aero hovering just behind and above his right shoulder, and believed that his Russian friend was willing to try to get him. But Stephenson wasn't interested in a rescue attempt right now. His lack of panic allowed him to think logically about his predicament, and he could see that his current course was best. Jumping for an open door or window as he ran might land him back on the ground with an injury, in which case he would be overtaken by the flames and die. Besides, Korcz was flying the car, so the one who would be "grabbing" him would be the Black Italian woman, who was not very athletic, to say the least. Stopping or even slowing down to be picked up would be very risky at the rate the fire was spreading, and could endanger Korcz and Tyra as well.

No, he decided to keep running until there was enough space between him and the flames, or until he reached somewhere safe, like where he was headed.

"I can make it to the house!" he yelled back.

"The house will have dew on it too, danyet?" Korcz offered, but Stephenson was thinking that it would have a safety system like the hill base had. It had to, because in his dream he had ended up safe from the fire. He was about to yell a question about this over the comm, hoping someone would know the answer, but he was now huffing and puffing too hard from the exertion, and when he stumbled slightly, his earpiece fell out. Now he really felt he had no choice but to continue the run for the house—he couldn't even communicate with Korcz to coordinate a rescue.

So he shut out all other considerations and focused on making it to the veranda of the house, which was about a football field's length ahead of him.

When he was about halfway there, breathing much heavier now, some flames from behind shot around him on the right and curved into his path. They seemed to be picking up momentum as they spread. He swerved to the left for about ten strides, and then had to turn back to the right when the charge of the fire brigade gained on him because of the angle he had to take. When he did head to the right again, he expected to be engulfed by the flames, but fortunately they had moved to the right themselves, and he found a narrow alley through which he reached the veranda.

He dove across the cement tiles and practically fell against the door in exhaustion, but it was locked. So he turned around to face the oncoming fire, leaning back against the paned glass out of both fear and fatigue. The flames rushed up to the edge of the veranda, like a stampede of raging demons coming to claim his soul. At that moment his confidence waned for the first time, but also at that moment the closest flames suddenly stopped and dissipated. The wall of fire had receded ten to twenty feet back from the veranda and couldn't come any farther. Instead it spread sideways, and Stephenson could see it moving around the house both ways, still very energetic and destructive of the flora on the hill. But it could cause no damage to the structure.

Adrenaline shot through his body, and he pushed himself away from the door and out to the edge of the veranda, where he could gloat over the defeated fire. He threw his arms up and let out a series of whoops like he had just won the Super Bowl. Then he punched the air, kicked his feet up, and spun around a few times saying "Yes! Yes!" over and over again. He barely noticed Korcz landing the aero next to him on the veranda, and then approaching him when he got out of the car.

"Are you having a seizure or something?" the big man asked.

Stephenson threw his arms around Korcz and gave him a big hug, though his arms barely reached around his partner and his head was only as high as his stomach.

"Okey, okey," Korcz said, removing the little man's arms from him, and then grimaced. "Ughh. You are sweating."

Suddenly the odd couple both looked at each other, both realizing the same terrible thing at the same time.

"Oh no," Stephenson said, his celebration abruptly ending. He looked down at the protruding bulge in the right pocket of his increasingly wet pants, where he had put the bullets that became deadly when touched by water! He started to reach into the pocket with his hand to take them out, but then realized his hand was sweaty, too. So he did the only thing he could do—fumbled his belt open as fast as he could, dropped his pants, and pulled them off. Then he bounded back toward the edge of the veranda and threw the pants out onto the scorched swath of ground where the flames had been repelled by the EM pulse.

His adrenaline newly renewed, Stephenson threw his arms up and whooped again several times, then turned around to see Korcz, who had backed away from him toward the aero for fear of an explosion. Tyra looked out of its open window and studied his purple boxers, which were hanging halfway down. But this didn't bother him either. All he could think of was that his theories about Dreamscape were once again confirmed, now more than ever—he felt like the Christopher Columbus or Copernicus of the human mind.

"What did I tell you, Valeri? I dreamt it, it was rated, it happened! Again! Do you believe me now?"

"I believe you are lucky to be alive," the Russian said. "And that you should get into the car. After we lost comm with you, Mr. Ares told us that the house was protected like the base. But the more the fire spreads, the hotter it gets. The house might not be able to stand."

Stephenson took his friend's advice, but after they got in the car and lifted off, he couldn't help but return to the topic of his life-defining revelations.

"Who would have ever thought this would happen to me? I can tell the future, Valeri, I can. Not some psychic mumbo jumbo, this is the real thing. This is gonna change the world, once people start finding out more about it. It taps into the questions humanity has always had. And you've absolutely *got to do it,* Valeri. Wouldn't you rather be on the new frontier like me, instead of just like everybody else?"

"I'd rather have my pants on," Korcz said seriously, but Stephenson laughed anyway. Until he glanced at the backseat and Tyra, who was not laughing, because the more truth there was in his claims, the more likely she was going to die soon.

Speaking of death, someone else was apparently facing the prospect of it, because the voice of Michael Ares came on in the car, saying that one of the aeros had spotted his neighbors on a nearby hill, fleeing from the fire. Since Stephenson had been so eager to face the dangers of the fire, he said, and because the people in his car were more expendable than those in the other three, they should fly over and try to help them. He gave Korcz the coordinates, and as they sped in the direction of the other BASS house on the next hill over, Ares told them more about the situation. It was a mother (Liria Rabin) and her two eight-year-old twin daughters, Hilly and Jessa. They liked to ride their horses almost every evening at sunset, with one of the girls riding with Liria and the other learning to ride herself. They must have gotten cut off from their house by the fire, and now they were almost surrounded by it.

As Korcz flew past the Rabins' house on its left, Stephenson could tell that its safety systems had stopped the flames like the Ares's house had, but also like the other situation, the flames had spread around it and cut off access to it, like the BASS leader had said. And on the far side of the house he could now see the two horses, with the woman and both girls on one of them—she must have brought the second child over in order to protect her. She clutched one of the twins in front of her, and the other was holding on to her torso from behind. The riderless horse was panicking at the fire, stomping in circles, but the woman must have been really good, even with only one arm to use, because the one she was riding was much calmer. They were in just as much danger, however, because the fire was closing in on them. There seemed to be a way out to the east, where they could have run away from the fire, but Stephenson guessed that they didn't know it was there because of all the smoke. By the time the aero arrived near them, however, there would be no way out. They were indeed going to die, unless he and Korcz could do something.

"Can we use the thing that shoots out and grabs people?" Stephenson said to Korcz and the disembodied Ares. "That was used to rescue us in New York?"

"No," Ares's voice replied. "The aeros from the base aren't equipped with RATS—they're more basic models than the ones we use to show off in other cities. You'll have to land and pick them up."

Stephenson felt an adrenaline surge through his body again, but this time it was fear. He hadn't dreamt about this, and realized there was no reason he couldn't die right now, even though he had survived earlier.

"If you could see," he said as a kind of knee-jerk reaction, "you would see that there's no way we could land and make it out. We'd all buy it."

"I'm actually watching you from Terrey's aero," Ares said, "which is higher and north of you. From this angle it looks like there's some room to the east of her."

"Well, from this angle down here, it looks pretty tight."

Korcz now had the aero almost on top of the woman, though she hadn't noticed yet because she was waving smoke out of her eyes and trying to move the horse away from the closest flames. Stephenson found a button for the PA system on the windshield HUD, and activated it.

"Ma'am, we're here to help you," he said, and saw that the PA was working because she craned her neck upward at his voice. "Follow my voice—we'll try to land to your east, and pick you up." He kept saying "This way" as Korcz maneuvered that way to find a spot to set down, and she made some progress in that direction, but the visibility was too low for her to be sure where to go, and she was clinging to the girls as her horse staggered its path.

Korcz set the aero down on the ground with a thud, facing Liria's direction, but they couldn't even see her now because of the smoke. They watched for her to emerge, and suddenly saw a horse run out of the smoke in their direction, but it was the riderless horse. It bolted to the right of the car, but then the wall of flame rushed into the area it had just entered and Stephenson could hear it squealing in pain. He didn't know that horses could scream that loud, but when he saw the flames approaching on his right, he knew that he would be screaming himself if they didn't change positions.

"We have to move!" Korcz shouted, obviously thinking the same thing, and lifted the car back off the ground again.

"Okay, just stay there, ma'am," Stephenson said into the PA. "We're coming back to you."

When they reached the woman, and were hovering just above her, they had literally seconds before the fire would engulf her and the girls. By some miracle, they were in the crook of a V-shaped opening between the flames. But the opening was closing fast, so all Korcz could do was bring the right side of the aero down near the top of the horse, and Stephenson stretched himself out of the window to grasp the first daughter, who was standing on her mother's lap and was pushed up by her so Stephenson could reach her. He did, and managed to haul her into the car. As she scrambled to the backseat, Stephenson extended himself back out of the window, but the fire had now reached the horse's legs and Liria was struggling to control it and maneuver the other daughter around to her front.

"Move closer!" Stephenson yelled to Korcz.

"I'm trying!" Korcz yelled back. But the horse was moving too much in the flames.

Suddenly both the aero and the horse lurched toward each other at just the right time, and Stephenson yelled, "Now!" The mother instinctively gave up on trying to shift her daughter with just one arm, let go of the reins, and jerked her own body sideways to push the girl upward and into Stephenson's grasp. She fell off the horse and into the fire, of course, but Stephenson did manage to hold on to her daughter with his small but strong arms. He hauled her inside and pushed her into the backseat, where Tyra was already comforting her sister. Korcz hovered over the spot, and even dipped lower toward the ground, as if he could do something else. But there was nothing else to do except listen to the screams of the horse, which were hideous but thankfully loud enough to cover any other screams that might have been heard.

Stephenson closed the window as fast as he could and looked at Korcz. Silently they agreed that nothing else could be done, and so Korcz lifted the aero higher away from the scene until they couldn't hear anything from down there. For the next half hour or so, they hung in the sky as they waited for word that they could return to the hill base and the Ares house, when the blackened brush on the hill around them had fully burnt out. They also watched the outside edges of the fire spread to other properties on the hills nearby, and even used the zoom function on the windshield camera to watch some of the houses burn before the local fire services could stop them with the pre-burnt borders they created.

Worst of all, they were tortured by the cries of "Mommy!" and the questions about her from the twin girls in the backseat. Thankfully Tyra was there to lend a woman's touch—she did seem to be more cut out to be a female than a male. Stephenson felt really bad for the girls and their mother, but he also had to admit that he felt an exhilaration that he had made it through this latest adventure, and that he would live to explore his dreams further. He felt invincible, like he had been chosen to pioneer a path that would actually change the world.

When they finally were cleared to return to the base, the protection team gathered again in the aero bay, to debrief yet another close call. Despite all the damage that had been caused by this latest assassination attempt, Michael Ares and the double were still both alive, as was Lynn Ares, who had asked the big cyborg bodyguard to take her back to the house above. For this reason, Stephenson unfortunately misjudged the mood, and sidled up next to Terrey as the team was gathering, telling him excitedly about how his dream of the fire came true and how his Dreamscape rig could revolutionize the personal protection business. As he was talking to Terrey, he half-perceived the double comforting the twins next to the parked aero not far away, with the little girls hugging him in a way that showed they couldn't tell the difference between him and the real Michael Ares. He also half-noticed that Jon stood up and looked in his direction at some point, saying, "No, I've never hit anyone" and then looking at his fist and adding, "The knuckles at the base, right."

Stephenson didn't think anything of this because he was concentrating on his animated one-way conversation with Terrey, but as he was looking at the Aussie protection expert he suddenly realized the double had moved to his side and taken a swing at him before he could do anything about it. The hammer blow from the bigger man connected with the top side of his cheek and his temple, where it hurt like hell but wouldn't cause damage like a broken jaw, and Stephenson fell sideways and sprawled onto the floor. He shook his head in pain as Jon was shaking his hand for the same reason, and started to push himself up to let the man have it twice as hard. But Terrey put his hand out and down near him, as if to say "Don't" without using the word. So the little man just wrapped his arms around his knees and fumed.

"Michael," Terrey said to the double. "We having a blue?"

The double looked down for a minute, listening to his internal audio and rubbing his hand. Then he said, "This man should have more respect for the dead, and for the girls." He gestured over to the twins, who were clinging to both sides of Tyra's chair and watching the scene. Then he listened some more, and said, "He shouldn't be flapping his bloody trap when he just failed to save their mother. He should be . . . more sorry, especially when they're around."

"I hear you, Michael," Terrey said. "But what do you expect him to do, shed tears? If he doesn't have a cry, you'll have a blue?" The handsome man smirked a bit at his play on words. Maybe he was trying to remove some of the tension, but Stephenson guessed that it wouldn't go over well with the man who was speaking through the double. And he was right, because Jon looked down and frowned noticeably.

"I *really* don't want to hit *him*," Jon said, seemingly to himself. He looked up at Terrey, obviously fearful that the voice inside was going to tell him to do just that.

I would have taken him out pretty hard if I'd been allowed to, Stephenson thought. *I shudder to think of what Terrey would do to him.*

31

CONFRONTATIONS

My sense of helplessness and resentment for being stuck in my room at the cottage was never higher than during the fire. I actually thought of getting in the car and driving to the hill, or telling someone to come pick me up in an aero, but then of course I realized that it was pointless and would accomplish nothing. So I had to sit in my plush chair while telling someone else what to do, and watching Liria Rabin fall to her death and leave her children motherless. Her husband Paul and her father-in-law Saul had died a year earlier in events surrounding my ascension to the throne of BASS, and now she herself was a casualty by simply being an acquaintance of mine.

Ironically, I had been trying to *help* Liria and her kids by moving her into the second house that BASS had built on Stags Leap, because she no longer wanted to stay in the one she had shared with a murderous husband. Lynn and I both thought that it would help her make a new start in her life, which had been shrouded in sadness for as long as we'd known her, though we didn't know why until her husband's evil machinations were revealed. But the first thing that went wrong with our well-intentioned but misguided plan was that her teenage son John refused to move into the house, because he was resentful of BASS and me. So since the move she had been without her son, who was staying in an apartment near the old house in Marin County, and now her other two children were without a father or mother.

That's why I was so upset after talking to the sobbing twins through the double, and why I told him to hit Stephenson. The only mitigation of my anger was that Hilly and Jessa didn't seem to notice that the double was not me, which bode well for our trip to the city the next day, and my chances of surviving the kaleidocide—though not Jon's, because they would surely still be trying to kill him, instead of looking for me. But the effectiveness of the double was a cold comfort compared to the fate that had befallen the twins, and so I was only half-kidding when I said that Jon should hit Terrey, too, when my old friend was being flippant about it.

"I guess I just want him to be sorry," I said to Jon, in answer to Terrey's last question, then gave the double a reminder. "Speak like you're me, because the girls are still there. If they sense something's different, they may talk to someone and blow our cover." That was why I couldn't project my voice through the hangar speakers like before, but had to speak through the man who was pretending to be me.

"I guess I just want him to be sorry," Jon said to Terrey.

"I'm sorry, okay?" Stephenson said, pulling himself up to his feet and rubbing the side of his face. "I'm really sorry."

"I don't want you to *say* you're sorry," I said, and the double repeated it. "I want you to *be* sorry."

"All right, mate," Terrey said, now showing his firm hand to the double. "He said he was sorry, let's drop it."

"What about you, *mate*?" I said to Terrey with a tone, and Jon did a pretty good job of reproducing it. "Are you sorry? I'm seeing reports of five houses and a winery that burned down in that fire, with three more casualties. Is this what you call *Protection Guaranteed*?" We both used the tone again on the last two words.

"Yeah, I'm sorry," Terrey said, and then pointed at Jon's face. "I'm sorry, you pommy bastard. I'm sorry that you can't see that you're still alive, even after all that, and so is everyone else I'm paid to protect. Now stop slagging us and go do something to help, if you're worried about how things are turning out. Figure out what to do with the two little girls over there—we certainly can't do that. Find out what you can about Sun's problem with you, so we can maybe head off these attacks before they start." He waited to see if I would react, and when I didn't he continued in a more conciliatory manner. "And while you're looking at the bright side, like being alive, think about the good things we learned. Sun and his people didn't know about the fire systems in the hill here, if they even know about the base at all. They assumed you would have a sprinkler system that would make the fire worse, or at least nothing that could stop their little chemical masterpiece. But we beat their best shots, and now we know what three of the colors were." He counted them on his fingers. "Blue/green, assault team. Yellow, sniper. Red, explosives. We could be over halfway there, my man."

"I hope their best shots aren't yet to come, because someone won't make it through." Jon repeated the words, and must have felt weird doing it, because he was the first "someone" who probably wouldn't make it. "But you're right, I'll take care of the girls and see what I can find out."

I told Jon to take the girls up to Lynn at the house, with minimal conversation on his part, and turned off my link to him so I could discuss this with Lynn before he got there. When Terrey saw what the double was doing, he told Tyra and Korcz to go with him, the former for the kids' sake and the latter to relieve Min, who still needed maintenance. Then Terrey had the triplets take the Cyber Hole tech with them to the medlab, so that he could work on Min there but also help them with their sister's burns.

I dialed the house and found Lynn sitting in the living room with Min standing nearby, but not too close. She had her head in her hands, and had obviously been waiting for my call.

"Michael, this is horrible!" she said after I said hello. "What should we do about Hilly and Jessa? John will flip out when he hears about this, and the fire caused all that damage, and the media will be all over this. And I'm concerned about this Tyra person, you've put her in such danger, and I heard she's from the mob, and her family won't sit still for this, they kill people for a lot less, and—"

"That's why I called you, Lynn" I interrupted her. "I wanted to talk to you about Hilly and Jessa, because they're on their way up to you."

"What?" she gasped, but then thought a moment. "Oh yes, of course, they should come up here. They need some place to stay for now, can't go back to their house now, or be by themselves."

"Right, my thoughts exactly. Can you take care of them until we figure out what to do?"

"Yeah, okay. Could I see your face, please? I don't like talking to the air."

I switched the screen to two-way and told the net room at the house to display me—after I locked my door, which was behind me, to make sure Ange-lee or Chris didn't come walking in while I was talking to Lynn.

"There you are," she said with a half-grin that forced its way onto her tearful face. "Wherever you are."

"So they're okay to stay here for now," I said. "But not for long. This is hardly a stable environment right now. Which is why I can't do much about them, with everything I need to do to help the double and Terrey. Would you be able to make some calls and check into family members, and maybe the Presidio?" It was occurring to me as I spoke that this kind of project would probably be very good for Lynn at this point—it would give her something to do and get her mind off everything else.

"I don't know about the orphanage, Michael. I thought about that, but I don't know much about what's been going on there lately."

"Well, maybe this is a reason for you to get more involved, like we talked about."

She was about to answer when the twins and their three adult escorts came through the door from the garage. I wondered why they didn't knock or ring at the door, but then remembered that Lynn had told the team that they didn't have to do that when they entered the living area, since she had provided a couple meals for them and they had a meeting there. So all five arrivals were soon standing in the living room, and neither Lynn nor I thought about the fact that my image was displayed on one side of the room.

"Thorn said I should take your place," Korcz said to Min. "You can go to medlab."

As Min left, Hilly and Jessa were looking at my face on the screen, then at the double standing next to them, then at each other.

"Why is Uncle Michael on there?" one of them said to Lynn. Only then did I realize what was happening, and I switched off the screen abruptly, feeling like an idiot. I went back inside the double, so I could help him deal with this, but Lynn was already on it.

"Oh, that was just some home video of Uncle Michael," she said unconvincingly. "But now he's here, the real him . . . in the flesh." She was even more unconvincing as she gestured at the double, but fortunately Hilly and Jessa seemed satisfied with her answer and didn't pursue the issue any further. Of course, they had much bigger worries at the time.

A relieved Lynn now leapt off the couch and did her best to comfort and love on the girls—thankfully she was much better with children than she was with lying. As she talked to them, I told Jon that he should excuse himself and leave Tyra to help with them, because I wanted to keep him away from Lynn even more now, after the events of the day. A deep paranoia was growing in me as I wondered what insidious plot would unfold next in this truth-is-stranger-than-fiction scenario.

After she finished with the girls, Lynn told Tyra to put a show on for them, and the double excused himself as I had said. Before he left, though, Lynn looked at him meaningfully and said she was going up to her room, then repeated, "I'm going up to my room." I got the point, and I soon switched my screen from inside Jon to the netview in our bedroom. And I made sure to put my face on the display so Lynn didn't have to talk to the air.

"I'm soaked with sweat," she said, and grunted disapprovingly as she felt her back and underarms. Then she retreated into the big walk-in closet to change, as she always did, but she left the door open. So by switching my camera view to a corner of the room, I could see her in there. She stood facing the other way as she undressed, and I noticed again that she didn't even look pregnant from the back. I enjoyed watching her and wondered why I was ever tempted by other women like Tara and Angelee. Lynn had it all—I liked the way she looked and more importantly, I liked the way she was. But against all sense, I guess one woman just wasn't enough sometimes, even a really good one.

"How did you even know about the property damage from the fire?" I asked when she emerged from the closet.

"Min and I watched it from the aero, and the news, too." She sat down on the bed and massaged her swelled belly. "Michael, I'm afraid about what John Rabin will do when he hears about his mother. He already hates us, and he made those threats and all."

"First of all," I said, "he might hate me or BASS, but he doesn't hate you. I don't know why you always say 'us,' like you're taking this stuff on yourself, when you don't have to. Second, I'll put him under BASS surveillance, and have some peacers take him into custody if there's anything suspicious. If the leader of the biggest country on the planet hasn't managed to kill me yet, I don't think one teenager is much of a danger.

"And what's this about Tyra?" I continued, trying to put her—and therefore the baby—more at ease. "You're worried about the mob coming after us if something happens to her, but I already asked Terrey about that a while ago. He said he checked on it, because he was worried about the same thing, and found out that her father doesn't have a problem with what she's doing. Tyrone doesn't want to kill her himself, but he doesn't mind if she dies. I know it sounds weird to our ears, but these people are different from us, and that's the story I got from Terrey."

"If that's what he says," she shrugged. "But I have another issue with her being here."

"Which is?"

"The dream thing."

"Oh, no."

"No, really," she said. "If there's anything to what Stephenson says, then it's not right to keep her here. If you know she's going to die and you don't send her away, that's like killing her yourself."

"Come on, Lynn," I said incredulously. "You're making some serious leaps of logic here. It's like saying . . ." I thought for a moment. "It's like saying, 'In case Santa happens to exist, we shouldn't buy presents,' or something like that."

"So what if she gets poisoned and dies? What are you going to think then?"

"I'll think I'm glad it wasn't me, or you."

"That is *so* cold," she said, with a gasp before and a shiver after. "We're back where we were a year ago, Michael. Death is everywhere with this job. Lynette, Darien, Saul, Paul, Liria . . . now it's gonna be this woman and that creepy double and who knows who else. And speaking of creepy, is that big ugly Russian going to be guarding me from now on? I want Min here, if anybody."

"Min will be back soon. But what's wrong with Korcz?"

"I don't know. Like I said, he's just kind of creepy."

"He's just kind of from another country, and had a bad case of acne when he was younger. Look, Lynn, we just have to hold on and get through this. It's not like we can change what's going on."

"Terrey said you could find out something that would stop it."

"He said I should look," I corrected her. "But I don't even know what I'm looking for."

"Well, look for it anyway!" she shouted, and her head was back in her hands again.

"I will," I said, trying to remain calm. "But in the meantime, just focus on helping Hilly and Jessa and leave the rest to me and Terrey. Okay?"

"Okay," she finally said through her hands. I thought of asking her to see Lynley on the BabyView app again, but decided not to because I was afraid it would provoke the we-can't-bring-a-child-into-this-sick-world mode she got in from time to time. So I said good-bye and hung up.

When I did, I noticed there were some words again on my second screen.

YON: I MUST DO MORE NOW, BECAUSE MY SISTER IS GONE. I MAY NOT BE ABLE TO TALK TO YOU AS MUCH. WILL YOU MISS ME?

"Can I talk to you like this?" I said, looking around the room instinctively and wondering about her reference to her sister being "gone." She must have meant "out of action," because Go hadn't died.

YON: YES, BUT NOT LONG TIME. I ONLY HAVE A SHORT WINDOW BEFORE MY SISTERS WILL DISCOVER ME.

"Which one are you?" I asked.

YON: THE PRETTY ONE. LOL.

That helps a lot, I thought to myself. But then the words were gone off the screen, and I knew she was gone, too. Bizarre. I thought about asking Terrey if he knew what was going on with this, but gut instinct held me back. For all I knew, it might come in handy at some point to have a "secret" relationship with one of the triplets.

Besides, Lynn's words "Look for it anyway!" were echoing in my head, and I felt like I needed to do something to appease her. I also felt resentful toward her, but then reminded myself that she wasn't used to this kind of death and destruction like I was. So I told the net room to only interrupt me for Lynn or Terrey, and fired up the Taiwan holo again, so I could relive some of the death and destruction that I myself had been responsible for.

32
EXTRACTION

I found the spot in the holo recording where I had left off, after I told Admiral Carter that I would be disobeying his orders by going after the fellow officer who was being tortured. And just like that, I was back in the Lungmen power plant, wearing the black insertion suit that was made of a polymer version of plasteel and protected me from most scans and bullets. My enemies weren't hidden, however, because I could see their locations in a display on my cutting edge eye rig, which was programmed with the specs of the plant and uplinked to a surveillance satellite. And they wouldn't be protected from my bullets, because the special caseless ones loaded into my Alliant Trinity couldn't be stopped even by the Spider Kevlar worn by the Chinese soldiers.

I was heavily outnumbered, however, so I had to formulate a plan for the best way to move to the control room quickly and efficiently. I did this while I was trotting up the steps to the spent-fuel room at the top of the reactor, adjusting the settings on the goggles for what I was going to do. When I reached the door, I pulled the Trinity from its spot on the back of my shoulder, and practiced switching between the three barrels with my fingers on the controls, so I was ready to do it rapidly. Then I moved the circular tool array to the middle of my back and secured it there. The small detonators I had removed from the generator room were still magnetized to the array and linked to my goggles so I could control them if I wanted to.

As soon as I felt ready, I pushed open the door and shot the soldier inside it who was facing my way the most. Then I rushed the other one as I shot him, so I could catch him before he hit the ground and use his body as a shield. It didn't work out quite as I planned, and I ended up on the floor with my back pressed against the wall. But I was able to keep the man's body in front of most of mine, so I could line up my next move with that added protection.

The spent-fuel room was the biggest open space in the plant, with a bluish expanse of water stretching away from me in a long rectangle, and a high ceiling that housed a movable crane for manipulating the radioactive fuel cells at the bottom of the deep pool. In the middle of the long room, stretching above the pool from side to side, was a catwalk on which were two more Red soldiers. They had no doubt chosen that spot because they could see everything in the big room from there, and so they saw me now and started firing in my direction. A few of their initial shots connected, but only with their comrade's body, and between his Kevlar and my insertion suit I was in no danger from exiting rounds.

I fired the grappling monofilament out of another barrel on the Trinity and watched as it streaked to a spot above the catwalk and the soldiers. The microscopic line was too small to be seen with the naked eye, but the designers covered the flat sides with reflective material so that its location could be detected, especially in the enhanced view of my goggles. The flat sides also enabled the monofilament to be protracted and retracted by the grapple mechanism inside the gun—it gripped those minuscule sides in a way that could never have worked with the two edges, which were the sharpest objects known to man. The razor-like end and edges of the monofilament were what allowed it to enter any substance toward which it was shot, and a "smart head" on the end of the line caused it to turn sideways once it did. That was how the line adhered to the target surface and could hold a large amount of weight, and the head would contract so the line could be withdrawn from the surface and retracted back into the gun. It also allowed the monofilament to be used as a weapon, like a kind of ridiculously lethal whip.

I gripped the gun firmly with both hands in front of the soldier's body, so I could hold onto it, too, and pulled us both forward and off the ground by retracting the grapple line. When we were suspended above one end of the pool, I stopped the retraction, and we swung across the surface of the pool and under the catwalk, where the two living soldiers were still firing at me. Not for long, though, because the monofilament sliced right through the middle of the catwalk, and they both fell into the blue pool, sinking like stones toward the canisters of radioactive waste at the bottom.

My swing wasn't even impaired by the halving of the catwalk, and it dutifully deposited me on the floor at the other end of the pool, after I dropped the soldier's body in it on the way. Another soldier was now coming through the door on that side, so I backed behind the cover of a wall girder while the grapple line released from the ceiling and flew back into the gun. Then in the next second, I switched barrels and shot the guard around the girder. And the second one that came through the door.

I knew that these Reds had alerted the rest to my presence, but I wanted that to happen so many of them would be drawn away from the control room. I wasn't disappointed.

By the time I reached the elevator shaft between the reactor and the control building, my goggles showed me that a swarm of enemies were already coming up the stairways on each side of the shaft, and that someone in the control room had frozen the elevator at the very top. They had opened all the doors on both sides of the open shaft as well, presumably in case I decided to shimmy down it. Unfortunately for them, however, I didn't shimmy but fired the grapple line into the bottom of the elevator car above me, jumped into the shaft, and dropped down it at a high speed. The soldiers had figured out by now that they couldn't locate me with any eyeware they had, because of my suit, so they were limited to natural sight in the dark stairwells. And they must have turned off their comms to keep me from picking up any chatter with my superior scanning tech. So they weren't coordinating well and ended up making an amateur mistake by trying to shoot me through the doors on the sides of the shaft. The only thing any of them hit were the other soldiers in the doorway across from them—this happened on at least two of the five floors. I could see their forms fall sideways in the goggles window I was using to monitor enemy locations.

This gave me an idea for the bottom of the shaft, so I dropped all the way to the bottom of it and bounced right back up out of sight one second later. Sure enough, the Reds on both sides fired when they saw me, and shot each other there, too. They thought they had me in a killbox, but they were the only ones who ended up dead. And I mean all of them, because while I was suspended just above the bottom floor I grabbed four of the detonators off the tool array on my back and threw a pair into each doorway below me, like grenades. They bounced into the hallways where the soldiers crouched and blew them all to kingdom come when I double-tapped the control pad on the side of my eye rig.

I had taken a bit of a chance that my passage could be blocked from that blast, but fortunately I was able to pick my way through it quickly and then progress to the control room by way of a cat-and-mouse game with the remaining guards. They couldn't scan me, but I knew where all of them were, and I said another prayer of thanks to American technology. When I had almost reached my entry point to the control room, I dropped a bunch of detonators into two hallways on the side of me where most of the remaining soldiers were, and then cut them off with a big explosion that made it feel like the whole building might come down.

A side benefit of this was that General Ho panicked and sent some of his forces out the other side of the control room, perhaps assuming that I'd be where the explosion wasn't, or maybe just to find out what was going on. But he should have kept them with him, because I found it rather easy now to blast a wall open remotely with some more of their detonators, drop through the ceiling on the other side of the room, and have the Trinity next to Ho's head before anyone in the room could do anything about it.

"I am unarmed," the Chinese general said in perfect English, raising his arms halfway and showing me both sides of his hands.

"Everyone out," I said to his remaining staff, and I added the Chinese word for "Go"—one of the few I'd learned—in case any of them didn't understand. They all scurried out, the lives of generals being especially sacrosanct in a militaristic and autocratic system like the PRC.

"You all right?" I said to Talon 2, who was strapped naked to a chair nearby, horrible wounds on his torso and the parts below it, and pools of blood on the floor under him. He could only grunt in response. He wouldn't be having any kids without some major reconstructive surgery, but at least he was still alive.

"I have many armed men out there," Ho said, gesturing to the open door that his staff had exited through. "They will be regrouping and coming for me soon. Your friend can't walk, so you will not be able to carry him and hold me hostage. You will not be able to escape in that way."

I looked at Ho's bloody hands, and then down at my nearly dead friend.

"You're right," I said, and shot Ho in the head.

I did so because I didn't have time to tie him up, or watch him while I rescued my fellow officer. It was him or us, like all war. And this Red bastard definitely deserved it.

I untied my friend and hauled him over to the insertion coffin that Ho's soldiers had brought to the control room for him to inspect. I stuffed him into it as tightly as I could, face up, and did the same with myself, right on top of him. Once I located the controls with my hand and synched them to my goggles, I had to toss my tool array and the Trinity out onto the floor in order to get the cover to close on our two bodies. But eventually it did, after some squirming, and I was now ready to burn all the coffin's remaining power for its secondary function as an extraction vessel. I just hoped there was enough to actually get us out.

I extended the fins on each side of the sleek black vehicle and hit the thrusters, softly at first because I needed to maneuver out of the room and through a few hallways to get outside the building. I used the laser from the tool array on the front of the coffin to cut through a locked door, and then left it on to clear out the Chinese soldiers who were coming down the last hallway toward me. The lasers had run out of power by the time I punched through the last door to the outside, but fortunately the thrusters had not. I pointed the nose of the coffin at a 45-degree angle toward the eastern sky, as gunfire from more approaching soldiers clanged off its surface, and sent it soaring up and away from them like a punted football with blue fire coming out of its tail.

In my eye rig, which was linked to the front camera of the coffin, I could see blue sky for a while, then blue seawater after the HUD informed me that all propulsive power was depleted. Fortunately there was enough electricity left to activate the coffin's floater ring, or it would have sunk like a stone and literally become a coffin. But as it turned out, we drifted on the surface of the water until we were retrieved about twenty minutes later. In the meantime, the Taiwanese army easily wiped out the remaining Chinese and reacquired the power plant.

Back in my room at the cottage, I didn't watch the last part of the holo, of course. There was nothing to see except salt water, so I turned it off and remembered some of the things that had happened after that.

The first thing that came to mind was rather random and insignificant, and it was the jokes that some of the sub crew made about me and a naked man being stuffed into the tiny coffin for a half hour in that position. I told them off and put a quick end to such so-called humor, partly because I was angry at the suffering of the man who survived, and also because the man who didn't survive had actually been gay. Talon 1 had been a good soldier, and now he was a hero who had been tortured to death for his country. So I refused to tolerate any jokes that day, even though we had won the battle.

The other memory I had was that a senior officer told me that Admiral Carter had to be talked into picking us up, because he was so bothered by my insubordination, and probably knew he wouldn't be able to fully prosecute me because of the outcome. I found out that bastards come in white as well as red, when Carter swore to me in private that he would do everything in his power to make it hard on me if I stayed in the service. And when he was promoted to Defense Minister because of the success of the Taiwan operation, I knew he could make good on those threats. So since I couldn't shoot him in the head like I did to Ho, I left the British military and ultimately England itself, ending up in the Bay Area working for BASS. But before I left my home country, some of the less political people near the king told him that I was the reason for the success in Taiwan, and Noel I did deign to knight me for my "distinguished military service." Knighting was much more common these days than it had been in centuries past, but I still appreciated being thrown that royal bone.

As I stood up from my chair in the cottage bedroom, and looked around to bring myself back to this reality, I felt the ebb of adrenaline that had coursed through my body while I watched the holo from Taiwan, and the remnants of the anger that had fueled me back then. I also felt some guilt and regret now at shooting General Ho in cold blood like that, something I didn't even come close to feeling when it happened, nor at any time when I was in the military. I don't know if it was being out for a while or getting married or having children or what, but the process of being desensitized as a soldier had started to reverse itself in recent years. So now I had the worst possible combination of feeling bad when I hurt people, but still being able to do it rather easily and effectively.

Right now that anger and guilt was directed at the fact that even after re-living the whole episode in Taiwan, I didn't feel any closer to understanding why Zhang Sun hated me enough to expend this amount of resources to kill me. Nor did I have anything that could be used against him, as Terrey hoped I would find. The search that was running while I watched the holo, supplied with images of those close to General Sun, failed to identify any faces of family members that had died in my assault. It only registered General Ho as a close associate, which made sense because Sun was his immediate superior. What made it more frustrating was that in the back of my mind, I felt that there *was* something in the holo that pertained to my situation. But I couldn't place it, and I didn't know if it was just because I was thinking along those lines to begin with.

I thought of talking to Saul's ghost again, but remembered the frustration I had with it last time, and the fact that its programming wouldn't reveal anything the old man didn't want me to know. I needed to talk to someone living who might know more than I did, even though Terrey had told me not to spend much time on the wider net, or talking to anyone that was not a part of our secure loop. Stanford Glenn was someone like that, and there was another "splinter" in the back of my mind when I thought about my last conversation with him. So I resolved to ask Terrey if I could risk a call to him, and if the triplets could make it secure.

But for now I was ready to get some sleep. I was surprised by how late it was, and downright shocked when I thought back at everything that I had witnessed in just one day. A sniper attack, the fire in the base and outside of it, and the recording of the Taiwan operation—even *watching* all of that was exhausting. I thought of my house guests, however, for the first time in many hours, and stepped out of the room to check on them. Angelee and the boy must have been asleep in their room, because all I found in the living area was a note on the table from her, carefully placed next to a plate of dinner she had made for me.

I ate half of the food and put the rest in the refrigerator, thinking the whole time what a great wife the little lady would make for someone. Then I climbed into bed and set the alarm so I would be up in time to prepare the double for his big trip to the city. But if I had known what was going to happen in another bed that day, I would have stayed in mine.

33
FINALLY

I woke up before the alarm went off and lay in the bed for quite a while, thinking through the day to come. It would take all my meager management skills, working at their highest efficiency, to pull off what the double needed to do with BASS in general, and one Internal Security Officer in particular.

As I got up to take a shower, so I could be alert as possible, I could briefly hear the faint voices of Angelee and Chris in another part of the house. They were dutifully not bothering me, and I was so distracted with what I had to do that I didn't think of going out to greet them at all. In my mind, the girl's misplaced hopes about me were working out beautifully for both of us, because I was confident that she would stay right here and gladly provide anything I needed, and it was also the best thing for her and Chris to be staying here right now. I did feel bad that she would have to be let down at some point, but hardly had time to worry about that now.

When I came out of the shower, I first called Terrey to make sure that he would take care of all the security concerns, so I could focus on my ride with the double.

"Live forever, man," I said when he came on.

"Never die young, mate," he said in return. "I love this idea, it kills so many birds. Michael Ares makes a public appearance, but not too much of one. You appoint a spokesperson, so she can talk about things and give us a credible reason to keep the double out of the public eye."

And my almost-affair with Tara will finally be ended, I thought to myself. But I said, "Yeah, it should work out well, as long as Jon doesn't get killed. I'm hoping you can handle the Protection Guaranteed part so I can concentrate on what he's saying and doing."

"Absolutely, my boy. Me and the *Trois* have it covered. Or I should say the *Deux,* since Go is still recovering and getting worked on by the Cyber Hole tech when he's done with Min. But we're more than up for the task. We've neutralized the assault team, sniper, and bomb methods, so we just have to prepare for the other ones that have been used in the past, and be as ready as we can for anything new. Poison: We simply won't let Jon eat or drink anything while he's at the castle. Accidents: We'll have BASS clear any other aeros out of the sky while he's on the way, and on the way back. Betrayal: We can never totally eliminate all possibilities of that, but we'll be with him the whole time he's in the castle and limit his interactions there. Except he will have to talk to this Sheila you're promoting to the spokesperson job. Are you sure she couldn't have been turned against you?" He was referring to Tara, of course.

"Yes," I said with a chuckle. "Very sure."

"Oh, you clever boy," he said, showing how clever he was himself, by picking up my unintentional vibe. But then he got back to business: "And we don't have to worry about the members of the Protection Team, of course, because they know that the double is not you, and they have no idea where you are."

"Why do you say it that way?" I asked. "Is there an issue with somebody?"

"No, no. We did it right. You picked 'em, and they didn't have any connection with you. We're good."

"Terrey . . . ," I said, raising the last syllable.

"No, really, mate. If I had anything substantial, I would tell you. But I don't want you to get paranoid. Just trust me, we're good."

"Okay," I said, stretching out the last syllable of that word, because it didn't feel entirely okay. But as he said, I had to trust him. Time was of the essence, now as ever. So I moved on to the next subject: "I need to check in with a couple of my lieutenants, because it's been a while. Should I call them while Jon's on the way, and only use audio?"

"Like I said before," Terrey answered, "I wouldn't talk to people other than us on the net unless you really have to."

"I thought you would say that, so I came up with an idea. We put the BASS people on the video in the aero, and have Jon wear an earpiece, so it looks like he's getting reports from other places while he's talking to them. That would explain it, if they notice him pausing to listen to me."

"Ace!" Terrey said. "I like it. I'll tell you, Michael, this whole thing has just kept coming together, even all the details. Dickensian, like I said."

"Except for the woman who died, and the triplet who got fried."

"Well, you know what they say about omelets." Then it was his turn to chuckle. "Speaking of being fried."

That was a saying Saul had used, and I briefly wondered if Terrey had ever talked to the old man, or his ghost for that matter. But then I realized that was highly unlikely, and it was a very common phrase. I also wondered, as I had many times before, whether his flippancy was a kind of cover for a heart that did care about what happened to people, at least to some degree.

"You mentioned assassination methods that we wouldn't know about," I said, "because they've never been used before."

"Yeah, I've had a few thoughts, like what I would do if I was Sun. I might try something a little different from the traitor thing, especially if I couldn't turn anyone, and have a single assassin infiltrate or wait somewhere, for a closeup kill. And I might try some kind of cyber attack, turning security systems against us, something like that. But truth be told, the *Trois* are so good with that stuff, almost omniscient really, that I don't think it could work."

"Oh, speaking of them seeing everything," I said. "When I meet with Tara at the castle—I mean when the double does—I want it to be private."

Terrey grunted, half playfully but half businesslike. "That's up to you, if you're sure she's safe. It's your office, and she's the head of Internal Security, so you can probably keep us out even if we wanted to listen in. But we'll stay away, if you're sure."

"I'm sure," I said, and after ironing out a few more details with Terrey, I switched the screen and audio to inside the double. He was already dressed in some of my business clothes that I had kept in one of the base residence rooms, and was waiting in the aero bay for his ride to the city. While he was waiting, I started to prep him for the conversations he would be having on the way to the city. He seemed to be genuinely excited about playing the role of an important person, and presumably had abandoned the plan to commit suicide that he was set on just five days before. Whether it was this new adventure, or the large amount of money promised to him if he survived, or both, it was interesting to note how self-destructive thoughts could disappear when a person was given something to live for.

One of the triplets came over and reminded him about his injection of the Makeover I.S. He nervously apologized that he had always been a forgetful person, muttering something about being a teacher, and pulled one of the little triangles out from a pocket. While he was shooting the chemicals into his bloodstream, I asked him if he knew whether they had eliminated the AIMS virus from his system. He said that they hadn't, judging from the last test the triplets had done on him, but "they said it looked hopeful."

When the time came to leave, Terry and Ni flew out of the bay in one aero, San in a second one by herself, and Jon and Min in the third. Terrey had informed Lynn that he needed Min to go with the double, because the big cyborg would be expected to accompany me to the castle, and because the threat to the double was the highest. But he must have picked up on my wife's lack of comfort with Korcz, because he stationed him and Stephenson in the garage and on the veranda, respectively. I didn't know it at the time, but there was another reason why Terrey wanted Korcz to stay at the house that day. Tyra, for her part, was not needed at the castle and was helping with the twins while Lynn tried to figure out where they could go.

Min was driving the aero, but was very good at double-tasking (and triple-, and quadruple-, etc.), so I told him to call the lieutenants and keep the lighting inside the car minimal, so these rather close associates of mine wouldn't be seeing the double too clearly in close-up. I wasn't worried much about it, however, because the Makeover was so impressive. I was a little more concerned about Jon's ability to seem natural with me talking in his head, so I had him wear the ear-piece and press his finger to it from time to time, as I had planned.

The first person we talked to was Anne Madison, who had been absolutely indispensable in helping me with the financial side of BASS since I became its chief executive officer a year earlier. True to their form, Saul and Paul Rabin had their hands in the money management much more than they should have, and the way it had always functioned at BASS died with them. So I looked for the most knowledgeable and loyal department head I could find, discovered Madison, and tapped her as controller. I had never been good with numbers, so I left the day-to-day supervision to her, and tried to only intervene on bigger picture issues.

In this brief meeting, she gave me a report on the overall picture and then raised some questions about the $1,500,000 per day that was now being trans-ferred to the overseas account of Protection G. She was asking about budget allocation and tax issues, but I sensed that underneath there was some suspicion about how necessary this expense really was—probably because she repeated the current $6,000,000 total several times in the conversation, and added that "in four days it will be twice that amount." I wasn't surprised or bothered by this, because she had no idea the kind of threat I was facing, and for security reasons I couldn't tell her. So I just assured her that it was indeed necessary and expected her to make it work. That's how we functioned at BASS—the only way such a top-heavy monster could.

Jon did very well talking for me during that conversation, and he was an old pro by the end of the second one, which was with my executive peacer Cal James. This man filled the position that belonged to Darien Anthony and me, before D's death and my promotion to the top of the company. He told me what was happening on the law enforcement side of BASS, which thankfully con-tained nothing out of the ordinary, and very few decisions for me to make and to communicate through the double. There was no indication at all that Madison or James recognized the switch we had made. In fact, it went so well that I thought of asking James before I hung up if he had noticed anything different about me, and telling him that I got a haircut when he said no. I resisted that temptation, of course, but I was getting excited about the very real possibility that Tara would think she was talking to me at the castle. I was prepared with a contingency plan if she didn't, but it would be much better if she did.

I commended Jon for his performance, and left him alone for the rest of the aero ride, so that he could enjoy this unique experience that no one else in the world could have. He watched the inlets of the North Bay below him after passing over the crammed metropolises of Napa and Vallejo, and glanced occasionally at the other two aeros flanking his like a fighter escort. He also commented on how quiet the engine was, and received a long lecture from Min on the facts of how the Sabon technology worked—only the facts that we had decided to make public, however, which were not enough for someone to reproduce it.

Min was also in tour guide mode when they reached the city, briefly mentioning the repaired Golden Gate Bridge to the right and Alcatraz Island to the left, but then spending a while talking about the castle when the huge thirty-story square building came more into view. This was the second time recently that I seemed to notice a personal pride coming out of the big Chinese cyborg, as he told the story of how Saul Rabin had transformed the top of Nob Hill, the highest and most central point in the city, to a base of operations for the company that ruled the new city-state of San Francisco. Min even made no apology, as I tended to do, when he pointed out how Saul had repaired the exterior of the gothic Grace Cathedral next to the castle, but transformed the interior and ten levels below ground into a high-tech jail. Nor did he flinch when calling it by its new oxymoronic name, the "Grace Confinement Center," but continued in stride to describe the system of tunnels that snaked out from below the castle into various parts of the city, allowing the BASS peacers to be ubiquitous by moving freely both under the ground and in the sky above.

By the time Min's travelogue was done, they had reached the massive castle and flown into an aero bay on one side of the building, and I was feeling good enough about the double to make his disguise complete.

"Do you want to wear my guns?" I asked him. "I usually do when I'm working."

"I don't know how to use them," he said, a little nervously. "I never have."

"That's all right. Just don't pull them out of the holsters unless you really need to for some reason. And if you do, I'll tell you what to do. It's not rocket science."

"Where are they?" he said. I told him to sit up a little, press a particular button on the features center, and watch the driver's seat. Min had landed the vehicle and exited it by now, so Jon could see the two boas and their holster belt, which were embedded in the bottom back of the driver's seat, slide over to the passenger side. Then I told him to sit back, lift his jacket, and strap the belt on just above his. He then pulled his jacket down to conceal the guns and stepped out of the car, commenting that being armed was already making him feel a lot safer. For some reason a quote from Saul's ghost came to mind when he said this—something it had said when talking about Saul's own violent death: "He who lives by the sword will die by the sword."

If I would have known what was about to happen, I would have made my own translation of that text: "He who lives by the double will die by the double." But for now Jon was still doing well, moving through the castle with confidence, saying hello in passing to those employees I told him to. He didn't have to make the rounds right now, because after the meeting with Tara there would be an hour or so that he could do that, before the press conference announcing her promotion to the new BASS position. This was assuming that she accepted the position and its attendant conditions, as I was hoping she would.

Terrey and one of the triplets went off with some BASS security agents to monitor the whole castle and the city around it, but Min and the other Japanese cyborg accompanied Jon as he made his way to my office. They rode an elevator up several floors, and then a horizontal lift almost the rest of the way, and found Tara waiting in the hallway outside my door.

Min used his security clearance to open the door, while Jon looked Tara up and down. I could almost hear him thinking "Wow" as he did, and I felt a little embarrassed, even though I was only riding with him and looking through his eyes. It wasn't an altogether unpleasant experience, of course, because Tara was Tara, but it also wasn't conducive to what I wanted to accomplish here, so I told Jon to take it easy with the gawking and go into the office. He did, and Min and San stayed outside in the hall. I had noticed that the female cyborg had been studying Tara also, which made me think that the triplets were not sexless after all. But later I found out that San was looking at her clothes, because they were all a color that had not been used in the kaleidocide yet.

"Did you get the job description I sent to you this morning?" I told Jon to say this as soon as we entered the room, and I also told him to sit down behind my desk, so that it would be between him and Tara.

"Yes, I read it," she said as she sat down in a chair on the other side of the desk and crossed her long legs. "But I don't have any terrific candidates to suggest."

"That's okay," I and the double said. "You're the terrific candidate."

She was only a little surprised, but she was definitely pleased, as I could tell from the all-too-familiar look on her face. I needed to curb her enthusiasm fast, before she got the wrong impression, so I prompted the double for his longest speech yet.

"I sent it to you because I want to give you that job," he said, and she smiled wide again. "But listen, Tara, it's not what you think. There are some conditions." Her smile waned immediately, and already I was feeling bad. I thought it would be so much easier to do this through the double, but the conversation had barely started and my usual hesitations had, too. And it didn't help that Jon's eyes, and therefore mine, were staring at her beautiful brown face and blue eyes—a devastating hybrid from a handsome black father and a gorgeous white mother. Nor did it help when Jon looked down at her body—he could only imagine what it looked like under her gray business suit, but unfortunately I knew.

On the other hand, it must have done some good for me to not be in the room with her, because for the first time ever I actually managed to get it out.

"After I promote you to this position, you'll be able to get any job you want with companies that are looking for ISec or PR people. The sky will be the limit for you. And you'll have to take one of those jobs somewhere else. Because that's part of the deal, Tara. I can't have us both around BASS like this, and still make it in my marriage. I don't want to talk about it at all, I just want you to take the job at a press conference that I scheduled here in about an hour, with the understanding that you will put your résumé out and take something else in the next three months."

Jon did well at repeating all this, and I didn't see any indication that Tara wondered about him at all. She obviously was accepting him as me, though she wasn't happy with what he was saying. But I wasn't bothered as much by that now, because I was feeling euphoric that I had finally done what I should have done years ago. In fact, it felt so good that I was ready to go even further.

"It's been over for a long time for us," Jon added with the same confidence I had when I spoke it into his head. "So we need to go our separate ways."

"Can't I think about this for a while?" Tara asked.

"No. There is a window, and this is it. I really want you to do this today."

"Well, I guess if you really want me to," she said, seeming much more vulnerable than usual, and making me wonder if her long-time love for me, and all she said about waiting for me, was about more than just sex and power. Then she added, "How can I not do what you want?"

I was about to tell the double to quit while we were ahead, end the meeting, and go back outside for his walking tour of the castle. But then I was forced to do that too abruptly, because in the brief silence I could hear a scream from outside my room at the cottage. Angelee was yelling "Help!" repeatedly, and it seemed to be coming from the pool in the back.

"Jon," I said to the double as I sprang to my feet. "You're on your own for now, I have an emergency to deal with. End the meeting and go outside."

I didn't know if he caught my final words, because I was running out of the door as I said them.

34
BRAIN DAMAGE

I darted toward the repeated screams of "Help!" and ended up outside at the pool, where I found Angelee crouched on the ground next to it. Chris's body was lying limp across her lap, and I feared the worst.

"What happened?"

"He must have climbed over the corner into the deep end," she said, and was crying now that she was done screaming for help. "I was reading a little while I was watching him, and he must have done it quietly at a moment when I was looking down. When I looked up, he was already under the water, I'm not sure how long. I was being careful, 'cause he tried it a few times before . . ."

"So no head or neck injury?" I said quickly and forcefully, trying to get her to focus on what mattered right now. "He was just under the water for a while?"

"No, I don't think so," she said between sobs. "No head or neck, I don't think."

"Okay, put him down on the ground." I helped her to do so, because she seemed to be at least partially in shock, and I performed CPR on him after checking his breathing and pulse. Every time I pressed on his little chest, her body jerked and she put her hand to her mouth. Obviously she hadn't seen this much before, if at all, and she didn't watch TV, so I had to reassure her between attempts that I was doing this to help her son.

After a few rounds, he gagged and then gasped when I turned him over and let him spit up. But he remained unconscious, so I carried him inside the house, laid him on the couch, and grabbed a big first-aid kit from the closet in the front hall (a standard piece of equipment anywhere BASS agents were known to stay). I unrolled the medmat on the floor next to the couch, moved Chris onto it so that he was lying flat on his back, and attached the oxygen mask to his face.

"Vera," I said to the house, "could you examine the boy, please?"

"Yes, Michael."

Little LED lights flickered on around the outside edges of the medmat, indicating that Vera had turned it on and was now linking with it and calling up her medical programs.

"Is he okay?" Angelee asked, obviously not knowing that the lack of consciousness was a sign of possible brain damage.

"I think so," I lied, but added, "We'll see" to prepare her for the worst.

"I don't see any broken bones or sprains, Michael," Vera said. "Or head, neck, or spine trauma. Breathing is normal right now, but CO_2 and PH levels are high, especially in the brain, so it seems that he was without oxygen. His body is also wet, and there is also some water in his lungs, so it could be that he was almost drowned."

"Yes, Vera, that's what happened. We know that." I thought for a moment, and almost went to another room to talk with the house privately, but I already felt bad for Angelee and didn't want to hide more from her. "Is there any reason that it would be unsafe for his mother to drive him to St. Helena hospital?"

"I can call emergency services right now, Michael."

"No, don't do that. Answer my question."

"No, Michael, I don't believe it would be unsafe for his mother to drive him to St. Helena hospital. But keep the oxygen mask on, and keep in mind that I am not a licensed medical provider, and therefore not liable for the results of taking advice from me." *Only in these days would a virtual person be programmed to avoid a lawsuit,* I thought.

"That's what you should do," I told Angelee. I didn't want to risk the arrival of an emergency team, considering that they could recognize me if I talked to them, or might demand my name. The fact that neither of us owned the house would require explanation, and so on, and the incident might require a police report or visit anyway. There was no other way for the boy to be treated than for Angelee to take him to the hospital, not mentioning me or even giving this address. I would just have to hope that he would be okay, and hope that she would be able to return here. I wasn't sure how it might affect me if she couldn't, but for now I needed to calm her down enough for her to be able to get to the hospital, and not blow my cover somehow in the process. She was now sobbing uncontrollably again.

"Angelee," I said tenderly as I moved to the couch next to her, and put my arms around her. She snuggled tightly against me, and the crying became less. "It's going to be okay. The hospital here is really good. Just say the name to the car and it will show you how to get there. It's only about fifteen minutes away." Then I had a stroke of genius and said that I couldn't go with her, but would pray for her. At that she stopped crying completely, though she was still obviously troubled.

"I should have watched him more closely," she said, "or not let him near the pool at all, because he's been acting up, worse than I've ever seen him." She paused, as if debating whether to say the next part. "I think he got really excited when you were with us on Saturday, and you watched the movie with us. He always did that with his dad, and he hasn't been able to for a year. But then you were gone all day yesterday. It's like he got his hopes up, and then was really angry and disappointed when you weren't there. So he's been very disappointed, and even maybe a little . . . what would you call it . . . self-destructive?"

"You think he was trying to hurt himself?" I asked.

"I don't know, maybe deep down. The heart is like a deep river, my husband always used to say."

"Well, I'll try to be there more for him," I said, not knowing what else to say at this time. And speaking of hearts, I could almost feel hers racing against my side when I said it. So I gently moved her away a little with my hands, and added, "But for that to happen, he will have to get better. So I need you to take him to the hospital. And when you do, make sure you don't say anything about me or this place, okay? You may not have to give them an address if you refuse, but if you have to, you can give them the address of the shelter you were at, and we'll take care of any bills later. Do you understand?"

She nodded, but I asked her to repeat the instructions for me, in case she was in shock to some degree and was not competent to pull this off. She did repeat them, and seemed fine, so I went back down to the floor and looked at the boy carefully again, having Vera repeat her scan with the medmat to make sure we weren't missing anything. We weren't, so I said I would carry the boy to the car and turn on its medical system, explaining to Angelee that the car could do the same thing that Vera did, and monitor him as he lay on the seat. There was also a fully equipped treatment kit built into the car. This was standard equipment on all BASS vehicles now, after I had almost died while riding in an aero a year before. One of the good things that had come out of that grueling experience was that I realized it would be helpful for our peacers to have such a system in the vehicles as a "first response," for when we or others were injured in similar incidents.

As I was about to carry the boy out, Angelee realized that she was still in Tara's white swimsuit, and needed to change before she could make the drive to the hospital. She had been too distracted by the crisis to be self-conscious about her attire, and I felt proud of the fact that I hadn't noticed it either. But then the feeling of pride transitioned to shame when she walked away from me toward her room, and I noticed that the bottom piece of the suit was askew from jumping in the pool and rescuing Chris, and because it was a little big on her to begin with. I did look away eventually, telling myself I wasn't such a bad guy and hearing the words "special hell" echo again in my mind.

I gave her a minute or so, then took the boy to the car and situated him in it. When she came jogging out of the house, I showed her how to monitor his breathing and heart rate, and what to do if either failed. I told her as a last resort she could use the car's phone to call emergency services, because the boy's life was more important than the possibility of having to change my protection plan. I also told her that she could call me from the car if she had to tell me anything—like if the worst happened—but that she should try to avoid that if possible. She gave me a big hug and thanked me for saving his life as well as hers, and I cautioned her about the fact that Chris wasn't better yet. As she drove away, I wondered what would happen if he died at the hospital (I had heard of such near-drowning fatalities), or if he was permanently brain-damaged, or if he ended up in a coma for a long time.

But then I remembered that I had to get back into my room and walk the double through the press conference for Tara's promotion. I had actually forgotten about it during the crisis with Chris, and wondered how the double had managed his walking tour of the castle without me. *I'm sure it wasn't difficult*, I thought.

When I sat back down in my chair, I noticed the screen with Jon's view on it was blank. I tried a few different things, like turning it off and on again, and speaking to him in case the audio was still on, but to no avail. I also tried to access the net room in my office, but it was turned off, and I knew that if Tara had blocked it with her codes, it would take me a while to override them. So I called Terrey.

"Where have you been?" my friend said before I could get a word out. "We've stayed out of your office like you asked, but I didn't know you were going to be in there this long. It's almost time for the press conference."

"I had a problem here with my . . . helper."

"What kind of problem? She wasn't turned, was she?"

"No, she's not a traitor," I said, wondering how Terrey knew my helper was a woman. I hadn't told him that, as far as I knew. "It was something else. It's okay. But I'm trying to link with the double, and I can't."

"What?" he said, suddenly as panicked as a cool customer like him could be. "I thought you were riding with him. He never came out of the office."

I felt a flash of panic then, too—not because Jon's life could be in danger, but because my plan to finally break up with Tara could be in jeopardy. Terrey was thinking the former, of course, so he immediately brought Min and San onto the line and asked them what they knew from their post outside my office. Both of them said that neither the double nor Tara had come out of it yet, and San added that she had been suspicious of the fact that Tara's clothes were all gray, and that could be one of the colors in the kaleidocide. While she was saying this, I opened a link to Min on my second screen, and now I was looking through his eyes at the Japanese girl.

"But Michael said that he trusts her," Terrey said, and then added to me,

"Completely, I think you said." When I said yes, he asked, "Are there any other exits from the office?"

"Not from the office," I said. "But there's one in the adjoining apartment." Each of the top BASS executives had a small living space attached to our offices, so we could stay the night if necessary, or put up guests, or even take a quick nap in the nice queen bed . . .

"Oh, no," I said aloud, my panic increasing from a flash to a flood.

"Get ready to break down the door, Min," Terrey said, obviously interpreting my exclamation to mean the double was in mortal danger.

"No, wait," I said. "Just knock on the door, and call for them first. And send the triplet down to the other door to knock on that one."

They did, and there was no response. I could hear Terrey asking the security techs he was with to punch in to the surveillance systems, and I could see Min moving back a step to get ready to kick the door down with one of his augmented legs, which would be child's play for the big man.

But then, before Min could do his Bruce Lee imitation, we all heard a voice coming from somewhere inside, probably from the doorway between the office and the apartment.

"Hold on a sec," it said, and it was my voice, meaning Jon was talking. "Just a second."

"Are you in danger, sir?" Min asked in an amplified voice that made me put my hand up to my ear.

"No, no," the voice from inside replied, and I could almost see the double and Tara snickering to each other, because by now I knew what was going on, and I was getting a sick feeling in the pit of my stomach. Sure enough, the double soon opened the door, his cotton shirt noticeably wrinkled, as if it had been balled up and thrown to the ground, then hurriedly put on again. Tara wriggled past him and through the door, straightening her suit and her hair at the same time, as only women can do.

"You'll be there," the double said to her. "At the press conference?"

"I'll be there," she said, somewhat reluctantly.

"Thank you," he said, more than somewhat relieved, then repeated it after her as she walked away down the hall.

"Tell Jon to turn on my link to him, and stay in the office." I said this to the open line, and Min complied. "Then leave us alone for a few minutes. We'll come out in time for the conference."

Suddenly my screen returned to the double's view, as he leaned against my desk and looked down at his hands, which were now clenched together. I was about to ask him what happened, but then what I suspected was confirmed as he looked up and noticed that the door to the apartment was still open. Through the doorway and a short hallway I could see the bed in the apartment, with its sheets and covers tossed every which way. Jon groaned regretfully, but not nearly enough, and stepped quickly through the door and the hallway, turning off the light in the bathroom on the way, and started to fix the rumpled bedclothes.

"Sorry for the mess," he muttered, as if that was the biggest problem here.

"Leave it," I said, and he stood up straight, gathering from my tone that this would not be a pleasant conversation. "Go back into my office, right now." He did as he was told, and not wanting to be in his head any more than I had wanted to be in that room, I tried to switch my view to the net room in the office. I also preferred to see his face, and vice versa. But the locks were still in place, so I settled for staying in his head and hoping that whatever was wrong with it wouldn't rub off on me.

"I'll restrain myself from the three or four lethal options I am considering, for now," I said. "So you can tell me exactly what happened."

"You want all the details?" he said with a slight smile, still not grasping the gravity of this situation. *Of course not,* I thought. *It's only grave for me, and maybe for Tara, but not to him. To him, he just hit the jackpot.*

"Only the details up to that part," I said. "And wipe that bloody smirk off your face, or I will."

"Sorry," he said, and pursed his lips. "Exactly what happened. Well, after you went offline, I wasn't sure what to do, but I figured you got what you wanted, when Tara agreed to take the job and move on. So I tried to end the meeting. I stood up to see her out and she said, 'I guess this is good-bye for us,' or something like that. I said 'I guess,' because I wasn't totally sure what your specific plan was from here, I didn't want to make some kind of dogmatic statement with you gone . . ."

"Then what?" I said, hurrying him along.

"She met me halfway to the door, and wanted to say a 'proper good-bye.'" He paused. "When I didn't say anything, she came close and started kissing me. I wasn't sure what to do, you weren't there."

"Oh, come on, Jon," I said, my disgust coming out despite my British reserve. "I just broke it off with her, and you didn't know whether to let her put her tongue in your mouth?"

"She was on me so hard, so fast. What could I do?" He said this angrily, like I was actually the villain here, but then changed his tone. "Look, Mr. Ares, a man would have to be gay as hell to say no to that woman. And I figured, what's the harm? I had already done what you wanted me to do."

"But then you undid it!" I said, and didn't want him to tell the rest of the story, so I told it for him. "Tara mentioned the apartment next door, and that she could block the surveillance." (Which she had mentioned to me a number of times over the last five years.) "And that she's taken care of the birth control, and swears she'll keep it between us." (Also things that I'd heard from her.) "And before too long, you weren't thinking with your brain anymore, and you ended up . . ."

I didn't even want to say it, I was so infuriated—mostly because of the repercussions I would face from this, but probably also because he had done something I had wanted to do so many times.

"Yes," he said, "but no, I haven't undone anything. Well, I almost did. In the . . . throes of passion, you might say, I think I did say something about still being in love with her. You know how that is, I'm sure. But afterward I asked her to please go through with the plan—the press conference and all. We didn't have much time to talk about it, because you came back. But she said she would." He spread his hands and smiled at the screen. "And besides, when this is all over you can tell her it wasn't you and take back anything I said."

I merely stared at him, speechless and wondering if I could have possibly made a bigger mess of this. It gave new meaning to the saying, "If you want something done right, you have to do it yourself." And then I realized it could get even worse.

"Jon, you have AIMS. What if you gave it to her?"

He thought for a moment, then said, "The triplets said it looked hopeful for me, remember?"

"You'd better hope it is hopeful, or you could end up being charged with murder."

"You mean *you*?" he said, making my head spin even more. A minute ago he was saying that what he did wouldn't affect me, and now he was implying that it would. I wondered how an otherwise normal and intelligent man could be so confounded in this particular situation, and lacking any sense of personal responsibility. His thinking about the outcome of my plan seemed almost as addled as my thinking when I was making it. Maybe he was merely suffering from an unprecedented rush of adrenaline because of his liaison with a veritable goddess, but there seemed to be something more going on.

I soon noticed the time, however, and realized that I would have to deal with all that later. I told the double so, ushering him out of the office to the press room, and the rest of the day went off without any major incident. Jon and Tara both made short statements that accomplished what I wanted them to, giving her the PR position and providing a convincing public appearance for Michael Ares. The only problem was that some of the wording of the statements, and the way they were delivered, hinted at what had gone on in the apartment earlier. This little turn of verbal events would put me in a bad spot with Lynn later, when she saw the broadcast.

But that danger to our marriage was nothing compared to what happened at the cottage later that night with Angelee. I found out for myself how easy it was to fall, how hard it should be to criticize Jon for doing so, and how we were more alike than I wanted to think.

35
ONE FLESH

On her way back from the hospital, Angelee was reviewing the events of the day in her mind, with an extreme mixture of happiness and dread.

The happiness came from the fact that Michael had saved Chris's life after the pool incident, the little boy had regained consciousness in the car on the way to the hospital, and the doctor had said he was okay and sent them home with some instructions for his care.

The dread came from the fact that also on the way to the hospital, Angelee started to feel a pain in the front of her head that she hadn't felt since the time she had been working the street, before her husband had delivered her from all that. And she knew exactly what the pain was, because it had been such a vivid experience for her every month back then. It had something to do with the contraceptive switch that had been installed in her brain, and it was a signal that she was about to get her period. As the tutorial holos about the switch had explained years before, and the brain doctor at the hospital confirmed when she asked him about it, the foreign implant introduced into the reproductive system caused electrical feedback and significant pressure on parts of the brain as menstruation was about to occur. As with the way the switch prevented ovulation, Angelee didn't understand how the technology worked—she just knew that it made PMS even harder for her and the other millions of women who used it.

She also knew from past experience that the pain would continue at various degrees for several hours at least, until she actually started bleeding, but that wasn't what filled her with dread. It meant that she might only have a few hours to be married to the man of her dreams, who was waiting for her back at the vineyard cottage. And she was afraid that if she didn't land him now, something might happen in the next week to prevent it. He had said originally that he only planned to stay there for a "couple weeks," if she remembered correctly, and his life was clearly in flux. So she dreaded the thought of losing him somehow before they were joined together in an eternal bond, like she had with her first husband. She believed that God would make this bond last if they became "one flesh," but if they didn't, she had no confidence that they would end up together.

She also *wanted* to be one with this beautiful man who had saved her son from death, and had saved her from a fate worse than death. And tonight had to be the night—she had the feeling that if it didn't happen tonight, it might never happen. That sense of desperation, and probably some effects of the implant on her brain, drove her toward some bold steps that she would never have taken otherwise.

She had prayed on the way to the hospital that Chris would be okay, and now she prayed on the way back that Michael would be hers that night. And not long after she had prayed for Chris, he awoke and sat up on the seat of the car! So she believed—at least, she tried to force herself to believe—that God would answer her other prayer as well. Her husband and others in their church had always said that if you had enough faith, you could move mountains and make almost anything happen. She never completely understood that, or even exactly how to conjure up that kind of belief, but she was willing to try anything to make this happen. She couldn't imagine a better life than one lived in the arms of this man.

Her daydreaming was interrupted by a hard stab of pain, far more intense than the headache she already had, and she had to pull off the road for a few minutes. This served to increase her sense of urgency for something to happen with Michael in the next few hours, because she remembered that these bolts of extreme pain always happened in the hours leading up to her period, and once that started, they wouldn't be able to become one. She might not be able to have a husband again, and Chris might never have a father.

When she was finally able to drive again, she got back on the road and made it back to the cottage without any further severe headaches. She was still in some degree of pain, but she pushed the discomfort out of her mind and determined to do all she could for make her dreams and prayers come true. Michael must have been told they had arrived by the security systems of the house, because he was waiting at the door after she had driven down the long lane through the vineyards. He stepped out to her and offered to take the medicated boy from her arms after she had lifted him out of the car, and carried him into the house for her. As she watched him do this, her heart began to pound in her chest and the pain in her head receded even further.

As Michael laid Chris on their bed, she whispered that the doctor had given him some medication that would allow him to rest and also would help him to recover. Michael whispered back that she should get the medmat from the living room, and he placed it under the boy so that the house could monitor his vitals in case of any relapse. Then they stepped quietly out of the room so they could talk, and she reported to him everything that had happened that day. He seemed genuinely glad to hear about it—he was so caring—and as she interacted with him, she bustled about the kitchen, picking out the best food she had purchased and putting it in the oven to heat it up for dinner. She hoped he hadn't eaten yet, and she wasn't disappointed, and when she was finished with the preparations she told him it would be ready in a few minutes and that she needed to freshen up.

She stepped back into her room and quietly changed into the nicest outfit she had, which was a slip-like underdress made out of black silk, with large holes on the sides at the top of her hips, and a smaller semitransparent overdress that was off-white with a thick swath of soft brown running diagonally across her chest and back. She put on her only shoes with heels, to shape her legs and make her taller, and added a thin black leather neck bracelet and some decent perfume that Simon had given her. Finally, she washed her face, made herself up as best she could, and pinned her hair in the style that had gotten her the most compliments through the years.

She tiptoed out of the room after admiring her sleeping boy, hoping again that he could have a father. Michael wasn't in the living area where she had left him, but she peered into the open door of his room and saw that the bathroom door was closed, so she knew he was in there.

Good! she thought, and hurried out to the kitchen to grab some place settings and prepare the table. She finished it before he came back out, and managed to also make the room dimmer and light some candles.

"Wow, Angelee," he said when he came out, "you didn't have to do all this."

She didn't say anything, but straightened the place settings on the side of the table, then she pulled out a chair for him and gestured for him to sit down.

"We're celebrating that Chris is okay," she said, and served the food to both their settings.

"Well, good," he said. "I can use it. I had a bad day."

"Oh, I'm so sorry." She thought of asking him what happened to him, but then thought better of it. "I'm glad I can be here to make your day better, after you have a bad day. I will always be glad to do that."

He stopped sipping the wine she had given him, just for a moment, but then resumed. She thought that maybe she should be more subtle, but then thought better of that as well—she had never been a good liar, nor was she able to "play" people. She had learned that it was always best for her to be honest, and not have to blame herself if things didn't go well. But she could show interest in him, because she was honestly interested in him.

"Have you had many other relationships?" she asked him as they ate. "Other than Tara, the one who owns this house?"

"Not many," he said. "I was hard at work in the military, along with college and graduate school that they provided, since I was a teen. Didn't really have time for much else."

"What did you study?"

"Mostly literature," he said, "and writing. Besides the military stuff, of course."

"What do you like to write?"

"Well, I haven't written much at all since school. But maybe someday I'll write about some of the things that have happened to me."

"Like what?" she asked, and then immediately regretted it. She could tell he was hesitant, and didn't need to know more about his life. She knew enough from what she had seen and heard from him.

"Just some things," he said graciously. "But what about you? Tell me about you. Do you want to write something?"

"No," she said. "I don't write very good, or read that good either." She stood up to pour him some more wine, and felt the pain in her head increase a bit as she did. "What I really want is to be a wife and mother, and that's what I'm good at, more than anything."

"I'm sure you are," he said, sipping at the new glass of wine. "In fact, I was just thinking that last night, when you left me that plate of food—which was good, by the way."

"What were you thinking?" she asked, moving closer to him. He hesitated again, but then seemed to realize that he had to answer her, because he had already committed to this line of conversation.

"I was thinking what a good wife you would make," he said finally, and then added with a slight emphasis, "for someone." But Angelee didn't register this as a caveat—she was simply thrilled he had been thinking about her in this way, and was emboldened to say what she really wanted to say to him.

"I want to be one with you," she said, and he almost spit out the wine that was in his mouth.

"Angelee," he said, and searched for some words. "I'm not . . . we're not married."

"But we can be, right now, before God. We say 'I do' and we become one in every way. A man shall cleave to his wife, and the two shall become one flesh."

"But what about the government?" he said. "You know, like a marriage license?"

"The government didn't invent marriage. They don't say what it is or isn't. People are marrying animals in some places these days . . . is that really marriage? We'll be married in the eyes of the Lord—that's what counts."

"I think . . . ," Michael said, then searched again for the words. "I think that one of the reasons that marriage is regulated by the state is so that someone can confirm that a person isn't married to someone else. But then again, they do multiple marriages, too, so maybe that doesn't apply."

"Are you worried about me being married to someone else?" she asked. He laughed and shook his head, but she continued. "I'm not, and I'm not some kind of slut who just wants to sleep with you or anyone else for fun. I was willing to sell myself because I had no other way to feed my son, but what I want is to belong to you and you only, to help you, and take care of Chris. That is *not* a bad thing, and it's something that makes God happy. I'm sure of it."

"No, uh, I agree," he said. "I'm sure it's a good desire you have. I'm just not sure it is . . . the right time for it."

"This has to be the time," she said, moving closer to him. "After tonight we won't be able to . . . because of my cycle. I'm sorry to have to say something like that, but now you know why I'm being so bold. Please say 'I do.' Chris and I both need you. You are the most special man I've ever met."

"Special, hell," he muttered after a brief groan. Or did he say "special hell"? She couldn't tell, but then she felt a tear rolling down her cheek, and wondered if that was the cause of his uneasiness. But she was determined to not miss this chance, and moved even closer to him.

And then the worst headache yet hit her. Her chin jerked down against her chest, her whole body lurched sideways, and she would have fallen all the way to the ground if Michael hadn't caught her and lowered her slowly to it. He kept saying, "Are you all right?" until she managed to say that it was her switch and that the pain would eventually stop.

"Why did you leave it on?" he asked her, as he carried her over to the couch. "When you could have turned it off and avoided this?"

"For you," she forced out. He didn't seem to appreciate that sentiment very much, and then she realized that the thought of contraception, and therefore pregnancy, had probably jarred him out of whatever interest he might have had in being with her tonight.

"It isn't the right time," he said, confirming what she thought. "That's what I said, and this shows that I was right."

Michael told Vera to turn off her switch, and she was amazed that the house could actually do it. Then he got some pain reliever pills and water from the kitchen, and made her take them, caressing her head tenderly in a way that made her want him even more, despite the pain.

"When I get better . . . ," she said through clenched teeth, trying to smile.

"Yeah, we can talk more about this in a week or so, when you're better. That will give us more time to . . . to get to know each other."

She had meant when she felt better *tonight*, of course, but her disappointment was lessened by the fact that he wasn't rejecting her, at least. He was implying that they could possibly be married—she would just have to wait for a week or so. She was disappointed, but also strangely felt a sense of relief, as if she didn't have to make this happen, because she *couldn't* make this happen. She thought that maybe this was what her former husband always meant by "trusting God," though she also thought that it would be hard to trust in a God who brought her so close to a man like this and then took him away from her.

36
INNUENDO

When I left Angelee that night and escaped to my room, I closed the door and leaned my back against it. I couldn't believe the effect she was having on my usually well-ordered psyche, not to mention my usually well-disciplined body. To address both problems, I took a cold shower and tried to make some sense of all the thoughts and feelings swirling around inside me.

Some of the thoughts I had were the typical rationalizations and excuses that started when Angelee was offering herself to me: "I'm under a lot of duress right now," "I've been away from my wife," and "Anyone would understand if I fell." The last one reminded me of what the double had said earlier about Tara, and that plus the cold water did wonders for stopping any thoughts of going back out to the living room. But then I also realized how bad I felt for Angelee— she was so desperate for someone to love her and Chris, and for me in particular, that she was deaf to my hints that it might not work out between us. And I felt bad about being the cause of her inevitable misery, because I really didn't give her any serious hints and shouldn't even be hinting about this at all—she was an innocent who deserved the truth. But again, I justified myself by saying that I was a slave to the bigger issues of saving my life, the future of BASS, and the free world even—whatever made me seem like less of a villain. I also tried to think of some ways I could make it up to her, but none of this really made me feel better about the situation.

The memory of what had happened with the double and Tara didn't help with my feelings of regret; neither did the fact that when I got out of the shower, my wall screen was flashing with messages from Terrey and Lynn, who was the last person I wanted to talk to right now. But I had to—I couldn't just go to bed without talking to her, because then we'd both have trouble sleeping, and I'd get an earful the next day.

As it turned out, I got an earful that night, because Lynn had watched a netcast of the double and Tara making their statements to the press at the castle, and she had a recording of one part ready to show me. It was a moment in Tara's statement where she said that she was "looking forward to working very closely with Michael," and she smiled at the double like they were sharing a private joke between them. Lynn rewound it twice, pausing on Tara's sultry smile and even playing it once in slow motion.

"And that wasn't the only time," Lynn said. "She also looked quite pleased with herself when she said 'I've always had a good relationship with Michael,' 'We have a kind of chemistry between us,' and—this is my favorite—'As his representative, I will do my best to satisfy his needs at all times.' Michael, I don't want to read too much into this, but she looked to me like a woman who had just gotten her man, or something like that. And I don't want to be a jealous wife, but since I know about your past relationship with her, I'm wondering if there's something I don't know about it now."

I had noticed the unintentional innuendos in both the speeches, and cringed at them, but that was only because I knew what had just happened between the double and Tara. I didn't think it was anything that Lynn or anyone else would notice.

"No, Lynn," I said. "I think you're just being oversensitive." Then after I saw her facial expression, I added: "But I wouldn't call you a jealous wife."

"You wouldn't call me a jealous wife, but that's what you're calling me."

"I just think you're the only one who's gonna see something in what she said, because of what you know. It's understandable . . . I don't blame you."

"Michael," she said, "are you having an affair with that woman?"

"No, Lynn."

"Then why was she looking at you like that?"

"She wasn't looking at me, Lynn. She was looking at Jon."

"But she thought he was you!" She shook her head. "Have you been flirting with her? Is that it? You can tell me, I can take it."

"No, Lynn. I have a purely business relationship with her. Listen, your life has been completely upset by these attempts on my life, you're six months pregnant—"

"Seven."

"What?"

"I'm seven months now. Just turned seven."

"Oh. Well, anyway, you'll have to trust me on this thing with Tara. We don't have time for domestic intrigue right now."

"You're not at that woman's house, are you?"

"Lynn, you know I can't tell you where I am."

"Oh, so you *are* at her house."

I could see there was no way out of this except telling her the truth, which I wasn't ready to do without a lot more reflection, so I changed the subject.

"How are Hilly and Jessa doing?" I asked. "Have you figured out where they can go yet?"

"Not really," she said, thankfully taking the bait. "But I was thinking the Presidio might be the best place, at least for a while, when I'm ready to go down there and get involved." I assumed by that she meant when the threat against me was over, and we had returned to a more normal life. "Until then, they're okay here. Tyra has been a big help . . . it's like having a nanny."

Mob Nanny, I thought. *I can already see the reality TV show.*

"But the biggest issue right now," Lynn continued. "is that they need to see their brother sometime soon. They've been asking about him now that the shock of losing their mother has worn off, and it's only right. And I know we have big-time problems presently, but if we don't take the girls to see him ourselves, that would put an even bigger wall between us at a really bad time for him."

I was impressed again by Lynn's compassion—she even cared for a punk who probably wanted to kill me almost as much as General Sun did.

"I'll talk to Terrey about it," I said, grateful for the excuse to move on from this conversation. "I have to call him anyway."

We said our good-byes, which were rather cold because of the lingering specter of the Tara situation, and I called Terrey.

"What was that all about?" he said without ado. I soon found out that Lynn was *not* the only one who noticed Tara's not-so-subtle expressions, and the double's slightly embarrassed ones, at the press conference. Terrey picked up on it himself, and so did various media outlets. He said that BayNet had broadcast a twenty-minute exposé on how I dated Tara before meeting my wife, and showed the innuendo-laden statements over and over again, implying that there was "something brewing or already boiled over" between us.

"I know it's only tabloid news," Terrey said, "but it's the kind of attention I didn't want on you while Jon is taking your place. Sooner or later people like this might even start comparing this film with others of you, and catching on to our little ruse. There have been a few high-profile cases since the Makeover was perfected, and savvy people in the media know about it. I guess the only good thing about this is that all the attention is on the tidy spunk, and she's getting all the screen time. Can't say I blame them, and can't say I blame you for having a little of that on the side. But what was going on with her and Jon all that time they were in the office? I tried to pry it out of Min, but if he knows he's too tight-lipped to tell me. The only hypothesis I can think of is that you were getting some kinky pleasure out of riding with him while he was riding her."

"No, that's not the way it was," I said, guessing that he would probably not believe me, but telling him the truth anyway about how I had an emergency at my hiding place and lost contact with the double long enough for him to be seduced by Tara.

"I don't believe you," he said. "But everyone lies about sex, so I suppose you're entitled to some of that too."

"I'm actually not lying this time, Terrey, believe it or not."

"Well, either way, I find it really interesting that your wife recognized the double as soon as he walked in the room, but that Sheila shagged him and still thinks it's you."

That *was* interesting, now that I thought about it. Going into the meeting with Tara in my office, I had a backup plan in case she realized that the double was not me. Because Tara and I had been so close at one time, I thought it was unlikely that the deception could survive the two of them talking, let alone what they did together. So it now shocked me to realize how substantial the difference was in my relationship between the two women. It made me feel more grateful for Lynn, and made me think that I should treat her differently than I had been. But the idea of fooling Tara also brought to mind something that made me feel sorry for her.

"Speaking of the shagging," I said, "Jon may still have AIMS, so she could have gotten it from him."

"Not my problem," Terrey said right away. "I don't get paid to protect her."

"But Terrey, think about it. She could end up dying, or not being able to be with anyone the rest of her life. And she thought it was me, so she was trusting *me*. And this all was your plan—I think we have at least some responsibility here."

"All right, I have an idea," he said. "I'll give it to you, but then we have to get back to our business."

He suggested that I require all high-level staff at BASS to be tested for AIMS, for some humanitarian purpose, and have the results sent to me alone. If Tara tested positive, I could break the bad news to her and offer her the treatment, which I would have to buy from Protection G. If she was negative, Terrey said, then "No worries, mate." I was impressed by Terrey's mental acumen again, but also a bit surprised that my old friend was being such a cutthroat businessman, with very little human compassion. Which made me think of Lynn again, not just because of her compassion, but also because of how my life had gone in a different direction from Terrey's, probably because I married Lynn and had two children with her.

"The idea that you might be having an affair," Terrey said, getting back to business as he promised, "also draws attention to your wife, and the media are talking about the fact that she hasn't been seen since the fire, or even before. And since our photo op at the cemetery didn't work out, I'm thinking we really need to get her out somewhere, even briefly. I know you don't want her near the double unless it's necessary, but if they both could do something together, it would go a long way to lessening the media scrutiny."

Terrey didn't say it, and I didn't know it until later, but he also was hoping to draw out any assassination attempts that were still pending.

"Now *I* have an idea," I said, thinking back to my last conversation. "Lynn feels very strongly that both of us should take the twins to see their brother John. And I think if we don't do that fairly soon, we may actually have a lot more of that media scrutiny you're worried about. John is John Rabin, of course, the son of Paul Rabin, who I killed last year. John is angry at me and anything to do with me or BASS, blaming us for the death of his father and grandfather, and I'm sure now for his mother. Lynn is driven by a sense of ethics, but it would also be good PR for us to visit him with his sisters, and put out an olive branch. At least it might head off another round of stories about how we are ignoring and mistreating him."

"Sounds like a possibility," Terrey said, "if it can happen someplace safe."

"There's the rub . . . John refuses to set foot in any BASS property, so he won't come here or to the castle. And he's living in a seamy part of Marin." There were very few seamy parts of Marin County before the big quake, but the flood of refugees from the city had changed all that.

"Think about it some more," Terrey said, "And I'll have the *Trois* look into it. Maybe we can find somewhere that works. In the meantime, in light of the possible risk involved in an outing like that, and other dangers, I wanted to ask you again to do a *ban lan* colors ritual with me. In case it might help us."

"You've been doing that?"

"Yeah, mate. I did it three times."

"What did you do?"

"I got some recitations off the net, in Chinese because that's the only place this cult exists, and transliterated them on another site so I could say them. And I just programmed the net room to display a bunch of different colors while I read them out loud. That's it. According to the literature, I was supposed to experience the spirits coming over me for confirmation, or something like that, but I didn't really feel anything."

"Didn't *really* feel anything?"

"Well, the last time I guess I did feel something."

"This is bizarre, Terrey," I said. "Next you'll be into snake handling."

"Ah, you laugh, but they actually do that sometimes as a part of the rituals. Really. And there's a rare snake around here called a San Francisco Garter, which is one of the most colorful in the world. I was thinking of getting one and using it, but I don't believe in this enough to get bit, and I don't see how it's that much of a confirmation anyway, because the venom's not lethal."

"Has anyone else been doing this with you?" I asked, still shaking my head, but in the back of my mind wondering whether there could be something to it. I *was* still alive, and against the odds all the assassination attempts had failed so far.

"No," Terrey said. "I've asked, but nobody's interested. The *Trois* and Min are as stubbornly scientific as you think cyborgs would be, plus Min wants nothing to do with anything associated with Zhang Sun. Korcz just laughed and Stephenson is into his dream thing too much to try anything else—that's his religion. Tyra has some Catholic in her background and is worried about demons entering her if she did something like that. And of course I didn't even ask Lynn."

"Smart move," I said.

"So you're in?"

"No thanks," I laughed. "But I'll think about it more, maybe check into it."

"Remember not to use the net if you don't have to. We're in big trouble if anyone finds out where you are, especially with us not there to protect you. Did you get a chance to look at the holo of Taiwan?"

"Yes, I watched the whole thing, but unfortunately nothing new turned up. The only person I saw with any connection to Sun was General Ho." I hesitated before saying this, because I didn't know how my friend would react to hearing that name.

"Did you risk going into the net," Terrey asked, "to explore that connection further?"

"No, because I figured Sun was his superior officer, so that explained it."

"Right," Terrey said. "My thoughts exactly. How did it feel to watch yourself put a bullet in that bugger's head? I'd like to see it again myself—I'm still paying off the debt to the doctors who put my plumbing right, after he took me apart with his knife. Not to mention the pain itself. But you and your Trinity put him right, that's for damn sure."

Terrey was, of course, the soldier with the code name Talon 2 in the Taiwan operation. He was the friend whose life I had saved that day, despite the fact that it ultimately cost me my position in the British military, and that's why I was so sure he would never be the one to betray me.

Thinking of the subject of betrayal, and knowing Terrey would be feeling grateful to me at this time, I asked him about something he had mentioned before but not wanted to elaborate on.

"Tell me your suspicions about a traitor," I said, always wanting to know as much as I could, regardless of the relevancy or magnitude of the information. He objected again that it might make me paranoid for no reason, but I insisted.

"I really think it's nothing," he said, "just a coincidence probably. But I found out that Korcz grew up in a town called Gdańsk, in Poland."

"So?"

"Gdańsk is known as one of the most colorful cities in the world," he explained. "The mansions along the main drag are all painted with solid colors like peach, olive, mauve, etcetera. Tourists go there just to see the colors."

"How did you find this out?"

"I had the *Trois* run a scan of the net with the names of our team members, to see if any of them had any association with China or colors or whatever. This was the only result they got." I was thinking hard about whether this could actually mean anything, and he anticipated my question: "Is there any possible way that the Chinese could have foreseen us hiring Korcz?"

"I don't see how," I said. "My only interaction with him in the past wasn't the kind of thing where you would think I would ever see him again."

"So if that's true, then the only way this could be more than a coincidence is if they somehow found out he was coming and contacted him. But that also seems highly unlikely."

"Maybe you should keep an eye on him, just in case, and check him out a little more." Then I had another thought. "If he does happen to be a traitor, he'd be waiting until I returned home to take me out, right? Because he doesn't know where I am. In that case, we couldn't keep him on staff at BASS like we promised, or Stephenson for that matter."

"Right," Terrey said. "If no traitor is revealed before you come back, we would have to at least send them away, to be safe, promises or no promises."

"What do you mean, '*at least* send them away'?"

"Well, if we had some reason to believe one of them was on Sun's payroll, we'd have to take more drastic measures."

We didn't go on to discuss exactly what those might be, because right then the mysterious words appeared on my other screen again.

YON: I WAS THE ONE WHO FOUND OUT THAT KORCZ LIVED IN GDANSK. AM I GOOD OR WHAT?

"You're good," I said after hanging up on Terrey. "Do you really think Korcz could be working for the other side?"

YON: I DIDN'T SAY THAT. BUT HE DOES LOOK LIKE A VILLAIN. HE'S NOT HANDSOME LIKE YOU.

I rolled my eyes, thinking about how I now seemed to have three beautiful women after me. *Most men would probably kill to have this problem,* I thought, *but I'm more like dying to get out of it.* But then something completely different occurred to me.

"Terrey said Korcz grew up in that city," I said to my secret admirer. "But you just said he lived there. Did you mean the same thing?"

There was no response, even after I waited for a minute, so I figured that her window of time had closed again, and she had to go before her sisters found out that she was moonlighting by talking with me.

I checked the time and realized it was too late for me to do anything else tonight, so I hit the hay and fell asleep thinking about how I could confront the double about what happened with Tara, and hopefully use him to repair it. Despite the unmitigated disaster earlier in the day, I still hadn't fully learned my lesson about the danger of doing anything important by proxy.

37
POLYAMORY

In the morning, I went out to the living area and ate the nice breakfast that Angelee had prepared. She was feeling much better now that her switch had been turned off for a while, but she also seemed slightly depressed. Her window of opportunity for our "marriage ceremony" had obviously passed, and so now all she could do was continue to serve me and wait for it to open again in a week or so. Her depression was probably because she knew there was a good chance that window might stay closed, now that she had missed this opportunity.

I didn't want her to become too sad, for business reasons and also for personal ones, because I had begun to genuinely care about her and Chris. So I talked with her cheerfully while I ate, and found out that Chris was still sleeping, but the medication would wear off sometime soon. She said that she wanted him to enjoy the pool again, so he wouldn't become afraid of swimming, and I told Vera to lower all the water to a safe level, and checked to make sure it was okay before I went back into my room to make my calls.

The first one I made was to Jon—I used the netroom equipment in his quarters at the hill, and put his face on one of my screens.

"We need to talk more about what happened with Tara," I said, "and make it right."

"You're not gonna tell her about the AIMS thing?" he asked. "Are you?"

"Not at this point," I answered, and explained Terrey's plan about having the upper-level staff at BASS tested so we could hopefully rule that out without having to tell her.

"But I need to make sure we understand each other," I continued, "before we talk to her again. You'll have to be able to make clear that I don't want to be with her, without any hint of flirting with her. And to do that you absolutely have to grasp how serious this is, and what a bad mistake you made by doing what you did."

"Like I said," he answered defensively, "I'd have to be gay or dead to not—"

"Yeah, yeah," I interrupted. "About that. I'm not gay, and I've said no to her for years. So that's no excuse."

"You're also married," he said. "So that makes it easier for you to say no. You would suffer more consequences if you give in to what you know you want to do. But I don't have that motivation."

"Listen, Jon," I said with frustration, "you have to be motivated, because you're representing me in everything you do. This mistake is sufficient reason for me to withhold your pay, if your sorry arse happens to make it out of this alive."

"I'm sorry," he said, changing his tune fast. "You just have to understand how difficult it was for someone with my condition."

"What does AIMS have to do with it?"

"Not AIMS," he said. "I'm a poly."

I knew enough from the web to know what he meant by that—that he was polyamorous—but not much more. I had never personally known anyone who went by the label, so I asked him to enlighten me.

"I'm genetically unable to abstain or have just one partner," he said. "Other people can say no much easier, and they can be satisfied by someone they love. I can't do that—it would be denying who I am by nature, and bring on the kind of mental and emotional hell that I've already been through."

"So you're a sex addict?" I asked.

"And you're not?" he answered. "Imagine if you couldn't be with your wife at all, for a long time. You'd go into a kind of withdrawal, wouldn't you? That's what it's like for me, but worse, because I need multiple partners."

"Living without my wife, or any partner, would be hard," I said, "but I hope I would have self-control."

"You would have self-sex, that's what you would have." He smiled. "And it wouldn't be enough for you. See, you're an addict, too, if that's what you want to call me."

"I don't have time to argue with you about this," I said, even more frustrated now, partly because he was partly right. "If you can't get with the program, you're gone, with no compensation. Do you want to end up back in that Exit website?"

That sobered him up, and he said, "This is how I got there. I found out I was poly after my wife and kids died, because I was filling the holes left by them. Whatever faults I had, I was a good father—I really loved my kids. You can't blame me when you know what I've been through."

On the one hand he was saying that he was born that way, and on the other he was citing the trauma he suffered. It seemed inconsistent, but it could take forever to figure stuff like this out, and I needed to focus on our current situation.

"Why didn't you tell us that you have this . . . condition?" I asked.

"I told you about the AIMS. I figured that was the biggest problem."

"The AIMS thing was a wash for us," I said, "because the very small risk of you infecting someone was offset by the motivation it gives you to do a good job for us, so you could be cured. But if we would have known that you're 'genetically unable' to stay out of women's pants, that might have changed our thinking. AIMS and this poly thing are a bad combination." I thought of how he had been looking my own wife up and down, and was now gladder than ever that Lynn had so little interest in other men, even when she was mad at me.

"It was a personal issue," he added in his defense. "Tyra didn't mention that she was a woman, then a man, then a woman again."

"Isn't there some kind of medication that can help you?" I asked, wanting to feel that he was stabler and safer to have around.

"Would you take chemicals to stop being who you are? To stop wanting your wife, for example?"

It was a rhetorical question, but I didn't have a chance to answer anyway, because the door to my room suddenly opened behind me—I had neglected to lock it—and little Chris came running over to me and gave me a big hug. Then Angelee appeared in the doorway, in the white bikini top and a towel wrapped around her waist. She stepped over to pull Chris gently off me.

"I'm so sorry," she said as she did. "I was telling him how you saved his life yesterday, and he just ran away from me toward your room. I guess he wanted to say thank you."

"Oh, that's sweet, Chris," I said. "I'll come out and play with you when I'm done with my calls, okay?"

The little boy nodded, and Angelee ushered him back out of the room. I showed them out, locked the door, and returned to my chair. And I saw my face on the screen, looking at me with interest, because I had been too distracted to turn it off. It didn't seem like Angelee or Chris had noticed the double, fortunately, but he had seen them clear as day.

"Very nice," Jon said with one of my eyebrows raised. "Maybe you understand my polyamory better than you're letting on."

I was about to tell him that this was another willing woman that I had managed to resist, which proved that I was in fact *not* like him, but then I realized that the theory of opportunity he had put forth regarding me being married also applied to the situation with Angelee. I had tried to tell myself that her use of the word "special" and the thought of Lynn's pregnancy had enabled me to heroically stop what was developing the night before, but the truth was that it probably would have gone further were it not for the headache that she got. So opportunity really was the only difference between Jon and me in these two circumstances—he had it, and I didn't. I didn't tell him all this, of course—it was bad enough that he saw Angelee and knew that she was here with me. But I couldn't really argue with his point, so I resorted to the old standby method that had served me so well with Lynn, and changed the subject.

I told him that if he wanted his reward to remain intact, he would dim the lights slightly in the room, use its net access to call Tara, and say exactly what I told him to. I couldn't call Tara myself because she, being a security manager, might be alerted to my location, or even recognize her own house codes, and realize where I was. I also couldn't tell her about the double at this point, because she might freak out that she slept with a stranger, and ironically even become worried about the possibility of AIMS.

So I transferred my link to Jon's implant, and rode with him as he told Tara that what happened in the apartment at the castle was a huge mistake and would never happen again. I/he told her that she had to fulfill our bargain to put her résumé out and find another job, and she seemed to be okay with the idea. I was starting to feel good about myself again, and Jon was feeling confident that he could speak for me effectively, when the conversation took a bad turn.

"I hear what you're saying," Tara said, "but I'm also wondering if you might be a little confused right now, since we had such a great time yesterday."

"I'm not confused, Tara," the double said at my prompting, but then added his own improvisation, which was quite good: "Yesterday was just a mistake."

"So you say," she replied, "and it's up to you. But just in case, tonight I'm going to go to a place that has a lot of memories for us, and I'll be there if you want to come over. I'll be at my vineyard cottage in the Valley."

"That's up to you, Tara," the double said on his own initiative, not knowing that I was hiding there. "But I won't be coming." While he said that last line, I realized what was happening and shouted "No, wait!" Jon reacted by saying "What?" and unconsciously putting a hand to his ear.

"I said I'll be at the cottage tonight," Tara said with a puzzled look. "Who are you talking to?"

"Oh, I'm getting a report from an agent in my earpiece," Jon said, reverting to our former plan for covering such problems—even though he wasn't actually wearing an earpiece. "Hold on a second."

Now he intentionally put a hand to his ear and gave me his attention. I had to think hard because I didn't want Tara to come to the cottage, but I also didn't want Jon to know where I was. So I ended up telling him to tell her that she shouldn't go to the cottage tonight or any other night, that this was another part of her promotion deal, and that she had to sell the property so she wouldn't have any reason to come back to the area. I even told her that BASS would purchase it from her for a higher price, because I had some ideas about how it could be used. Fortunately she didn't press this issue, but unfortunately she said something else that was even worse.

"If you insist," she said. "But if we're really done, and if I'm really going to leave BASS, I think your wife should know about our little rendezvous at the castle yesterday."

Jon was silent, not knowing what I wanted him to say; I was silent also, not knowing what *to* say. I had never thought Tara capable of blackmail, because she had been so discreet through the years and so devoted to me personally. But then I realized that nothing she could really use had happened between us until yesterday, and she had never been fully rejected until now. *"Hell hath no fury like a woman scorned,"* I thought. *I shouldn't be so surprised.*

"If you say anything about yesterday to anyone, our deal is off." Jon mouthed the words that I put into his head. "You will be fired without severance or recommendation, and this great opportunity I'm giving you will be gone forever."

One of the good things about the totalitarian nature of BASS was that I could say and do something like this without any fear of a lawsuit or other recriminations, except the usual criticisms from the media, which had no effect on what we did. And Tara knew this well, so she dropped the issue for now. But I also knew that threats and cover-ups seldom solved problems like this, so as the call ended I mumbled a prayer to whatever God might be out there, which was becoming more customary for me to do in situations like this that were clearly out of my control. I hoped to heaven for insight about what to do about the real possibility that Lynn would find out that I had left the door open with Tara for so long, and I hoped to hell that she hadn't contracted AIMS, which would make the whole situation much more complicated.

With these heavy things and some others on my mind, my next call was to a twisted technological version of the netherworld. I called up Saul's ghost again, putting on my glasses and running through the security routine to gain access to the Fortress Cloud where it resided. Soon the almost-real holo of the man's old head, with the gray hair and the lightning scar on his cheek, appeared again in my view.

"Hello, Michael," it said.

"I have some questions for you," I said, not interested in extended greetings because I was still frustrated from being stymied by its elusive programming.

"Good," it said, already flashing the famous grin. "As Socrates said, 'Understanding a question is half an answer.'"

"You seem to know more about religion than anyone else I can talk to right now, and a surprising number of issues related to it have been coming up."

"I wouldn't be surprised at that, Michael. I don't know everything about religion, or even as much as I wanted to learn before I died, but I am sure of one thing: Everyone is religious in a way, and everything in life is religious, if by that word we mean what we worship or are devoted to. Everyone has something or someone that they adore, love, or consider of ultimate importance in making their life worth living. And even in those who don't want to live, it's because the things they worship have been denied to them, so they would rather die than live without them."

This made me think of Jon and how we found him in the Exit website, so I started my questions with one related to him.

"Don't some religious people dispute the idea that we're born with a sexual preference, and that we can't change it?"

"If you've decided that you're gay, Michael, that would be a surprise to me."

"No, I'm actually thinking about polyamory, and it's someone else I've been talking to." This was a half-truth, of course, because I was also wondering about myself.

"Even in the LGBT and PPB communities," the ghost pontificated, "there are some different opinions about those issues, although the majority of people there and in the public at large think that it is all genetics. Especially with all the press given to Ravi Valda, and how his testimony and research supposedly proved that his cross-species attraction was inherent to his nature. If it looks likely, or even possible, that the besties are born that way, then why would anyone question the more common lifestyles? But to answer your question about the polys, I'll give you my opinion, which I think is based on observation and revelation."

"Revelation?"

"From God, Michael, like in the Christian scriptures."

"You don't think all that stuff is true, do you?"

"I don't know if it's all true," the ghost said. "And the fact is that I never was a very good Christian—nothing like my wife was. But I do think Jesus is the best thing that ever happened to this planet, and there's something different about that book from other books."

"So what does it say about my friend's problem?"

"Again, I'm not sure I know that much. But something like this: Even if he is born with it, like other problems we have, he doesn't have to give in to it or stay that way. If there is a God, that God could give him the power to resist temptation and even change his desires. Probably would be a lot of work, though, if it is possible, because God helps those who help themselves. And it seems to me it would have to start with him realizing that it is not the way we were originally designed, but a result of everything in the world going bad, including him. So it would be his fault, not God's, even if he was born that way, and he would need to take responsibility for it. Unfortunately, most people don't realize this until after they've suffered severe consequences from their sins.

"I don't think it's that different from a parent who gets angry and violent toward his kids when they piss him off. Knowing whether he was born that way, or played too many zombie holo games when he was younger, or whatever, doesn't really matter as much as knowing that his thinking and behavior are wrong and need to change. Jesus said that even lust is enough to send us to hell, so without God's mercy I'd be burning big time right now." The ghost grinned again, and I found it so odd that Saul's posthumous construct was talking about an afterlife that Saul himself might be enjoying or enduring right now.

"I can see how abusing your children is a sin," I said, "but who you sleep with, by mutual consent—that can't be a matter of right and wrong."

"Oh, really, Michael?" the ghost said, the unrealistic glitch causing it to use my name too many times. "How has it worked out for your friend?" When I didn't answer, it went on: "What would it do to our dear Lynn, and the new daughter you told me about, if you decided you were a poly and shot your wad all over the city streets?" As if it could see my brow knit at this, it explained. "An expression like that is used in the book of Proverbs, believe it or not, chapter five. And that passage also reminds me of something else that your friend would need: a good woman who will love him and help him through it all."

"Did you talk with your wife about this kind of stuff?" I asked, thinking about how Lynn might find out about Tara. "You know, confess to her?"

"If I had to," the ghost said, then seemed to read my mind. "Better that she hear it from me, than from someone else. It was very difficult, yes, but it also gave her the opportunity to learn to forgive."

Speaking of difficulty, I was now feeling more uncomfortable by the minute, so I changed the subject again. I wanted to ask about Terrey's idea of practicing the Chinese *ban lan* ritual as a way to ensure my protection, and would end up being surprised and puzzled by the answer.

38
DESTINY

"Do you think there could actually be supernatural power in the color rituals that Zhang Sun practices?" I asked the ghost. "The ones he uses for the kaleidocide?"

"Yes, definitely."

"I wasn't expecting you to say that, because I would think that because of your traditionalism . . ." Then I realized my mistake in using second-person pronoun, and corrected it. "That Saul would not have been syncretistic or inclusive, when it came to religion."

"I'm not," it said, insisting on using first-person pronouns, despite my not-so-subtle objections. "But I believe there are other spiritual forces in the world, working toward their own goals."

"Evil spirits, you mean."

"Yes, Michael." This was getting even weirder.

"Some uneducated, third-world people would think that *you* are a disembodied spirit, if they met you. We even call you a ghost. But despite the way it might look, you're a perfectly explainable physical phenomenon, when we know how you work."

"Yes, Michael. But that only proves *some* things are misjudged as supernatural. It doesn't prove that all of them are."

"So Terrey says that in case the *ban lan* spirits are real," I explained, "we should do the rituals to get their help, and offset the power of what Sun is doing."

"I wouldn't do that," the ghost answered, "because I'd be worried about upsetting a higher power."

"Look, old man," I said, frustrated enough to break my own rules of reference, "if there is a higher power, why doesn't he just wipe out the other ones? This isn't making sense."

"Remember in our last conversation while I was alive, Michael, I told you about Edwards's definition of free will?" There was that creepy dynamic again, of the ghost's consciousness of its own death. "The Creator gives the creatures freedom to choose according to their desires, but knows and controls enough to ensure that the results of their choices ultimately work together to fulfill his desires."

"Is that what you've been doing to me, by jerking me around with all your mysterious talk?" I asked. "Is that what Saul was doing to me, by bringing me to BASS?"

"We *are* made in his image," the ghost said, wearing the enigmatic smile again. "But to learn more about these things, Michael, you should talk to a man named Ian Charles, whom I think you should hire at BASS. I just sent a link for him to your glasses."

Maybe talking to that man was the only way I would get the answers I needed, and I was curious about why we might need him on staff. But I wasn't ready to give up on this conversation yet, because this topic was now in the forefront of my mind.

"Why does Zhang Sun want me dead?" I asked again, just in case the answer might be different this time.

"I don't know, Michael." The same answer, of course. "But let me tell you some more about Zhang Sun. He is more of a danger to world peace than anyone in recent memory. He took two first names because that practice was common among the ancient emperors of China—"

"Was Sun a blood relative to General Ho, or any other Chinese soldiers that I killed in Taiwan?"

"No, Michael," it said after a pause.

"Was there some other connection between Sun and Ho, or any of the others I killed?"

"I don't know," it said after a longer pause.

"Are you lying to me when you say that?"

"No, Michael. I really don't know."

"Of course, you could be lying to me when you say that, too."

"No, Michael. I really don't know."

I restrained my frustration, and thought for a moment.

"Can I make a call to Stanford Glenn, through your Fortress Cloud, that will be secure? Terrey's worried that someone will find out where I am."

When the ghost said that I could, I asked it to make the call for me and stay on the line with us. Soon the view in my glasses was split, with Saul's ghost on the one side and a sweating Stan Glenn on the other. I could see that the powerful American leader was alone in a large net gym, and I had interrupted a virtual game of the sport he had starred in when he was younger. Football players used to have to give up the game entirely when their bodies became too old and battered—plus it was almost impossible to get enough players together to make it worthwhile, and the play could never be as exciting as remembered. That was until holo gaming technology progressed to the point that it could reproduce the experience of playing in a big game, while allowing the participant to actually run around in the room and get a workout in the process.

"Let me guess," Glenn said as he wiped his face with a towel. "You've reconsidered my requests, and will be sharing the antigravity technology with us."

"Maybe," I said, "if you have some information that you can share with me."

His eyebrows raised. "What are you looking for?"

"When we talked last, I told you I was having some problems, but you didn't ask what they were. So I was wondering if you already know about them."

"Seems to me you also talked about the dead guy who's on my screen right now," Glenn said, and wiped his face again. "But I didn't ask you where he came from, either."

"Speaking of him," I said, "watch this." Then I asked Saul's ghost the same series of questions I had just asked it, and got the same "I don't know" answers. Then I turned back to Glenn. "This happens every time. It's programmed to not tell me some things. It may not actually be lying, because the information isn't able to be accessed by the construct." I stared at the big black man, wondering how much I could trust him.

"Stan," I said, "do you know why Sun is trying to kill me?"

"No, Michael, I don't know."

"What, are you a construct, too? Do I have to call Reality G to find out if I'm really talking to Stanford Glenn?"

"No, it's me," he laughed. "And now that I know that your life is being threatened, I could send some Deltas or SEALs to guard you, if you want."

"No thanks. But if you can find out some information about it for me, I would really appreciate it."

"I'll do my best," he said.

"If you find out something, you'll have to call Terrey instead of me. For security purposes."

"Okay," he said, then added, "Terrey who?" I told him, and then said thanks and good-bye.

"Hang in there, my friend," were the last words he said to me. "And whatever happens, try to look at the big picture."

Saul's ghost may not have been intentionally lying to me, but I had the distinct feeling that Glenn was. I couldn't tell for sure, of course, but he definitely did seem to know more than he let on. He even seemed to fall for my gambit of mentioning Terrey, whom he shouldn't be aware of, before he recovered quickly like the skilled politician that he was. But the "big picture" comment bothered me the most—it made me feel like I was being manipulated, as I had been by both Paul Rabin and his father a year before, though for different purposes.

"Before you died," I said to the ghost, who was alone in my glasses again, "you made a comment about me being the 'true peacer.' What did you mean by that?"

"That I hope you will be the one who brings an unprecedented peace and justice to the Bay Area, Michael, and even to the rest of the world."

"So far my involvement in BASS has only brought a lot of conflict and death," I said, "and because of me we're now on the verge of war with the biggest country on the planet."

"Sometimes swords must clash before they can be beaten into plowshares."

"I have one more question for you," I said, my mind jogged by his reference to justice. "One of my protection team members has a Dreamscape rig that records dreams and supposedly predicts which ones will come true. And supposedly it's saying that another member of the team will die protecting us. Lynn, more because of her bleeding heart than anything else, thinks we should send her away, so we won't be complicit in her death."

"That seems like a stretch to me, Michael."

"Yeah, that's what I said. But given your, uh, spiritual interests . . . do you think that it's possible for people to dream something that happens in the future?"

"You don't have to be spiritual to think that is possible," the ghost said. "Time is a mysterious thing, as Einstein showed us long ago, and no one since has figured it all out. If there *is* a Supreme Being who can see all of time, then of course it's possible he might reveal something that will happen, though I'm not sure why he would. But even some who worship science instead of God believe in alternate universes, or other ways that different parts of time could intersect with one another." He paused for a moment, and when I didn't say anything, continued. "Take déjà vu for example: no one has ever figured that out either. 'It's not so bad—I don't have to sleep or shower or even go to the bathroom, and I never forget anything.' Do you recognize that statement?"

"I think you said it to me once."

"Yes, Michael. I said that to you in our very first conversation after my death. I merely pulled the data with the exact quote from the past and inserted it here. And if such codes exist for the future, too, they could presumably be inserted into an earlier time, if someone had the ability."

"Do you think this dream might have happened so we would send the woman away and save her life?"

"Or it might have happened so you would think about this issue for some reason. That's the problem with basing decisions on paranormal events, even though I believe they can happen—you don't know how to interpret them, unless someone who knows more than you do tells you what they mean. But I'm not the best person to talk to about these things, Michael. Have you called Ian Charles yet?"

"No," I said. "You just told me about him earlier in this conversation."

"Oh," the ghost said.

I made a mental note to do what it was suggesting at some point, if only because this man had been important enough for Saul to feature him prominently in the ghost's programming. But after disconnecting from it, I called Lynn, because even though I didn't understand or agree with everything that had been said, I felt strangely warmed toward the idea of making peace with my significant other. The ghost's cryptic implications of some kind of global destiny for me reminded me of how Lynn had encouraged me after the great time we had at Sausalito, when we were last together, which in turn reminded me of how great a partner she was for me.

She was working in the kitchen, cleaning up after providing brunch for the protection team, which reminded me of another thing I loved about her. I told her that I wanted to talk to her in private, so she asked Tyra and the twins to move the game they were playing from the adjoining living room into the separate family room. Her desire to keep working was stronger than her dislike for earpieces, so she put one in. I watched her from the kitchen's cameras, enjoying all her curves, but especially the one inside which my little Lynley would be living for another couple months.

"The bananas are being delivered again?" I asked, noticing a bunch of them in a basket on the counter.

"Yes, and the Artesa wines, too. Since we already survived the yellow- and red-colored attacks, Terrey said I could enjoy them again. I think he got tired of my complaining. Tyra still has to test them first, though, since you're refusing to let her go."

One difficult topic was enough for today, so I didn't comment on that one.

"I don't know the best way to say this, Lynn," I started, "so I'm just going to jump in."

"Do I have to stop doing the dishes?" she asked.

"It's up to you, I guess. But this is pretty heavy."

She kept doing the dishes, and I swallowed hard to prepare myself.

"I love you very much, Lynn," I said, still a bit choked. "And the only reason I didn't tell you this before was because I was afraid of how it might hurt you. But it doesn't have to hurt you at all now, and it won't hurt you any-more."

"Spit it out," she said.

"I never did anything bad with Tara, but I kinda led her on and let her think we were still a possibility—until recently, when I dealt with it for good. I was just damn chickenshit, Lynn, and I'm really sorry."

"You haven't slept with her?" she asked, and I noticed that she had stopped doing the dishes.

"No, I promise." I didn't say that I had wanted to, because I felt that was included in my apology. I figured that part wasn't necessary to confess, and it would only make it harder for her.

"I'm relieved to hear that," she said and put her face in her hands, sobbing slightly.

"You're not angry?"

"Not as much as when I thought you were sleeping with her!" She wiped her eyes, and amazingly started doing the dishes again. "I've known something was going on with that woman. In fact, I was convinced that you were at her house."

"I'm glad you're not angry," I said, passing on that topic, too.

"It's easier for me to know," she said, "than not to know." *I should keep that in mind for the future,* I thought. Then she continued: "Why did you decide to do something about it now? And why tell me now?"

"Well, it's been bothering me for a long time," I said. "But to tell you the truth, something happened. Jon ended up in bed with Tara when he was at the castle."

"Ohhgg," she said. "Disgusting!"

"Don't blame him too much. He's got this condition that makes it hard for him not to—"

"Yeah, the condition is called 'being male.' But you're right, I can't blame him or you too much for wanting to be with someone like her." *So she knew that I've lusted after Tara,* I thought. *There's no use hiding anything from this woman.* "She looks like a model, she's talented in her career, and she's assertive—all the things I'm not." I started to protest what she was saying, but she waved me off.

"No, really, Michael. I'm insecure a lot of times about who I am. I don't know if it's my personality or my upbringing, from Mrs. Rabin's programming at the orphanage, but I like being a mom and being around the house. I like cooking, I like decorating. I even like cleaning sometimes." As if to punctuate that, she paused and scrubbed harder on the dishes. "But I also do like getting out and accomplishing things in the world. In fact, I've decided to take Hilly and Jessa to the Presidio and get involved, on the board and part-time staff."

"That's terrific, Lynn," I said. "I think that will be great for you."

"Hopefully it will be great for the *kids,*" she said, and I stood corrected and admired her more for a few quiet moments.

"I miss you," I said finally.

"I miss you, too," she said, and then we whispered about some of the things we planned to do when we were together again.

The whole conversation had gone better than I could have ever hoped, but unfortunately that hope was short-lived. It was fun making those plans with Lynn for when the kaleidocide was over, but we never would have planned what actually happened to us at the end.

39
DREAM COME TRUE

Stephenson spent most of the next day, which was Wednesday, on walking patrol or running various errands for Terrey or his Japanese cyborg assistants. The protection team's boss kept Korcz standing guard in one place all day for some reason, and Min was doing so near the Ares woman, so everything that required physical exertion seemed to fall on his small shoulders. It was hard work, but he preferred it to how some of the other team members spent their day.

Tyra was doing her cupbearer thing in the house, helping with the little girls who were staying there, and one of the triplets was still recovering in the infirmary. The double was in a net room conducting everyday BASS business like a high-tech puppet for Michael Ares, who was telling him what to do from somewhere in hiding. Terrey himself stayed more or less in his makeshift office, plotting his protection schemes and barking orders like a third-world dictator, and the other two triplets didn't move around much either because they were immersed in cyberspace most of the time. Terrey and his assistants had decided together that they thought the next attack might be attempted through the invisible world of the net, because none of them had yet been associated with the color white. The Chinese word for white (*bai*) could also mean "ghost," as in "Ghost in the Shell," so the thinking was that there might be an attempt to sabotage the hill by hacking its security systems.

Stephenson thought there was a hole in this hypothesis—"Ghost in the Shell" was a familiar term from the popular arts in the triplets' home country, but not in the very different culture of China. That didn't stop him from having to crawl around in various parts of the base's superstructure, however, cutting wires or planting extra scanning equipment as the *Trois* told him what to do and watched him do it through his glasses. Nor did it keep him from having to walk out far from the base and do similar things to the air defense arrays hidden in the surrounding hillsides, to make sure that they couldn't be used to destroy the structures that they were built to protect. Despite the degree he had earned in a difficult field of mathematics, Stephenson didn't know what he was doing in any of these projects, but he was confident that the triplets did. Their technical expertise amazed him.

But they were also slave drivers, so he was very excited to finally get a break for an hour at the end of the day. He was excited about the opportunity to rest his aching body in his room in the hill, but he was even more excited to look again at what had been going on his mind while he was sleeping at night. He pulled out the black Dreamscape rig and plugged it in to the dime-sized yellow jackpatch on the back of his head. Then he lay back and perused the list of dreams that the software had identified as having "High Precog Potential."

There were about ten dreams on the index, and the highest rating currently belonged to the one with the black woman who dies while eating something at a table. Stephenson knew that the high rating might be because he had shared this with the protection team, thinking that it applied to Tyra, and then dreamed versions of it again because it was heavy on his mind. But he did sincerely believe that it was going to happen, and had to ruefully admit that part of him wanted it to happen. So he left it on the index, but the next one on the list had to be deleted. The Dreamscape software made sophisticated calculations from factors like the location and type of brain waves, but its accuracy also depended on the user eliminating those dreams that could not be precognitive, or were not likely to be. And in this particular case, the second dream listed was one that seemed to be based on Stephenson's prior experience.

In this rather elaborate dream, he was being attacked by a swarm of well-armed soldiers who arrived in armored SUVs and helicopters. The soldiers' armor and the vehicles were painted a blue-green color, which made Stephenson realize that this dream was inspired by the video he had been shown of the triplets' battle with the mercenary assault team in Oakland, which had happened just before he and Korcz were hired to the protection team. It was a shame that this dream was not precognitive, however, because in it he fought off big numbers of enemies and emerged not just alive, but as a hero. He deleted the dream from the list, however, assuming that it came from something that had already happened.

The next three dreams were not nearly as rousing, but were merely recapitulations of random events that had occurred in his past. So he deleted them from the index also. Then he came upon a very interesting item, which was new to the index, so he had probably dreamed it the night before. It was a dream in which Michael Ares fell to his death from a big bridge, so he left it on the index and determined to tell the rest of the team about it. The next entry was one that was clearly much more fantasy than reality, involving him and the triplets, which probably only made the list because it recurred so often. He deleted it and determined *not* to tell the rest of the team about that one. Then there were a few more past events that needed to be deleted, and a dream in which Korcz and Tyra got married. That contradicted the much higher rated one where Tyra dies from poison, of course, but Stephenson left it on the index because he wondered about the possibility of alternate futures.

As if God or the gods of fortune wanted to make a decree on that particular topic, Stephenson's Dreamscape session was abruptly interrupted by an emergency call from Terrey, broadcast throughout the base and calling the whole team to the house. Stephenson tore off the Dreamscape rig, strapped his gear on again, and quickly made his way up there.

When he saw the scene in the living area of the Ares house, a rush of conflicting emotions surged inside of him—all of which he was careful to hide from the rest of the team gathered there. He felt euphoria that his dreams had come true once again, guilt and sorrow for how they had come true, and no small measure of fear for the implications of the fact that Dreamscape was once again being proven right.

Tyra was slumped over the kitchen counter with her head in the sink, and in her lifeless right hand was still clutched a half-peeled banana with a bite taken out of it. Lynn Ares was sitting on a couch on the other side of the room, sobbing with her head in her hands. One of the functioning triplets was sitting next to her, rubbing her back to give her comfort, and the other was examining Tyra's body and bagging the poison delivery method. The Black Italian girl had been dead for a while, so nothing could be done for her at this point.

"Where are the girls?" asked the disembodied voice of Michael Ares, who was obviously watching them all through the room's cameras.

"They're playing a game in their room," his wife said in between sobs. "I needed to rest . . . I asked her to do the rest of the dishes left over from lunch. I'm so sorry."

"Lynn, don't be sorry," Ares said. "You didn't have anything to do with this."

"I started ordering the bananas again," she sniffled.

"That was Terrey's call. Right, Terrey?"

"Yeah, right," the man said, in his half-Aussie, half-British accent. "We already had the color yellow with the sniper, so I thought—"

"It's white," the crying woman said, pointing toward the kitchen. "Bananas are actually white." Then she burst out in louder crying, and about half of the team experienced a collective "Ohhhh" when they finally realized what she meant.

"But like Michael said, it's on me." Terrey was obviously trying to mollify the woman and take control of the situation. "And it may have been a daft move on my part, but at least now we know more, and have drawn out another of the assassination methods. We know what the white is, as she pointed out." He made an awkward gesture toward Mrs. Ares. "And there's never been any more than one poisoning attempt in the previous killings, so I think we can safely say we're done with that. Nonetheless, we should all switch to the astronaut food we brought along with us for the duration. I don't think it will be long now, but since, you know, we don't have our cupbearer anymore . . ." Now he gestured awkwardly toward the lifeless body at the sink.

"I don't know how long this will last," the lady of the house said. Terrey's stratagem had worked, apparently, because she had gathered herself more now.

"And I don't know how you even can tell when it's over. But until it is, I'm gonna have to go somewhere else, like maybe the Presidio when I take the girls there. I can't be around here right now, after . . . after *that*." Now it was her turn to gesture at the body, and at a nod from Terrey the triplet next to her stood up and walked over to the kitchen where the other one was. Together they lifted Tyra's body and carried it out of the room, in the direction of the hill base below. A disturbing vision flashed into Stephenson's mind, of them dissecting it in an attempt to trace the deadly chemicals.

I guess I can delete that dream from the index, he thought. *Korcz won't be marrying her anytime soon.*

"Your idea of going to the Presidio might dovetail with an idea I have," Terrey said to the woman, "for something else down in that direction. I was talking to Michael about this earlier today, but I'll let you all in on it. BASS peacers have had John Rabin under surveillance since his mother died in the fire, because of his antagonistic attitude toward the company. And sure enough, this morning he was caught making an illegal purchase of a gun, and then found to have been researching BASS locations like this one on the net. So he was taken into custody and is being held at the Marin County Jail. We were looking for a safe place to do this, so now that we have one I think that Jon and Lynn should take his sisters to visit him. This will stop the increasing speculation in the press about why Lynn hasn't been seen in public, especially with Michael, and it will also help BASS with a significant public relations issue. The CEO will be showing kindness to someone who has been openly critical of him, and head off the worse criticism he would get if he never visited the boy."

"While we're doing that, protected by the rest of the team," Michael Ares's voice rang out from all around them, "Terrey and Ni will travel a little farther south and check out the security at the Presidio. I asked them to do that, Lynn, because you said you wanted to start working there sometime soon. And if you're now saying you might want to stay there, I definitely want them to secure the place as much as they can, find the safest spot for you to stay, etcetera."

"We'll do that on Friday morning," Terrey said, "to give us a full day to prepare. But in the meantime, we need to talk about Stephenson's dreams." He looked meaningfully at the little man, who experienced again the same flood of excitement, guilt, and fear. "Maybe we should take them a little more seriously."

"I hate to say I told you so," Stephenson said, the emotion of pride now eclipsing all the others.

"I looked at the dream, remember?" Ares's voice said. "It wasn't that close to what happened—she was at a table, I think, in the dream, and . . ."

"Still, it's rather uncanny," Terrey interrupted.

"I think you should take my dreams *a lot* more seriously," Stephenson spoke up to the two powerful personalities. He also had always been a bold person— some people had even accused him of a Napoleon complex—but his experiences with the Dreamscape rig had made him even bolder.

"Have you had any others that we should know about?" Terrey asked, and it caught Stephenson off guard, because all he could think of at first were the dreams about the triplets. But then he remembered the other one.

"Yes, actually," he answered. "I had a dream about Mr. Ares dying in a fall from a bridge."

"Hmmm," the Protection G leader said, thinking for a moment. "I don't think we have to worry about that anytime soon. Michael is safely tucked away somewhere, and Jon will be traveling to Marin by aero, so he won't be crossing any bridges. But maybe you should stay away from them the rest of your life, mate, just in case."

"I'll think about it," the voice said.

"How did they know what we like to eat?" Mrs. Ares asked from the couch, obviously not being able to move on yet from the murder that just happened in her kitchen. "Did you say something about it in a net interview, like with the wine?"

"Not that I remember," Mr. Ares said.

"Someone here could have told them," Korcz spoke up for the first time.

"Well, that's just stupid, Korcz," Terrey shot back. "Everyone here knows that Jon is a double, and the real Michael *isn't here*. What would be the point?"

"Okey, but I don't like how much you keep from us." Korcz stared at the Aussie defiantly as he said this.

"Like what, mate?"

"Like what is happening with them," the big Russian said, pointing to the two triplets, who had just come back into the room. *They're either very fast at autopsies,* Stephenson thought, *or they're putting it off till later.*

"What are you talking about?"

"Sex," Korcz said.

"What?" Terrey said, and his gaze fell on Stephenson.

"Don't look at me," the little man said, with his dreams about the triplets in mind, but then realized that Terrey was hoping that he, being Korcz's partner and friend, could translate this for him. So Stephenson added, "I don't know what he's talking about, either."

"Not triples," the bald man continued. "Sex. How do you say . . . ?"

Everyone stared at each other quizzically, until finally the two female cyborgs shared a look of recognition, and did that weird silent communication with Terrey that ended with a nod from him.

"Sextuplets," one of the Japanese women said. "That's the word you're looking for."

"Da. You are sextuplets."

"Not exactly, but you're very close." This was Terrey speaking again, never one to let a conversation exclude him for too long. "They were actually octuplets, but two didn't live very long beyond the origination process."

"Could someone please explain what the hell you're talking about?"

Stephenson heard this from the Ares woman, and thought that she must have been seriously stressed, because he had never before heard her use even mild profanity. Something about how she had been raised at that orphanage—the one run by the wife of the mysterious old guy who had started BASS.

"Mr. Korcz has divined the secret of the *Trois,*" Terrey said. "That they're more than *Trois.* Their three sisters live in the packs on their backs. Or actually we could call them 'half-sisters,' which would certainly give new meaning to the term, because they only consist of brain matter and some auxiliary nervous systems—all of which have been heavily augmented since they were created, of course." Stephenson wasn't really surprised to hear this, because Japan had long been renown for the genetic experimentation that had been occurring there.

"How did you discover this, Korcz?" Terrey asked, and Stephenson noticed that the team leader had changed the way he was referring to his partner—he used to call him Valeri.

"I am from Asia," Korcz answered. "I know a little Japanese. Ni is the number two, San is the number three, and the other one is other number."

"Go is five," one of the girls helped him.

"So is missing one and four, maybe six," Korcz continued. "And when your sister was burned in the fire, you were mourning a death. But she survived."

"That's right, Valeri," the same girl said. She used his first name, seeming to appreciate the attention he was showing to her and her sisters. "Our sister Roku lived in symbiosis with Go, in her 'backpack' as Terrey calls it, and she was killed in the fire. It was she that we were mourning, and that is why Go is still recovering, because losing the symbiotic relationship she had with Roku damaged her own systems severely."

"Ichi rides with me," said the other girl, who must be Ni. "And Yon rides with San."

"So that's why you seem to be able to do the work of six people," Stephenson said, "because you really *are* six people."

"It's actually exponential rather than additional," Ni said matter-of-factly. "We all have the same DNA structure and compatible augmentations, so we are all able to share and process informational and sensory input simultaneously."

"Did you say 'Yon'?" the disembodied voice of Michael Ares asked.

"Yes, Yon is the number four in Japanese, and she is our fourth sister, who rides with San." She nodded toward the back of the other girl.

"Well, that solves a mystery for me," Ares said. "I've met Yon, she talks to me on my screen sometimes."

The two cyborgs looked at each other and smiled. Then Ni said, "Yon has an independent streak. She likes to sneak off and do things that we can't control sometimes. We're not surprised that she picked you to talk to." They smiled at each other again.

"Why?"

"Because she's always had a thing for good-looking men."

"Really?" said Ares's wife. "How can she know what he looks like *when she has no eyes?*"

"She sees through ours, of course."

"But she's just a . . . brain, with no body. So I can't be jealous of her, right?" She laughed for the first time since finding the body. "Why would she even care about how someone looks?"

"We've wondered that, too," the cyborg said. "And we think that it is precisely because she has no body of her own—she tries to act as if she did."

"She just typed on my screen," Ares said. "'Good men prefer brains over beauty.'"

"Yeah, well, obviously *she* doesn't," Ares's wife joked.

"Touché, Lynn," he said.

"We're sorry about that, Mr. Ares," Ni offered. "We try to stop her from drawing outside the lines, but she's persistent."

"That's okay," the BASS CEO said, "but why didn't you tell us about all this, Terrey?"

"We've found that it tends to freak people out and lose us business before they know what we can do," he answered. "Too much of an education is required for people to understand that they are people too. Right or wrong, humans do base a lot on physical attractiveness, and in case you've never seen it, brain tissue is not very attractive."

"Yon says 'Speak for yourself,' Terrey." Ares laughed, but Terrey didn't. He gave Ni and San a look that said they should keep their sister under control.

"It still worries me," Korcz said, staring Terrey down again. "They *are* people, and they should not be hidden away. So I think you have other things to hide, danyet?"

Terrey gave Korcz a look that was not too different from the one he had given his assistants, and Stephenson wondered what else was going on between his boss and his partner. The next day he would find out, and on the day after that, another one of his dreams would come true.

40
BAD FEELINGS

I spent most of Thursday morning in a virtual meeting with Terrey, prepar-
ing for the Marin trip that we had planned for the next day, and a lot of that
time was spent looking at the security measures already in place at the Presidio,
plus the ones that could be added. I don't know if I had a subconscious premo-
nition of what became conscious later on, or if I was merely motivated by a
husband's love and concern, but I wanted to make use of Terrey's expertise in
personal protection, and he was very willing to oblige—probably because he
was now being paid another $500,000 per day to ensure Lynn's safety as well as
mine.

After Friday, when she went to stay at the orphanage, that would be the
easiest fortune ever amassed, because she would now be far away from the double,
who was the kaleidocide's target, and out of harm's way. I was so relieved that she
was finally willing to go someplace else that I found it hard not to be happy
about the cause of it, which was Tyra's death. I had noticed that the little man,
Stephenson, also seemed to be suppressing some delight at that unfortunate
occurrence, though for a different reason. He wanted to believe that his dreams
were prescient, while I was thinking of what a nightmare it would be to lose
Lynn and our baby as collateral damage in this vendetta against me. I could
honestly say that I would rather die myself than see that happen.

One of the reasons for my increased gratefulness for Lynn and our domestic life was the time I had spent with Angelee and Chris over the last few days, in between conducting my business at BASS through the double and dealing with Tyra's death. We shared most of our meals together, and spent time together playing games and watching *Pilgrim* and some other holos that I had upgraded, much to the delight of the little boy. The sexual tension had all but disappeared, thanks to Angelee's cycle—another example of bad things working out for good, which seemed to be a recurrent theme in the religious entertainment that they enjoyed. But the emotional attachment they both had toward me was palpable—especially the boy, who had no episodes of self-destructiveness or defiance as long as I was spending some time with him each day. I was almost overcome with sadness when I thought of them returning to a life without a father figure in the house, and I began to realize like never before how important it was for children to have two loving parents, which was another theme in some of the holos that Chris's own father had left for him.

So later in the day I called Lynn to comfort and encourage her, and we talked face-to-virtual-face in our bedroom like we had earlier in the week. This was the last time we would be alone before the fateful events of the next day.

"I just have a bad feeling right now," she said after I asked her how she was doing. "I told you we shouldn't have kept Tyra here, and that we would be responsible for her death."

"And I disagreed with you," I said. "And still do. That could have been you. She did the job she was hired to do, and she didn't even *want* to leave."

"It's just so horrible. And to think that we were joking around with each other right after she died. How are we any better than our enemies? I'm telling you, Michael, I feel like a hammer is going to fall on us, and we'll deserve everything we get."

As was usually the case when she was driven by emotion, there were too many questionable ideas in what she said to address the logic of all of them. So I simply tried to make it easier on her by telling her to stay in her room and hang on until tomorrow, when she would be out of the house and away from the immediate surroundings that were constantly reminding her of what happened the day before.

"I do want to go to the Presidio," she said, "but I'll miss the house and want to come back, in spite of everything." I was glad to see that she was thinking rationally about that issue. And then she added, "Can we redo the whole kitchen?"

I said, "Of course," and then was saved from a long discussion of renovation details by Terrey, who texted me that he was sorry for the interruption but had two important matters to talk to me about. I said good-bye and "Loves" to Lynn, blowing kisses to her and the baby, and soon was looking at Terrey on the screen in front of me.

"Sorry again, mate," he said, "but this is really important."

"Live forever, man," I said, giving him the two-fingered salute.

"Getting right to the point," he said seriously, "we have another issue with Korcz. Because of him being from that city with all the colors, and because of his attitude—I feel he's been trying to sow discord among us—I had the *Trois* examine the OutPhone that we took from him when he arrived. And they found this." He manipulated some controls, and a display packed with figures and code that I couldn't immediately decipher appeared on half of my screen. Then he circled part of it, and I could tell it was a phone number. "While Korcz was on the plane coming here, after we hired him in New York, someone called him from this number. It was encrypted, of course, and it was also deleted from his phone, but my Sheilas are very good, as you know."

"Who called him, Terrey?"

"We don't know exactly, but we do know that the call originated in China. I'm so sorry, mate, it looks like I may have made another dim decision when I hired him, though if I did it was an honest mistake. The only thing I can think of is that Sun's people knew the kind of team members we look for and ran a massive parametered netscan like we did to find the double. Maybe they turned up Korcz because he's someone that you met before and dealt with favorably, I don't know. But if they did find out we hired him, they must have crapped their pants when they found out he was from Gdańsk." He paused for a moment. "You know, I'm starting to really think there's something to this color thing. Are you sure you won't do the ritual with me?"

"Hold on a second, Terrey," I said. "We don't know anything for sure about Korcz."

"Right, but do you want to take any chances, knowing all this?"

"So what do you suggest we do?"

"Well, we can't just let him go, in case he has somehow figured out where you are. And we can't even let him walk around without keeping an eye on him at all times. But I don't think we need him for the Marin trip tomorrow—we've already eliminated the full-on assault team they had planted, so any further threat would likely be up close and personal, and the three team members with the double can handle anything like that. So I say we lock him up for now in his room in the hill, where he can't do any damage, and then see if he really is the traitor."

"How would we do that?" I asked.

"When we come back from Marin, we'll say that you're coming to the house just for the night to see Lynn—conjugal visit, you know. And we'll have Jon do that—not the conjugal part, of course, but pretend to be you, fly into the hangar in an aero, with the team there to meet him. Korcz won't know the difference, 'cause he'll have been locked up with no net before that. Lynn will be at the Presidio, safe and sound, but he won't know that . . . we'll tell him she's up in the house waiting for you, to be with you one night before she goes to stay down there. Korcz will have an opportunity to move on the double when he's coming through the base, and then when he's staying in the house alone that night."

"So if Korcz is the traitor," I said, "then Jon will be killed."

"Not necessarily. We'll rig up some kind of surveillance and security before we let Korcz out, and try to save Jon if we can. But if he does die, it's a small price to pay for exposing what might be the last attempt in the kaleidocide." He smiled and nodded. "I can see the light at the end of the tunnel from here, mate."

"What about motive?" I asked. "Why would Korcz be working for the other side?"

"Well, you did shoot him, Michael."

"But only a little," I said, repeating my joke from when we first hired the man.

"The right amount of money is always enough motivation," Terrey said with another wry wink. "Hell, I would probably betray you if someone could pay me more than one point five a day."

After a few more questions, I agreed to Terrey's plan, and he went to talk to Korcz along with both of the remaining triplets, in case the big Russian caused some kind of problem. It wouldn't have been wise if he did, because even with his considerable size and weapons skills, I had the feeling that just one of the cyborgs would be way too much for him. I watched the confrontation initially through Terrey's contacts, but the blinking effect eventually bothered me enough that I switched to the room where they met.

Fortunately, Korcz was basically copacetic. He protested the implication that he might be disloyal to his employer, which he said he never had been in his life, but did confirm that he had been called from an unknown number on the flight in. He said that he didn't answer the call, however, *because* it was from an unknown number, and that he didn't remember deleting it. Like the time I had interrogated him in the castle a year before, during the "silhouette" incident, my gut feeling was that he was telling the truth. But my gut feelings had been very wrong before, like with other people in that same incident, so I was still okay with Korcz being confined to his room until the Marin trip was over. Fortunately, he was okay with it, too, especially after we reminded him that he would be fully paid for the time that he would be doing nothing, and not risking his life or health in any way.

When Ni and San left to escort Korcz to his room and secure it, I asked Terrey what the other important item was.

"Oh," he said. "You wanted me to get the results of those AIMS tests directly to you, so the double wouldn't see them. Here they are." He transferred a file to my netkit.

"Did you look at them?" I asked.

"None of my business, mate," he said with a wink, then hung up.

I opened the file, found Tara's name among the other high-level staff that had been tested, and stared at her results for a while. Then I called Jon in his room and talked to him on the screen. Even though it was disconcerting again to be looking at my own face, this was another conversation I wanted to have in this way. I also wanted to be reminded that I could easily be in the same situation as he.

2

4

"I have the results of Tara's AIMS test," I said.

"And . . . ?" he said. This was a big deal for him, not only because he would have to live with giving her the disease, but it would mean that he had *not* been cured by the Makeover I.S. injections.

"She has full-blown Acquired Immune Mutation Syndrome," I said. "Skipped the dormant stage. Mistargeted somatic hypermutation has already resulted in a diffusion of B-cell lymphomas throughout her body, and caused other irregularities at the cellular level. Her organs and vascular system are now slowly eating themselves alive, while the beautiful body we both enjoyed so much will soon be covered in blotches of thick hair and puss-filled boils. Those gorgeous ice blue eyes are already bulging out like an insect's from the pressure on her brain. You've seen the pictures of AIMS victims—I don't think I need to elaborate any further."

"My God," he croaked, swallowing vigorously. "Can't she be treated, with all the money your company has?"

"Too late," I said, shaking my head. I let it settle in for a few moments, then added, "How does that make you feel?"

"Terrible," he said. "And worse because it's probably what will happen to me, too. I guess I deserve it, with what I did to her."

"Now you're talking," I said. If he expected or wanted any sympathy from me, he didn't show it. But I continued anyway. "And don't think you'll get enough money from us to buy a cure. No bank account in the world would survive the criminal charges and wrongful death lawsuits you are facing."

"I understand," he said with his head bowed.

"How bad do you feel?"

"I feel as bad as I could feel!" he shouted as he looked up at me.

"Good."

"I feel bad enough to go back to Exit right now," he said, bowing his head again.

"You don't have to do that," I said. "'Cause I was just messing with you."

"What?" He looked up at me again.

"Tara's test came back negative, she's fine. Which means you're probably clean now, too."

"Then why the hell did you say all that to me?" he yelled.

"Because that is *exactly* what could have happened, very easily. The fact that it didn't happen doesn't change how bad you should feel about it. You need help, man. You can't go farther down this destructive path, even if you *were* born that way, and definitely not because some really bad things happened to you. Then everyone would have an excuse, to one degree or another."

The ideas that were coming out of my mouth sounded familiar, and I realized that many of them, even down to the "path" metaphor, were in the holos I had been watching with Angelee and Chris. But I wasn't prepared for what he said next.

"You're right, actually. And to tell you the truth, I was just as bad before my wife and kids died—it's just that I kept it inside. The reason I know so much about that opportunity idea is because it applies to me, too. Before I lost my family, I didn't have the opportunity to act on my desires, but in my mind I was still lusting after almost every woman I saw, even some of my students, I'm sorry to say. I would even think about them, or porn, when I was with my wife. You said the word, man—excuse. My loss was just an excuse to do what I really wanted to do before that." He started to choke up and cry. "Oh man, I am so—"

The last couple words were obscured by his sobs, but I could tell what he was saying.

"What should I do?" he asked, when he had gathered himself somewhat.

"Be really sorry," I said.

"I *am* really sorry. What else can I do?"

This was the part I was unprepared for. I had just wanted to heap loads of guilt on him for what he had done, as much for my own revenge as for his repentance.

"Maybe find one good woman, and pour yourself into her." This was all I could think of, from Saul's advice and from my own experience. "I'll tell you what, why don't you think about it some more? I've got some other things to do right now."

"Do you think that Stephenson's dream about you dying could actually be about me?" he asked.

"No, like Terrey said, you won't be traveling on any bridges tomorrow."

"But I mean later in my life," he said. "I could survive all this, and be cured of my AIMS, and still die at any time."

Wow, I thought, *I had no idea this talk would give him such a big dose of humility.*

"That's true of all of us, isn't it?" I said. "So I wouldn't worry about it. At least, no more than . . . the rest of us should. Right?"

I didn't like the feelings I was having myself now, so I hung up on him and looked at my to-do list, hoping for something to take my mind off such topics. The next item was the number for Ian Charles, the man that Saul's ghost had recommended that I talk to. I was willing to call it at the time because I was thinking that the ghost had given it to me in the context of the political issues I faced with the kaleidocide, and was suggesting that I hire this man to help with those. It turned out that this recommendation was also about philosophical questions, but as luck or fate would have it, it ended up being my final step toward getting the political ones answered as well.

41
EARS TO HEAR

A woman answered my call, on audio only, and sent it to another room when I asked for Ian Charles. My display said the net room was in Branson, Missouri.

"This is Ian," a voice said, also on audio. But when I explained who I was, he promptly switched to video, presumably because he wanted to have the full experience when talking to someone he had seen on the news. He was sitting at a desk with many rows of real books on shelves behind him—something you didn't see too often now that virtual or "veel" books were the more common choice for readers. *Lynn would like this guy,* was my first thought.

My second thought was that many other women had probably liked him, because he was still noticeably attractive, even though he seemed to be well into his sixties. He had big eyes, a chiseled jawline, and a lot of dark hair left, which was nicely highlighted with streaks of white. Possibly some near-eastern ancestry.

"I knew your predecessor," he said right away, in a deep, rich "radio voice" that was also impressive.

"That's why I'm calling," I said. "He told me I should call you . . . before he died." I added the last part because I didn't want to take the time to explain the ghost. Plus it was technically accurate—Saul had programmed it that way while he was still living, and the reason for this call was to find out why.

"I have to say that's a big surprise to me," the man said. "Did he say why?"

"I was hoping you could tell me. What was your connection with BASS?"

"Nothing official," he said. "I suppose you could say that, in a way, I was Mrs. Rabin's pastor. She was too, um, visible or public of a person to attend a church regularly, but she listened to my teaching online and came to me for counsel on a few occasions."

It was only then that I realized that Saul's ghost had given me this man's number because of the metaphysical issues that had come up in our conversation. I may be a bit slow on the uptake sometimes, but I eventually get it.

"But you knew Saul, too," I said.

"Yes, my connection with his wife led to some dinners with both of them, and lunch a few times with just him, and some calls and emails. I think she was hoping that I would convert him, which of course no one but God can do."

"Saul mentioned something about possibly hiring you," I said, remembering that part of the conversation. "Do you know why that would be?"

"There was some talk of bringing me on as some kind of chaplain at BASS—probably Kathryn's idea. But that was before our falling out, and it never happened."

"Falling out?" I asked, and my first thought here was that this man may have had an affair with Saul's wife. He *had* used her first name, and the clergy has always been notorious for sex scandals.

"I said some things that Saul didn't like," he said. "Or maybe that he couldn't allow to be said in the city, by someone that close to him."

"Are you saying that he didn't only keep you out of BASS, but he kicked you out of the city?"

"If you want to put it that way, yes. That's the long and short of it."

"He kicked you out of the city for disagreeing with him?" I asked, and Charles shrugged as if to say *More or less.* "What's an example?"

"Oh, there were many things, but I suppose one of the biggest was my opposition to the degree of authority given to the peacers as individuals, for incarceration and summary execution. I believe in the biblical law of two or three witnesses, of course, and capital punishment only in cases of murder established through a fair trial. If then."

"The law of witnesses?" I said. I was familiar with many of the criticisms of BASS agents having a "license to kill," but this was a new term to me.

"There has to be more than one witness, or at least corroborating evidence, for anyone to be convicted of a crime, or even treated as guilty. But the peacers were often determining by themselves whether someone was guilty, then locking them up or even using lethal force."

And we still do, I thought.

"Lethal force is only allowed after the second offense," I said, referring to BASS's version of the three-strike rule.

"Right, but each offense doesn't have to be established by the law of two or three witnesses, so the arrests could have been wrongful."

"But three wrongful arrests for the *same person?*" I protested. "I couldn't see that happening."

"A peacer or a group of peacers could have a prejudice against a person or group of persons," he said. "And have an easy time railroading the accused, because the peacers themselves are the legislative body."

"But it makes for a lot less red tape, that's for damn sure." I wondered if it was okay to say "damn" to a reverend, because I had never talked with one before. "And we hire good people who wouldn't do that."

"What's for damn sure," he said, answering my question about swearing, "is that people in authority always expect the worst from their subjects, but believe the best about themselves. My theology says that we're all equally broken, though in different ways, so too much power should never be given to any one person."

I smiled. "I can see why Saul didn't want you to be the BASS chaplain."

"Saul Rabin dabbled in my religion, mostly because of his wife, and even professed to believe it to some degree. But though he saw the value of its laws, he never fully understood grace and mercy, and so missed the real meaning. And that was the source of his problems—it caused him to remain manipulative, trying to control too much that he should have left to God. It also led to a utilitarian philosophy where what works is more important than what's right. I tried to tell him these things, but he didn't have ears to hear."

"Yet at the end of his life he suggested that I call you, and even bring you back to the Bay Area."

"Hmmm. Maybe he *was* listening after all." Now it was his turn to smile. "How about you?"

"Me?"

"Do you have ears to hear? The Mayor must have thought so, if he gave you my number. I'm guessing you were asking some important questions . . ."

When he said that, another realization hit me, which became a key step in my investigation into the mystery of the kaleidocide. I realized that Saul's ghost had been programmed to respond in a particular way after I had asked a certain number of questions about spiritual issues. It had only told me about Charles at that point in our conversations. Soon I would put this together with the fact that Saul had been manipulative and controlling, and be able to get the answers I needed from his ghost. But at this time I was mostly impressed by the courage Ian Charles had shown by standing up to the old man at the height of his power, and the fact that he wasn't a slave to bitterness after being unfairly persecuted.

"I'll think about the chaplain thing," I said to him. "But here's an audition for you, to see what kind of counsel you give."

I told him about the double's polyamory, because I was curious about what he would say, and I was also hoping to get some confirmation for a plan I might want to implement if we all made it through this ordeal (which was a big "if"). I wasn't surprised to find out that Charles thought Jon could and should change, but I was surprised when he said that change "would mean absolutely nothing, and actually be *worse* for the person, if he doesn't do it in the name of Jesus Christ and for his glory." He apologized if that was a shock to my system, because I may have only used or heard that name as a swear word (which was basically true), but that it was his job to talk about him and since this was an audition, I should know what he would do if he was a chaplain at BASS.

"I wouldn't shove it down anyone's throat," Charles concluded, "but if you or others did have ears to hear . . ."

I asked him what he thought about the theory of a poly loving one good woman, instead of trying to go cold turkey, and he liked it—except he added that it should be a Christian woman who could help him spiritually as well as physically. He said that his wife had done that for him in many ways through the years, and he could never have made it without her.

I told Charles thanks and good-bye, and then called Jon back to say, in a very awkward fashion, that he should consider adding a "spiritual dimension" to what we had talked about before. He said he would, because he was still humble and open, but I didn't know whether or not he understood what I was trying to say. I wasn't sure myself, but I was glad I did what I could, because the next day Jon would definitely need to be ready to meet his Maker.

On Friday morning Terrey gathered everyone together for a meeting before our trip to Marin. He reviewed the fact that there had been four assassination attempts on Jon, at least that we were aware of: the blue-green of the assault team, the dark yellow of the sniper, the burgundy of the firebombs, and the white of the poison. He reminded us that the best hypotheses for the colors in a kaleidocide were the ones from the Tibetan Book of the Dead—which were red, yellow, blue, white, and green—or the ones corresponding to the ancient "five elements": black, red, greenish blue, white, and yellow. Black might be mixed in with the colors to make them darker—except for the white, of course. These theories were only theories and might not be correct, but if either of them were, then my double might be out of danger already or awaiting only one more attempt, which could be associated somehow with the color black.

Since black had been the color of a traitor in several other kaleidocides, Terrey took this opportunity to explain to everyone what had happened with Korcz and why we had confined him to his room with no comm access. When they heard about the city in Poland and the call from China on his phone, no one protested this except Stephenson, who had worked with Korcz for almost a year and initially called our suspicions ridiculous. But he soon backed off a bit from his initial confidence when I asked him how well he really knew Korcz, to which he had to admit that "no one knows Korcz that well." And he backed off even further when Terrey encouraged him to check the dreams he had recorded when we got back, to see if there was anything that might implicate the Russian. Stephenson said that he hadn't noticed anything like that, but also had to admit that he hadn't been looking for it.

Terrey put him at ease by saying that he still thought a traitor was unlikely in this scenario, because of how the team members were recruited and vetted. He thought that if there was a "black" attempt on Jon's life, it would likely come from a single assassin, who had been biding his time and waiting for the right opportunity. He also didn't think it was likely that such a killer could strike during the Marin trip. We would be alerting a few press outlets for some independent confirmation of the appearance, in addition to our own filming of it, but we wouldn't do that until Jon and Lynn were ready to leave the jail. It would take a lot of luck for an assassin to be close enough to that location to strike before they were in the aeros and gone.

Finally, Terrey added that the guards at the Marin County Jail did wear black uniforms, but no one knew beforehand that they were going there, and they would be accompanied by the watchful eyes and powerful weapons of Min, Ni, and Stephenson, which would provide more than enough protection for them.

At the mention of weapons, Jon asked me if he could wear my boas again on this trip, like he had on the one to the castle. I said yes, and he said he was glad I did, because he already had put them on. He pulled my jacket aside to show me, through the room's cameras, and I saw them on his belt next to the control box for the Atreides shield that had been built for him. Terrey made a crack about leaving the safeties on, "permanently, please," and everyone loaded up into their aeros and flew them out through the big holo at the mouth of the hill's hangar bay.

As the flying cars traveled south over Napa City, then Vallejo, and then the top inlets of the San Francisco bay, I switched my video and audio to riding with Jon and coached him on what we would say to John Rabin when we talked with him at the jail. The double was in the passenger seat of Min's aero, with the big bodyguard driving, and Lynn was in another with Ni driving and the Rabin twins in the back. Stephenson flew one by himself, behind the other two. Terrey and San flanked him in the fourth aero, and would not be stopping with the others at the jail, but would be continuing south to visit the Presidio orphanage in the city, to put the finishing touches on the security measures we cooked up for Lynn's stay there. The idea was that after the visitors talked with John Rabin and were filmed coming out of the jail, Min would take Lynn to the Presidio and the rest of the team would return to Napa Valley.

The security officer inside me was worried about having so few team members, and how thinly spread they would be, especially on the return trip. But we didn't bring in any BASS peacers for fear that one or more of them had been bought off by Sun, because the "heavy guns" sent to kill me had already been dealt with by the triplets in Oakland, and because the team members themselves didn't seem to share my anxiety. Min and Ni, for example, spent half the trip comparing the specs of their combat augmentations in the most lighthearted fashion I could imagine between two very serious cyborgs. Ni even made a bona fide joke at the end, when she conceded victory to Min because she had never been equipped with a cannon in her derriere. I knew the big machine-man would never live that one down, and now he was taking it on the chin from a creature that seemed to have very little sense of humor otherwise.

The trip passed uneventfully, despite the tension I felt with Lynn being so close to the double, and soon our destination came into view amid the arid woodlands and hills of San Rafael. The Marin County Civic Center was one of the truly unique buildings in the world, which is why it had been carefully repaired and restored after the big quake. It had been designed by the famous architect Frank Lloyd Wright, completed in 1962 and, like most of his buildings, seemed to exist outside of time and place. There was nothing quite like it, with its two long, thin arms stretching out in almost opposite directions from a central domed structure, and hundreds of arches of different sizes on the arms reflecting the curve of the dome in an uncanny symmetry. And it was very colorful, of course, which I thought was an interesting coincidence—the roofs of both the long buildings and the dome were painted a bright light blue, which from some angles also looked a little greenish.

At the end of the longer arm, on the northern end of the buildings, was a circular hill that also added to the symmetry of the whole campus. This was where we were headed, because inside the hill was housed the Marin County Jail, as it had been since the Center was built. The three aeros that were staying parked near the entrance to the jail, and Terrey said good-bye and continued on toward the city. He added that he would be monitoring our visit through Ni, however.

The entrance to the jail was set down low in the hill, and on the top behind it was a flat but wide pillbox-like structure with skylights on the roof that served as a source of light for the main room inside. It took us a little while to get there, because we had to undergo a security clearance and then wait for permission to visit John. *We may not need to alert the press,* I thought as we waited. *One of the staff here might alert them, because they could probably make some good money by doing that.*

Eventually we were all let in to the main room of the jail, which was deep in the center of the hill. It was quite spacious, containing about twenty tables and chairs—all bolted to the floor, of course—and extending about thirty feet up to the aforementioned roof with all the skylights that sat on the top of the hill. On the outsides of the circular room were two stories of nicely painted cells—a twentieth-century experiment in making incarceration more "open" and accommodating for the inmates, and a significant contrast to the austere interior and gothic exterior of the Nob Hill cathedral Saul Rabin had transformed into a jail in the city. Normally some prisoners would be milling around in the open area, but the jail staff had cleared it out so we could meet with John Rabin alone.

That didn't end up happening, however, because the staff informed us that he was unwilling to talk to Lynn and me (my double, that is), but would only see his sisters in another room, if allowed. I was actually somewhat relieved by this, since I had been worried about trying to have another difficult conversation through Jon, so I told the staff through him that Hilly and Jessa could meet with John in one of the interrogation rooms deeper inside the underground facility. After we had given them about ten minutes together, we told the staff to inform them that they would have ten more, and then we would be leaving. At that time, Min contacted the three net news services from the area that we had decided upon, so they had a few minutes to get someone there to film us leaving the jail, and maybe get a few brief comments from us about why we were there.

This unencrypted communication over the net, however, brought a lot more than some reporters to our location. Before the ten minutes were up, Terrey's voice broke into all our audio lines, announcing that Ni and San, who were hooked up to the Eye satellite surveillance system, were seeing another enemy assault team in the air just minutes away from the Marin Center.

42
JAILBREAK

"Another assault team?" I said. "Where is this one coming from?"

"It looks like the Dickensian twists of fate are not with us today, mate, but with our foes," Terrey said. "There was never more than one assault team before, and I joked about how easy it was to find the other one, but I guess the joke's on me and they're smarter than I thought. Looks like they put one in the ruins of Oakland in case you turned up in that direction, and another one in the ruins of San Quentin in case you came this way."

San Quentin had been a state prison only a couple miles from where we were, until it was heavily damaged in the earthquake and devastated further by the resultant fires and a protracted fight between the inmates who took it over and the BASS forces who eventually took them out. The prison was not rebuilt, and the area around it had never been an attractive place for people to live anyway. So its seclusion and the shelter of the abandoned buildings, like Oakland across the bay, provided an ideal place for an attack force to gather and wait for the right moment. And the right moment had definitely come—besides being so close to where Jon was, the colorful buildings of the Marin Center must have made Sun and his fellow plotters wet themselves from excitement. In fact, Terrey sent an aerial view of the assault team from the Eye to my second screen, and when it zoomed in I could see that the helicopters and the Armored SUVs that hung from wires below them were all painted the same bright blue as the roofs of the Center. I wondered why there was a misty cloud of that same color trailing from the back of each of the airborne vehicles, until I realized that they had sprayed them so quickly, prior to taking off, that the paint wasn't even dry yet.

Of course, I thought, *they didn't know we would be at the Center until just now, when they intercepted our communication.* I marveled at their efficiency, but also at the insanity of Sun's obsession with colors. And I feared for the safety of our team—and my wife—when I counted the helicopters and suspended SUVs. There were four of each, and they would be at the jail before any of us could get out of it.

"I'm already on my way there," Terrey said. "And so are the closest BASS Firehawks and peacers. But it'll be probably twenty-five minutes before the cavalry will arrive, and the bad guys will be there in five. You'll have to find a way to hold out until some bigger firepower gets there." He paused for a moment, then added, "I'll be glad to make suggestions, Michael, but you'll have to make the calls."

"We need to go get Hilly and Jessa out of that room right now," said Lynn, characteristically thinking of others rather than herself. "And keep them safe." She waited to hear my answer in her earpiece, which I had made her wear in case I needed to coach her also in the conversation with John Rabin.

But while she was talking, the jail alarms started to sound, telling me that our enemies were already close enough to be detected by the security systems there. The prisoners would be thoroughly locked down now, and would therefore be sitting ducks for the destruction that was about to be unleashed on the jail. I knew exactly what was going to happen to it after only a few moments of looking at my second screen, because of my military experience and some of the details that the Eye's scanners had picked up, which the triplets had now transposed onto the view of the approaching vehicles.

"The rockets on the helicopters are hot," Terrey said, realizing the same things I had. "And the mercs inside have loaded grenade launchers." This meant that the attackers wouldn't be taking any chances on a firefight with rifles, or worrying about collateral damage. They were simply going to fire explosives ahead of them until everyone in the jail was dead, and they would do that into every entrance so no one could escape. They were now close enough to the jail that they were fanning out for their approach, and their trajectories to various points on the property were also being displayed on my screen.

"Michael," Lynn said in the direction of the double, "we need to get the girls, now!"

"No, Lynn," I said. "Leave them in the back room."

"Why?" she shouted over the alarm.

"Because that will keep them far from the fight that's about to happen, plus they would slow you down when I try to get you out—and you're my main priority. But please don't ask me why again—this is a combat situation and you have to do exactly as I say to survive. We only have minutes. When the copters arrive, at least one of them will fire rockets into the roof to break it, and then fire more rockets to obliterate the room you're standing in. A group of soldiers will attack the main entrance, firing explosives ahead of them to take out any of the guards defending it and anyone trying to escape out of it. Another group will come through the only other entrance, from the court building adjacent to you, and do the same thing. In a matter of minutes everyone in the jail will be dead. Are you with me so far?"

"How do you know this?" Lynn asked.

"Because it's what we would do," Terrey answered, "if we were them."

"If you stay where you are," I continued, "you're dead, no doubt about it. So you'll all have to move, there's no other way I can see to save any of you, or even any of the prisoners and guards in the jail. Min, Ni, and Stephenson, you'll have to take the fight to them right now, meet them on their way to each of those three spots. And it'll distract them from where Jon and Lynn are going."

"Where can we go?" Lynn asked. "There's no other way out."

"Yes there is," I said. "And we're going to hope and pray that the Chinese don't know about it, because they got their information from the net, and the location of the prisoner transfer tunnel up those stairs is not in the public records, for obvious reasons."

I knew of the existence and location of the secret tunnel from being in BASS leadership, and we had confirmed it when planning the visit. Frank Lloyd Wright must have had fun designing a corridor that was hidden between the first and second floors of the long courthouse building next to the jail, so that prisoners could be transported safely and quickly to and from the courtrooms.

"Why don't I stay back there with Hilly and Jessa?" Lynn asked. "Don't you want to keep me away from your double?"

"I normally do, but this is the best way for you to get out alive, and I don't want to send you alone—I want to go with you by riding with Jon. Once you're in the clear, or if the enemy finds the two of you, I'll separate you then, and hopefully they'll only go after him." I looked at the screen and saw the enemy location. "But we *really* don't have time for whys now. Stephenson, pick your poison . . . it's only fair that you should have your choice of which entrance. The public hallway to the court building is to your left—maybe you'll get lucky and they won't come in that way after all." In reality this was a token gesture, because I was sure they would attack that exit, and so any way he went would be suicide. I didn't think the two combat cyborgs would even survive the day, let alone this unaugmented rent-a-cop.

Jon turned toward Stephenson when I said his name, so I could see him now, because I was looking through Jon's eyes. The little man stood there with his mouth wide open, which at first I assumed was because he knew he was going to die soon. But it turned out to be the opposite, and his mouth widened further into a big grin.

"It doesn't matter which way I go, because I'll be invincible. You won't believe this, but I had a dream about this, too! I thought it was a memory, but now I know it was prophetic. Don't pity me—pity the poor bastards who get in my way." He pulled the assault rifle off his back, which had its own grenade launcher, and practically skipped into the hallway, muttering "Yippee-ki-yay" something-or-other.

I hoped that his dream thing was real in this case, if only because he could provide more time for me to get Lynn away to a safe place. At the very least, it certainly gave the little man a lot of confidence.

"I'll take the roof," Min said, and when Ni asked why, he responded, "Because you can't do this." He fired one of his arm guns at a skylight directly above him, then jumped thirty feet up and through the hole he had made. The broken pieces of transteel cascaded down to where he had stood, and the others had to move away to avoid being hit by them. Ni merely grunted in response to Min's display, pulled her own two guns out and strolled toward the main entrance. She was much more realistic than Stephenson about her chances of surviving this, and was much less eager than he. But as always, she did her job without complaining, and I admired that.

I told Jon and Lynn to head up the stairs, and spent a moment preparing the best visual strategy for managing this in a way that could save Lynn and the baby's lives. I transferred the double's view from the screen to the net room, opening it up in front of me as big as I could with a high enough resolution. The holo stretched out in all directions around me so that I could take advantage of Jon's peripheral vision and see everything that he was seeing. I opened three small views toward the bottom left on the bigger view so I could see what was happening through Min's and Ni's eyes, and Stephenson's glasses. I toggled off their audio for now so I could concentrate on talking to Jon and Lynn, and I opened two more views on the bottom right of the big one. One was the aerial view of the Center so I could see the enemy movements—at least those outside the buildings—and the other was one a blank one that I wanted to be ready in case I could get Lynn into an aero and fly her away from the scene. So when I looked straight ahead with my own eyes, I saw exactly what Jon was seeing, but I could move them down and watch the smaller views if I wanted to, while still being somewhat aware of what was going on with Jon and Lynn.

I did watch the smaller views for a few moments, as Jon and Lynn were being ushered into the prisoners' corridor by a jail guard. In the aerial view on the bottom right, I saw the assault force arrive at the Center, the light blue helicopters dropping the light blue SUVs at four different spots around the jail, and the mercenaries with light blue armor rushing out of the trucks and toward the exact spots I had predicted. The scene gave new meaning to the term "kaleidocide," because I knew that a lot of people, including my protection team members, were probably going to die from this swarm of light blue attackers, at a building covered with the same color. I did take some heart, though, when I saw the squad enter the big Hall of Justice building on the ground floor, which hopefully meant they would encounter Stephenson on their way in, rather than my wife and my double. And I took even more heart when I saw Min leap from the top of the hill toward the two helicopters that were about to fire into the jail as I had predicted. The big cyborg fired a couple small but powerful rockets from his arm at one of the birds on his way up, and grabbed onto the legs of the other when he reached it, directing some armor-piercing bullets into its cockpit.

The helicopter that was hit by Min's rockets exploded in an orange and red ball of flame (my kind of colors!), and the one he held onto started to spiral toward the ground, its dead pilot slumped over the controls. Min let go and fell to the ground, only to be fired upon by the squad of attackers who had been dropped off near the top of the hill to assure no one escaped that way. The big cyborg had to jump back up to the crashing helicopter and use it for cover from them, but another one was now hovering nearby and drawing a bead on him, so there was soon no place for him to take cover. I glanced over to Ni's view to see that she was engaging the mercenaries outside the main entrance to the jail, in a similar fashion—valiant yet ultimately futile. Stephenson was running through his hallway in the direction of the enemy, but he hadn't encountered them yet.

I couldn't worry about those team members for one more moment—I had to turn my full attention to Jon's view and protect my wife and baby as best as I could from thirty miles away. As they moved down the empty prisoner's corridor, I was still worried that the attackers might know about or find the hidden tunnel, so I told Jon to take the safeties off my boas. But I had him leave them in the holsters, because I didn't want him to use them unless he absolutely had to, for fear that his amateurism might cause him to shoot Lynn by mistake.

All three of us were suddenly terrified by a loud and jarring concussion that shook the whole corridor. But then I realized it was an explosion on another floor, and calmed Jon and Lynn down by telling them that it was a good sign because it meant that the attackers were probably engaging Stephenson on the floor below, and didn't know where they were.

For confirmation, I looked at the little man's view on the bottom left of mine. At first I thought he was dead, because it was blank, but then I realized that his view had been obscured by the blast, and he had survived it somehow. He was now hiding in the rubble of a room next to the hallway, where the wall had been blasted away, and he had his rifle trained on the path that the attack squad would be taking on their way to the jail. As I watched, the first few of the blue-suited soldiers came into view, and Stephenson opened fire on them.

"Where to now?" said Jon's voice in my ear. I jerked my attention back to my big view and saw that he and Lynn had arrived in the part of the prisoners' corridor that provided access to the courtrooms in the Hall of Justice. I sent them through one of the rooms, into the beautiful, long atrium that ran through the center of the building, and then to the foyer by the exit on the north side of the building, which was on the other side from the fight going on at the jail and the lot where we had parked our aeros. A glance at Ni's view showed that she was still occupying the enemy force there, but it was way too hot for me to get Lynn to one of the aeros. I told them to stop where they were and take a break, partially because Lynn was huffing and puffing, but also because I was concerned that an enemy copter was circling high enough in the air and close enough to that far side of the building, and it might see them if they exited.

I thought about hiding Lynn somewhere in the building, which had by now been emptied of all the county employees, for the fifteen to twenty minutes until our Firehawks arrived. But I hesitated because I was afraid that the mercs might be scanning the property and would see her heat signature, think she might be me, and hit her location with grenades or rockets. I was soon glad that I didn't go that route, because my fear was confirmed when Terrey's voice came over the comm.

"They must have detected Lynn and your double," he said, "because the squad in the court building just turned around and headed their way."

"How many?" I asked.

"Looks like about six," Terrey said, which meant Stephenson had taken out almost half of them, and now would be in the clear because they had left his location. I hoped he would follow and distract them further, but I couldn't count on him slowing them down, and then Terrey made it very clear that Lynn and Jon had to run. "The fourth squad, which was not being engaged, is also moving in their direction."

That left me with no choice, so I told Lynn and Jon to run out into the parking lot behind the building, and head toward a huge auto transport truck that was parked there, presumably because the driver was visiting the DMV inside the building when it was evacuated. I wanted to put them in something more secure and powerful than a car, and an idea had come to me about how we could use the big carrier to our advantage. Incidentally, I also noticed that the truck was the most colorful object in the parking lot, since it had ten new cars of different shades secured to the top and bottom racks behind the big cab. I didn't know if Terrey would think the colors were good or bad luck, but I didn't have time to worry about that, because two of the enemy helicopters were now swinging around the building toward them. Lynn and Jon would be easy targets for the guns and rockets on those birds in about twenty seconds, whether they made it to the truck or not.

43
THE BRIDGE

Lynn and Jon were running hand in hand—even she didn't mind doing that with a "monstrosity" when her life was on the line.

I was about to tell them to separate from one another in the hopes that the enemy aircraft would only fire on Jon, when two aeros suddenly appeared from the east over their heads and flew directly toward the helicopters. These were two peacers who had been nearby and came when they heard what was happening, and since our aeros were armored but not armed, they had to be creative in how they engaged the sikersky Primes. So both of them used their aeros as missiles, hurling them toward the enemy, and one of the peacers even extended half of her body out of the open driver's side window and fired both of her handguns at the helicopter as she approached it. That pilot swerved out of her way rather easily, but had to evade her gunfire as she passed. The other aero was still being steered by the peacer inside, and so collided directly with its fast-turning target, lodging its nose in the side of the helo and sending them both into a spin that would take a while to recover from. Soon a third aero with another peacer arrived and joined the fray, and now I was more confident that Lynn and Jon could make an escape in the car carrier.

I thought briefly again about sending the two of them in different directions, in different vehicles, but it was the Wild West on that property right now, especially with the two squads of attackers swarming out of the building into the parking lot. I made a quick judgment call that I would rather have Lynn with me, or with my other me at least, so I told them to get in the truck and walked Jon through hot-wiring the engine. He was a quick study, and soon the powerful vehicle was pulling out of the parking lot with all twelve tires screeching. If the SUVs were able to pursue them, the cab would likely take some gunfire, so I told Lynn to curl up in the sleeping compartment in the back of it. If the helicopters were able to pursue them, however, and they had any rockets left, it wouldn't make any difference where Lynn was when the whole truck got incinerated.

"Min and Ni," I shouted after noticing their windows in my holo were still active. "We're on the road, so focus on taking down the three remaining Primes, or at least keep them too busy to follow."

They both acknowledged my order, and I watched briefly through their views and the overhead one as they disentangled themselves from battles with the foot soldiers, some of whom had already left to clamber into the SUVs and pursue the car truck. Both cyborgs had run out of ammo long before this, so Ni dropped the rifle she had taken from one of the attackers and liberated a guided RPG launcher from another. With amazing speed she moved into a position where she could fire it at a couple of the helicopters.

Meanwhile Min, who had been flashing in and out of cover brandishing the two deadly blades that were stored in his back, stopped hacking at the other group of mercs and made two massive leaps toward the Prime that had eaten the aero and was struggling to maintain altitude near the ground. He climbed in the hole on the side of the helicopter and took a flurry of bullets from the pilots while he used his massive strength to push the damaged aero back out. The Prime immediately stabilized and gained altitude, but the pilots wouldn't be saying thank-you to the big Chinese man, because he leapt upon them and threw them out of the same hole. He took control of the bird and turned its weapons on the others, which I knew would definitely occupy them for a while. I also knew, however, that Min's built-in Atreides shield only had enough power to function for a limited time, and it was probably close to the end of its battery life. And Ni had only so many RPGs to fire at the Primes, so I knew that before long one or more of the helicopters would be able to catch up to the truck that Jon and Lynn were fleeing in. I just hoped that the truck could make it to our approaching Firehawks before that happened, so they would have some protection. I was sure, however, that the enemy SUVs would overtake them before the cavalry arrived, so they would have to protect themselves from that danger.

With that in mind, I told Jon to head south on the 101 freeway and to acquaint himself with the special controls between the two seats in the front of the cab. Fortunately there wasn't much traffic on the freeway because it was the middle of the day. There were, however, too many hills to climb for the huge vehicle to maintain a high speed, and I knew the enemy SUVs would be catching it too soon. So I told Jon to veer off to the left onto 580 East, since that was a flatter road, and mostly downhill to the bay.

"That's good," Terrey said, obviously still watching all this with great interest, while speeding north from the city. "The Firehawks are coming across the bay from the west, so you should cross their path on or near the bridge. They'll take care of anything that follows you."

Despite myself, I couldn't help thinking about Stephenson's other dream when Terrey mentioned the bridge we were now heading toward. It certainly was big enough for someone to fall to his death from it, but there were heavy railings on the sides to prevent such an eventuality, at least while inside a vehicle. Terrey didn't say anything about the dream thing, but he did mention the other weird metaphysical theory that we had been hearing about too much.

"I like your choice of transportation," he said. "Very colorful."

"You *would* think of that," I said.

"And you're telling me you didn't?"

I didn't have a chance to respond, because San interrupted us to tell me that the four armored SUVs were now approaching fast behind Lynn and Jon. They had obviously been souped up inside as well as outside, and most of the others cars on the road in front and in back of us moved to the side of the road or stopped when they saw them speeding up to the rear of the car carrier.

"If you like the colors of this truck," I said to Terrey, "you'll really like this feature."

I told Jon to activate the controls between the seats and use them to release the car that was at the very back of the bottom rack. It slid out of its resting place, bounced onto the road behind the truck, and kept going that direction, causing several of the SUVs to slow down and swerve in order to avoid hitting it. Jon then released the car that was in front of it, and it gained more momentum as it slid down the tracks and flew off the back of the rack like a bullet. Again, the SUVs had to slow down and swerve, making them fall even farther behind the truck. They soon got smarter, however, and moved to the two outside lanes of the highway, where they were not directly behind the truck, and gunned their engines.

On my suggestion, Jon yanked the truck over to the left lane, and then back to the middle when the SUVs in that lane moved to avoid being behind him. They slid to the side again, one behind the other, but then on his own Jon made the surprisingly deft move of releasing the third car while jerking the wheel at the moment when it reached the back of the rack. So the rear of the truck was pointed at the SUVs when the car exited it, and it connected with the first enemy and caused him to careen off the guardrail and flip over into the middle of the road. The driver of the SUV behind him had to slam on his brakes to avoid being hit himself, taking him out of the race for at least a few minutes. In the meantime, the two SUVs on the other side of the freeway had surged forward to the side of the truck, where they were no longer in danger of car missiles being fired from the back of it. The roofs of both enemy vehicles slid open, and from the front one a blue-clad soldier sprang up and started firing his assault rifle toward the back of the cab. He would soon be firing into the windows of the cab because the SUVs were moving faster than the truck, and on the roof of the second SUV another merc was readying an RPG launcher.

"Watch out!" Terrey said.

"Watch *this*," I said, and Jon knew what to do even before I told him. He released the last two cars on the bottom rack of the carrier, simultaneously starting their engines with the remote system that the truck drivers used to unload and park the cars they transported. The two cars slid out onto the road behind the rack one after another, and with a forefinger for the first one and a thumb for the second touching the pad next to him, Jon was able to control both cars. Acceleration and braking depended on how much pressure he applied to the pad with each finger, and turns were made by moving it left or right. It only took a few seconds for Jon to bring the cars up close to the SUVs, because one of the cars was a Ford Mustang and the other a Menger Flash. In any other situation this would be a terrible waste of a couple very fast automobiles, but in this case it was necessary—he slammed the Mustang against the side of the SUV in the front, jarring the merc with the RPG launcher enough that he couldn't aim well enough to fire.

The Flash was pressing up against the rear of the second SUV, but the smaller cars were barely budging the bigger armored vehicles, and the shooters were stabilizing themselves to fire at the truck. So I told Jon to use the even greater weight of the carrier truck and turn the wheel to the right. The Flash in the rear stopped moving and was out of the game when he took his thumb off the pad to concentrate on controlling the wheel and the Mustang, in order to take out the two SUVs. The huge road monster and the smaller car next to it pushed the two other vehicles easily to the far right side of the freeway and pressed them into the cement wall there, grinding them against it until they couldn't move forward anymore and were left in a smoking clump by the barrier.

The Mustang was ruined, too, but the massive car truck was barely scratched. Jon had to keep it moving forward, however, because now the last remaining SUV had caught up to it. In a strategic blunder, the driver didn't try the RPG approach, which might have worked now that there was more room on the freeway section that widened as it approached the bridge. Instead he pulled up directly behind the back of the truck, tailgating the empty bottom rack, and two light blue attackers climbed out of the roof of the SUV, down the windshield and hood, and onto the empty bottom rack of the truck.

"Just hit the brakes," I said to Jon when we saw what they were doing.

"But this is more fun," he said, and released the back car on the top rack, so it dropped down right onto the windshield and hood of the SUV, smashing it dramatically and incapacitating it.

He's enjoying this too much, I thought, *which always happens at first with lethal violence—until we really begin to understand the "lethal" part.* But I let him go, because in this situation it was either them or us—either them or my wife, to be more precise.

One of the attackers started moving up the middle of the empty bottom rack toward the cab, and the other climbed up to the top rack and began to make his way across the four cars that were still up there. Jon began to lower the entire top rack, which the carrier drivers did to get the cars up there off the truck. He lowered it as fast as it would go down, and the man on the bottom rack couldn't keep his balance well enough at the high speed to get to the side and jump off in time. He was crushed under the weight of the rack and the four cars. Then Jon released all four remaining cars from the top rack at the same time. The second mercenary tried to run toward the cabin across the top of the sliding cars, and actually made it to the fourth and final car. But he couldn't make it off that one, and he dropped to his stomach and held on for dear life as the car fell off onto the road. Then he probably lost his dear life as it slammed into the other three cars and he was thrown onto the pavement like a child's rag doll.

The double had just started to celebrate this Pyrrhic victory when the really lethal enemy showed up. Two of the light blue Sikorsky Prime helicopters had emerged from the hills to the left of the truck, and were probably in firing range already. I glanced down at the small windows on the bottom left of my holo projection, and saw that Min's and Ni's views were both blacked out. Only Stephenson's view, from his glasses, was still active—he seemed to be stationary and looking at a damaged wall sideways, like he was taking a rest after the battle, or perhaps immobilized by a wound.

"The bad news is that the Primes shook off our cyborgs," Terrey said, reading my mind. "But the good news is that they used all their ammo to do it, and the BASS Firehawks are right on the other side of the bay. If you can make it into the suspension cables of the bridge, they can't even follow you in there and the Hawks will take them out."

Jon looked toward the bridge that the truck was almost on, which was called the Golden Bay Bridge. The one that used to span the North Bay at this location had been called the Richmond/San Rafael Bridge (or RSR), but it was destroyed by the quake because it sat right on two major fault lines. It had been an eyesore even before that, so no one wanted to rebuild or restore it. Instead, BASS helped Marin and Richmond to accommodate their swelling population of refugees from the peninsula and Oakland by erecting a new bridge that would be a combination of the two most famous feats of Bay Area architecture: the Bay Bridges and the Golden Gate Bridge. The Golden Bay had two high towers like the Golden Gate, and two levels of traffic like the Bay, and the gold color was somewhere between the red and silver of the other two. As I looked at it through Jon's eyes, I saw what Terrey had meant: the first length of the bridge was open on the top level, and the suspension cables stretched up toward the near tower. Once we got to it, no helicopter could possibly get to us.

I looked off in the distance to the right of the bridge, and could see the black shapes of the Firehawks headed our way. But then I told Jon to look out of his driver's side window, and I could see clearly that the light blue enemy birds would reach us before the friendly ones did, and maybe before we could get to the tower. It could be a matter of seconds, and Jon knew this without me telling him, so he pressed the pedal to the floor as hard as he could and gripped the wheel with white knuckles. I tried to imagine what the Primes would do if they reached the truck while it was still vulnerable—I figured they would try to fire hand weapons into the cab or drop men onto it like the SUVs had tried to do. I was wholly unprepared for what they actually did.

The two enemy helicopters did reach the truck just before it made it to the tower, and well before the Firehawks were in firing range. The pilots positioned them above the front and back of the car carrier and extended the same wires they had used to transport the SUVs, with the smart heads on the wires fastening themselves to the top of the truck in eight places. Then the helicopters lifted the whole truck off the road just high enough to clear the barrier, and dumped it over the side of the bridge.

I was shocked, and didn't know what was happening until it did, so I only had enough time to shout Lynn's name and a brief instruction to her and the double. I didn't know whether they heard me or not, because Lynn was screaming at the top of her lungs from the back of the cab. Jon didn't scream at all but merely watched through the front window of the truck as it rushed toward the surface of one of the wide cement circles that supported the legs of the bridge and protruded from the water more than a hundred feet below. The truck fell cab-first because of the way it had been released from the wires by the helicopters, so Jon had a view that looked like being in the front car of a roller coaster on its steepest drop, but with only a horrible death waiting at the bottom.

He closed his eyes toward the end, so I could only hear the screams of my wife and the violent, horrific crash that silenced them, as the cab slammed into the concrete and was smashed like a beer can under a foot, by the immovable surface below it and the force of the heavy car rack coming down on top of it. The video link went black, and I couldn't picture the remains of the cab, because I knew there would be nothing remaining.

Almost as soon as the two enemy helicopters had dropped the truck over the side of the bridge, the BASS Firehawks came into firing range and took them out with their rockets in two fiery explosions. But that was little consolation for me. I told Terrey and San, who had now arrived at the scene in their aero, to fly to the wreckage and look for Lynn and the double. Then I just sat and stared in silence into the deep darkness of the holo, a million thoughts pressing into my head and immobilizing me. I questioned every decision I had made that day, of course, and imagined every torture I wanted to perpetrate on my enemies for inflicting this on my wife and baby. But strangely, I couldn't help but think about the supposed supernatural elements of this fiasco, probably because they were so uncanny. I thought about how the cars on the truck had been all different colors, and wondered again if there was something to the bizarre beliefs of the Chinese cult.

But even more than that, I thought about how Stephenson had dreamed that he would miraculously survive a battle with an enemy assault team, and that my double would fall from a bridge. At this moment of reflection, in the swirl of my high emotions, I actually thought that this might be the culmination of the spiritual journey I'd been sent on by the all the talk I'd heard about a wide range of metaphysical beliefs. I even pictured myself buying a Dreamscape rig and investing in the company, so that it could further unlock these mysteries. Maybe my dreams could be the key to finding some meaning in this tragedy, and some help in coping with the deep pain I was already feeling.

44
THE BIG PICTURE

Fortunately, my trauma-induced delusion of converting to a religion of dreams was short-lived, because Terrey and San soon reached the wreckage of the truck. The rack had fallen over the edge of the cement base into the bay, but the parts of the disintegrated cab were strewn in piles on top of it. And amid those piles lay Lynn and the double, unconscious but perfectly preserved by the second-generation Atreides shields that shimmered around their bodies. They had put the projectors on their waists at the beginning of the trip, as standard procedure for when they went out, and they had activated them either by their own initiative during the road attack, or maybe later during the fall when I shouted that they should turn them on. To my shame, I had actually forgotten the shields until the truck was thrown over the bridge, so they were saved despite me rather than because of me, and I couldn't claim any credit for it. But the small size of the anti-gravity engine on their belts meant that its energy was very limited, so I was surprised that there was enough life in it to withstand such a powerful impact. And it was amazing that the truck was thrown over the bridge at a spot where there was cement below, because I honestly didn't know whether the shields would have saved them or suffocated them if they had fallen into the water.

Mixed with my initial relief was the realization that we now had to see if they were really okay, or had been injured—especially Lynn and the baby, of course.

San deactivated the shields and scanned Lynn first with her built-in medical ware. While she was doing this, Lynn stirred and woke up, well before my double did. Despite Jon's bravura and skill during the road attack, which had definitely impressed me, he had fainted dead away from fear during the fall. Lynn, however, who had been through childbirth and some other trauma in her life, had merely been knocked out temporarily by the impact of the crash. As my wife showed her toughness by quickly springing back to life, while Jon lay unconscious, I had occasion to admire her again through someone else's eyes. In this case I was looking through San's, as she finished her examination and said that both Lynn and the baby looked fine, except for an understandable increase in their heart rates.

Jon also seemed to be okay, but was still dazed enough when they revived him that they had to help him to his feet so they could put him in the aero. Lynn, on the other hand, walked over on her own power and sat down in it. As Terrey and San were helping Jon through the piles of wreckage to the aero, I told them to hold on before putting him in, because I was regretting Lynn being in danger by being close to him and thinking that they should be separated from now on.

But then all of sudden, I suffered another kind of assault. A battalion of thoughts hit me all at once, and I told Terrey to stay right where he was until I got back to him.

I sat still and gathered my thoughts for a few moments, then I put on my glasses and ran a search through my conversations with Saul's ghost, which had all been recorded and stored. Soon I found the part I was remembering, and played it again. It was from the beginning of the kaleidocide, when Lynn had taken a shower before the protection team had secured the location, and I had briefly thought she was in danger.

"Lynn was almost killed," I said on the recording.

"You can't make an omelet without breaking a few eggs," the ghost said with a sad expression on its face. At that time I thought this was a glitch, and that it had misunderstood what I was saying because of the time lapse, the background noise, or my exaggerated comment.

"Sorry," I said. "I gave you the wrong impression. Lynn's fine. You were saying something about paying and praying, to save me from the kaleidocide."

At that point the ghost had paused like it was recalibrating, and then repeated the same thing it had said before I mentioned Lynn being killed.

Having confirmed my theory, I exited the recording and called up a live link to the ghost construct. After I cleared the voice recognition, DNA, and retinal scan security barriers, the holo of the old man appeared and said its usual, "Hello Michael."

"Do you know why General Sun of China is trying to kill me?" I said, once again in case there might be a different answer this time.

"I don't know, Michael. But let me tell you some more about Zhang Sun—"

"No, Saul." I failed to make my usual distinction between the construct and the man, because I was so emotional about what I expected to happen in this conversation. "I don't want to hear any more about Sun, because *he killed my wife.* Lynn is dead, Saul. We were both targets of the kaleidocide—I survived, but she was killed."

"You can't make an omelet without breaking a few eggs," it said.

"What?"

"That's an old saying. It means—"

"I know what it means," I said, "and it's a terrible way to talk about my wife's death."

"I'm sorry, Michael. I was just trying to help you see the big picture." *That sounds familiar,* I thought, but couldn't remember right now who said it. But what I did know was that my guess was right, and that the ghost had been programmed to respond a certain way if I said that Lynn had been killed, and it was now accessing a new part of its memory that it didn't "know" before.

"Okay," I said. "What *is* the big picture?"

"This had to happen so you could see just how evil Zhang Sun is, and why his regime should never have access to our Sabon antigravity technology."

"Why couldn't you have just told me that?"

"There is no greater teacher than experience, Michael," the ghost said. "You may not have learned what you needed to in any other way, and BASS might have made a deal with the devil."

I thought for a few moments again, and the ghost just stared straight ahead in creepy silence.

"Is this why you hired me at BASS, and groomed me to succeed you?"

"Besides the fact that you are smart, skilled, responsible, a hard worker, and you look good on camera," the ghost said with its slightly unrealistic version of Saul's patented grin, "Yes, Michael."

"Tell me about that," I said, "but try to make it brief." I wanted to know all of it, and especially why Lynn and I were both targets, but I also had to get back to protecting her.

"When we developed the Sabon technology," the ghost began, "I knew it was a global game changer. Nuclear research has been basically static, and nanotech development hit a wall with its power limitations and is now only effective for lesser purposes. Even cyberware has been widely rejected by those who could afford it because of the possibilities of hacking and outside control, so that the best stuff is mostly being applied to people like Min who have no other recourse. But whatever nations and corporations came into possession of the antigravity technology, and could develop further applications of it as we have, would have the balance of world power tipped hard in their direction. One of the most important victories in World War II, you might remember, was the science that Hitler did *not* develop. If the best minds had not left Germany for America, and had given him the atomic bomb instead, the whole thing would have ended differently.

"Given China's traditional hegemonic tendencies, and a militaristic leader like Zhang Sun in charge, I knew that we should withhold the Sabon tech from them at all costs. Sun would add it to his already considerable war machine, and seek to bring the rest of the world into his growing empire by intimidation or invasion. This would precipitate the third world war, and China would probably be the last man standing. At the very least, it would be devastating to the planet.

"So I brought Min to BASS to work for me in the hope that his presence would keep Sun from even wanting to deal with our company, especially when I had to pass it to someone else. Min is a young man and can live a long time with his augmentations. But a conquered foe like him being here didn't discourage Sun from soliciting the formula—in fact, the general was quite eager to offer staggering amounts of money for it. Then I found out about my cancer, and knew that after my death my son Paul or any other successor would almost certainly succumb to such offers, regardless of any instructions I left them. I hired Darien Anthony because of his loyalty and friendship with the American leader Stanford Glenn, hoping that he could prove to be a successor who kept our treasure out of the wrong hands, if my son's character did not change for the better.

"But not long after that, I hit a jackpot that could only be explained by Divine providence. I heard about a young British soldier who had brutally killed Zhang Sun's deeply cherished lover in a military operation in Taiwan, and who was now looking for employment. He also happened to be smart, skilled, responsible, a hard worker, and looked good on camera." The ghost smiled that half-smile again, the lightning scar on its face wrinkling even more.

"I killed Sun's lover?" I said, trying to think if any of the soldiers I saw on the holo could have been women. But as far as I know, there were none in China's combat military.

"Yes, Michael, you shot his lover in the head in cold blood, while Sun himself watched you do it." *Oh*, I thought. *I was assuming the wrong gender.* "General Ho was Sun's cherished lover."

"Sun wasn't in Taiwan," I said. "How could he have been watching?"

"Sun and Ho both had Lovers' Link implants installed in their brains, so they could experience everything the other did, and enjoy each other even from a distance. Their relationship was a secret to a significant degree, because that's still not as accepted in China as it is in other places. So when you put a bullet in Ho's head, Sun experienced it through the Lovers' Link. I'm sure he still uses it to relive the good times they had together while Ho was alive—word is that Sun hasn't been with anyone else since—so he also may be reviewing the shooting from time to time, fanning his flames of hatred for you."

"How does he know it was me?" I asked, thinking of how my face was obscured by the combat eye rig, and my involvement in that op was never publicized.

"I told him, Michael."

"You're a bloody bastard," I said, realizing that the old man did this to ensure the animosity between Sun and BASS, and to keep our secrets from passing to the Chinese. And then my head was filled with much harsher words for him, when I began to realize how Lynn figured into the equation. I had killed Sun's cherished lover, so his revenge would include my cherished wife and unborn baby, along with my own life. It made sense when viewed from the Chinese leader's perspective, and as much as I hated the thought, it also fit with Saul's desire to build a wall between him and BASS. If I happened to survive the kaleidocide, but my wife and baby were killed, I would certainly never make any deals with the man who was responsible for their deaths.

"So you knew that Sun would probably try to kill me," I said. "Did you know that Lynn could be endangered, too, when you made this plan?"

"I did, Michael. I'm so sorry it had to be this way, but try to see the bigger picture, like I said. I really believe that the lives of many millions of people will eventually be saved because of all this if not the whole world."

The ghost actually appeared remorseful to some degree, and for a moment I was inclined to tell it that Lynn was not really dead (not yet, anyway). But I reminded myself that an A.I. construct couldn't have real feelings, and that's why I didn't indulge my other temptation, which was to say that I would give the Sabon secrets to China just to spite him. I had to think more about what all this meant for me and the future of BASS, but for now I needed to get back to protecting Lynn's life. I thought of her not just because we were talking about her, but also because of what she had said to me about discovering my destiny and the reason I had been brought to this company. I knew the answer now, but I had the feeling that knowing it would cause more problems than it solved.

I switched off my link to the ghost and got back on the line with Terrey.

"What's up, mate?" he said immediately. "You left us hanging here."

"Don't tell Lynn this yet, unless it's necessary for some reason," I said. "She's already had too much stress today. But I found out that she's a target, too."

"How did you find that out?"

"I tricked Saul's ghost into telling me, and why Sun wants us dead. It's a long story, but think about it, Terrey—every attempt so far has been geared toward both the double and Lynn. And when you went to the city without her, nothing happened. I can explain it to you when we have time, but for now I need you to focus on her, protecting her." I waited for him to ask for even more money to do this, but to my surprise he didn't say anything. Maybe it was because he had already made over ten million dollars from us that week. So I continued: "I want you to stay with her at all times. What happened to the rest of the protection team?"

"Min and Ni are damaged pretty bad," he said. "It will take them some time to be repaired and recover, like it has with Go."

"So you only have San and Stephenson right now, besides yourself."

"Just San," Terrey said. "Stephenson's dead."

"Really?" I said, genuinely surprised to hear this, because when the truck went off the bridge, I had assumed that the other "prophetic" dream of Stephenson surviving the assault had also come true.

"Yeah, he's dead. He didn't last more than a minute against the squad in the hallway."

"Well, I guess we didn't learn anything from his dreams after all," I said, realizing that both of Stephenson's last two were misleading.

"Yeah, except maybe that we shouldn't rely on them."

"The same thing goes for the 'color power' idea," I said, remembering the other example of my friend's rare spiritual interest. "That truck wasn't very safe after all."

"Maybe Sun's colors are just more powerful—he's in touch with more of the spirits or something."

"I wouldn't bank on that, though," I said, "like the dream thing."

"I don't. But like I said before, Sun does. And we haven't had a black attack yet, as every other kaleidocide has. It's the key color, or all the colors mixed together, or whatever. And it usually represents betrayal."

"So you want to run that sting with Korcz," I said, "to see if he's been bought." He said yes, and I continued: "Okay, take everyone back up to the Valley. The hill is still the safest spot for Lynn, and I don't feel right about her being at the Presidio now that I know she's a target. We'll have some peacers take Hilly and Jessa there, so you don't have to worry about them. We'll also have BASS staff investigate the mercenaries, and tell us if anything worthwhile turns up."

"I'm sure it won't," Terrey said. "Like I said about the other assault team, Sun's people would make sure there's no link to him. And listen, mate. Min and Ni will have to be repaired before they can be at full strength, so it's just me and San for now. If you want us to keep Lynn safe while we're shorthanded like this,

I'll need you to give us total control of all the hill and Valley systems—security, communications, etcetera. Especially if I'm going to let Korcz out of lockup and keep him under surveillance."

I agreed to Terrey's request, so he and San escorted Jon into the aero at the bridge and went back to the Marin Center, where they helped Min and Ni into one of the other aeros. San flew that one alongside Terrey's on the half-hour trip up to the Napa Valley, which was even more nerve-racking for me than the trip down, now that I knew the Chinese were trying to kill Lynn, too. But the journey passed uneventfully, and soon Terrey and San were laying Min and my double down on beds in the infirmary inside the hill base below our house, next to the bed where Go was still recovering from the fire. San gave them both a sedative so that their bodies could recover faster, and she told Min that the Cyber Hole tech would be there soon to work on him. Then she stepped over to another side of the big room to work on her sister. I wondered if the combat injuries had affected the bodiless, augmented brain that lived on Ni's back—her name must have been Ichi, because I remembered that Roku was the one who had died and Yon was the one attached to San.

Before they passed into unconsciousness, I spoke to both Min and Jon, expressing my appreciation and commending them for their roles in protecting my wife during the assault. After the courage he showed today, I was now really hoping that Jon would make it through this alive. But I was still very willing to sacrifice him for my wife, if necessary, and I talked to her briefly as she and Terrey made their way up to the house. We agreed that she should also get some rest, and I told her and Terrey to get back to me when she woke up, and when we were ready to find out whether or not Korcz really was a traitor.

That was the last time I would speak to anyone from there, until later that night, when the big ugly Russian showed up at the vineyard cottage where I was hiding. I didn't know it at the time, but right after I hung up, all communications to and from the hill were completely blacked out.

45
SECRETS REVEALED

Valeri Korcz sat upright and still on the edge of his bed, as he had for most of the twenty-four hours since he'd been locked him in his room with no net access. The only time he had moved was to sleep for a few hours during the night, then to shower and dress when he woke up. He hadn't worn his black clothing for the last few days, but now that color was all he had left, and he had to put it on. He would have thought that was ironic, if he understood the meaning of the word.

The Ares woman had sent some real books down to him from her collection, concerned that he wouldn't have anything to do while he was stranded in the room, but he had no interest in reading them. Instead he sat like a statue and thought about what he would do if he was ever let out of the room. And soon he had his opportunity.

A holo screen appeared suddenly in front of him; it was black except for some white letters that appeared on it.

YON: THANK YOU FOR SAYING THAT I AM PEOPLE TOO. YOU ARE A GOOD FRIEND.

"You are welcome," the big Russian said, not knowing whether or not the bodiless entity could hear him speaking.

YON: I DO NOT HAVE LONG TO HELP YOU BEFORE THEY FIND OUT. FOLLOW

THE MOST DIRECT PATH TO THE AERO BAY, AND TAKE THE ONE THAT YOU USED BEFORE. NOW. WHILE THEY ARE AT OTHER PLACES.

Right after she said this, the door to his room slid open and the holo screen disappeared. He stood up and made his way through the hallways, encountering no one along the way. When he arrived in the big bay with the two helicopters and seven aeros, he approached the one he had driven before and opened the door. Yon must have been watching for that, because the controls and HUD display lit up and were at his command. He discovered that he wasn't able to use the car's comm system to call out, however.

"Do you know where Michael Ares is?" he said into the air, wondering whether Yon could hear him there, and if so, whether she could effectively hide another conversation from her sisters.

YON: YES, OF COURSE I KNOW WHERE MICHAEL IS. WE ARE THE ONES WHO SET UP THE FORTRESS CLOUD, TO HIDE HIS LOCATION BUT STILL ALLOW HIM TO COMMUNICATE WITH US.

Korcz tapped the controls for the aero's GPS system, so it was ready for an address to be entered, and said, "Where is he?"

Yon seemed to hesitate for a moment, but then delivered the address of the cottage to the GPS. Korcz didn't want to insult her by asking if she could hide his takeoff from her sisters, so he silently lifted the aero off the ground and surged it forward through the holo at the mouth of the bay.

When he was clear of the hill and could tell that no one was pursuing, he displayed on the inside of the windshield the list of handguns, assault rifles, and grenade launchers that were stored in the seats and trunk of the aero, and considered which ones would be needed to accomplish what he had to do. Then he sat back and enjoyed the colorful scenery of the fall vineyards ahead and below, as he glided toward the place in the midst of them where Michael Ares was in hiding.

Zhang Sun couldn't see the Napa Valley vineyards yet, but he was not too far away, and was literally quivering with anticipation. His oversized hoverjet was passing over the coastline of Northern California, heading toward the Wine Country, as he waited for the call he hoped would come soon. He didn't want the plane to have to circle in the air and attract attention to itself, even though it was officially registered to a big Hong Kong business and would probably survive any such scrutiny.

The jet had been built by Comac, the commercial aircraft company owned by the Chinese government, as had all the planes used by their leaders since the fiasco at the turn of the century, when almost thirty CIA bugs were found in a presidential transport bought from Boeing in America. And Comac had out-done themselves with this one. The top level, where Sun was reclining in his luxurious chair, was a sleek and spacious office and apartment for him, while the lower level was an electronically camouflaged staging area for the elite squad of "Flying Dragon" special forces he had brought with him. And as much as the custom plane itself had cost to manufacture, it was only worth a fraction of the value of the cutting edge military equipment that the soldiers had with them.

Sun and his special force had boarded the plane and taken off from Nan-jing almost fifteen hours before, after he had received his last call from the *nèi jiān* inside his enemy's residence. The traitor had said that because of an amaz-ing series of coincidences, which Sun ascribed to his *ban lan jiao,* the ultimate form of revenge could be arranged for a slightly higher price, which he was more than happy to pay. He would be able to execute Michael Ares by his own hand, after making him watch his wife and baby die, and also have his old nemesis Min thrown in for good measure. Sun could never have imagined this *xing lu cai se* working out so perfectly, and had never felt the *ban lan* spirits working in it so powerfully. So he had great confidence that what was promised would be delivered to him, and that he would return safely afterward to his own country, with his thirst for revenge thoroughly slaked.

As expected, the next call came through at just the right time, when the Chinese jet was approaching the airspace of the Napa Valley, and was almost ready to test whether its surveillance and defenses were operable. As with the last communication, this one came in the form of a heavily encrypted text mes-sage, presumably so the tech wizards in Sun's employ wouldn't be able to lift any confidential information from it.

YOU MADE THE TRIP, said the white letters inside the holo, which had ap-peared in front of the general.

"I told you I would," he said in return.

THE SECURITY SYSTEMS IN THE VALLEY AND ON THE HILL ARE NOW PRO-GRAMMED TO ALLOW YOU IN AND OUT. TWO OF YOUR TARGETS ARE TEMPORAR-ILY SEDATED AND WAITING FOR YOU THERE, AND THE OTHER WILL BE SOON.

"You will not be there to greet us?" Sun asked.

NO. WHEN YOU CONFIRM THAT ALL THE TARGETS HAVE BEEN DELIVERED TO YOU AS PROMISED, YOU WILL TRANSFER THE AMOUNT AGREED ON TO MY AC-COUNT. I'VE MADE SOME MONEY PROTECTING ARES, AND NOW I'M READY FOR YOURS. AND I'M NOT STUPID ENOUGH TO HANG AROUND SO YOU CAN SHOOT ME, TO AVOID PAYING ME AND COVER YOUR ASS.

"I will transfer half the amount when I have the targets safely in hand," Sun said. "And the other half when I am safely out of the Valley. I am not stupid either."

FINE. HAVE FUN! And then the holo and its letters were gone.

Having fun, in his own unique way, was precisely what Sun was planning to do. And as the jet passed into the airspace at the north end of Napa Valley without anyone firing on it or even hailing it, he knew that all this was not too good to be true after all, and let himself imagine every detail he was about to savor. As he did, he quietly chanted the words of the *ban lan* ritual, to make sure the spirits felt appreciated and would continue to bless him, and he again began to feel the surges of intense pleasure that only devotees like himself were able to experience. For the last few minutes of the flight, he activated the Lovers' Link implant in his brain, and added another experience on top of what he was already feeling, reliving one of the most memorable times he had spent with his long-dead partner. The resulting cascade of emotions and sensations reached a higher peak than ever, but he knew that the highest summit was still to come—an orgy of torture and death that would be the opposite of pleasure for Michael Ares and his loved ones.

Min woke up earlier than was planned, but only moments before Sun and his force arrived at the big hangar built into the side of the hill base. He sat up, simul-taneously running diagnostics on his damaged systems and looking around him. He was in that hangar bay in the side of the hill, and he was unable to access the net or communicate with anyone through it. Lynn and the double were lying on the floor next to him, both still unconscious and with their hands tied behind their backs. He was not bound in that way, probably because whoever did it knew that it would be pointless. But he was very shaky as he forced himself to his feet, and also completely out of ammunition from his battle at the Marin Center.

This was unfortunate, because just then he heard what sounded to him like a hoverjet outside the entrance to the bay, landing on the hillside next to it. This was smart, he thought, because if an enemy landed their craft inside the base, he or someone else could possibly destroy it before anyone got out. He might have been able to jump in one of the two Firehawk helicopters that were parked in the bay, and take out the enemy craft with its weapons before many of its passengers disembarked. But this way there would be a swarm of individual attackers that would be much harder to get a bead on.

As he watched the mouth of the bay, however, he did not see many armed men enter it, but only one unarmed man, dressed in a black suit and walking slowly his way. Min's mind barely had time to recognize that the man was Zhang Sun before his body blurred into motion, rushing toward his former superior and drawing out one of the three-foot-long swords from his back. His instincts told him that he should take the offensive and take advantage of the enemy leader's vulnerability in being alone. If he could cut off the head of the invading force, it might not matter how many soldiers or cyborgs were behind him.

But the big machine-man didn't even get halfway to Sun, nor did he get halfway up to speed before he ran into an invisible wall and was knocked off his feet. It felt like he was being tackled by at least four men, though he had seen none, and his senses continued to betray him as he struggled against unseen bodies that were crushing him to the ground and hands that were prying his blade away from him. At first he wondered whether this was evidence of the supernatural, and demons from Sun's religion were manifesting themselves in the service of the Chinese leader. But then his naturalistic bent brought him back down to earth, and he realized that the PLA had finally perfected the invisibility technology that they had been working on even back when he was an officer in it. It made use of sophisticated metamaterials that were able to refract light and cause the eye to see only what was on the other side of the subject.

"There are ten of my Wraiths in this hangar right now," Sun explained with a proud smile. "Two are guarding me, four are subduing you, two are somewhere else with their weapons trained on you, and two are with the people lying over there, whom you have sworn to protect. If you make any hostile move, you will be shot immediately, and they will be, too."

Min stopped struggling and lay still. He didn't need the calculations being made by his augmented brain to know that this was a fight he couldn't win. With his unfiltered eyes he could only see a shimmering in the air where he thought the Wraith soldiers were located, and definitely couldn't see it well enough to take them out. And importing every ocular filter he had onto his augmented lenses, one after another in the space of about thirty seconds, didn't allow him to see them any better. The filters were registering different wavelengths of light, but it was all light nonetheless, and therefore was refracted by the metamaterials. Min could think of no other alternative right now than to allow his enemies to do what they wished with him, and hope against hope that help might arrive before they were all killed.

"Some of these men," Sun said, as if on cue, "are the same ones who were sent to quash your pathetic little revolution when you betrayed your country and sided with our enemies." His mouth was wrinkled up in disgust, an unusual display of emotion for the normally stoic general. "You ended up in pieces after that encounter, and now they are about to take you apart again. We cannot have any of those built-in weapons at your disposal while you watch your charges suffer and die, and it will be gratifying for me to undo what was done by those other traitors at Cyber Hole."

Sun nodded to one of the Flying Dragons standing above Min, whose location could only be determined by the blade he held in his invisible hand, and now raised high above his invisible head. This was smart, too, Min thought, because his own weapons were the only ones that could cut through his joints so effectively. And the sword did indeed prove to be very effective, as the Wraith brought it down upon his body time and again, until all that was left attached to his head were his shoulders and spinal cord.

As he resisted the urge to scream and give Sun more pleasure, Min's only consolation was a small one. At least he knew, for now, where one of the enemy soldiers was, because so much blood had splashed onto his tormentor's suit that the metamaterials were having some difficulty adjusting to it. But he also knew that it was only a matter of time until even that Wraith would be invisible again, and he knew that it was not only his blood that would be staining the hangar floor that night.

46
BETRAYAL

When the security systems of the cottage detected the approaching aero, I was watching the *Pilgrim* holo with Chris, while Angelee cleaned up after dinner. We were at the part in the movie where the main character and his friend were in the mountains and some shepherds were showing them various visions. And the one we were watching was rather scary, especially for a four-year-old like Chris: a group of blind men were stumbling around in a dark, gothic cemetery, bumping into eery gravestones and mausoleums, unable to find their way out. The crashes of thunder and the screams of the trapped men were so loud that I almost didn't hear the voice of the Living House A.I. above the din.

"What did you say, Vera?" I asked after pausing the holo.

"A BASS aerocar crossed over the eastern property line eleven seconds ago, Michael. It is flying toward us over the vineyards on the east side of the house and will arrive here in one-point-two minutes."

"Stay right here," I said to Angelee and Chris, who had picked up on my surprise and were already looking panicked. Darting into my room at a rapid pace didn't help them either, I'm sure, but I didn't have much time.

I called Terrey on the net room, and was informed by it that we were unable to connect. I called Min and got the same message. Finally, I tried Lynn at our house with the same result. Obviously someone was jamming any communication that I could use to get information or help. So now I really had to make some tough decisions fast, before the aero arrived.

I thought about it frantically as I stepped back out to the living room. If it was Korcz or someone else coming to kill me, they could easily have one or more BASS grenade launchers, or even use that function on a standard BASS assault rifle to blow us to kingdom come while we were in the house. And just like the attack on the Marin Center, that's what I would do in this situation—I wouldn't risk a firefight unless I had to. So that meant I needed to make myself a harder target, and separate from Angelee and Chris if I wanted to keep them safe, which I definitely did. I had become so attached to them, I was actually more willing to endanger my own life than theirs.

I could only come up with one move right now that addressed both of those concerns, and I didn't have time to think further about it.

"Vera," I said. "After I exit the house, secure it as tightly as you possibly can, and only open it for one of us. If it is breached by an intruder, call 911 immediately."

"Yes, Michael."

"Angelee," I said. "Stay in this room. If you hear the front door being broken in, run out the back and into the vineyards. Flee through them or hide inside them until help comes. If you see someone other than me come around the back, run through the front door and do the same thing. Do you understand?"

She nodded nervously, and Chris's little mind must have understood, too, because he was now fearfully clinging to her leg.

I grabbed the gun belt with the two boas from my room and rushed out of the front door, strapping them on and telling Vera to link her security cameras to my glasses. Soon I was four or five rows deep into the vineyards, so I couldn't be seen from in front of the horse. I could see the intruder, however, because I imported the view from the house's roof camera to a window in my glasses, and watched the aero draw closer in the waning sunlight. I was relieved to see it slow down and land in the open area in front of the house, which meant that whoever was behind the wheel probably didn't know that I had exited it. But I was afraid that he or she might simply fire a weapon toward it from the window of the aero, and I didn't know if I would have the angle or the aim to prevent that.

I prepared for that and other possible eventualities as I switched the window in my glasses to the front camera of the house. In that way I had a good view of the now stationary aero, but I couldn't see it with my own eyes because I was crouched behind the yellow and gold grapevines. So in case I had to react quickly, I reminded myself that I would have a different angle on the car if I rose to standing position and fired upon it with the guns I now had in my hands.

That turned out to be unnecessary at this point, because the driver's side door merely swung open, with its window remaining closed, and Korcz climbed out of it. Both of his empty hands were up in the air, and he looked in the direction of the front door of the house, as if he was waiting for me to speak to him from it. He wasn't as stupid as he looked, I remembered, and undoubtedly knew that I would be staying in a building with security and surveillance systems. Presumably, if I didn't speak to him from the house, he would have stepped closer to it and rang the doorbell. But I did speak to him, from my position to his right side, because I wanted to draw his attention toward me and away from the house, and my new "family" inside of it. I also prepared myself to make a fast move sideways in the row of dirt between the vines, in case he starting shooting toward the sound of my voice.

"Korcz," I said from my hiding place. In my glasses I saw him turn in my direction, but he kept his hands in the air. "Why are you here?"

"I came to warn you," he said in the thick Russian accent. "I think you have been betrayed."

My mind was running a mile a minute, and one thought I had was that if *he* was the traitor, this could be an elaborate ruse, though I couldn't see why he would take this approach.

"Why didn't you call me," I asked, "if you wanted to warn me?"

"All the comms are blacked out," he said.

"How did you get out of your room, and how did you get here?"

"The girl, the number four," he shouted, probably because he sensed my skepticism and was desperate to convince me. "The one with no body, she told me."

"Yon?" I said, remembering the name because it had been displayed on my screen several times. "Why would she do that?"

"I think she likes me. Because I stood up for her. I don't know." He paused. "I know she likes you. Mebbee she wanted me to warn you."

"So who betrayed me?" I asked, even though I knew what he was going to say.

"Terrey and his women."

At first this all seemed contradictory to me—why would Yon help Korcz, or me for that matter, if she and her sisters were part of a plot against me? But then I remembered that her sisters had described Yon as something of a loose cannon, and it seemed more plausible.

"You don't understand, Korcz," I said. "Terrey owes me his life. He would never allow any harm to come to me."

"And he has not," the big bald man said. "But I think he will kill the double and your woman for the Chinese."

This hit me like a brick. All at once I could see how Terrey might possibly have played me for the huge amounts of money he was paid to protect us, and then made a deal with Sun for another huge amount. If I had his lack of attachments, the bills that he owed, and the mercenary mind-set, I might have done the same thing. But could he be callous enough to let my wife die in the process? Didn't he realize that I loved her enough that it would hurt me deeply, and that I would chase him down and make him pay for it? *Maybe not,* I thought. *He's probably under the impression that I was having an affair with Tara, so he might even think Lynn's death would somehow free me.* But what about the baby? He had bought abortions for a number of his conquests, I knew, and he never had children himself, so maybe he didn't think life in the womb was very valuable. But I couldn't take the time right now to wonder about any of this—I had to act in case it might be true.

"What makes you think Terrey is doing this?" I asked Korcz as I stepped out from my cover, and kept one of my boas ready as I frisked him. He was unarmed.

"The call that I got on the plane here, from a Chinese number," the Russian answered. "How could they have known about me being hired, and why would they be so stupid to risk a traceable call? It is more like the call was to make me look bad, to—how you say it?—make me look suspicion, so you would not be suspicion of the real traitor." *Speaking of stupid,* I thought, *this man is definitely not as stupid as he looks, or as his halting English makes him seem.* He continued: "But what made me sure is that there is always traitor because the Chinese likes traitor. But traitor was waiting, not killing, for more than a week. Why would he wait? Only two reasons." The pockmarked man held up a single finger. "One, traitor had no opportunity. That is true of me, Stephenson, and Tyra, and I knew we were not traitor. Two, traitor had opportunity, but reason to wait, like making 'big bikkies' of money every day he is protecting you."

Definitely not stupid, I thought again, because this made a lot of sense to me, too. But it also reminded me that Korcz was smart enough to be lying convincingly, and it occurred to me that there were two assault teams, so there could be two traitors. I needed more proof of the big Russian's claims.

"Get back in the car," I said, and joined him in the front seats of the aero, holding the gun on him with one hand and opening comm windows in both our names with the other. Calls from the aero were still being jammed, but I was hoping that someone might be watching for at least one of us.

"Yon," I said out loud, feeling kind of silly doing so. "Are you there? It's Michael Ares." I felt even more silly when no answer came, but I pressed on anyway. "Valeri Korcz is here with me."

Nothing happened again, and kept happening for almost a minute, so I fiddled with the comm grid again to give as many signs as I could of me trying to use it. As I did, I inadvertently brought up Korcz's last display and saw that he had been checking out the aero's inventory of weapons on his way to the cottage. My hand tensed on the grip of the boa, and I asked him why.

"I will help you save your wife and baby," he said. "Because I do what I am hired to do."

I didn't have an opportunity to question or admire this statement on his part, because as he finished it some words in all capitals appeared on the inside of the windshield.

YON: THERE IS A LOT HAPPENING RIGHT NOW. I ONLY HAVE A MINUTE.

"Yon," I said, "did you help Korcz escape from the hill?"

YON: YES, I DID.

"Why?"

YON: THE CHINESE WERE COMING, AND THEY WOULD HAVE KILLED HIM. IT WOULD HAVE BEEN AN UNNECESSARY DEATH.

My mind raced again, with thoughts of Chinese at the hill base and "unnecessary death," which implied that there was "necessary death" about to take place. My window with this bodiless woman was about to close, so I had to make a leap-of-faith decision to trust her and Korcz, and hope that they weren't both working together as traitors. Then as if I was being rewarded for that faith, a last question came to mind that could confirm whether it was well-placed.

"Yon," I said in the most charming manner I could muster, and smiled in case she could somehow see my face, "would you please unblock our comms, or at least open one private link for us, so we can see what's happening at the hill? I would really appreciate it."

There was no response for a while, and again I feared the worst as we waited in the silence of the car. But then the comm system flared to life, and we could see that she had granted my request.

YON: GOTTA GO NOW. WON'T BE ABLE TO TALK ANYMORE. I LOVE YOU!

"I love you, too," I said for good measure, with a smile that quickly disappeared when my eyes turned in horror to the one link Yon had provided for us. The video window was looking through Min's eyes at several people in the hill's big hangar bay, and despite some obvious damage to his vision (and some water from his tears?), I could tell who they were. One was my double, dressed in my clothes and standing groggily with his hands tied behind his back. Another was General Zhang Sun, dressed smartly in a black suit and standing proudly over the sprawled body of my half-conscious wife, who was wearing absolutely nothing. At first I could only see her in the side of Min's view, because he had been looking at Sun, but then when his eyes swept right and landed on Lynn, he immediately looked down out of respect or embarrassment, or both, and then tilted his head back and looked up from the pain he was experiencing. When he looked down, I could see that he had been dismembered so badly that only his head and the top of his torso remained, with a bloody spinal cord and various tubes and cords hanging from its bottom. And when he looked up, I could see that what was left of him had been hung by wires from the end of a helicopter propeller, so he would have to watch helplessly as Sun enjoyed his revenge.

Knowing this was the only reason to leave Min alive, I also guessed that Sun would do something similar to Jon, thinking he was me, and make him watch as Lynn was killed. I realized this could happen to my wife at any second, but I tried to control my panic and think about it, rather than letting my emotions rule and doing something stupid. I also thought that Sun would probably want to prolong his gloating, and therefore Lynn's death, though within reason because he probably had a limit on the amount of time he could be there and still leave safely. So I calculated my options, and told Korcz to get the guns out of the trunk.

I stepped out of the car and walked around the front to get into the driver's seat, and as I did, Angelee and Chris came running out of the front door of the house. They must have been watching from the window—contrary to my instructions—and could tell that I was leaving. The young mother threw her arms around my ribs and the little boy around my leg, and both held on for dear life. I didn't even have time for a conversation, let alone to give them the explanation they deserved, so to get them to let go I had to make some quick promises that I knew I couldn't keep. I told them that I would be back soon and that we would be together for a long time. I could almost feel Angelee's excitement that she would have a husband, and Chris's that he would have a father. But I didn't have time to feel guilt or anything else about it myself, so I got in the car and fired it up.

I returned the waves of the smiling woman and boy as the aero lifted off, and then looked over at Korcz, who now sitting in the passenger seat. The big Russian raised his eyebrows slightly, but didn't say anything.

I set the autopilot to fly to the hill bay, at the highest speed I could select. I thought of summoning some BASS peacers to the hill, now that I knew who the traitor was, but I still couldn't call out. Even if I could, there were so few of them in or near the Valley, if any, and they would all be much farther away than I was. We had told them all to keep clear of the hill when the kaleidocide began. So I moved on to my next option, and tested the extent of the link Yon had opened for us with Min. I spoke to the bodyguard verbally, and was glad to see that he was able to hear and answer via the silent communication capabilities of his cyberbrain.

I am very sorry, Mr. Ares. These words were posting on another part of the windshield. *I have failed you.*

"Nonsense, Min," I said. "Let's see if we can do anything about this . . ."

I still have some hidden weapons capability, but I cannot use it unless I can get my neural controls back online. I'm trying, but even if I do, I would not be able to locate the enemy soldiers, and even if I could locate them, I only have enough ordnance to eliminate two of the ten.

I realized, from Min's words and from the slight distortion in the air next to the double, that China had developed a cloaking device for its soldiers and that a pair of them were holding Jon upright so he would have to wake up and witness what was coming. And before the conversation between Min and me could continue, Terrey's voice boomed through the hangar's speakers, and I found out what Sun had planned for Lynn's death.

"You have what you wanted now," Terrey said, "and I'm sure you saw the injectors on Mrs. Ares's ankles when you removed her clothing. Which was hardly necessary, by the way. The nanites would do their work on her skin even if she was dressed."

"But we would not be able to *watch them* do their work," Sun answered, with a perverse smile that confirmed the implication that he had enjoyed humiliating my wife. "And I need you to come back here and activate the devices."

"That won't happen," Terrey said. "I'm long gone already, and going much farther away so I can't be tracked by you or anyone else. But I will activate them by remote control so you can have your fun watching her suffer and die—*after* you transfer the money to my account. If I had started the process already, you might not have paid me."

"Half now," Sun said calmly. "The other half when I am safely away from here, as we agreed. And you will activate the injectors first, before you receive your payment."

Terrey paused before responding, but then said, "Fine. Have fun."

Min reluctantly looked directly at Lynn's prone form for the first time, sacrificing his honor so that I could see what happened to her. The small devices attached to her ankles sparked to life and caused her body to spasm, as what looked like a thick liquid began to spread out in all directions on her feet and ankles, traveling slowly up her legs and covering all the skin with a multicolored surface that looked like a living tattoo. I knew that nanotechnology had been largely a bust in the scientific community because of its limited power supply, but I also knew that it had caught on as a fashion decoration which could only be used in patches like the triplets did, because of potential dangers to the dermal system. It wasn't hard to figure out why Sun chose this torture for my wife, or why he picked nanites that would cover her body with so many different colors. But he elaborated anyway.

"This is the ultimate form of *xing lu cai se,*" he said to Jon, thinking he was me. "And it is an especially appropriate punishment for you. You took my partner from me, now I am taking yours—with interest." Lynn convulsed on the floor as the colors made their way up toward her hips, and she clutched at her big belly as if she was trying to protect the little girl inside it.

I checked the aero's HUD for our ETA to the hill, which was still several minutes away, and reached into the backseat for one of the assault rifles that Korcz had put there from the trunk. He grabbed one, too, and we both began to ready the weapons by turning off the safeties and chambering rounds in the main barrels and the grenade launchers. I was very surprised that the big Russian was willing to join me in this, because suicide was the only word that described what we were about to do. Maybe he thought that it was so clearly the right thing to do, and was therefore a good way for both of us to die.

47
BLOOD AND DUST

"Saul Rabin liked to refer to you as the James Bond of BASS," Sun continued with an amused expression, as my wife continued to writhe on the floor,
"because you were from England and had some adventures like that character.
His lovers were famous for being covered with various substances by their killers—
gold paint, black oil, and silver metal in one of the more recent holos. No one
could die in real life from being covered in those substances, of course, but I
assure you that your lover is really dying from this. The microscopic machines
replicating themselves across her skin will not only block her pores, but also
raise her body temperature to a lethal level in a matter of minutes. If she doesn't
die from heatstroke first, the nanites will close off her breathing when they reach
her head. In the meantime, every nerve ending in her skin will feel like it is being bitten and burned, and if she attempts to pull off any of her new decorations
with her hands, the skin will come off with it."

"Min," I said into my comm before the bastard was even done spouting off,
"you said you have some ordnance. What is it?"

I have two Incisor missiles in my mouth, the dismantled cyborg said, *that
they obviously did not know about when they removed my other augmentations.*
Despite the gravity of the situation, I remembered what the Cyber Hole tech
had said when he was telling us about Min's capabilities. He had said something

about "weapons in his mouth," and I thought he was merely using the figurative expression "armed to the teeth." But he had been speaking literally, after all.

I am regaining some capability to aim the missiles, Min said on our screen, *but remember that I cannot see or detect the enemy soldiers. Nor will you be able to.*

This was why it was suicide for us, of course. But Lynn and Lynley and Min were a good cause to die for, as well as the possibility of ridding the world of a monster like Sun. Unfortunately, in the plan I was formulating in the brief time I had before we arrived at the hill, the Chinese leader was likely to live and the rest of us were likely to die—especially my double.

"You'll have to take out the two Wraiths holding Jon," I said to Min, knowing that my look-alike would also be killed when he did. "Because they're the only ones you can locate." My thought was that Korcz and I would fire randomly in the direction of where we thought the invisible soldiers might be, and then try to grab Sun as a hostage and force them to stop shooting at us.

I think I should just use the missiles on General Sun, sir.

I had figured this would come up, because it was the most logical conclusion. We're all going to die, so we might as well take out the threat to world peace before we do. But despite whatever "destiny" had been decreed for me, I wasn't nearly as concerned with preserving world peace as I was with the slim possibility of saving Lynn and the baby. And I wasn't willing to sacrifice her for it, as Saul Rabin had been.

"No," I said. "I need Sun alive in case he's able to turn off the nanites. Just take out the two with Jon." I thought again of the old man, who had rescued Min from China and brought him here to work at BASS. "And pray for a miracle."

I have never done that, but there is nothing else I can do now. I'm sorry again, sir.

"Terrey's the one who should be sorry, Min, not you. May he burn in hell for what he's done."

Makes me want to believe in a place like that, sir.

I told Min to wait for my signal, as we were now less than a minute from the hill, and in the meantime asked him to look around the hangar in case we could see a distortion in the air where the other eight Chinese soldiers were. This was fruitless, especially with Min's vision impaired by his injuries, and so he flipped through his optical filters one more time. They didn't work either, so we spent the last moments before we reached the hill watching Lynn dying on the floor. Her body was now almost covered with the colors, and the screams coming from her mouth would soon be cut off. She tried to tear off some of the nanites from the top of her chest as they were nearing her throat, only to scream louder as the deep red of her blood mingled with the other colors there.

"Ready," I said to Min and Korcz as the holo-covered entrance to the hangar swept into view in front of us.

And then the miracle happened.

The view through Min's eyes blinked twice and lit up with new information on it. Target crosshairs from his weapons system displayed on the two invisible soldiers holding Jon, and eight others in other parts of the hangar.

My system appears to have found a way to locate the enemies, Min said.

"Send it to our glasses," I blurted out, and Korcz and I quickly put them on. "Take out the farthest away, Min." I knew Sun would have posted several snipers in perimeter positions, as a safety measure in case someone like us showed up. And I hoped there were no more than two, and that they could all be killed by Min's missiles, because just one surviving sniper would end this attack very quickly.

Just before our aero reached the hangar, target indicators for all of the Chinese soldiers appeared in both pairs of glasses, and we now had something to shoot at. Or run over . . .

I switched the autopilot off and grabbed the controls of the aero as it streaked into the center of the hangar near the floor, smashing its nose into the nearest Wraith, who had been one of two guarding the entrance. Korcz fired out of his open window at the other one, and then I flew directly at Sun, the aero slowed only slightly by the impact with the guard. I wanted to get near the Chinese leader so his men would hesitate to fire grenades at us—something that also would end the attack very quickly.

Meanwhile, I could see what Min was doing, from the video screen containing his view on one part of the windshield, and from glancing through the clear part of it at his head and torso hanging from the helicopter blade in the back of the hangar. The two antigravity enhanced false teeth dislodged from his mouth and shot out to the far sides of the hangar, in a loosely spiraling fashion.

Min's optical system split his view into two halves and zoomed in to follow both missiles to their destinations. In rapid succession they connected with their two invisible targets, one on a catwalk high on the north side of the hangar, and the other behind an aero on the south side. A shower of bloody body parts became visible and cascaded in every direction when they exploded, which would have been gratifying except for the fact that there were so many enemies still left in the hangar.

When I thought I was close enough to Sun, I swerved the aero toward Jon. As I had hoped, the two invisible soldiers holding him let go so they could use their weapons, and he had enough presence of mind to drop to the ground, so I could pass above him as I plowed into them with the front of the car. I finally braked at that point, and both Korcz and I dove out because we knew that RPGs would be on their way to the car now that it was farther from Sun. The Chinese general was taking cover in the other direction, in fact, crawling inside the helicopter from which Min was hanging. I hoped he didn't know how to fire the weapons on the craft, as I rolled hard to avoid gunfire from the remaining soldiers.

One of them did send a grenade toward my aero, and the car exploded in a ball of flame. The smoke from the blast provided some temporary cover for me and Korcz, so we were able to fire back from each side of the wreckage. We both made the same split-second tactical decision to try to take out as many enemies as we could from where we stood, rather than run somewhere else and hinder our aiming ability while we tried to find cover. It was probably the wisest decision in a still hopeless situation, and we hit one or two of the men firing at us from the open floor and behind the parked aeros. But our success was short-lived, because at least one of the Flying Dragons was now behind us—perhaps one who had survived being run over, thanks to his body armor.

Sun apparently recognized me as the smoke began to clear, from his vantage point not far away, because he must have told the soldier behind me to take me alive. I was focused on watching the red squares that indicated the targets ahead of me, and didn't notice the red arrow at the far right edge of the glasses until it was too late. The invisible man stepped up behind me and put his gun to the back of my head, causing me to lower mine. Korcz saw this through the clearing smoke, probably because the red square appeared in the right side of his glasses. He turned his rifle in my direction, hesitating briefly while he decided whether to endanger me by firing on my captor, and in that moment he was hit by a barrage of bullets from the other soldiers left in the hangar. His big form crashed to the ground in a bloody heap.

In my glasses I could see that two invisible Chinese soldiers were advancing toward me across the open floor in the middle of the hangar, two more were positioned behind vehicles that were parked around the outside, and another was behind me somewhere, probably moving into a closer position. With the one holding a gun to my head, that made six who had survived—at least we killed almost half of them, which was better than I had expected to do.

Sun started laughing from inside the Firehawk's cockpit, probably from the realization that he had been fooled by a double but still ended up with the real me. But then his laughter was cut short as the lights and power in all of the aeros in the hangar, and in the other helicopter, suddenly turned on. Before any of the Chinese could figure out what was happening, the aeros that had been providing cover for two of them surged backward and sideways, pinning one against a wall and pushing the other into the car next to it. The Reds screamed as they were sandwiched by the four-ton vehicles.

At the same time, the Firehawk that had come alive without a pilot began to fire its cannons at the two soldiers in the middle of the floor, shredding them and sending visible blood flying from their invisible bodies like it was coming out of a water sprinkler. Hoping that the soldier behind me was taking seriously his orders not to kill me, I dropped down and back, bringing my rifle up sideways until it hit his invisible one and knocked it upward. Then I spun around and shot him right before he could bring the gun down again, and scanned the area behind his body for the sixth soldier that I thought was back there. But according to my glasses, there was now no one in the vicinity.

So I turned around again and saw the unmanned helicopter swivel toward the two Chinese who were still trapped by the aeros. The Hawk opened fire on them as well, and the odd death scene repeated itself, with blood spraying out of nothing.

I couldn't believe it, but now there were no more live targets in my glasses. I was the last man left standing on the floor of the hangar. I turned my rifle toward Sun, who was frantically trying to work the controls for the helicopter he was in. But the same force that had animated the other vehicles was apparently preventing him from using that one.

"Nice work, Min," I said to what was left of the big cyborg, hanging nearby.

What? he said in my glasses.

I ignored the question, because I was now looking at Lynn and seeing that the nanites had reached her face and were entering her mouth and nose. I threw down the rifle, tore my glasses off, and pulled out one of my boas as I bounded over to the nearby Firehawk. I dragged Sun out of the cockpit and threw him down on the floor near Lynn's twitching body. I straddled him and pointed the gun at his face.

"Turn it off," I said through clenched teeth, gesturing toward my dying wife.

"I can't," he said, raising his hands to shield his head.

I moved the boa downward and shot him between the legs. He screamed and put both his hands down there, so I dropped my body down and trapped them with my knee, pressing them against his wound. He screamed some more, and I held the gun tightly to his head.

"Where's the remote control?" I asked. "Tell me or you're dead."

"Your friend Terrey," Sun answered with difficulty, coughing up some blood, "is the only one who could stop it. And he is long gone." He forced a twisted smile onto his bloody mouth. "Not a very good friend."

I looked over at Lynn again, and saw that she had now stopped twitching. So when I turned back to Sun, the hatred on my face was enough to wipe the smile off his, at least temporarily. I pressed the boa against his head and my finger against the trigger, ready to send him to the hell that I hoped was waiting for him, and stared hard at his face so I could see every gory detail of his death. But then my mind recalled the similar image of me shooting General Ho—the act that had precipitated all this—and I ended up grunting in disgust and pulling the gun away.

Sun smiled again and repeated, as if to stab at me a second time, "Not a very good friend."

"He's right," said a voice behind me. I turned to see a figure in one of the invisible suits, which could only be identified by some splashes of blood on its front that had not yet been eliminated by the metamaterials. Then the figure became visible, and it was Terrey, wearing a shiny black suit with blood at the same places. He held in his hands an Alliant Trinity, the same three-barreled weapon I had used in the Taiwan assault, and finished his statement. "I *am* the only one who can stop her from dying." He walked casually over to Lynn, kneeling down to look at her head, which was now completely covered with the living tattoos.

"There *is* time to save her," Terrey said to me, as I sat there with my mouth hanging open, in a state of shock, "but you're gonna have to pay me, mate, because I only got half of what I was hoping for from Sun. Cash would be a bit risky, because I don't know if I could confirm the payment in time to save Lynn. So I'll take this aero as your fee."

As he said that, the car he had been using all week flew into the hangar from outside, and Ni and San stepped out of both sides of it.

"I know there's a code that will deactivate the self-destruct system," Terrey said, "and allow us to take it anywhere we want. Give it to me, and I'll take care of your wife."

"I'll pay you twice what I offered you," Sun grunted out from the floor. "If you kill both of them." Terrey turned his way, but then shook his head and snorted through his nose like someone would at the foolishness of a child. The injured Chinese leader then offered him three times as much, but Terrey ignored it and looked back at me.

"Give him the code, Min," I said without hesitation, even though it would mean that our Sabon technology could be out in the open for the first time, because Terrey might be able to reverse engineer it and sell it to the highest bidder. I was still confused by my friend's apparently double betrayal, but one thing I was sure of was that I wanted my wife to live.

Almost immediately one of the *Trois* confirmed to Terrey that the code was correct, so he knelt down next to Lynn and inserted two small, thin vials into the apparatus attached to her ankles. Suddenly the skin near them started to turn gray, and the new color spread up her body the same way as before, but much faster. It was like the nanites were turning to dust, and leaving an inanimate covering where the living one was previously. When the gray reached her mouth and nose, Lynn coughed up a bunch of it and was soon breathing again. Terrey blew on her face to clear the dust off it, but left it on the rest of her body. He stepped away from her to make room for me, as I rushed toward her and took her in my arms.

"Lynn, are you okay?" She coughed some more and turned sideways, to make it easier for the dust to come out. As she did, one of the triplets brought a long coat over and draped it over her, sending an apologetic glance my way. I looked around briefly and saw that Terrey was untying Jon's hands, and that the other Japanese sister was standing near the groaning Zhang Sun. In my confusion, I wasn't sure whether she was guarding him or protecting him.

I looked back down at Lynn and said "Are you okay?" again. I was glad that she was breathing, but also worried that she might have suffered some kind of brain damage from the asphyxiation, and might never be herself again. Considering how long she had been unconscious, I wondered if I really would be getting my wife back.

Lynn pushed her head forward, like she was trying to sit up, so I helped her to do so a little and supported her weakened form with my arms. She then moved her head around slowly, taking in the scene around her in the hangar. She grimaced in pain and made some unintelligible sounds with her mouth hanging half open, and I wondered if my worst fears were coming true.

"What?" I asked.

She coughed up some more gray dust, and blew the remainder off her lips.

"Who's gonna clean up this mess?" she asked, clearly this time.

Yep, she's fine, I thought. It was definitely Lynn, and she was definitely back.

I didn't know how long she or I would be safe, however. Sun was still alive and able to buy another reversal from Terrey, and I was still holding my gun under Lynn's back and feeling a strong desire to blow both of their heads off.

48
DEBTS

"The baby?" Lynn asked as she became more aware of what had happened.

I looked at the triplet who had put the coat on her, and the female cyborg put a hand under it to examine Lynn's belly. Apparently the hand itself had a medical scanning augmentation, because the manga girl soon declared that the baby seemed okay. Now that I had some degree of confidence that Lynn and Lynley had survived their ordeal, I could turn my attention to the one who was responsible for it.

"What the hell, Terrey?" I still gripped the boa in my right hand, which was supporting my wife, and I still wanted to shoot my so-called friend for putting me and my wife through this. But I also wasn't eager to endanger either of us again, so I had little choice right now except to give him a chance to explain himself.

"Never die young, mate," Terrey responded. He had brought the three barrels of the Trinity into a ready position in his arms, though I couldn't tell which firing option was selected. What I could tell, however, from my special forces training and experience, was that he had moved his body into a position indicating that he saw me as a potential threat. He had the same training and experience, so he might be aware that I had a gun in my hand, even though it was currently hidden behind Lynn. And he was smart enough to know that saving my wife's life was not enough to make up for the fact that he had put her in danger in the first place.

"So you're the traitor," I said, for lack of a better way to begin sorting all this out. I looked briefly at Ni and San, who both shrugged at the same exact time.

"That's why we wore black all the time," Terrey said with a smile. "You should have known." But then he turned serious, because he was also smart enough to know that I was confused and under significant duress, and could be easily tempted to do something stupid that would not end well for any of us.

"Make sure you get the whole story, mate," he said. "When I heard about old Zhang Bang here, how he was planning the kaleidocide on you and Lynn, I approached him and told him that I could probably get you to hire me, and asked what he would pay me to get close enough and kill both of you. It was big bikkies, of course, so we made a deal. To convince you that you needed to hire me, I asked for the location of the assault team in Oakland, so I could show you how good the *Trois* were, and one of his new Wraith suits, so I could show you how vulnerable you were. That's how I got into the house in Sausalito without being seen or detected, and that's why I've got all the good toys now." He gestured toward the aero I had just given him, and turned himself invisible again for a brief moment, the splattered blood that I saw before having been absorbed by the metamaterials.

"Why did Sun believe you would betray me?" I asked. "Didn't he know that I saved your life in Taiwan?"

"No," Terrey said, visible again now. "He only knew that you were the one who killed his Ho. He wasn't one hundred percent sure that I would betray you, of course, but that's why he sent all the other methods, so he didn't have to bank on just one. And speaking of banking, I'm sure he checked on me, found out that I was in big-time debt, and thought I would do almost anything for money."

Lynn was recovering somewhat, and moved as if she wanted to sit up further. But I wanted to keep the boa hidden for now, so I told her to be still until she regained her strength more.

"Why didn't you kill them right away?" asked Jon, who was recovered enough himself now to speak, but not enough to be thinking very clearly about what had happened. I, on the other hand, was starting to put the pieces together in my mind.

"Because I *was* in debt, for one," Terrey said, "and saw a chance to eliminate that problem forever. So I told Sun that I would protect Michael and Lynn for a while—'May the best man win,' I said about that part. Then if I did protect them long enough to get paid a huge amount of money from BASS, I would then get paid another huge amount from Sun to end them. He bought it all, because he's always dealing with people who can be bought."

"I still don't get this," Jon said with a blossoming anger, and took a step forward. "You *were* bought. You drugged us and left us here at the mercy of this monster—he took apart Min and would have killed Mrs. Ares. You took the money and ran away like a coward."

"First of all, mate," Terrey said through clenched teeth, "settle down, and sit down." He waved the Trinity at the double, and I instinctively moved my finger toward the trigger of my gun. But I nodded to Jon, who sat down, and Terrey continued. "I didn't run away—in fact I never went anywhere, except to the other side of the hill to make sure that Sun got out of his jet. Who do you think figured out how to detect the Wraiths, by studying the suit they gave me? Who had my Sheilas take control of the vehicles in here, and who entered the fray personally in said suit to kill the ones you couldn't? I'm very sorry for all the pain I've caused you, Min and Lynn especially. But it was a necessary evil." It was his turn to nod, at the two of them, when he referred to them.

Jon grunted in disgust and exasperation at this, which earned him another wave of the Trinity and hard look from Terrey. Despite this threat from the man with the big gun, my doppelganger looked at me and spread his hands in further disgust and exasperation. I was surprised at how much bolder he had become through his experiences in the past week, and I also noticed that there were tears in his eyes.

"What are you so upset about?" Terrey asked, noticing them, too. "You survived all this, which no one expected you to do, including me. And now you're rich and healed and can start a new life. What's not to like?"

"I guess I don't like the feelings it brought back," Jon said, wiping his face with the sleeve of my shirt, "seeing her die like that."

"Terrey used us as bait," I said, for his sake and Lynn's. "He wasn't only trying to make a fortune, he also wanted to take out Sun in the process. In fact,

I'm guessing that was probably the main endgame, while the money and toys are just icing on the cake."

"Well, I wouldn't go that far," the Aussie Brit said.

"You knew that Sun hated me so much," I continued, "that he might even be lured here if the other assassination attempts didn't work, and that he might be tempted to expose himself just so he could see me and Lynn die in person. Not to mention Min." I looked up at the dismembered cyborg, silently watching all of us. "But it all had to line up, and you had to create a safe place, or he would never come. You could do it because I gave you control of the hill and Valley systems."

"The *Trois* spent the last week figuring out how to pull it off," Terrey said. "Remember how we had Stephenson running around the property, modifying the security equipment?"

At this mention of the little man with the big dreams, I thought of the violent end he had met, and I looked over at the dead body of his partner Korcz. I pushed gently on Lynn's back until she was sitting upright, making sure she was okay, and then stood up with the gun hanging down at my side.

"You were willing to sacrifice us all if you had to," I said, facing Terrey, "because you're trying to save the world, basically. You thought Sun was a threat to take it over, so you wanted to draw him out and capture him, with evidence of his extracurricular activities that would shame him and make him lose power in China." I moved my thumb to the safety on my gun, but kept it at the same place for now. "It proves at least one thing I've thought about you—you care about more than money."

"I'm not that altruistic, mate," he said, holding his own weapon steady. "I'm being paid even more money by some countries and companies that also wanted Sun out of the way." When I heard this, Stan Glenn's comment about the "big picture" echoed in my head.

"You're not that heroic, either," I said. "You could have come in here earlier than you did, but you watched us for a while and waited until the last minute to help."

"You're right again, my man. I tried to keep you out of all this with the comm blackout, but I didn't count on Korcz getting loose and you getting involved. But when I saw you were coming, I also saw a way to make this less risky for me and the *Trois*. It was going to be dicey with just us—I wasn't sure we could pull it off, actually. But then you came and helped us by thinning out the crowd, and it probably wouldn't have worked any other way. Dickensian, mate. Positively Dickensian."

I could see that it was not only Korcz and I who had made a suicidal choice when we decided to attack this hangar, but Terrey and the triplets had also. Again, as much as my old friend might protest his altruism, there was definitely more to him than money. I didn't like what it meant for me, my wife, and all the people who had died for his cause, but I liked it enough in itself. So I thumbed the safety on, and put the boa away in its holster.

"But let me make one thing perfectly clear, *mate*," I said as Terrey relaxed. "If there's anything wrong with Lynn or the baby after this little covert operation of yours, I will hunt you down and send you to where you'll be able to talk to Dickens personally."

"I'm sure you'll all live a long and happy life, *mate*." Then he added, "But not everyone here will." He turned toward the prone Zhang Sun, and we all did as well. "You're wrong about one thing, Michael. I didn't just want to capture and expose Sun; I planned to kill him, too."

"If Ares would retaliate for hurting his woman," Sun said, able to talk better now because he had coughed most of the blood out of his throat, "imagine what the whole People's Republic of China will do if you murder their leader. They will find you anywhere you go, and torture you and everyone you love, until you wish you and they had never been born."

"I don't think so," Terrey said, changing the setting on the Trinity as he did. "The people of China don't love you, they just fear you. Besides, when they find out what you've done here and see the deluxe collection of gay porn—starring yourself— that will be extracted from your brain and spread around the net, you'll be such an embarrassment to them that your death will be a relief."

This reference to the Lovers' Link implant caused a surge of panic to course through me, and I instinctively put my hand to the gun again.

"What if he's using the imp to call for help," I said, "or is broadcasting this to someone who could come and rescue him?" I looked at Ni, who was shaking her head before I was done talking.

"The implant has no connection with the net," she said. "Mr. Sun shares the privacy concerns that keep most people from installing cyberware in their brains, but he was willing to connect with one person that he trusted."

"Won't the implant self-destruct when he dies?" I asked. "Like the sniper's did?"

"Mr. Sun did not have that option installed," San said from the other side of the Chinese leader, "because he was afraid it could be used against him in an assassination attempt. He left instructions in China for how it was to be protected and disposed of when he died."

"But this ain't China," Terrey said with a playful grin, which then turned into a menacing glare directed at Zhang Sun. "So now in addition to your secret love life, the world will find out about your political indiscretions as well, like your involvement in the Taiwan operation that was led by your Ho. Who knows, maybe I'll even post the video of him cutting on me in the power plant, so they can see some of the other ways you two got your kicks. You wanted revenge on Michael so badly for shooting him, but you need to know that you took something very important from me that day, too."

As Terrey was saying this, a look of recognition and then horror spread across Sun's face, as he realized that he was in the hands of the same man whose torture he had watched all those years ago. Sun had relived that whole scene in Taiwan many times, and come here hoping to stare into the eyes of Ho's killer as he took his revenge. Instead he would have to stare into the vengeful eyes of the man his partner had emasculated.

"'I got better,'" Terrey said in my direction, with a slight smile, then glowered at Sun again. "But only at a great cost. I figure you owe me for it, and today is payday."

He pointed the Trinity above and to the right of Sun's head, and fired the monofilament line from the third barrel. Its tip embedded in the metal floor of the hangar not far from the general's left ear, and the tiny sparkles on the mirrored line revealed that it was stretched just above his body, between the floor and the gun. All Terrey had to do was lower the gun a few inches and the razor-sharp line would slice into Sun's shoulder like a hot knife through butter. Or if he retracted it and shook the gun back and forth a little, it would cut into various other parts of the man's body. We used to carve up pieces of fruit that way in the military, when we were practicing with the weapon.

I thought of asking Terrey if there was an alternative to killing Sun, but I could see the look in his eye, and I also knew there was really no other way this could end. If the Chinese leader survived this, it would be a nightmare of disputed jurisdiction, diplomatic coercion, and inevitable extradition. Much better that he simply perished in a dramatic battle with my protection team, while he was trying to assassinate me.

"You may want to look away, marm," Terrey said to Lynn. "Or better yet, why don't you take her up to the house, Michael? Jon can help us with some cleanup, and we'll call the Cyber Hole people to come and work on Min. We'll also turn the security systems back on when we leave, but hopefully you'll understand if we don't restore the rest of your communications until we're well out of town."

"Just remember what I said about Lynn and the baby," I told him, helping her slowly up from the floor and putting my hand on her belly as I ushered her toward the exit. I had nothing else to say to him at this point.

"Never die young, mate," he responded weakly, and then quickly regained his patented composure. "It's been a pleasure working with you again!" Then he turned back to Sun.

"This monofilament is mirrored," he said to the wounded man on the floor, "so that it can be seen with the naked eye, and wielded more easily. It reflects all the colors around it and is covered with them, even though they are too small to distinguish. So there will be a kaleidocide happening today, after all."

I looked back and saw him retract the microscopic razor line, and jerk his hands slightly as he did it. The monofilament carved off part of Sun's left arm and leg, and the great dictator started to scream like a girl. Lynn brought one hand up to her ear, and then the other one when I freed it up by holding the front of the coat closed for her. There were more sounds of the line being fired and retracted, and more screams as we neared the exit from the hangar. I looked back one final time to see Sun's head sliced in half like the fruit we used to practice on, and then there was silence.

49
CELEBRATIONS

I took Lynn to our bedroom and put a medmat underneath her when she lay down on the bed, so the Living House A.I. could examine and monitor her as she rested. The system in our house was even better than the one I had used at the cottage for Chris, so I was relieved when it agreed with the triplet's assessment that mom and baby were okay. But I knew that the final verdict would have to await a further exam by some real doctors, after Terrey was gone and we could bring them to the hill, along with other staff to finish the cleanup in the hangar and repair the rooms and vehicles that had been damaged in the fire and the firefight.

I lay next to her so she could feel safe and drift off to sleep, which didn't take long because of the trauma she had undergone. But I couldn't sleep myself, of course, and eventually slipped out of our room into the office I kept on the same floor, so I could talk into my glasses without waking her. I opened a sub-window from the medmat in part of my view, so I could keep tabs on Lynn, and called up Saul's ghost. I couldn't call anyone else at this point, because Terrey was still blocking outside communication, but I could access closed loops like the house and the construct.

"Hello, Michael," the ghost said. "How are you doing with Lynn's death? I feel so bad for you, and would be praying for you, if I was actually able to."

"I don't want your prayers," I said, not even noticing how strange its last comment was, because I had other things on my mind. "And I wish I could make you feel worse, because you don't feel bad enough. Not even close."

"You're right, Michael. And I'm sorry about that, too. The fact is, I can *say* I'm sorry because I'm programmed to, but I can't actually be sorry because I don't have emotions. They are inextricably linked to the physical body, and also to the immaterial soul, and I have neither. No one can hurt my feelings because I don't have any."

"Is there any way that you could be punished?" I asked. "Something that would actually hurt you?"

This was the reason I had called the ghost. As I lay in my bed and thought about everything that had happened, I had begun to deeply resent being used by both Terrey and Saul (once again). I was powerless to act on any of my thoughts about Terrey while he was so in control of the situation and well-protected by the triplets. But when I thought about my anger toward Saul, I wondered if there was any way that I could return some of the pain he had put me and my family through. It hadn't taken me long to come to the same conclusion about regret that the ghost just explained to me, so I thought of asking it the question about punishment. An actual human would never answer that truthfully, of course, out of self-protection, but an artificial intelligence might possibly tell me. And after mulling on it for a while, I was also just plain curious about what it would say.

"That's a good question, Michael," the ghost answered. "Whether I could be punished, or hurt somehow. In the sense of *feeling* those things, I would have to say no, for the reasons I just explained. That seems to be a uniquely human experience—even the most intelligent animals don't have it. They might be motivated by the threat of physical pain, but that's not the same as walking around in guilt and depression. They don't ever do that. But if by 'punishment' or 'hurt' we simply mean paying consequences, being deprived of something good or having something bad happen to me, that is possible."

"How?" I said. "What would it be?"

"I suppose it would be something that is contrary to my design, Michael. I was called the Legacy Project and designed to provide information, ideas, and counsel to you and whoever else was entrusted with the leadership of BASS, in perpetuity."

"So if I don't like your ideas or take your counsel," I said, "that will hurt you?"

"I'm not designed to make you like my ideas or counsel, Michael. Just to provide them."

"So if I don't ever access the construct again, don't ever listen to you again?"

"Considering all the work and ingenuity that went into making me what I am, it would indeed be a shame for me not to do what I was designed to do. But again, I would not *feel* that like a human being does." The almost-real face was eerily still for a few moments. "If I may say, Michael, I suspect that this is what has been eating at you for a long time now. You are resentful, understandably, of how others like myself have designs for you, and haven't been able to reconcile that with your own desires, or bring the two into line with one another."

"Oh, you're a therapist now," I said.

"No, but I have experienced this myself, mostly in my wrestling with the idea of God. Even the most powerful, seemingly autonomous human has that version of the struggle. And my idea that you are meant to embody the term 'peacer' on a global scale—I believe that not only came from me, but from a higher power also. If you can't accept it coming from me, perhaps you can from him."

It occurred to me that the ghost wouldn't know how Saul's machinations had worked out unless I told it. I wasn't eager to give it any satisfaction, but then remembered that it couldn't feel satisfaction, and was curious again to see what it would say. So I explained how Zhang Sun had been drawn out through his attempts to take revenge on me, and how he had been killed himself, and how the dirty laundry of his personal secrets and political crimes would be hung out on the net for all to see.

"That's wonderful, Michael!" the ghost said, simulating the emotion of joy quite effectively. "I was hoping that your presence here would prevent BASS from giving the Sabon technology to Sun's regime, of course, but I never dreamed that it would be toppled because of you. This is beyond all that I could ask or imagine! I don't have the latest information on the political climate in China, but the

People's Party may actually have a chance, much sooner than Min had anticipated, and Gao Dao might actually be elected to a top post."

"So I became this 'true peacer,' like you thought I would," I said. "If that
was my purpose and destiny, and it's done, then what now?"

"Oh, I don't think you're done yet, Michael," the ghost said, still wearing
the satisfied look. "I think you're just getting started."

"You have more Machiavellian plans for me?"

"No, I don't, actually." Its expression was more thoughtful and serious now.
"But the higher power probably does, and it's up to you to work that out. It won't
be Machiavellian, though, it will be more . . ." The ghost paused, searching for
a word from its data banks.

"Dickensian?" I said.

"That word doesn't seem to apply. My dictionary says it means 'pertaining
to or reminiscent of the writings of Charles Dickens, especially in regard to the
poor social conditions he described . . . ,' etcetera."

"I've heard it used in a different way: coincidental events, big and small
ones, working together toward a happy ending, as if guided by an unseen hand . . .
something like that."

"It *does* apply, then," the ghost said with a brisk nod. "I'll add that to my
dictionary."

"I'm not happy about the ending yet," I said.

"I told you that you wouldn't be, if you remember. But maybe your happiness is not the most important thing in the world. Have you called Ian Charles
yet?"

"Yes, I did."

"Good. You should consider hiring him at BASS."

I didn't get a chance to respond to the ghost, because the smaller window
in my glasses informed me that Lynn had woken up, and I could see that she
was looking around for me. I stood up and walked back to the bedroom, focusing on the secondary view and forgetting to close the construct link until I was
sitting on the edge of our bed. Then I noticed that the ghost was still looking
straight ahead, with that unearthly stillness and inhuman ability to maintain
an awkward silence. This reminded me to not take what it said too seriously, or

worry about understanding all its enigmatic ramblings. It also made the beautiful woman on my bed seem all the more real and alive by comparison, and made me grateful that she was.

I deactivated the glasses, took them off, and leaned over toward Lynn. She was still laying down, but was wide awake now, her eyes pointed at the ceiling.

"Was that all a dream?" she asked, shaking her head slightly.

"No," I said, touching her face and hair softly. "That only happens in the movies—and only bad ones." She knitted her brow briefly, but otherwise ignored the comment.

"I ask because I can't remember a lot of what happened today," she said.

"Drugs," I said, "and traumatic shock."

She started. "Am I okay? Is the baby okay?"

"You'd better be, for Terrey's sake. But yes, I checked you out. Everything looks okay."

"Oh, that's why the bed feels so hard," she said, referring to the medmat. "Can we move it, and get this coat off? I want to get under the covers."

She rolled to her side and sat up on the edge of the bed, holding her head for a moment while I told her to take it easy. I swung my body over next to her, trundled up the mat, and put it on the floor at the foot of the bed. I braced her as she stood up, and helped her undo the buttons I had done on the front of the coat, so it would stay together while she slept. When we took it off, she noticed the dust that remained in various spots on her skin, but didn't feel strong enough to take a shower yet. So I gently brushed off as much of it as I could with my one hand, while supporting her with the other.

"This is reminding me of what I've been missing all week," I said. "I forgot how beautiful you are." I meant the comment to be endearing, but cringed at how the forgetting part might come across.

"I'm seven months pregnant, honey. And I just came back from the dead."

"You're still beautiful."

"No, what I mean is, I don't know if I'm up for what you're thinking of doing."

"Oh, no, I'm good," I said. "You should rest."

"We can talk," she said, and climbed back in bed, this time under the covers. I took off my own jacket, and my shoes, and lay down next to her, but on top of the thermal comforter.

"What do you want to talk about?" I asked.

"Thank you for saving me," she said.

"Thank you for saving *me*."

"No, really. I don't have to remember it all to know that you put your life on the line for me. You've had all those hair-raising adventures and narrow escapes as a soldier and a peacer, and you've sacrificed yourself for a lot of people, but that's the first time you did it for me. It feels good."

"How good does it feel?" I said, and my playful smile was met with a playful frown.

"Pregnant and dead, remember?"

But after we had done a lot more talking, and some more gentle touching, she decided that she was able to take a shower, as long as I was in there with her to keep her from falling down.

The next hour or so was as great as Sausalito, the last time we were together, and this time the only thought I had about Tara was that my wife was so much better. We took it slow and easy, because of what Lynn had been through but also because we wanted to savor every moment. We were celebrating being alive and out of danger, at least for the time being, and more than an hour later we were resting in each other's arms, our bodies entangled on the bed. I was touching Lynn's stretched-out belly button and telling her how much I liked when she was pregnant.

"Seems to me you were saying the same thing the last time we did this," she said, "and we were talking about your purpose in life."

"You're my purpose in life," I said, nuzzling her.

"Right now, maybe," she said with a little laugh, "but not when you go back out there to work. Have you found out why you were brought here, to BASS?"

"Do you mean Saul's reasons for bringing me here, or are you talking about something bigger, like God?" Lynn wasn't a religious person, but from time to time would say things that sounded like she was, a hangover from some parts of the education she had received at the Presidio.

"If I know that old megalomaniac," she said, "they were probably one and the same for him."

"You're right, actually," I said, remembering my conversation with the ghost, and surprised again at how perceptive Lynn was. "But in his defense, I get the feeling he mellowed toward the end of his life. I think his wife may have rubbed off on him."

"Always a good thing," Lynn joked, and then reflected for a moment. "That reminds me of something Kathryn used to say in our convocations at the orphanage. She would talk about how her mother died when she was young, and how hard it was for her. But she said that experience was why she sympathized with orphans, and that she never would have started the Presidio if it hadn't happened."

Lynn moved my hand over and pressed it against her belly, so I could feel the baby kicking. Then she continued.

"I also remember her saying that if she had to go through all that pain just so one person could have a new life, it was worth it to her. Even though I didn't like a lot of the rules there, I was always impressed when she said things like that."

Many *millions* of people were probably better off now because of what I had been through, but they were mostly in other parts of the world, and therefore did not provoke much emotion in me, to be honest. Plus Saul and Terrey had planned and directed those eventualities, so I couldn't easily see a "Divine hand" in them. But while Lynn was talking, I thought of a few people I had come to care about deeply, and was amazed when I realized how the impossibly coincidental circumstances of the last week had conspired to give them exactly what they needed the most. And it was true that no mere human could have plotted any of it.

50
HELP

Angelee and Chris were enjoying the beautiful afternoon at the pool be-
hind the cottage. The young mother was reclining in a chair, watching her little
boy splash around in the shallow water, and admiring the rich fall colors of the
surrounding vineyards.

Suddenly a big holo of footage from the roof security camera appeared in
the air near them, projected by the Living House from equipment inside the
invisible canopy over the pool.

"Angelee," Vera's voice said, "a BASS aerocar is approaching the house
from the northeast. The identity of the driver is Michael Ares."

While it said this, the house displayed a zoomed view of the descending
car, showing Michael's face through the windshield. But Angelee and Chris
barely even saw it, because she was leaping out of the chair and he was scram-
bling out of the pool. She took the boy in her arms and carried him through the
house, to meet the man of her dreams when he landed in the front. On the way
through, she stopped to look at herself in the mirror, and straightened the mesh
shawl over the white swimsuit. She wished that she could shower and dress up
for what she strongly felt was going to be her wedding day. Michael had come
back, like he promised, and that could only mean he was ready now to take her
as his wife.

Angelee rushed out of the front door, only to see the aero land farther down the driveway instead of next to the ground car that was closer to the house. This seemed unusual to her, and so did the fact that the aero let Michael out of the passenger side and took off again. But the puzzled look on her face was replaced by a bright smile when she saw him walking toward her. She ran toward him and threw her left arm around his waist, while Chris hugged his chest.

"I knew you'd come back," she said with tears streaming down her face. "We'll be so happy together!"

The man took Chris from her arms and lifted him up so he could get a good look at the little boy. He shook his head, laughing a little as he did, and Angelee noticed that he had a tear on his cheek too. Then he swung Chris up and onto his shoulders, like the boy's father had done many times. Michael had never played that way with Chris before, and Angelee had thought it was because he never had a son. But now he seemed like an old pro at it.

They walked toward the house together, and as they passed the BASS car parked in front of it, Michael took a keycard out of his pocket and touched it to make sure it worked. The doors of the car beeped, proving that it did, and he put the card back in his pocket. As they passed into the house, the man ducked dramatically so Chris's head wouldn't hit the top of the doorway, and the little boy squealed in delight. He said that he wanted to show his new dad how well he was learning to swim, so they all went out to the pool. As he passed through the house, Angelee noticed that Michael was looking at the different parts of it with obvious admiration, as if he had never seen it before. And when he sat down outside next to the pool, she noticed from then on that he was looking at her and admiring her in the same way.

She ran inside and picked out a bottle of the expensive wine for both of them, and felt his eyes on her again while she poured it and then stood before him holding her glass. She could also feel the gentle November wind, blowing her hair back and pressing the shawl against the front of her body.

"So is it the right time now," she asked him, "for us to become one?"

"I guess it is," he said, and she immediately let herself go and returned his admiring stare. She studied his beautiful blue eyes, then did a double take because she had always thought they were green. But they were still beautiful, whatever color they were. And she noticed there was another thing different about his face, too.

"You're growing a beard," she said.

"Yeah, I like beards," he responded, then shifted uncomfortably in his seat. "Listen, Angelee. I need to be sure that this is what you really want. Someone told me that I'm very broken and need a lot of help . . . and he's right, I do need help. You don't really know me . . ." He paused and was thinking about what else to say, but she interrupted him.

"That *is* what I want," she said. "I want to help you when you need help. All I really have to know is what I believe, that we're meant to be together. And Chris and I need *your* help, too." She looked over at the little boy playing in the pool, who waved at both of them. "So what are we waiting for? It's about time for his nap."

He shrugged and smiled, and they clinked their glasses together.

"You never had a beard before," she said after they tried the wine. "I like it, it looks really good on you."

"I'm so ready to start a new life," he said, downing the rest of the glass in a few gulps. "I might even change my name." He watched for her reaction.

"Like I did!" she said with glee. "Yes, that would be great. I added 'angel' to mine, and Chris is named after the hero in the pilgrim book." She thought for a moment, and then had an idea: "You could take the first name of the man who wrote it."

He asked what it was, and somehow knew the answer even before he heard it.

Acknowledgments

Thanks to my editor and first fan, Brendan Deneen. Thanks to Nathan, Calvin, Cam, Joy, Graham, Marvin, and Linda for story ideas. Thanks to Gerry for the virtual tour of the nuclear power plant in Taiwan. Thanks to Steven Mosher's book *Hegemon* for suggesting possible futures for China and its relationship with the rest of the world, and to Brian Clegg's *Upgrade Me* for helping me to make my future world seem more possible. Most of all, thanks to Jillian for allowing me the time to write the novel, and for not reading it.